MW00682491

PROSPECTS

ROBERT W. SPENCER

Prospects
Copyright © 2020 Robert W. Spencer

ISBN: 978-1-63381-217-8

This is a work of fiction. Names, characters, places, and incidents either are the product of the author's imagination or are used fictitiously, and any resemblance to actual persons, living or dead, is coincidental.

Cover photograph:
Primus, photographed by Andrea Mason for the American Museum of Natural History

Designed and produced by:
Maine Authors Publishing
12 High Street, Thomaston, Maine
www.maineauthorspublishing.com

Printed in the United States of America

To my three beta readers: Gere, Kay, and Doreen,
and Eleanor Yerbury Spencer (1919–2019)

Acknowledgments

Special thanks to the Waterford Historical Society, from whose three books and archives are drawn valuable research, such as the North Waterford Fire scenario in Scene 91 of this work.

And to historians David Sanderson and Nancy Marcotte for their guidance and suggestions.

And to Jane Perham for her encouraging words.

The author thanks Maggie Kroenke of Maine Mineral and Gem Museum and Jennifer Kane of the American Museum of Natural History for working to provide the image of the *Primus* tourmaline used on the front cover. Use of the image without permission from the American Museum of Natural History is prohibited.

Author's Note

"Based on a true story" begins the review of many films and fictions. Many of the characters in my tale are based on the lives of actual individuals involved in the life of Oxford County, Maine, at the turn of the twentieth century. These are the little people of whom little is known, not the rich and famous. Like you and me, each of them has stories to tell us about what life was like at that time. They give me permission to tell the tales. I make no claim that it is true history. Several characters, locations, and events are taken from history and adapted to my fiction.

Contents

Prologue: Striking It Rich

Elijah Hamlin and Ezekiel Holmes strike it rich in Paris, Maine. The two college students are out for a hike on Mount Mica the day that summer vacation is ending in 1820. They come upon a fallen maple tree within whose exposed roots are embedded several radiant green tourmalines the size of a thumbnail. The crystals gleam so brightly in the fading sunlight that the young men know for sure these must be as valuable as emeralds in a queen's crown. When they return to the site in the spring, they each carry home bucket after bucket of gemstones.

Blacksmith Henry Timmons strikes it rich in Canada.
He is setting sections of track near the town of Sudbury, Ontario, for the Central Ontario Railroad in 1890. He throws his ten-pound hammer at a fox that is trying to steal his lunch pail. When he retrieves the tool, he sees that it has broken a chip off a gray boulder, revealing that the rock contains silver ore. As he scans the area, he notices that all around him the ground is littered with very large boulders of silver ore. He is suddenly very, very wealthy.

In 1928, farmer Cummings strikes it rich.
He is cultivating potatoes in Albany, Maine, when his hoe hits a huge green stone. As he digs at the stone, he discovers that it is a crystal of the emerald mineral beryl that is nineteen feet long and four feet wide.

Frank Perham strikes it rich in October 28, 1972.
At the Dunton Mine in Newry, Maine, Frank Perham, Maine's Gem Man, squeezes his torso into a small pocket in the pegmatite.

As his flashlight sweeps over the stony enclosure, the beam glints off large green and orange crystals. He and partner McCrillis expand the opening and remove two hundred pounds of gemmy tourmaline.

There are so many such true stories about mining that get-rich-quick fantasies fill the minds of every miner, whether professionals who move from prospect to prospect looking for the mother lode, or amateurs who tote bucket, spade, and hammer out to an abandoned mine on weekends. "If only," they say as the hammer snaps off a piece of quartzite, or a blast of dynamite opens the bowels of the earth. "If only I could be one of those who finds their fortune in an instant."

1

March 1895

MILLETT'S AMERICAN DESIGNS said the sign hanging above the porch of a colonial three-story house. Next to the front door stood a mannequin dressed in a sky-blue dress, with a purple scarf wrapped around her neck. Bright-green floor-length drapes, tied back by golden cords, hung in the first-floor windows. This was a dress shop and showroom located on busy Forest Avenue in Westbrook where customers might purchase fashions designed and produced by Miss Lizzie Millett. The proprietor sat at her worktable immediately inside the front door, working on an original pattern for a yellow cotton lady's jacket, part of a new fall line that would soon be shown at retail shops in Portland, Boston, and Manhattan, as well as in a small clothier's shop owned by her husband, Moses Webber, in Saco, where her main material, cotton cloth, was made at the Pepperell Mill. As Lizzie sketched and cut sheets of translucent tissue paper, attaching the pieces together with common pins, Moses descended the stairs from their second-floor apartment.

The sound of his walking: one footfall followed by a cane tap and then another footfall, had become a familiar sound in the many weeks they had been at their Westbrook house. They had not been to their Saco town house since the tumble he had taken at work nearly two months before. Moses, a partner at the mill, had taken a leave of absence from the job of Paymaster, but he still dressed for work every day, donning his office outfit of tan waistcoat over a white linen shirt and worsted woolen trousers.

"This letter came for you yesterday, Lizzie," said Moses as he hobbled into the shop.

"Thank you, dear" said Lizzie as she glanced at the envelope. "It's postmarked from Waterford. I've not been there for years. Who would write me from there? The return address reads Aphia Stevens, but I don't know anyone by that name." Opening the envelope with sharp cloth shears, she began to read:

Miss Millett,

Please forgive me writing to you after so many years. Since our last confrontation, my irrational behavior toward you has been a bother. Perhaps it was my sense of guilt that my late husband had abandoned you to marry me which drove me to be so belligerent. Believe me, it was not my intention to knock you down. My purpose was to return the letter which you had written to him, but he had never seen. As you may not know, Henry Greene deserted me just before your arrival. That was almost fourteen years ago. He has never returned, so I consider him to be dead. I have retaken my family name.

Believe me, you were most fortunate to have been abandoned by that man. If you had wed, you would likely have suffered the same as I from such a harmful relationship.

Just as you wrote in that letter so many years ago, I write to you to assuage the guilt that I feel about my actions toward you in hopes of quenching some of my many demons.

In respect for you, I am
Aphia Stevens

Tossing the page onto her drawing table, Lizzie rose to clear a chair piled high with fashion magazines, so that Moses might sit. She passed the letter to him.

"Dear, please read this odd letter. It stirs up many buried memories. This is the woman my former fiancé married in order to get a farm from her grandfather. I told you about that frightful meeting she and I had in Waterford City. She is much more bothered by the past than I have ever been."

Moses read the letter and passed it back to her. "Yes, I remember that tale now. She knocked you to the ground, then mounted her horse and rode away in a huff. She sounds to me like a tormented soul. She still feels guilt about her dead husband's actions toward you."

"She thinks him dead. He may have just run out on her for all I know. After all, he did the same to me."

"That is a possibility, but she seems sure that he is dead."

"I wonder why she's so sure of that. I wonder if Nathan knows anything about this. He is in Waterford quite often. I have always told him not to speak to me about Henry Greene. I didn't want to be reminded of the past. Now I'm curious. Perhaps he has heard rumors."

2

The next time Lizzie saw her brother-in-law, Nathan Hallett, he had just returned from a visit with customers and clients in the Oxford County towns of Waterford, Bethel, and Rumford. It was late summer, so corn shops in the area needed cans from his clients in Portland. The operation in South Waterford was particularly busy and had made a special order that Nathan had agreed to deliver. As a jobber or middleman he made a very good living buying and selling all manner of manufactured goods throughout New England. He made no products of his own, but created jobs for many others. Liz had decided to visit the Halletts in their home on High Street in Bridgton. She would enjoy the company of her beloved sister Hattie, niece Francena, and nephew Nathan Jr., as well as delve into news about the fate of her former fiancé. As she tethered her horse to a hitching post next to the barn, Hattie ran to her and enveloped Liz in her arms.

"My dear Lizzie. How is it that you seem to grow taller each time I see you? I thought we used to be the same height."

"No, no, Sis. It is not I who grow taller, it is you who are growing shorter." Both laughed as Lizzie pointed to her stylish new leather boots with stacked heels and lacing that ran nearly to her knees. "These are the latest style. All the rage in Boston. Very Italian, you know."

"You are always so modern. Here in the country, we are still getting used to those flat-heeled ankle boots. I so envy you sometimes. Your dressmaking business does keep you in touch with the latest fashions."

Hand in hand, they walked to the house laughing and chatting. Hattie's two children rushed out the screen door, letting it slam behind them, to greet their favorite aunt, whom they had not seen since Christmas. Young Francena, now sixteen, curtsied gracefully before hugging Liz and placing a soft kiss on her cheek. She had become a beautiful young woman much in the image of her namesake grandmother, Francena Fogg Millett. The sisters' mother had died so young that Liz and Hattie were the only ones in the family able to remember her ethereal beauty.

"My sweet Franny" said Aunt Liz. "You have the unusual allure of your grandma. Your parents must be constantly on guard against the boys."

Franny blushed as her younger brother shoved her aside and reached for his aunt's hand. He kissed it and then hugged her around the waist. At thirteen, he was a small boy who had only recently begun to shoot up in height. His long pants were rolled up nearly to the knees, his bare feet stained with dirt. The visor of his cap was set to the rear.

"Aunt Lizzie," he said loudly, "Franny is a good girl, not like her friends who flirt with the boys all the time."

Liz pulled at her nephew's cap. "What a good lad to come to your sister's defense."

3

That evening after supper, Liz and Nathan sat on the front porch. He waved to neighbors who walked by in the cool of the dusk. The aroma of his cheroot reminded her of Moses's pipe tobacco.

"It is a pity Mr. Webber was not able to accompany you on

this trip. He and I always have intriguing conversations about our mutual business interests. He has such great commercial experience that he can teach me a lot of the world."

"Moses wanted to come with me, but his broken ankle makes it very difficult for him to get around the house. Such a long ride would have made him very uncomfortable."

"I was at the Pepperell several weeks ago and expected to see him. One of his assistants told me he had not been at work for some time."

"Yes, working at the plant requires long hours of standing. It will take a while for him to be able to return. Neither of us has been in Saco for nearly two months. Lack of contact with the partners has led to a decrease in contract work."

"Do you have enough work to keep going?"

"Thankfully, demand for our custom creations keeps the shop busy. We're working overtime to complete new styles for the upcoming season. Buyers from New York visited us last week to check on the progress of their orders."

She sipped Spanish sherry from a small crystal glass. Both were silent for a moment, listening to the children singing inside while Hattie played the piano.

"Nathan, many years ago, I told you never to speak a word to me about Henry Greene. However, a letter from his wife, Aphia, came to me two weeks ago. It has piqued my interest in hearing what you might know about his disappearance. She believes him to be dead."

"That woman is quite a strange case. She stays to herself, a hermit in the cave of her small farm. Never is seen in town unless it is a short visit to buy provisions. She is still a beauty, though her clothes are worn and her hair quite wild-looking. My client Bill Watson says that there are rumors she has become a witch of sorts, growing herbs which local women use as medicines."

"But what of her late husband? Has he passed on or is he still alive somewhere?"

"There are many in town who think he is dead and that she

knows the details of how it happened. Her brother Ron told me about a visit he made to her a few years ago. She was 'spooky'—that's how he put it. Didn't want him to stay. Ron mentioned that when he attempted to walk into a pasture near the house, she blocked his way. If you ask me, there is something tormenting her to this very day about Greene's fate."

He changed the subject to a more pleasant topic. "Another reason I am sorry that Moses isn't here is that I want to share an investment opportunity with both of you. There's a gent in Rumford, Mr. Hollis Dunton, who has purchased large tracts of first-growth forest in Newry, up near Bethel. He is planning to build a modern sawmill, clear the forest, and produce huge quantities of board to supply the coming building boom."

Liz said nothing for several minutes. Nathan was always getting involved in new ventures. His excitement was contagious, having led several times to investment by herself and Moses.

"I'm sure Moses would be interested. He's much more knowledgeable about business opportunities than I am. Unless the business is related to fashions and dressmaking, my guard goes up."

"If you would be kind enough to mention this new operation to him, I would be ever so grateful. I may stop in for a visit in a few weeks when I'm down Portland way. Surely he is aware of how many homes and warehouses are being put up right now. More and more projects come on line every day. Dunton's family made hundreds of thousands clearing Mount Desert Isle downeast and selling the lumber to builders throughout the region."

"He is sure to have an interest. That latest fall has injured him so that we will likely be in Westbrook for the foreseeable future. You know he's had a number of mishaps recently, and his eyesight is failing him. Doctors say it's the diabetes."

"I'll make you an offer. If you have clothing ready for delivery to Boston or New York by the time I visit, I can arrange to hand deliver it direct to your customers."

"That sounds good, and I will pay you just what I would have paid to ship the boxes. And please, if you are in Waterford again, check for news on that girl and Henry Greene."

They shook hands to close the agreement and went inside to retire for the evening.

4

Nathan was intrigued by the conversation about Aphia Greene's letter. There was no pressing need for a trip to Waterford, but he really wanted to dig for more information about what had happened to Henry. At dinner the following Thursday, he suggested to his family that they might take a few days off together and make the short trip to South Waterford, where they could stay with his friend Mary Monroe at her Bear Mountain House.

"What a wonderful plan!" said Hattie. "We've not had much time together as a family in such a long time. You are away so much, and the kids have been so busy with their friends during summer vacation. I haven't been to Waterford in many years. So much must have changed."

"Well, it's easier to get there since the roads have been improved, but the village will likely seem little changed to you. Several mills still operate. The lakes are still crystal clear. Maybe a bit more dairy farming being done now."

"But that was so long ago, dear. I don't expect 'twould be as backward as it was then."

Franny and Nate sat silently at the table looking at each other and making sour faces. Noticing the frowns and grimaces, Hattie asked, "And what do you two think of your father's plan? You've never been to your mother's hometown."

As if he knew that his opinion would have little effect on the decisions made by his parents, Nate was mum and went back to eating. Franny was the first to answer. She spoke slowly, searching carefully for each word.

"I suppose it would be quite nice, but only for a couple of days. What would we do there for fun? Father, is the place all about business and farming? Are there any shops and restaurants like we have here in town?"

"Waterford is much more rural than Bridgton. The children there have to make their own amusement. There are many small ponds and lakes where the water is purer than our Highland Lake, and their hills are easier to climb than Pleasant Mountain."

"So, would we be swimming a lot?" Nate chimed in. "I like swimming. But what will Franny do? She never goes swimming."

"I will go in the water. Maybe I don't know how to swim, but Auntie Lizzie made me a very modest bathing dress. Perhaps, brother dear, you might *teach* me to swim."

Two days later, the family climbed aboard a stylish brown four-person surrey with a fringed top; Nathan often used this carriage for his business trips around Maine and New Hampshire. A dark-gray quarter horse drew them out of Bridgton on the road west toward Fryeburg, until they turned onto Sweden Road. At Sweden Four Corners, they turned to the right on Waterford Road. For the next two hours, some of the most beautiful farmland views opened up before them. At one point where the road made a sharp curve, Pleasant Mountain in West Bridgton rose beyond a spacious apple orchard. Nathan stopped and, pointing back toward the road they'd just traveled, directed them to look at majestic Mount Washington.

They passed through a village where many houses and sheds clustered on the steep banks of a small brook. Piles of lumber, barrels, and metal gear wheels lay along the roadside. Chickens pecked among the debris, and sheep grazed behind barbed wire strung along the watercourse. As the wagon slowed to cross a split-stone bridge, a tall bearded man stepped from a two-story shingle-clad building, waving to Nathan. The man was William Watson, owner of the sawmill from which he'd appeared, and also Postmaster and Selectman.

"Nathan, what a surprise to see you. Hopefully you've not come to arrange for shipment of the next box order to Boston. We are only halfway done."

"No, Mr. Watson, I've brought the family here for a holiday before the school year begins. This is my wife Hattie, Francena, and young Nathan. You likely know Hattie. She was born over on Mill Hill. She's a Millett. Her grandfather was your good friend Hiram Fogg."

"Oh, yes. Miss, I was sorry to hear of your grandfather's passing some years back. He was a good man. Made good jobs for many men in this area."

"Bill, may I take just a moment of your time?" interrupted Nathan. "We're on the way to Bear Mountain House, but I must have a moment of private conversation with you."

Stepping away from the wagon, the two men walked toward the brook, where water spilled over the mill's split-rock dam. The waterfall was so loud that they had to stand very close and talk loudly to be heard.

"Bill, I'm not sure that you would remember Hattie's older sister, Lizzie Millett. She was the girl Hiram Fogg rescued from her father's second wife, Rose Haskell."

"No. I can't say as I remember either of the sisters. But my memory isn't working as well as it did before I got so old," said Watson with a big grin.

"Fogg told me that you and the Selectmen took the woman's two babies, the ones Lizzie was taking care of, and found a proper home for them."

"Well, yes. I do remember that part." Watson wanted Nathan to come to the point. "Friend, what is it that you wanted to know about your wife's sister?"

"Not about her sister, really. I'm trying to find out what happened to a friend of hers, Mr. Henry Greene. He was a local man who worked for Hiram in Westbrook, but then returned to Waterford and bought the Whitcomb farm. He married Abe Whitcomb's young granddaughter, Aphia Stevens."

"I remember Greene very well. He worked here making boxes for me a few years back. Wasn't too regular at work. I had to let him go."

"Have you seen him in town recently?"

Watson glanced back at the sliding barn door of his mill, which he had left open. A cloud of sawdust billowed out in their direction.

"No. I can't say I've seen Mr. Greene for a number of years. There was a rumor that he had deserted the wife, but then he returned to attend old Abe's funeral. Seems to me he went back to living on the farm. Then he just disappeared from the face of the earth. You might check with Mr. Jones Hall, but he's been quite ill and staying with family in Norway. Nathan, forgive me, but I have to get back to work. Your customer in Boston will be looking for his order soon."

5

By the time the Halletts reached the Bear Mountain House, both children had fallen asleep. Hattie had her arm around her husband's waist, and her head rested on his shoulder. She was exhausted, but the excitement of being in her home village once again kept her awake. As they turned off Waterford Road onto a wide driveway, she saw a big white house set in the center of an open pasture. Two horse-drawn carriages were tethered in front of a gigantic barn. A young man dressed in denim overalls and work boots was wiping down one of the horses. He motioned Nathan to tie up at a granite hitching post beside the barn. Nathan nodded, but drove up to the wraparound porch first, where his passengers disembarked.

Hattie's breath was taken away when she turned and saw a panoramic view across the field and down the length of Bear Pond in which were reflected bright white puffy cumulus clouds and the towering bald face of Bear Mountain. A young man in short pants and suspenders greeted them at the front door and asked to take Hattie's bag. Just inside, at an open door, a tall, heavyset woman carrying a plate of teacakes gestured for her three new guests to follow her.

"Good afternoon; my name is Mary Monroe. Please join our other guests in the parlor for tea. My John will hold your bags at the front desk until I get a room ready for you."

Surprised by such hospitality, Hattie and Francena curtsied and Nate bowed at the waist. Entering the door to this scene, Nathan broke into a wide smile. "Mrs. Monroe, as you can plainly see, my family is domesticated. We will be no trouble to you for the next three nights."

Three other guests sat at one of four tables in a small parlor that was brightly lit by late-afternoon sunlight entering a huge double window. The tables, each covered with fine linen cloths and napkins, were arranged about the window so that all guests would have a grand view across the pond. A handsomely dressed man with two lovely ladies sat closest to the window. The man rose from his seat and held his hand out to Nathan.

"Welcome, sir. My name is John Ritchie. This is my wife, Mary, and our daughter, Lottie. Please join us for tea. You have selected a fine establishment for your vacation. Mrs. Monroe is the perfect hostess."

"I am sure of that, Mr. Ritchie. I've been her guest many times in the past. Is this your first visit to Waterford?"

"Yes. We had planned to stay at the Lake House in Waterford Village, but there were no vacancies. The proprietor there highly recommended Mrs. Monroe. We have been here for a week now."

"You're fortunate to have such a long stay."

"Well, we plan on being here for another fortnight. A friend from Bethel is coming down to stay with us for the weekend."

"Mr. Ritchie, allow me to introduce my wife, Hattie, our daughter, Francena, and our son, Nathan Jr. We have driven over from Bridgton Center."

Hattie shook hands with Mr. and Mrs. Ritchie. Lottie curtsied, and Franny did the same. Young Nathan simply doffed his cap before sitting down to devour a small cupcake.

Over the next three days, Francena and nineteen-year-old Lottie spent much time together. During walks to the pond and lunches on the porch, they chatted as if they had been fast friends for years. The Massachusetts girl told Franny of her life in Winchester, just west of Boston. There were debutante balls, sailboats on Cape Cod, and nights at Symphony Hall. The Maine girl listened with envy about experiences she could only imagine.

One thing that Franny was able to do that her new friend could not was swim in Bear Pond. Dressed in her new brown cotton bathing dress, complete with pantaloons and matching umbrella, she took her brother's hand to enter the water from a small sandy beach. Nate instructed her in freestyle strokes, but her arms just wouldn't cooperate with her legs. Settling for a dog-paddle lesson, she swam round and round in the shallow water while he went out many yards from shore.

Lottie shouted out to her friend, "Franny, please have your auntie make a swimming dress for me. My friends in Winchester would be red with envy. I think I could learn to swim pretty easily—I'm a natural athlete."

She removed her Mary Janes and stood in the cold water. Nate saw an opportunity for a prank and began to splash her. Then he ran back to shore and pushed his sister's new friend into the drink. She screamed at him and pulled him in after her. All three of them ended up sitting in the water just two feet from shore.

"You devil!" Lottie scolded Nate as she made her way back to shore. "How dare you do this to me? My mother will kill me when she sees my soggy dress!"

As Nathan and Franny stood up, Lottie jumped at them and rolled with them back into the water. From the back of the barn that sat above them on a knoll, Mrs. Ritchie cried out, "Lottie Adelaide Ritchie, you are little more than a country bumpkin yourself! Look at you! Come up here immediately."

The three soaked friends looked at each other for a moment. Lottie was ashamed that her mother might have offended the Halletts. Francena could think of nothing to say. Nate just stared at his new playmate and finally said, "Lottie Adelaide Ritchie. What a highfalutin' name!"

6

On the second morning of the holiday, Nathan arose at dawn and invited Hattie to go for a walk along the brook that ran through the woods behind the barn. She decided to stay in bed until breakfast, so he set off by himself. It was his habit at home, if he rose before her, to make a cup of coffee and work on accounts at his desk until she came down to the kitchen to make breakfast. Now on vacation, he was trying to enjoy his time away from business concerns.

As he stepped out into the dawn, sunlight was just beginning to break through the pine forest east of the house. A recently mowed pasture between the barn and clusters of maples lining City Brook lay soaked in the morning dew. The scene reminded him of fields he and his father had mown together many years ago at their old farm in Gorham. He could almost see the old man swinging a scythe in the early morning in order to beat the afternoon heat. Following a sandy path that led to the stream, he breathed in the cool, clean damp air of country life. Walking down the slope through the maples toward the brook, he listened to the sound of its gently flowing water. He reached the water at a spot where the course split around a jumble of large stones and boulders that he thought must have been deposited by the departing glaciers 15,000 years before. Sunlight was streaming through the canopy and reflecting in rippling waters where shadows played on a sandy bottom.

Nathan perched on a lichen-covered rock and stared into the current. Such a peaceful feeling came over him that he lost all sense of time. Freed for a moment from thoughts of work and responsibility, he reflected on what a good life he had. I want to share this tranquility with Hattie, he thought. She is always telling me to slow down and relax, to let the rest of the world go by…

He rose and walked back toward the inn, unaware that he had been sitting by the brook so long he had missed breakfast. Hattie, who was tired of waiting for him, had walked halfway down the slope to meet him. He grabbed her up in his arms and

swung her lovingly in a circle around him. She laughed as he
placed a kiss on her forehead and set her down.

"Husband, where have you been for so long? Mrs. Monroe
held a place for you at the table, but when you didn't return, she
put everything away."

"Lovey, I have found the most perfect place to sit and forget
my duties. It's beside a babbling brook where one can lose oneself
in reverent thoughts."

"You sound so religious!" she exclaimed.

"Come. I'll show you the spot."

"No, Nathan. I came to bring you back to meet someone. Mr.
Ritchie has a visitor whom you might be glad to meet. He is down
from Bethel and is apparently a partner in that same lumbering
venture which has drawn your interest. We can go to your secret
spot later in the day."

7

John Ritchie sat on the porch next to a large man with a handle
bar mustache. The man was dressed in a gray business suit of
worsted wool and smoked a meerschaum pipe. Smoke drifted in
John's direction.

"Dr. Abbott, perhaps we might switch seats. The pipe smoke
is blowing right in my face."

Dr. Hiram Francis Abbott, a wealthy resident of Bethel,
looked surprised at the irritation in his new acquaintance's voice.
He was not accustomed to men who did not smoke. It was something that all his friends did, and the failure of this man to do so
made the doctor think less of him.

"Yes, of course, Mr. Ritchie. By all means. Hate to make a man
uncomfortable," he said as he rose from his comfortable stuffed
chair. "My wife sometimes is bothered by my tobacco habit. However, it is something that I enjoy."

As they resettled in their seats, Abbott resumed the discussion. "As I was saying," he said with a slight tone of annoyance at

having to start over. "Mr. Dunton has purchased two very large properties in the town of Newry, a small village north of Bethel. Only a handful of farmers live there, and those who do have a difficult job making the land pay. Two of those residents grew tired of working their land and have given Hollis Dunton a bargain on four hundred acres."

"Was that only one lot or the two in total?"

"That was the largest of the two. The plan is to harvest the first-growth forest which occupies most of the land and supply lumber to feed the building boom in that part of Oxford County. There is a great deal of money to be made by anyone who invests in the operation. A mill has already been built in Rumford Falls in preparation for producing millions of board feet. This is a similar plan to the one Hollis's father used to clear the first-growth forest on Mount Desert Isle downeast. The family made thousands on that operation."

"I assume you have already invested, Dr. Abbott."

"Yes, yes! I was the first one outside of the Dunton family who made a commitment. I am not a foolish man when it comes to making a good return on my dollar."

Just then, the Halletts strolled up to the porch arm in arm. John Ritchie called out to Nathan. "Mr. Hallett, you might have some interest in our discussion here. I don't think my associate would mind speaking with another potential investor."

When the couple approached, both men stood, bowed to Hattie and shook hands with Nathan. John introduced the doctor. "Nathan, this is Dr. Hiram Abbott from Bethel. He has been telling me about a Mr. Dunton and his proposed lumber mill. "

Abbott interrupted. "If Mr. Ritchie thinks you are a man who is interested in making the most from your capital, I would be happy to include you in the discussion. Mrs. Hallett, if you would excuse us…"

It was Nathan's turn to interrupt. "Sir, my wife is my partner in making decisions about the best way to increase our fortune."

Abbott was surprised. It was highly unusual to speak of business with women. They did not usually have an interest in such matters, but, if the husband was the type of man to allow such things, he would have to go along with it even though it meant that he would not be able to smoke.

Ritchie drew two more chairs around the small wicker table. Nathan sat next to Abbott and restarted the discussion. "Dr. Abbott, I am highly pleased to make your acquaintance. I have already met with Hollis Dunton in his office at the new mill, so I am very aware of the tremendous opportunity offered by his venture."

Abbott reached out to shake hands with Nathan once again. "Mr. Hallett, Dunton has spoken very highly of you. What a coincidence to meet you here in Waterford."

Hattie then spoke. "Gentlemen, what do the owners of the land plan to do with it once the lumbering operation is completed?"

"Such a good question," said the doctor, shocked to get a comment of value from her. "There is already talk of building more homes and businesses in a brand-new town center. Also, there is speculation that a section of the smaller lot may contain a pegmatite deposit. Perhaps, like the mine discovered on Mt. Mica in Paris, it may yield valuable minerals and gemstones."

Hattie was excited about the prospect of her husband's involvement in a lumber business that had the possibility of becoming a gem mine. When they returned to their room, she expressed her feeling to Nathan. "I'm sure that your intuitions about Dunton's lumbering venture are well founded and that we will prosper by being early investors. The prospect of finding a lode of valuable gemstones beneath the cleared land could prove to be of greater value."

"You may be correct, but such a possibility is purely theoretical. The trees are real. We know their value. Your stones may lie buried and invisible beneath tons of overburden. I'm not disagreeing with you. No, such a prospect is very exciting. Let's just place our investment in the Dunton Lumber Company for now and consider the Dunton Mine if and when it comes along."

"I know. I know you're right. So rational about these business matters."

"Did you notice how quickly Abbott brought up the possibility of the future mining venture? Hollis Dunton told me that the good doctor is an incurable mineral collector. He has a collection of specimens from all over the world. You can be sure that the man will be on watch for interesting rocks amongst the stumps."

8

On the final day of the holiday, Hattie, Mrs. Ritchie, and Lottie walked up Waterford Road and then down Back Street to a stone bridge across City Brook. On the way, they passed the Waterford Creamery, where a farmer was unloading gray milk cans onto a raised dock.

"Mrs. Ritchie, these folks have won many prizes for the quality of their butter. It's the best in the area. Waterford Butter is shipped in large quantities to Portland and as far as Boston. Perhaps you have seen it in your local stores."

"Can't say that I have," answered Mrs. Ritchie, "though, to tell the truth, we use only butter from a Belmont dairy. The quality is unparalleled. I am sure this shop makes the best for your area, but it can't be as good as the Belmont."

Lottie had her own opinion on the matter. "Mother, if the butter we have been eating at Mrs. Monroe's is from this plant, then I would have to say it is as good or even better than what you buy. Sometimes I think you are biased against country life. You're always saying our life in Winchester is better than the life they live here."

"Young lady, when you have lived as long as I have, you will realize that the rural standard of living leaves much to be desired. I am not biased, just wiser in the ways of the world. Food here is exposed to so much more dirt and farm debris that disease is more common than in our more sanitary environment. You don't see as much manure in Winchester."

Hattie held her tongue for as long as she could. She had already seen the big difference between the mother, who was a snob and never seemed to enjoy herself on their vacation, and the daughter who relished being in a more bucolic environment. Finally, she had to interject.

"I am reluctant to take sides, but 'twould be remiss of me not to agree with Lottie. While you may see more run-down homes here in Maine than in the part of Massachusetts where you live, people who are producing butter, meat, vegetables, and other foodstuffs here are just as diligent to deliver high-quality, clean products to their customers. Our way of life may be a bit slower than is your own, but that is the way we like it."

This statement brought an abrupt conclusion to the discussion, and the women continued their walk in silence. At the bridge, both Hattie and Lottie played at kicking dust from the road into the brook on the upstream side and running to the other side to watch the cloudy patch of water float by. The haughty mother stood off to the side and never said a word.

9

Nathan was settling up the bill with Mrs. Monroe while his children packed their bags. After counting out payment, he asked the innkeeper about Henry and Aphia.

"Mrs. Monroe, you've lived in South Waterford your entire life. You must know Henry Greene."

"I knew him as a young man when he was still living with his father in North Waterford. We didn't see him much down here in our village. Occasionally, he would come down to work for W.K. Hamlin in the carding mill or for Watson's box factory. His mother died very early on, I believe, so his dad raised him and a brother. He left for a year or two, but returned a few years back to buy a farm up on Blackguard Road. Haven't seen him in years."

"I heard he married a young girl from Norway. She still lives up on that farm, I think."

"Yes, old Pastor Shaw married them in the Wesleyan Chapel. It was funny that the service was on a workday. No one could go. Seemed odd to me."

"Do you know if the couple got along? I've heard rumors that he ran out on her."

"Can't say. I did hear from Clyde Bellows, who has a mill in Harrison, that the old owner of the farm, Abe Whitcomb, had a tragic loss of horses some time back when lightning struck and killed his herd. Greene was sent down to see if Bellows would render them all, but Clyde couldn't handle so many. He said that Whitcomb had to burn and bury them."

"So tragic," said Nathan. "That must have been a horrible job."

"Yes, you know how it is with the dead. If you don't bury the bodies deep enough, the smell comes up through the shallow soil for many years. Hope they were able to do the job right."

Nathan didn't like the way the conversation was going, so he said his farewell and went to the barn to get his horse and surrey. Soon Hattie returned and climbed up in the wagon with the children. Just before they were to leave, Lottie Ritchie ran over to grab Franny's hand.

"My new friend," she said earnestly, "I will never forget you." She handed Francena a piece of stationery. "Here is my address. Please be sure to write to me as often as you can."

As Franny took the young woman's hand, Hattie said, "Lottie, I'm sorry if I offended your mother. If she forgives me, perhaps she might allow you to come visit with us next year during the summer. We would all love to entertain you and show you how we live."

"Yes, Lottie, yes!" said Franny. "Come live with us for a time. It would be so wonderful!"

10

Liz sat at her design table plotting a new dress for the spring season. It was only September, but she wanted to keep ahead of the competition. Nathan had been promoting her creations all over New England. Demand for her women's, men's, and children's clothing had increased so dramatically that partners Maeve Cain and Mary Flaherty were unable to keep up with new orders from large department stores. Two part-time seamstresses had recently been hired, and the workroom was so crowded that Will Cain, Maeve's husband, was building a new shed addition in the rear. Liz was working the same long, six-day weeks that she had worked years before at the Pepperell, but she could not complain. Business was very, very good.

There came a knock at the door. Before she had time to answer, Will came bounding into the room with his young son, Owen, at his side. In the nearly thirty years Will had been her friend, Liz hadn't noticed him aging a bit. There was some gray showing up in his hair and beard, but he still stood straight and tall. She thought he remained as handsome as the day they'd first met. The boy, now six years of age, was going to be the spitting image of his dad except for the shock of red hair, which he got from his Irish mother.

"Lizzie, could you please do me a favor?" asked Will. "Could you keep an eye on the boy for me while I meet with the building inspector? With Maeve working so much these days, I'm having to care for all the children. Mary is taking care of little Anne, but she wouldn't take both. It will only be for an hour at most."

"Of course! I can use him to help me. How would you like that, Owen?" The boy ran to her side and placed a sweet kiss on her cheek.

"Where are the other two?" she asked.

"They're in school for another few hours. James has choir practice after school, but Janey will be home at two. I should be done before that. Caring for children is a lot of work, I'll tell you!"

"We all have a lot of work to do, don't we, Will?"

Doffing his cap, Will said, "Thanks so much, Lizzie dear. Don't you look forward to winter coming? The pace always slows down when the snow flies."

She did indeed look forward to a little rest, but not before the new designs were completed. There had been no time to visit the Halletts for several months. Letters had come from Hattie, so she knew that the family was doing well. Nathan had been so busy launching a new venture, in addition to servicing his regular clients, that their income was booming. However, he did not have the time to visit Westbrook. Liz was dying to hear if he had learned anything about Aphia Stevens and what had happened to Henry Greene. Life had taken many twists and turns, but she knew that, without a doubt, her own life was better by far than Aphia's cursed existence.

Owen sat to her right and held the long sheet of pattern paper on which a new dress design was being created. He watched as his "Auntie Liz" drew long flowing lines of a full skirt across the sheet just under his nose. The smell of ink irritated his nostrils, and he gave a little sneeze, dropping the paper.

"Sorry, Auntie Liz. Did I get anything on your drawing?"

"Don't worry, dear. That happens to me every once in a while. But don't wipe your nose on your sleeve, Owen. Here, use this piece of cloth."

Then came another knock. This time she rose from the table and opened the door. To her surprise, Nathan stood there with a bouquet of roses in his arms.

"Nathan, I was just this minute thinking of you, and you pop up at my very door. What a great surprise."

"Hopefully, I am not disturbing you, but I was coming back from Portland and wanted to make a quick visit. Oh, I see you already have a male caller," he said, pointing to Owen, who was still wiping his nose. "I saw these flowers in a shop in Commercial Street and just had to get them for someone."

She took the bouquet and placed a short affectionate kiss on her brother-in-law's cheek.

"Oh, yes," she said. "My life is filled with gentlemen callers today."

"Liz, I can't really stay for long. Hattie is expecting me home for a dinner party with several new friends. They are involved in that new venture I mentioned to you. One of them is a young man from 'the Provinces' who has come south to look for work. The other is an opinionated old doctor from Bethel. I am afraid I'll be protecting my wife from his demeaning opinions of the weaker sex. If I miss that dinner, I'll never be allowed to forget it."

"Oh, please step in; at least rest your bones. Can I get you a root beer?"

"No, thank you. I wanted to stop in and report on what small amount of information about Greene I learned during our recent vacation."

"Please, then, please sit down for a moment so that I can give you my full attention."

He related how little he had been able to find out and how evasive several people had been to his questions. He told how William Watson had fired Greene a few years back because he failed to show up for work. Was it a drinking problem? Watson was unwilling to say. Had the man been around recently? Again the question was left unanswered. Talk with Mr. Jones Hall was all he said, but Hall was not currently living in town. When he spoke with Mary Monroe, her answers were either misleading or reflected a failing memory. She recalled the Greenes' wedding, but other than that, she had no knowledge of whether Aphia was living alone or not.

"Liz, I am sorry at the disappointing report, but I will do my best to track down that man Jones Hall next week when I'm in Norway. I might even drive out to the farm in West Waterford and see for myself what the woman is doing there."

"Nathan, don't put yourself out. After all, it's simply a personal whim to put more pieces of my past to rest. I much appreciate your efforts, but we all have more important work to do than play private detector. Now, you have to go, and I have left my helper holding that pattern. He must be tired or bored."

She and Owen said goodbye to Nathan and went back to their work. Presently, Will returned and explained to Liz what had transpired with the inspector. All was going according to the permits, and they could continue closing in the walls of the addition.

"Liz, I thought I saw Nathan ride out of here in a hurry in that fancy surrey of his."

"You did. He couldn't stay around long. My sister is expecting him for an important dinner party. He was just telling me about a recent visit he and his family had in Waterford for a short holiday."

"Been years since I was out that way. Not that far away, but a bit off the beaten path."

"He says that the place is thriving with businesses, hotels, and such. They stayed at an inn run by a Mrs. Monroe."

"Mary Monroe. Of course. I know her well. My father used to do some work for her late husband, Samuel. Perhaps I might show the family a good time at that inn next spring. Right now, there is too much work to do before winter sets in. Come on, son, let's get out of the lady's hair."

At that moment, Moses entered the room, and Liz was surprised and pleased to see that he was not holding himself up with the cane. His leg must be healing. Soon they might be able to travel to Saco, and he might be able to resume reduced duties at the mill. That would make him feel much more useful, and they would be able to check on possible orders for the spring lines.

"Moses, my dear. You are looking quite healthy today. No cane!"

"Yes, Lizzie, isn't it wonderful for me to be able to toss that stick aside! It's been weeks since I fell. Took so long to heal this time." In the fourteen years since their marriage, Moses, who was twenty-five years older than his wife, had aged quickly because of arthritis and diabetes. On good days, their relationship was lively and amorous, but on days when he suffered, he played the role of patient with her as his nurse.

"My love, I apologize for being such a burden to you these last several weeks. You've been so kind and patient to this invalid."

"No. No, dear. You have needed the space and time to recover. You've done the work to heal yourself. Let's hope that you're getting back to being your old self."

"Old, you say? Liz, you make me feel so *young*. I'm not old when you're with me!"

He stood behind her chair, large hands tenderly resting on her shoulders. As she reached up to touch his arm, he leaned down and kissed the top of her head. They held that pose for several moments, each with their eyes closed. Then he walked across the room and landed heavily in a creaking maple pressed-back chair barely strong enough to hold his weight.

"Dear, Nathan was just here."

"Yes, I saw his chariot run off trailing a cloud of dust. He certainly does get around. Why didn't he stay? He and I have business to discuss."

"He could only stay for a moment. Hattie expects him to be in Bridgton in time to entertain two of their partners in that lumber mill in Rumford."

"That was one of the topics I wanted to discuss with him."

"Oh, I'm sure he will have time to meet with you and discuss that. Perhaps we might soon visit the Halletts and get a direct report."

Then she rose from the drawing table, walked to him, knelt by his side, and put her head on his ample lap. "It is so wonderful to have you back to your old self. Let's plan on traveling to Saco next week and then to Bridgton for a few days."

He stroked her long tresses and said, "We can go both places, but first I want to take you in my arms and show you that my love is still young."

11

Aphia Stevens did not expect a response to her letter to Miss Millett. It had been her intention to apologize for her past behavior to this perfect stranger. She did not want to start a conversation with the woman who was much more fortunate than she was to have been rid of Henry Greene. If only she herself had realized what a curse marriage to the man would become. When she'd met the seamstress, right after the man's death, Aphia had still been angry and stressed. She was finally rid of him—who had attacked her several times—but the willful confrontation with Millet was the last thing she'd wanted to do. Now, standing in the kitchen of her small farmhouse, she placed an envelope on the kitchen table. It was a letter from Lizzie Millet that had been waiting for her at the North Waterford Post Office that morning. A Westbrook return address and delicate woman's handwriting made it clear from whom it had come. She set a kettle to boil for tea, removed muddy knee-high riding boots, draped a worn denim jacket over a stuffed easy chair, and submerged a small, hand-tied bag of herbs from her garden into boiling water. Once her long legs were comfortably folded underneath her, she broke the seal on the envelope.

As she read the letter, a dark frown spread across her face. It hadn't even been her idea to reach out to Millett. Bert Learned, a friend in West Waterford who had known Millett from the time she was a child, had suggested that Aphia's growing anxiety was a result of both a horrible marriage and how hurtful she had been to the seamstress. He thought that a letter of apology might quiet her own mind. What a fool she had been to follow Bert's advice.

Dear Miss Stevens,

Forgive me for being so slow in responding to your recent letter. So much time has passed since we met that I was unsure who you were and why a stranger would write me. I don't think I ever knew your family name, as Henry only referred to you as Aphia in his "dear John" letter to me. Or perhaps I had blocked out any recollection of our confrontation along with the pain we both received at the hands of that man.

As memories of that day have come back to me, I do recall that you pushed me to the ground. Perhaps I lost my balance when I realized he had never read the words of my own letter to him. I had hoped to pierce his heart with words which might stay with him until the end of his bitter life. Please be sure that I harbor no ill will toward you, who wished to greet me as a woman who shared Henry Greene's cruelty and greed. Friends tell me that you still own the farm which Henry got from your grandfather after deserting me. As I am often visiting with my sister and family in Bridgton, it would be easy to meet you there at your farm. You might also visit me here in Westbrook, if you are ever traveling out this way.

Please do not feel remorse any longer for what passed between us so long ago.

Sincerely,
Lizzie Millett

"Pierced his heart! End of a bitter life! Yes, yes!" she shouted. "Missy, you may have cursed at him, but I made your wishes come true."

Angered by the unwanted letter, she ran from the house into the cold afternoon air. Dark clouds rolled down from the top of Beech Hill, and dampness in the air suggested that rain or snow would soon follow. It was only when she stepped into a shallow puddle near a break in the fence surrounding the horse pasture that she realized her feet were bare. Yet, the cold water did not slow her pace. To the left of the gate, the grade climbed abruptly onto a small hillock where dark-green vinca and twisted grapevines grew wild. She yanked up a vine and, waving it in the air around her head, began to laugh so loud that it sounded like a scream. Up and down Aphia jumped on the ground cover. She tried to kick up dirt in one bare patch of ground, but her foot caught in another vine. She lost her balance and fell face first into the damp soil.

"Fie on you, Henry Greene!" she yelled. "On you and on the woman you left behind when you took me to be your wife. If she dares to come here, we will see if she might join you in Hell."

Heavy rain driven by a sudden gust of wind soaked the anguished woman and splashed mud over her clothes. Rising up from the ground, she struggled back toward her house against the force of the wind. At the door, she stripped off all her muddy, soaked clothing on the threshold. She turned to face the storm completely naked and held her arms straight up in the air.

"Henry, you devil, you have held me alone in this curse for too long. Now I wish to share it with others!"

12

Hattie stood at the door and watched as two men dismounted their horses and tied them to the hitching post. Nathan had promised to be home before they arrived, but he was late. She now would have to prepare dinner *and* entertain his business partners, one whom she disliked and one of whom she had never met. This was not at all fair.

"Mrs. Hallett," Dr. Abbott hailed as the two approached. "I'm afraid that we are a little early. The road down from Bethel is so much improved that the ride was easier than I remembered."

"Come right on in, Dr. Abbott. You have made better time than my husband, but you are certainly very welcome. Would you prefer to secure your horses in the barn rather than leave them tied to the post? There are blankets there to keep them warm in this early autumn chill."

The second man, a young, handsome man with a full beard, bowed in her direction. "Aye, that would be something I could do. Please, Doctor, allow me to care for your horse as well as mine."

"Thank you, Mr. Potter. That would be very kind of you. This old back of mine could sorely use a little rest. Though the way was easy, the ride from Bethel is always long."

Hattie watched the young man unhitch the horses and lead

them into the open barn. He was a short man who looked to be no more than in his mid-twenties. His build was that of a blacksmith: broad shoulders and arms so muscular that they drew the sleeves of his coat very tightly around them. He wore trousers of homespun cloth and a heavy vest of the same knobby material. Such material was seldom worn in Bridgton anymore except by the very old or those living in poverty.

Remembering that Abbott would likely want to smoke, Hattie led him to the front porch. "Dr. Abbott, Nathan and I do not like to have tobacco smoke in the house. Please feel free to sit out here and enjoy your pipe. I know it will help you rest from your journey."

"Thank you so much. Would you first direct me to the privy?"

She smiled and said, "Oh, sir, we no longer use an outhouse. We have running water pumped from the well and have the latest bathroom sink and toilet. The door is just over there." She pointed in the direction of the kitchen.

Abbott, though impressed by modernity, was nevertheless embarrassed to say that he had never used a flush toilet before. "Mrs. Hallett, would you please be so kind as to instruct me in how to use the contraptions? Even in Bethel Center, we do not see such improvements."

It was now her turn to be embarrassed as they headed toward the bathroom. She had not meant to boast and make the man ill at ease. As they entered, she demonstrated how to fill and empty the bowl. Flushing made such a noise that he jumped back in surprise. "I'm not sure I will ever install one of these in my house. The noise would make me forget what I was doing in the place."

How strange, she thought to herself as she closed the door on him. We don't usually have conversations about our private business.

When she returned to the kitchen the second man was warming himself by the cookstove. "Madam, permit me to introduce myself. I am Clarence Leslie Potter from Yarmouth, Nova Scotia.

Ye have such a modern home. Surely your husband works very hard to keep his family comfortable."

He spoke with an accent that Hattie had not heard before. All the people she had ever met from Canada either spoke French or had a very distinct French accent. Potter spoke English very clearly, but with diction and pronunciation very much like Maeve Cain and Mary Flaherty.

"Mr. Potter, welcome to our home. Nathan and I try to keep up with all the newest amenities, but I can assure you there are many neighbors here in Bridgton that have more lavish residences. Please make yourself comfortable. Dr. Abbott will soon be sitting on the front porch so he can relax and smoke. You might like to join him there until my husband returns."

"I deny myself the smoking that so many others seem to enjoy, but I am ready to sit with the doctor as you request."

"Sir, I don't mean to pry into your life. I don't know you well enough for that, but by your accent, I would take you to be Irish. Pardon me for asking. It is just that my sister has two business partners from that country who speak very much as you do."

"No, Mrs. Hallett, I was born and raised in Nova Scotia. My grandparents came from Scotland originally. They have Scottish Gaelic as a native tongue. When I was a child, my family had that same tongue at home, but we were taught English in school. Now I have both languages, and yes, there are some similarities between Scots and Irish."

They looked at each other in silence for a few seconds as if each would like to know more about the other's life. Hattie then excused herself to prepare dinner, while Clarence joined Dr. Abbott on the porch. Perhaps she was being too pushy about keeping the visitors outside until Nathan arrived, but it was not her responsibility to entertain them. They were his guests, his partners in both the lumber and mining businesses. Besides, it was her job to finish preparing the roast beef dinner, and their presence in the kitchen would be a distraction. Thankfully, as Abbott exited the bathroom, Nathan bounded up the front steps. He was quick to ask the men to join him outside, where he might show them around the property before dinner.

13

Following an exceptional dinner, the three men retired to the porch to chat while the doctor smoked his pipe. A chill had set in during the meal as a brisk northerly wind picked up from Highland Lake.

Nathan was curious about the Canadian. "Mr. Potter, you have traveled quite a distance to be with us tonight. Will you be staying in the area for a while?"

"Sir, please call me by my given name. The hospitality you and your family have shown me today has made me feel at home. Surely, I would want to extend my stay here in your country for a longer time, but I am only here for a fortnight and must away to home quite soon."

"Winters must be harsh in Ontario," said Nathan. "Must be hard to find year-round work there."

"Yes, it is for many men. The man I work for, Mr. Albert Warren, keeps me busy. He has paid me to travel here. You might have heard of him. He is an American from Ohio. A very wealthy man who now owns the Canadian Central Railroad and two iron mines in Quebec Province. He has been very good to me, taken me from the dead-end prospects of a Nova Scotia miner and given me the chance to make a better living building the railroad. I'm now managing a team of welders in Ontario. With the winter setting in on us early this year, I was able to get away for a time."

Abbott knocked ashes from his meerschaum onto the porch floor and began to question the purpose of Potter's visit.

"Mr. Potter—er, Clarence—I did not know you were a miner," said the doctor.

"Sir, any interest I have in mining is personal. After reading about the discovery of very valuable gems at Mount Mica here in

Oxford County, I wish to see what possibilities might be here for me and my family."

"Do you have children back in Canada?" asked Nathan.

"My wife Emma and I have three young children. My wage is better with the railroad than it was as a Nova Scotian miner, but it is not enough to guarantee my children have a better life than I have."

"So, you are both a miner and a blacksmith?" asked Abbott. "There might be a job for you at a mine in the future."

"Oh, I would be so grateful, sir. If such a mine might produce gems of as high quality as those taken from Mount Mica, the future for all involved would indeed be very bright."

Hattie, who had been standing quietly at the front door, overheard the mention of Mount Mica and joined in, saying, "Mr. Potter, I agree with you completely. Nathan and I are excited about the prospects for the new Dunton Mine."

"Ma'am, I have personally seen the wealth that a good mine can return to its owners and operators," said Potter. "Mr. Warren and his partners have become millionaires. They now own over 700,000 acres of copper-rich Ontario wilderness and have begun to produce a metal called nickel, which is so hard you can shoot bullets at it and it will not even dent. They didn't even know about nickel before I discovered it mixed with the copper ores."

"I'm not one who knows anything about either copper or this new metal," said Hattie. "Not even sure what mica is. However, if the tourmaline gems from Dunton's land are as good as the ones those boys found by the bucket in West Paris, we will surely be rich."

Nathan stood from his chair and said, "Come, everyone. Let's retire to the parlor where I may light a warming fire. Mr. Potter, when you decide to move down here, I'm sure we will be able to find you both a job and a place to live. Your many skills would fit precisely with a number of my customers and clients."

14

By the time Clarence returned to Sudbury, Ontario, winter had wrapped itself around what meager settlements had been made by miners and railroad workers. His train had been halted twice by icy snowdrifts towering above the locomotive. He and other passengers had to disembark and work with shovels to clear enough space to pass. This was his first experience with winter on the plains of the north where unchecked winds blew down from Hudson Bay and Manitoba. In Nova Scotia, where he had been raised and had lived for most of his life, maritime winters were less harsh. The house his family had vacated in Yarmouth to make a better life in the West of Canada was much more comfortable than the one-room cabin in which they now lived. Theirs was one of three identical cabins clustered around a stack of snow-covered railroad ties. The other two were vacant for the season, abandoned by workers who were perhaps wiser than they were in not wanting anything to do with Ontario winter.

No one met him at the makeshift train station, which was little more than a wooden platform set to the side of the tracks with a small hand-painted sign swinging back and forth in the wind. The dirt roads that led in the direction of his home were so drifted over that he had to lift his legs up to the side and swing them over the snow as he walked. The duffel he carried was such a burden that he kept tossing it as far ahead of himself as he could, then picking it up and repeating the process. The only way he was sure which cabin was his was that smoke rose from only one metal chimney, and pale light shone through the small windows on either side of a bare plank door. Before he could enter, he kicked snow aside so that none would get in through the open door.

So as not to frighten Emma and the kids, he knocked three times and waited for someone to answer. When no one answered, he entered to find everyone huddled in one bed. Four-year-old Hazel jumped from the covers and ran to him with arms spread. Before he could shake the ice from his coat, her younger sister toddled across and wrapped her arms around his wet boots. Emma stayed beneath the covers nursing baby Clyde. At last she rose to greet her husband who had been gone for so long.

"Husband, how were you able to get here in such a blizzard? We have been lying together for heat all day. The fire makes little difference. The blasted wind just sucks the heat right out of the wood as it burns."

Indeed, the place was so cold that his breath condensed in front of his face and the snow was slow to melt from his clothes. After a quick hug and kiss from Emma, he went to the stove. No wonder it was so cold—the fire was nearly out. Thankfully, there were two large stacks of cordwood just outside the door where he had piled them before leaving for Maine. Soon the fire was blazing and stew was bubbling in a cast-iron pot on top. Carrying Clyde, Emma came to stand beside him. The two toddlers sat on the floor very close to the stove and began chattering to each other.

"Clarence, this weather will be the death of me, mark my words. I'm wondering why we even left that good strong house, our family, and our neighbors in Yarmouth."

"Yes, the weather is wicked here, but look around you. Did we ever have such a wood pile in Yarmouth? Did we ever have so much food in the larder? So much good clean water? I was working so hard back there just to survive. Here we have more of what we need to improve our lives."

"If so, why do you leave us and travel so far? I need you to be here. I can't do this alone," she said, gesturing to the wee ones on the floor and at her breast.

"I am so sorry to have left you for these few weeks. I didn't know how fast and how bad the weather could turn. I'm here now and will not leave again. Be assured."

She passed the baby to him and stirred the stew. Her plan had been to greet him with open arms and a hearty meal, but at least he would be able to enjoy some hot food after a terrible trip.

Clarence sat at the wooden table nestling his lovely son onto his chest as the other two moved away from the fire to sit at his feet. He knew that Emma would never be able to understand why he had gone south to Maine. She did not have the imagination he did about what could be done to improve their lives. He had tried to explain his big plans to her many times, but in her mind, they were all fantasies that had nothing to do with their day-to-day needs. Like him, she had grown up in poverty. Her father and brothers were coal and iron miners who had no future but a hole in the ground. Someday, he said to himself as she served the stew, "someday she will see that my plans will pay off, and we will live the lives that we deserve."

That night, the couple lay together under warm quilts that Emma had made. The room was much warmer, and the children were in their own beds sleeping soundly. Clarence drew his wife so close to him that he could feel her heart beating. He did not want to disturb her, yet, over a month had passed since they had last slept together. He touched her breasts through the flannel nightdress and she stirred. He kissed the side of her face and whispered, "I have missed you so much these last few weeks. Please forgive my absence," as he reached down to touch her belly. Rolling over so that her back was up against him, she coughed and then sneezed.

"Dear Clarence, I have missed you, too, and wanted to give you a warm welcome. Instead you found a cold house with little more than a stew to eat. That is not the meal I had planned before such a blizzard came."

"You can still give me a warm welcome," he said, smiling in the darkness as he placed his hand on her buttocks.

"I know, but that will have to wait. When my time of the month arrived while you were away, the bleeding never stopped. I fear that something is wrong, but with such a winter, I haven't been able to get to the doctor in Sudbury Center. My mother had the same problem at times. Her mother died very early from her bleeding. The old ones used to say that it's a curse put by God on certain women because they enjoyed sex too much."

"What can it be? You've had no lasting problems from Clyde's birth. That was a year ago, and you've been healthy, haven't you?"

She rolled back to face him and placed his hand on her lips. "Yes, we have had no problems with our lovemaking, and I've been regular with my cycle. I've felt a little weak lately, but I'm sure that's because you were gone. Now that you've returned, I'm sure to get my energy back. Please, let us sleep soundly together tonight. Perhaps we might try again tomorrow."

Emma returned to sleep, but Clarence lay awake worrying about her and dreaming of a day when they would be far away from this rugged wilderness.

15

The spring of 1896 arrived early, just as the winter had. It was only March 20th and already the snow was gone and buds had begun to appear on the aspens. Clarence stood at the window watching a flock of robins peck at the muddy roadway. It was mud season, but at least he could get outside without being blown about by a northern gale. Since his return from Maine, he had thrown himself into making the family comfortable: keeping the fire burning, lugging buckets of water from the spring that never froze, and sharing the care of the children. He had also begun an exchange of letters with Nathan Hallett, with whom he shared a belief that his future lay in Oxford County, not Ontario.

Several times in his correspondence, Nathan had mentioned the progress being made by Hollis Dunton in Newry, near Bethel, and suggested that Clarence might want to return to Maine to speak directly with Dunton. One letter had come from Abbott, a short note in which he expressed a willingness to house the Potter family temporarily in his own home, if and when they decided to move.

Given more time to herself because of her husband's help, Emma's health improved during the late winter to the point where she was able to enjoy their life together once again. Then, in late February, as the weather moderated, she began to plan her new vegetable garden, thinking that as soon as the snow cleared, she might lay out the beds. One night after supper, she went to the pantry, climbed up on a wooden stool, and pulled a large earthenware jar from the top shelf. In it were all the seeds she had brought from Yarmouth.

Clarence sat by the stove writing another letter to Nathan. In it, he explained that Emma and her parents back in Nova Scotia were against them relocating to Maine anytime soon, but that he would visit again in the spring. A loud crash sent him running to the kitchen. The seed jar had fallen to the floor, and Emma was crawling around trying to gather up the scattered seeds. As he joined her on the floor, she cried out, "We must gather every seed! Can't lose a one—these are my hope!"

Tears slid down her cheeks as he grabbed her by the shoulders and looked directly into her eyes. "Em, it's all right. We'll get them all. Please don't worry."

"I know how foolish I may seem. These are only seeds to you, but to me they're like the family blood in my veins. You believe in a better future, not like me who looks to the past for my dreams. These seeds came from the garden of my grandmother. If they are lost, my hope will be, too."

When the seeds had all been found, the two sat down to sort them out by type: one pile of squash, another of corn, another of turnip. When there were many little piles on the table, Emma took empty envelopes from Clarence's writing box and began to label them to hold the seeds. As he was about to chastise her for using his good stationery, his eyes spotted a red dot on the floor beneath her chair.

"Em, are you bleeding again? Look on the floor there. Is that blood?"

She looked at the floor, then at her dress. There was a red stain on the fabric. "Oh, no! It has come again. I thought 'twas gone away for good, that I was healthy. Oh, no!"

"We'll be off to Sudbury Center tomorrow to see this doctor everyone says is good, Em. For now, let me finish putting the seeds away for safekeeping. You can clean yourself and rest until the morning."

"What of the children?"

"We'll be gone for only a few hours. I can light and bank the fire to warm them. They will be safe."

"But what if I am unable to return?"

"Even if the doctor keeps you overnight, I will come back."

Neither of them slept that night. Emma was up every hour to wash blood from the rags pushed up inside her. Clarence was wracked with worry, and before dawn, he saddled a horse borrowed from the mine stable. After banking the fire and making sure the children would be safe, they began the long trip to town along a road so muddy that the horse's hooves slipped in the mire. It took three hours to get to the doctor's house, and by that time, Emma had weakened so that she was barely able to hold her arms around her husband's waist. He lowered her to the ground, telling her to steady herself by holding fast to the saddle horn until he could dismount and lead her to the door. He knocked, but no one answered. He rapped again and then tried the door. It swung open as Emma fell against it.

Just to the left of the door was an office with a big desk, two chairs, and an examination table upon which Clarence laid his wife. Her eyes were closed, and she seemed to be asleep by the time a tall bearded man entered the room.

"Are you Dr. Jeffers?" asked Clarence. The man stared past him to the woman on his examination table.

"Yes, I am he. What is wrong with this woman?"

"My wife, Emma, has been dripping blood on the horse all the way from the mining camp where we live. It won't stop."

Jeffers strode to the table, raised Emma's eyelids, and lifted her hand to check her pulse. "Sir, your wife is dead."

16

This will be the day I get caught up on my bookkeeping, thought Lizzie as she descended the stairs from her apartment to the first-floor office. With completion of the new spring lines, the seamstresses had been given the day off. Moses had already left for Saco, so there would be no interruptions. When she completed her chores, she would be able to follow him to their town house and enjoy some free time in Portland and "Spindle City," as Biddeford/Saco was called. She had been concerned about Moses traveling alone, but when Will Cain offered to drive him to the train station, it set her mind at ease.

On top of her small oak secretary desk were two trays, one of invoices and one of receipts, piled so high that the papers overflowed. In the rush to complete so many orders, a month had passed since ledger entries had been recorded. It wasn't that she tried to avoid balancing the books. She had been taught at an early age by her late mother, Francena, how to keep a household budget. Business records were very much the same to her. The noise of early-morning traffic was building on Forest Avenue when she heard the sound of a horse's hooves coming up the driveway. For several minutes, she waited for the bell to ring at the locked door. Hearing nothing, she walked to the front window. Tied to the porch railing was a most beautiful Morgan, its skin shining in the morning sun. Beads of sweat dripped from its haunches as if it had been ridden hard for a long way. Its rider stood unseen behind the animal. Lizzie could only make out the person's high boots. With such boots, it must be a woman, she thought, but why has she not come to the door?

Lizzie went to the door, opened it, and peered at the as-yet-unknown rider, who then stepped clear of the steed. It was Aphia Stevens dressed in the same denim she had worn the first time they had met back in 1884. Liz was speechless and stepped back into the room waiting for her visitor to approach. Standing on either side of the threshold, the two women eyed each other suspiciously, Liz with her mouth agape, Aphia with a toothy grin.

"Well, Miss Millett. I'm betting I am the last person in the world you expected to see at your door this morning." She began to giggle.

"Miss Stevens, you'd be a winner on that bet. And please, my last name is Webber. I'm married."

"Oh, you found a man after all, did you? I would think that after your first experience with a man you would remain a spinster. Why does the sign not say '*Webber's* American Designs' if you are really married?"

"I don't think that is any of your business, Miss Stevens. What are you doing here?"

Usually Liz would have invited a visitor inside by this time, but there was something about the woman's demeanor that was suspicious. The boots were mud-spattered, although it was a dry day. Her jeans and jacket, too, were filthy and nearly worn through at the knees and elbows. Nathan's description of her riding wildly through the town of Waterford came to mind. Something was wrong with this woman.

"I've been wanting to speak directly to you ever since your letter came. Why don't you invite me in? I've ridden all the way from West Waterford today and would like to sit for a spell."

"Oh, forgive my lack of matters. Please come in. You must have been on the road since before dawn. Can I offer you coffee and breakfast toast?"

"No, Miss. I only want to rest before returning to my home. Just need to sit and perhaps have a cup of water, if you would be so kind."

Perhaps I'm wrong about her, thought Lizzie. I can at least give her a drink and a place to sit in the office. Perhaps I'm overreacting.

Aphia sat in a pressed-back chair next to the desk as Liz went for the water. When she returned, the woman was at her desk going through the trays.

"Please step away from those papers. They are none of your business." She startled herself with the loudness of her own voice.

The intruder again began to giggle as she turned around. She accepted the cup and returned to the chair. "I have a gift for you, Miss Whatever-your-name-is."

Pulling a worn and wrinkled piece of paper from her jacket pocket, Aphia tried to force it into Lizzie's hand. "This is the letter you wouldn't take from me when last we met, the one you sent to my late husband when he deserted you for me. After you and your sister left the village, I returned and pulled it from City Brook." Again she giggled, but this time the laughter became loud and quite wild. "Dearie, you offended me those many years ago. I only meant to give you back your pathetic letter."

"I did not want the letter then, and I surely do not want it now. The woman I was those many years ago was weak and unhappy. That letter carries the words and thoughts of someone other than me. You are the one who seems to carry the hurts of our youth deep in your heart. Best to leave all that behind and start a new life."

Throwing the scrap of paper on the floor, Aphia stepped on it, moving her heel back and forth as if she might be crushing the memories of her late husband. Then she bolted from the room, untied the tired Morgan, and mounted.

Before riding away, she shouted out, "Missy, you are never to see me again! If you bother me, I will make sure you share the curse Henry has laid upon my life!"

And with that, she was gone.

Much relieved, Liz closed the door and returned to her desk, but she was unable to start the task at hand. She worried about the possibility that Aphia was dangerously mad and that Nathan needed to be warned. As she would soon be in Saco and unlikely to see him for several weeks, she pulled a box of stationery from the desk drawer, pushed the two trays aside, and penned a letter to him. As she wrote, Mary Flaherty entered the office accompanied her young niece, Faith Cain.

"Mary, did you catch sight of a woman on horseback speeding away on Forest Avenue? I want to make sure she has left and does not return."

"No. I didn't see anyone. Faith and I walked over from Maeve's house, so we were not near the highway. Who was it? Anyone I know?"

"No. And you can be glad you don't know her. It was that woman Aphia Greene, who married the man to whom I was engaged so many years ago. You remember that story. Hattie and I went to visit our old home in Waterford, and the woman pushed me down in the mud. I told you and Maeve about it long ago."

"And sure you did. I recall that. But what in the name of God was she doing here in Westbrook?"

"She rode all the way to threaten me and warn me to stay away from her. As if I would *want* to be near her! She is mad."

"I will warn Will about her being here. He has mentioned her before and is curious about what happened to her husband. I'm sure my sister does not want her husband to poke his nose into her business. He could get his nose bit off."

Lizzie couldn't hold back a laugh at Mary's comment. "You are so funny, my friend. You certainly see things in a different way than I do. But yes, please advise Will on what happened. God knows if she might resent anyone who knows me."

"Yes, that's me," Mary said in her Irish lilt. "Good old funny Mary." She winked and stuck out her tongue as Lizzie reached for her hand.

"Don't you ever change, dear. You are a ray of Irish sunshine."

"I think I'm more American than Irish now. I've nearly lost my accent. If it wasn't for the freckles, you would think me a native Mainer, like young Faith."

Riverton Trolley Park. *Amusement park on the Presumpscot River at the junction of Forest Avenue and Riverside Street. Opened by Portland Railroad Company in 1897. Casino design by architect John Calvin Stevens of Portland. Photo in* Portland, Maine, and What I Saw There. *Portland: Chisholm Bros., 1906.*

17

Unable to finish her bookkeeping at the office, Lizzie carried it with her to Saco. She was sure to be able to find time to work on it in the town house where she would be living for a month or more. Her big trunk was filled to the top with clothes made in the shop to meet every possible occasion. The weather in Saco was so changeable and her social life so busy that she had to be prepared for anything. Moses often referred to her as his "fashion plate," a term that had bothered her at first, before she realized that the description was apt and complimentary. He was proud of the clothes she made and pleased to show her off to others.

Will Cain loaded the trunk, a large valise, and two duffels onto his two-horse wagon. He had offered to drive Lizzie to Riverton on the banks of the Presumpscot River, which marked the town lines of Portland and Westbrook where a trolley park had recently been opened. There she would be able to ride the electric trolley back to Union Station for the connection on the Boston and Maine to Biddeford/Saco. The Cains were planning to spend a family day in the park, so the wagon would be somewhat crowded, but the ride would be fun for all.

The conditions were ideal for a late fall day, warm with bright sun filtering through remaining foliage of reds and yellows. Faith, Owen, and Patrick sat atop the luggage and were tethered to the wagon railings for safety. Will drove with the two women crowded in on the bench seat. During the short ride to Riverton, the children sang a round that they made up about riding in a buggy. Over and over, they repeated the chorus of "Clip, clop. Clip, clop. Clop, clip. Clop, clip. What a day to take a trip."

"Children, children, your Aunt Lizzie might not appreciate your loud singing," said Maeve after a while. "Why don't you just pay attention to the scenery and rest your voices. We are nearly there."

"Let them be, Maeve. I love the sound of their cheerful voices. You are so fortunate to have such a happy family. Moses and I love them as if they are our own."

"Never too late to try, you know."

"Oh, believe me, we do try, but it may be too late for us."

"Hush, now. How old are you? Me mom had me when she was in her forties. I came out okay. Well, didn't I? You don't have to answer if you don't want to."

"Yes, you came out great. It's not so much my age that keeps me childless, but Moses is so much older that I don't think he would be able to keep up with a young one. Plus, our way of living is not well suited—always moving between one house and the other. Where would the nursery be?"

"My dear, as long as you are happy with your life and with Moses, that's what counts the most. Like your sister, Hattie, I could hardly wait to have a family. It's the most important part of life to me. Couldn't be without the young ones. Will here is good to me, so I'll keep him, too."

They crossed the river and entered Riverton Trolley Park through a lovely wrought-iron gate held by two stone pillars. Families were disembarking from a four-car trolley. The women were dressed in gay outfits, the men in vests and bowler hats. Youngsters carried kites and balloons. A multicolored gazebo could be seen nestled among the trees on a bluff overlooking the riverbank. On a pier that extended out nearly to the center of the Presumpscot, a line of people had formed waiting to rent canoes.

"Oh, what a great day you will have!" said Lizzie as she stepped down from the wagon. "I'm tempted to stay here and enjoy such a gay scene."

"Yes, Liz. Please join us for a while," said Will. "You won't find any threatening types here, I'd venture. Just a fun place for a warm fall day."

"Did Maeve tell you about my visitor?"

"Yes, she did. I saw the woman riding away at a fast gallop. Nathan told me several years ago that Aphia had become mad, and that she rode around town some nights hollering to herself. He related a story he had heard from a man who did some work for her on the farm. He said that her barn was full of bundles of dried herbs hanging from the rafters. And that she cooked up potions on the kitchen stove. She seems to have expanded her mad rides to include our part of Westbrook."

"Madness is the right word for her. I can't figure why she has not been able to free herself from her demons. There must be something more to her husband's disappearance than we know, some factor that drives her to distraction. I know I expressed an interest in finding out more, and that you and Nathan said you would investigate, but please do me the favor of forgetting my request and stay away from that witch."

"A witch, you say. Hmm. That just might be true. Another story I heard was that Postmaster Watson was concerned about a number of packages she was posting to addresses all around New England. He asked her what the parcels contained and, following several arguments, she told him that she was sending herbal mixtures to her 'customers.' Liz, don't worry about me. My guard is up about that woman."

"Will, you are a dear to bring me this far. I have to catch a train at Union Station in the afternoon, so I must be leaving. Can you give me a hand with the luggage?"

As he handed the last bag to her on the trolley she touched his arm tenderly. "You have always been the one who helps me travel. I remember you so many years ago lifting that huge chest when I first left my grandparents to go to Saco. We've been friends a long time. Now your family is so dear to me. We have shared so much."

"Lizzie. Safe journey to you. I'll always remember our experiences together with gratitude." He gave her a gentle hug.

Maeve watched the brightly painted open-sided trolley pull away. She had never considered the possibility that there might be something between her husband and her dear friend until now. The manner of their farewell struck her as very affectionate for old friends. After the entire family had climbed down from the wagon, she reached for Will's hand as the kids scampered before them.

"Willy, how long have you known Lizzie?"

"She was just a child when first we met. Perhaps thirteen or fourteen years old. I remember her being so sad and bedraggled when her grandfather brought her home for the first time. She had a very rough beginning in life."

"Yes, she has told me those tales about losing her mother so early and some of the problems she faced with her father and stepmother, but she has turned out well for one with a bad start."

"You have known her nearly as long, haven't you? She must have been only sixteen or so when she moved to Saco and roomed with you and Mary. You know as much about her life as I do."

"Perhaps, but you two seem to have a much closer bond than she has with Mary or me."

"Not jealous, are you? Hey, relax. We are close like brother and sister or cousins."

"Just as long as it's not kissing cousins."

"Maeve, come on, now. I get enough kisses from you. Don't need any more from anybody else." He put his arm around her shoulders and touched the auburn bun of her hair. "How could you be jealous? I'm concerned with her welfare, aren't you? The surprise visit by that mad woman has me worried. There is too much mystery about Miss Greene or Stevens or whatever she calls herself now. What happened to her husband? No one knows for sure, but it's mysterious. Now, out of the blue, she shows up on Liz's doorstep, warning her to keep away or else. Good reason to be concerned, I'd say."

"I know you're right, Will. It's just that you two act so close, almost like lovers. Back home in Clare that kind of affection would be okay, but here? I guess I am more an American now than I thought."

"You are my only lover, Maeve. Have no worry of that. After all these years and the many experiences Liz and I have shared, she is like a sister, and I want her to be safe and happy, just as you wish for your sister Mary."

"I'll say no more about this," she said. "My life with you is a most precious gift from God, one that I do not wish to hurt with foolish suspicions."

18

Francena Hallett had maintained regular correspondence with her new friend Lottie Richie ever since they'd first met in South Waterford. Hattie and Nathan were pleased that their young daughter had become such a letter writer. Until recently, she had not been an avid student. Now she had become very studious about penmanship, spelling, vocabulary, and diction. Her teachers remarked that her "pen pal" should be awarded for encouraging such diligence.

One Saturday morning, as her daughter sat writing a letter at the kitchen table, Hattie sat down across from her.

"Franny, what would you say to inviting your girlfriend up for a visit this summer? If her parents approve, we might entertain Lottie for several weeks."

"Oh, Mother, that would be so wonderful. I love her so. But she has such an exciting life in Winchester, it might bore her to be with us for a time."

"You can't be sure of that. After all, she seemed to love their visit to Mrs. Monroe's. Why don't you just invite her and see what comes of it?"

The letter she was writing then became an invitation:

Dearest Lottie,

My mother has come up with a splendid idea. She wonders if you might get permission from your parents to visit us in Bridgton after your classes are done. You might stay for as long as you wish. We would show you a wonderful time here in Maine. We will go hiking, swimming, picking berries. We could read books to each other and go to the theater here in town. A climb on Mount Washington would be thrilling. There is so much to do. You might stay until you got bored.

Please do consider a visit.

Your true friend,
Franny

Only a week later, a letter from Massachusetts arrived addressed to Francena. When she returned from school, Hattie handed the envelope to her. Franny ran to her room without removing her coat and boots, threw herself on the bed, and opened the letter with a sharp opener she had purchased with her allowance.

My Dear Sweet Franny,

I love your invitation. On the day it arrived, I read it to my parents at the dinner table. Mom chastised me for not concentrating on my meal and didn't like the idea at all. Dad convinced her that it would be good for me to get away after graduation and before I start classes at Burdett School of Business. She still objected until I agreed to stay for only two weeks and have her travel with me on the train and stay herself for a couple of days. I think she wants to get away from Dad a little bit.

So, YES!! I can accept your kind invitation, if Mom's coming along is acceptable to your parents. Your mom and mine didn't seem to get along all that well, but it will only be for two days.

Dad wanted to know if you would be allowed to travel back with me and stay with us for a week or so. I would love to show you off to all my friends. And take you around to all my favorite places. Please think about that.

My high school classes end in very early May. Graduation is May 20th. Perhaps I might be able to be with you for Memorial Day. That would be so swell. Let me know if that is acceptable.

I love you so much,
Lottie

The stage was set for an exciting exchange of visits. Hattie was not so sure that Mary Ritchie would be a joy to entertain, but she believed it would be worthwhile if the two girls could become fast friends. Nathan said that he could schedule a trip to his Boston area clients and accompany Franny back to Winchester with Lottie.

19

Clarence grieved, not so much for his dead Emma, but for himself. How could he work for the Central Ontario Railroad and raise three children by himself? With spring coming on, he had to make some quick decisions. Emma's parents might be willing to welcome him and the children back to Yarmouth, at least temporarily, but there was no way he could earn enough money at home to take care of the family's needs. As he saw it, there were three options. He might stay in Ontario working for the railroad, but he would need to find a new wife right away. Or he might return to Yarmouth and live with in-laws who would help with the kids until he found a new wife. Third, he could leave the children temporarily in Yarmouth and return to work laying track, then reunite the family when he had a new wife.

Since it was unlikely that he could remarry immediately, he decided to take the second option. Not being one to carefully work out all the details, he packed up four-year-old Hazel Merle, two-year-old Bessie Mildred, and one-year-old Clyde Conrad. They traveled to Yarmouth, first by stage and then by ferry, arriving unannounced at the door of Matthew and Ellie Sherman three days later at dusk. The two youngest were crying loudly as Clarence knocked. Mr. Sherman opened the door, but in the dim light, he could not clearly make out what he saw.

"Can I do something for you?" he asked. The elderly miner was not wearing his glasses. He still had on the pit outfit, heavy denim coveralls spotted with rust. His bare arms showed cuts and bruises earned by long hard labor many feet below the ground.

Years of listening to jackhammers and the strikes of sledges had dimmed his hearing.

"Father Sherman, it is Clarence Potter," said Clarence.

"Who do you say? Are you sure you have the right address?"

"Matthew, it is me, Clarence Potter. Your daughter has died, and I need your help."

Finally, the old man recognized Clarence. "Mother, please come here. It's Potter and the grandchildren."

Ellie, a tall, gaunt woman who wore her hair pulled back in a tight bun, stepped onto the threshold. "What do we have here? A family visit? Come in, please. Come in! Where is Emma?"

"Ellie, your daughter is dead. I buried her three days ago."

Matthew and Ellie threw their hands up to the low ceiling and began to cry. The woman lost her balance, falling to the ground. Wailing and keening, she lay there until Clarence put down the baby he was carrying and offered a hand to her. She refused his help, rising to a kneeling position before her husband put his hands under her arms to help her up. Then both glared at Clarence without saying anything.

"She died from a hemorrhage. That's what the doctor said. There was nothing to be done. It may have come on as a result of damage done to her insides during Clyde's birth, but no one knows."

"Did you not do anything to help her? Just let her die?" asked Mathew.

"I carried her to the doctor's office on horseback. It was the only means of transport we had. *He* said it was too late to do anything. I tried. I am so sorry to tell you this."

"And now I suppose you're here to live with us. Is that it? You let our daughter die out there in the wilderness, and now you want us to take care of you all. Is that it?"

"Please, sir, I did what I could for Emma. I loved her like you loved her. Without her, I cannot give these children the care she would want them to have. Can you find it in your heart to help us for a short while?"

"What do you mean by a short while?" said Ellie. "You know we are barely able to take care of our own needs. With him only able to work a few hours each week, we can't afford food all the time. How are we going to feed another four mouths?"

"If you could only care for the children until I find a job and a place to live here in Yarmouth, I would be ever so grateful. I'm young and strong. They'll hire me in the iron mines. I can contribute money to your household. Perhaps Matthew may not even have to work."

"Potter!" yelled the man. "You come here and tell us you've let our daughter die after stealing her away and moving her to the frontier! You want us to take care of her children? You want us to believe you will pay us to do it? I don't believe a damn promise you make!"

"Yet, you know we would not turn Emma's children away," said Ellie. "How could we do that and leave them to your neglect? You are playing us for fools!" She was shouting now. "Go do what you must to support your family, but do not turn your back on us."

Clarence deposited all three children in chairs at the kitchen table. Then he went outside to retrieve their clothes and a few toys. He said goodbye to them and then turned to thank his in-laws.

"Begone with ye," said Ellie. "The next occasion on which I hope to see you will be when you return with money for us. If you can't help, then you might just go away and forget you even have children. You devil…"

Matthew said nothing as he gestured toward the door. As Clarence exited, the old man slammed the door behind him.

20

It was May already, and Aphia knew she needed to do something to keep flies from swarming again this year. It was during late spring and late summer that dark clouds of the insects invaded the house every time the doors or windows were opened. She was sure the smell rising above the little hill at the edge of her pasture drew them. She cursed her grandfather, Abe, who had buried six Morgans there after they were struck by lightning. At the time, she had named it the "Hill of Death." Abe, Henry Greene, and she herself had only been able to dig away enough earth to make a shallow grave. The smell of decomposing flesh continued to this day.

Two years ago, she had convinced her friend Bert Learned to deliver several loads of soil to cover the area, but he had failed to complete the plan before disappearing. The one load he *had* delivered had stayed piled in one section of the field until she spread it by herself. She was afraid to bring anyone else in on her secret problem. Yes, it was good that Henry had died and Bert had disappeared. Now she was the only one who knew about the Hill of Death.

The problem of flies and smells would not go away by itself. Perhaps there was someone else who might lend a hand to make the hill higher, the graves deeper. Perhaps Mr. W.K. Hamlin or Selectman Watson might have a worker with time to help her for a couple of days. It would have to be someone new to the area, someone who would know nothing about Henry or Bert.

The next day, she rode into South Waterford to inquire. Hamlin's carding mill was closed, so she went on to Watson's box factory, where she found the owner in conversation with a handsome young man in a worsted business suit. As she approached, the two stopped chatting and tipped their hats to her.

"How do you do, Miss Stevens?" greeted Watson. "What a fine day to be out for a ride." The other man stood off to the side and said nothing, but he was watching her very closely.

"Sorry to interrupt your business, Mr. Watson. I was wondering if you might have a hand who would do some field work for me."

"No interruption at all. Ma'am, this is Nathan Hallett. He gets me a lot of business."

Nathan still had not said a word, which made her a little nervous.

"What type of work do you want doing?" said Watson.

"I want to spread a good thick layer of soil and gravel on part of my pasture to stop it from eroding. Should take a couple days to dump and spread. That's all. Do you have a new man working for you, one who's new to town?"

"Yes, in fact several who I've just hired to fill Nathan's new orders."

Nathan stepped forward and introduced himself to Aphia. "Good day. I've heard your name mentioned about town several times. You have that fine herd of Morgans out in West Waterford, if I'm not mistaken."

"Why, yes, you're correct. Do you live around here, sir?"

"No, my wife and I live in Bridgton Center on High Street, but I'm here in Waterford quite often. Perhaps you know my wife, Hattie. She is a Millett and grew up here in the village with her sister Lizzie."

At the mention of the sisters, Aphia's face flushed bright red, and she stammered when she spoke. "W-w-ell, n-no. I have not heard that name before. N-n-n-ice to meet you, Mr. H-H-Hallett. Mr. Watson. P-please see if you can have a man work for me on Thursday and Friday next. I will pay him very well. In cash, not trade."

She said not a word of farewell, but climbed back on her horse and rode away at a trot. As the men watched her disappear in the distance, Nathan said, "That is one strange woman. You'll not find me having anything to do with her. I don't trust her."

"I would have to agree with you, Nathan. On the surface, she appears to be an attractive woman. Several local boys have been attracted to her and have tried to pay court, but she's un-approachable. She blows them aside like a sudden gust of wind. You may know one of the boys. Bert Learned was quite smitten with her, though he was much older than she. I believe he even proposed marriage. She rejected him outright and in such a cruel manner that he was apparently shamed into moving away. Just up and disappeared."

Nathan said nothing more about the woman, finished his business with Watson, and climbed back into his surrey for the trip home. I must tell Lizzie that strange story about Mr. Learned, he thought. She knew the man from long ago.

21

Moses surprised Lizzie when she returned to Saco. He greet-ed her at the station in their one-horse chaise and present-ed her with a giant bouquet of white mums. He had picked them from the old plants that grew on the south side of their house in garden beds planted many years before by his late first wife.

"Oh, so lovely!" she exclaimed as he passed the flowers to her and placed a peck on her cheek. "Did you pick these yourself?"

"I did. And I've been working in the gardens these last sever-al warm days. It's wonderful to have my energy back."

"You are such a dear, Moses, but be careful not to overdo it. We wouldn't want to have a relapse," she said pointing to his leg.

"Yes, yes, I know what the doctor said, and I am being careful. It's just that the warm spring weather drew me outside, and you know how I love to garden," he said as he helped her into the carriage seat. "Now, let's go to dinner at the hotel. I've made early reservations."

As they drove to the hotel, Lizzie told the story of the strange visit from Aphia. He listened intently but said nothing. Moses had planned this happy welcome for his lovely wife, and nothing was going to spoil the occasion. At the Saco Hotel, a young man helped Liz from the chaise, took the reins from Moses, and led the horse and buggy to the stable. It was just like the days when they had first met and he was flush with cash and recognized as an important man about town. For the last few years, though, he'd felt that youth had left him and that people were wont to treat him like an "old fella" who had seen better days.

Seated at a table near the floor-to-ceiling windows, the couple watched the busy world pass by. Both of them were pleased to see several young ladies walk past wearing dresses made in their Westbrook shop, very modern outfits reflecting European styles that were the vogue in Boston and New York.

Dinner was splendid: leg of lamb, potatoes au gratin, and a watercress salad. So different from the simpler fare that was customary for restaurants in Westbrook or Windham. Moses chose an apple tart for dessert and café au lait for himself, while Liz sipped Darjeeling tea with lemon. It was all wonderful.

22

"My friend, welcome back to our humble abode," said Moses as he shook Nathan's hand. Fresh from a long ride from Portland, Hallett stood in the entryway of the two-story brick house with dust covering his long tan canvas coat and wide-brimmed hat. He dropped a satchel on the stone floor and scuffed dirt from the bottom of his shoes on a boot jack just outside the door.

"Thank you, Moses. Thank you. I've been trying to find time to visit you and Lizzie for quite a while. You two move around so much, one hardly knows where to find you."

Lizzie entered from the sun porch where she had been reading the latest issue of *Godey's Lady's Book*, a fashion plate magazine from New York City that featured drawings of the latest fashions. When Nathan saw the magazine, he laughed loudly and gave his sister-in-law a big hug. "Don't you ever stop working? Looking to steal new designs for your fall line?"

"Shame on you, Nathan, for thinking that I don't come up

with original designs of my own," she said in jest as she flung the magazine on a nearby sofa.

Moses picked it up, looked quickly at the front cover, and said with a grin, "Sir, the designs from Millett's American are all originals, never copies! Give me your bag and I'll take it to the guest room."

As it was well past eight o'clock, Liz set out a platter of cheese and fruit for her guest on the parlor coffee table. Moses poured glasses of port for himself and Nathan and topped off his wife's sherry. They exchanged pleasantries about family and the latest news until Nathan had relaxed enough to remember that he had come for a specific purpose.

"Lizzie, I just returned from South Waterford, where I met with William Watson. You know him, I'm sure. He's doing very well supplying a big horseshoe nail manufacturer in Boston with secure shipping boxes. I had a new order from him for Watson. As we were talking, Aphia Greene interrupted us with a strange order of her own."

"I believe she calls herself Stevens, now. Uses her family name again," said Lizzie. "That was how she signed her most recent letter to me. You may not know that she visited me in West-brook just before I left to come here."

"No, that's news to me. Isn't she a strange one? Still quite pretty and all, but her eyes were wild, hair close-cropped like she had cut it without a mirror. Both Watson and I agreed that she smelled bad, as if she had been standing in smoke from a fire."

"Yes, she certainly has become an oddity."

"As I was saying, she interrupted us to ask if Bill had a hand that she might pay to deliver and spread topsoil for her. Normally I wouldn't have thought that strange, but when she asked him to only send a man who was a newcomer to town, I began to be suspicious. After she left, he told me a story about your old friend, Bert Learned."

"Didn't you tell me that Bert had left town and moved out west somewhere?"

"I did, but Bill told me your friend's departure was a bit mysterious. He had done some field work for the woman last year and taken a shine to her. Will Cain told me some time ago that the man had lost his wife in a fire and had remained single ever since. Perhaps he was looking for a companion and, with such a beautiful young woman available and close at hand, he thought to make the most of the opportunity."

"Did he not know of the suspicions about Henry Greene's disappearance?"

"Who can say? But he may have tried to get close to her. Maybe even asked her to marry. That's what Watson mentioned as a possibility. Anyway, after Learned left so suddenly, the rumor was that she had rejected his advances and, in shame and disappointment, he left town in a hurry, not letting anyone know where he was going."

Moses poured a second port for his guest and himself. "Lizzie, you must tell us the details of her strange visit to you last week. The two of you are painting a very dark picture of this Aphia. She's beginning to sound dangerous."

Lizzie poured herself another sherry before sharing her own story. At the end, she leaned forward in her chair so she was face-to-face with Nathan. "I know that I have asked both you and Will to investigate Aphia for me, to see if you might learn any details of what happened to Henry. Now you tell me that old Bert has disappeared after being with her. I hereby withdraw that request. Whatever happened can be forgotten, as far as I am concerned. It is of less interest to me now than is my concern for the welfare of you both and your families. My intuition is that Henry met with foul play at her hands. Leave her alone, Nathan. It is not worth the danger."

Their discussions had gone on for several hours and all three were ready to retire. The business that Moses had wished to discuss would wait until morning.

23

Clarence was very disappointed. He walked all over Yarmouth looking for a paying job only to find that nothing but part-time positions were available to him. He inquired at a small tin mine in his father's hometown, Clementsport. His name was recognized, but there was nothing for him. He searched in all the small villages outside of town, asking for work at each blacksmith shop. He told each smithy that he was a skilled welder and former, but the only offer came from a man several miles from the Shermans' house. It was as a part-time farrier to shape and fit horseshoes, and even though such a job paid far less than a man with his experience desired, it would have to do for the time being.

When Clarence reported for his first half day of work, a local farmer who watched him file his animal's hooves mentioned that gold had been discovered in the coastal town of Kemptville, a few hundred miles to the north. Reports were that the mine had yielded several hundred ounces of gold ore in its first months, as well as a smaller amount of silver. The owner of the David Cowan mine was hiring. Leaving his new job and moving so far away would be risky and would require leaving his children behind, but the possibility of a well-paid full-time job would be worth the risk.

The three adults and the two older children sat at the crowded wooden table set up close to the big open fireplace made of rubble stone. Little Clyde, who was colicky and running a slight fever, slept fitfully in a rough wooden shipping crate that had been adapted as a crib. Ellie Sherman swung the kettle crane forward from the fire and removed a cast-iron pot of mutton and potato stew. As she set it on a trivet before the family, Clarence offered a blessing.

"May all in this house be healthy."

Ellie stared blankly at him, then bowed her head for a moment before speaking. "You may pray for health on all of us, yet in the week you have been here, you have not delivered a penny to feed us. How can your children grow healthy on the meager gruel that we have to give them?"

Not waiting for an answer, she ladled thin stew into the children's small bowls, then into her husband's and her own. Clarence then received whatever was left, barely half a serving, which he accepted without comment. Matthew, who had been laid off from the mine and was now working as a stable hand, ate in silence, his eyes nearly shut. The new work was hard, but it was above ground in fresh air. He earned just enough to keep things going, but was exhausted at the end of each day.

Bessie and Hazel spooned the meat and potatoes in the stew quickly into their mouths and then held up the bowls, pouring broth down their throats so eagerly that some dribbled down the corners of their mouths onto the table.

"Slow down, girls," Clarence instructed. "Your grandparents will think that you're wild animals if you eat like that."

"Don't bellow at them," said Matthew. "They eat nothing all day. Hunger makes them wild. If there was more to eat, their manners might be better."

"Father Sherman, at the end of this week, I will get my first pay. All of that will be turned over to Mother Sherman, and I hope it will be used for better provisions."

The old lady rose from her chair and returned the pot to its crane. "I'll not accept any complaints from either of you men about the food I place in front of you. Especially from you, Clarence. Your money will be used to the best of my ability, but with six mouths, all that you provide will likely be inadequate."

Clarence bowed his head in thought before speaking again. "There is a new job for me in Kemptville, where a new gold mine has been opened. My pay would be much better, and I will be able to provide you and my children with more food."

"Kemptville, you say? Dear, did he say Kemptville?" said the old man. He cupped his hand behind his left ear and blurted,

"For God's sake, man, that's over two hundred miles away! What if there's no job when you get there? You know how temporary these mine jobs can be."

"I knew it! I knew it!" Ellie exclaimed. "You'll leave us now, abandon your children, and leave us to our poverty! I knew you would go away. We'll end up on the poor farm, and your children will become wards of the Province. Just wait and see."

"Mother Sherman," said Clarence quietly, "you will see. I will make sure you are well provided for until I find a new wife and take the children to my own home."

"We shall see about that when the time comes," she said bitterly.

24

Francena mumbled to herself as she paced Bridgton's Depot Street station platform. The train carrying her new friend Lottie and her mother from Portland was an hour late. The weather is good, she thought. What could be the problem? Perhaps she decided not to come or her nasty mom forced her to stay home.

She stared eastward down the tracks and breathed deeply to calm her fears. When she spied puffs of smoke beyond a clump of evergreens lining the narrow-gauge track, she knew it was the train at last. Hitching up her long skirts, she raced to the front of the platform and stood beneath the arrivals sign. She wanted to be the first to greet her visitors. As the single passenger car slowed, she saw that the two women were the only ones aboard.

A young man in a conductor's uniform of brown pleated pants, white linen shirt, and blue waistcoat slid the heavy door aside and gestured for Franny to step away from the car, which was still moving.

"Young lady, please step away from the door. We've luggage to unload. You might get hurt if you're in the way," the man shouted. "You, there!" The conductor hailed a boy who was sitting in the station office and paying no attention to the arrival.

"You, young man. Help these two fine ladies get their luggage from the rear of the car."

When the young man emerged, Franny was surprised to recognize a classmate of hers. He recognized her and stopped to tease her about her "lady's outfit." Anticipating that the Ritchies would be dressed in the latest styles of travel wear, she had chosen to wear her best church clothes.

When Lottie and Mrs. Ritchie finally disembarked, they were costumed in completely different attire. The woman wore a yellow bonnet and a long blue denim traveling coat over a lovely brown dress to her ankles. Her daughter, however, wore a pair of denim pants, a tight matching jacket, and a baseball cap. Her leather ankle boots were scuffed as if she had been out riding or feeding cows. Franny was embarrassed that she herself had overdressed.

Mrs. Ritchie was the first to speak. "Why, Lottie, look at your little friend. She is so well dressed. I told you to wear that blue dress and your new boots, but you just had to have your way. As usual."

"Mother, stop harping. You've been complaining about everything all the way from Boston. If it isn't my clothes, it's the weather or the 'uncomfortable' seats or that 'rude' conductor. Please stop. If I wasn't so excited to see my Franny, I'd say you nearly ruined the trip for me." She rushed to her pen pal with arms spread out like she was flying and grabbed the smaller girl around the waist, lifting her feet from the platform. Franny squealed with delight.

"Oh, Lottie! How you have grown! So tall, and stronger than I remember. It's been so long since we were together."

The friends held hands and danced around each other, oblivious to the woman who had turned her back on them and followed the porter. She harangued him as he unloaded their luggage. "Be careful there, you clumsy oaf. Don't drop our trunk. You will pay for any damage. Mark my words!"

When she heard the commotion, Lottie called out, "Mother,

will you please stop your tongue-lashing? He's *helping* us, for God's sake. Let him alone."

Franny could not believe that she was witnessing such a family argument. If she were to speak to her own mother like that, she would be punished severely. Yet, her mother would not likely act the part of a shrew like Mrs. Ritchie. The boy stood for the longest time taking it all in. He didn't know what to do with the bags and he was not about to interrupt. Franny caught his attention and gestured for him to take the things to the front entry of the station, where Hattie would arrive soon to take the guests to the Hallett home.

"Mrs. Ritchie, Lottie, please come with me," said Franny, trying to bring an end to the shouting. "My mother will be here shortly to get us in the buggy. I'm sure you both will feel better when you clean off the travel dust and change into more comfortable clothes."

Both women walked through the station with arms held stiffly at their sides.

What a way to start a visit, thought Franny. Thank God Mrs. Ritchie is only here for a couple of days.

25

It was a pleasant change for Clarence to have money in his pocket. Many weeks had passed when he couldn't afford even one cigarette or a piece of candy. Even with all the problems that plagued him, Clarence knew that someday he would have a better life—better than his father and grandfather had lived. Better than what he himself had known in his life to this point. Emma had been a good wife, and he missed her terribly. Together they had started a family and would have taught their three children to grab on to the best of things. She had been less of an optimist than he, but they balanced each other, the positive and the negative. If only she had not died...

Clarence stood inside the head house of the Kemptville gold

Ore Breaker. *Gas-powered breaker used to crush ore during the early twentieth century. As seen in Jerome, Arizona. 2019. Photo by author.*

mine, waiting for his men to walk out of the tunnel. It was the end of the week, and he had pay envelopes for each man as they emerged from the darkness. It had been a very good week in the mine. A lead that the men had been following for two weeks had finally started to produce tons of yellow ore of high quality. He was sure the partners would be pleased. Of course, the quality of the yield would only be proven after slag had been removed at the breaker, but he was sure the results would be very good.

When he had reported to the Kemptville mine, the foreman had asked if he had any mining experience or if he had ever managed a crew. He told about being a manager in two small iron mines back in Clementsport and how he had his own crew of track welders on the Central Ontario the previous summer. He was soon given the position of full-time crew leader. Now he was able to rent a room in town, send money back to the Shermans every week, and still have a good bit of bob in his own pockets. He knew that soon a beautiful woman would come his way, one that would catch everyone's eye when he walked into a room with her on his arm. She would be a looker for sure, but also a good mother for the children. Yes, life was looking up.

After handing out the pay, he pulled a satchel from his locker and headed for town to board a train bound for Yarmouth, where he would be able to spend the Dominion Day summer holiday with his children, whom he had not seen in a month. In addition to the clothes he carried, there were three boxes of candy for the youngsters and a purse filled with coins for the Shermans. He was sure that such gifts would be cause for great enjoyment. In a small cloth bag hidden in his inside vest pocket was a contraband of golden nuggets taken from the conveyor at the bottom of the breaker. He was not sure what to do with these, but the jiggling against his chest made him feel wealthy.

26

In early dawn, Clarence tried to open the Shermans' door, but to his dismay it was locked. The plan had been to make his visit a complete surprise and to be sitting in front of a hot fire when the family woke. He tapped lightly on the door several times, but with no result. Disappointed, he sat down on the stone step to wait. Looking down the dirty street, he could clearly make out a small white church with its thin steeple rising high above all the other buildings. Beyond, waves breaking in Yarmouth's harbor threw spray on the rugged cliffs lining the shore. The town was so still and beautiful at this early hour that he realized how much he had missed such quiet after the constant noise of his job.

There was a scratching noise behind him and, when he turned, he was surprised and delighted to see five-year-old Hazel Merle's head peeking through the slightest of openings. Her hair was long and tangled. She rubbed the sleepers from her eyes.

"Hazel, you look like you've seen a ghost," he joked. "Don't you remember your father?"

Her head moved up and down and a smile began to curl across her mouth. She opened the door wider, holding her finger to her lips as a sign for him to keep still. As he entered the house, she reached out for his hand and then wrapped herself around his legs. He was overjoyed to see her, but still wanted to let the others sleep. Dropping to his knees, he kissed her cheek and whispered, "My lovely Hazel. I've missed you so."

Together they coaxed a bed of embers remaining on the hearth into a full, warm fire; then she sat on his knees while he combed the kinks from her blond curls. Much about her face and complexion reminded him of lovely Emma, especially the hair color. As he smoothed each snarl, he kissed his daughter's head. Neither noticed Matthew Sherman enter the room.

He stood silently behind them taking in the tender family scene. He was bothered that Clarence had come back after all these weeks with no notice, yet he did not want to disturb the intimacy of father and daughter. After a few moments, he stepped forward, acknowledged his son-in-law with a curt wave, and tapped Hazel on the head. Clarence set the girl down on the hearth, rose from the chair, and placed a purse of cash in the old man's hand. They were both staring at the purse when Ellie came into the room.

"What? Clarence? You devil. How dare you show up in our lives with no warning! You come and go as you please, don't you. No consideration for the rest of us. No letters or cards. You leave my man and me to take care of these three with no help from yourself. Then you arrive like God's gift." Even when her husband opened the purse and showed the cash to her, she continued to rail. "I don't know what my dear departed Emma saw in you. I told her that. It was no secret between us. You are a dreamer. Perhaps that's what she fell for. But you don't have the strength to make those dreams come true. Charlatan! Faker!"

Her loud curses woke the other children. Bessie, the three-year-old, led Clyde by the hand. They both wore stained diapers, and their feet were bare. The old lady ran back into the bedroom and grabbed two small blankets, which she wrapped around the two children. When Clarence went to pick them up, she threw up her thin arm to block his way.

"These children are ours now. You have done little to deserve to be their father. Yes, you bring a few dollars to tide us over, but that's not enough to keep your family together. I will never forgive you for letting my Emma die, and I will never let you have the chance to mistreat her children."

Both Clarence and Matthew stood away from the fire and stared at the angry woman. With his head hung down, Matthew laced up his tattered boots and pulled on a light jacket in preparation to leave for a morning of work at the stable. Clarence, disregarding the harangues, sat down at the table, pulled the small sack from his vest pocket, and spread out a handful of yellow nuggets for all to see.

"Matthew, you'll not be needing to work today or perhaps

any other day. Mother, these pieces of gold will make life easier
for you all. Please take them."

The old man hesitated for a moment to peer at the gold, but
then departed without a word.

"What shall we do with these? Tell me," Ellie challenged.
"They are worthless to the likes of us. If we try to sell them, they'll
say we are thieves and jail us. Best you keep those for your own
betterment. We will keep your money and hope that there will
be more to come. But don't think that your coins can pay for my
forgiveness."

From behind an earthenware crock on the mantel she pulled
a letter and handed it to him before turning her back.

Not wanting to stay in the house alone with Ellie Sherman
while her husband was at work, Clarence stuck the letter in his
vest pocket and gathered the children together for a walk into
town. It had been a long time since he had cared for the three, so
he had to ask for help in dressing them. When all were prepared,
he took Clyde in his arms and instructed the two girls to hold
hands and follow close behind.

As they were leaving, Clarence noticed that Ellie was smiling
as she filled a clay pipe and sat down by the fire. He was sure
the smile was for the pipe and not for his being reunited with
his children.

Out on the street, the parade of four Potters made its way
between a row of cottages until they reached the town cemetery
at the end of the residential neighborhood. Clarence led on to the
wharf area, where a huge ship was nearing completion. Riggers
climbed back and forth across the mainmasts, guiding heavy
ropes through a series of pulleys. A pile of folded sail lay on the
pier next to the ship in front of a row of wooden crates on which
the family came to rest. As there were no rails along the edge of
the pier, Clarence secured all three children on a length of cord
and tied it to his waist. The little ones sat on the rough wooden
wharf boards watching the men above and two lobstermen who
were repairing traps.

Clarence peered at the return address on the folded envelope. Seeing that it was from Ohio, he assumed that it was from an old friend from his hometown of Clementsport who had moved to South Ohio in Nova Scotia. When he opened it and began to read, he was shocked to see that it had been sent by his boss, Mr. Albert Warren, from Albany, Ohio, USA.

Dear Clarence,

I send this letter to you addressed to the "The Shermans" in Yarmouth because I know of no other place to locate you. I just heard about the death of your wife through foreman Mr. Quincy in Ontario, who tells me that you have left our employ and are trying to find a good home for your children. Please accept my deepest condolences and prayers that Emma is now with God in Heaven.

If your plight had been known to me before you left the track crew, I might have given you an advance to make it possible to stay in Ontario. You have been a valuable employee for the Central Ontario Railroad and the Canadian Copper Company. If you could see your way to return, I would be very pleased and could offer you a foreman position at higher pay.

I want to request that you do me the favor of returning to Maine during the summer to inspect several businesses in which I wish to invest. Dr. Abbott, whom you know, advises me that two mines have recently been started up which offer to be good prospects. With your mining experience, you would likely be able to serve as my eyes and ears in Oxford County. I will pay your expenses and a generous retainer for your willingness to assist.

You may reach me at the address on this envelope or, if you have access to a telephone, the number at my office in Ohio is Albany140.

Sincerely yours,
Albert A. Warren

My God, said Clarence to himself. Am I to be so trusted by this man? I cannot question such good fortune, but I wonder how this came about.

He thought back to a time nearly twenty years before when his father, Alfred, was working to lay track for the Central Ontario Railroad into wild territory near Lake Tameskaming. A group of American investors had purchased vast acreage of forested land there and proposed to cut, mill, and distribute lumber throughout Canada around the Great Lakes. To do this, rails had to be extended, and Alfred was hired to supervise a crew of metal workers in the job of setting and welding track. Clarence, at thirteen years of age, had spent two summers with his father learning the skill of welding. In 1883, a smithy associate of Alfred's, Thomas Flanagan, had discovered deposits of copper along the track right-of-way. Clarence and his father, who had spent many years working in Nova Scotia iron mines, assisted the Americans in setting up several mines. By 1888, both Potters were working for the Canadian Copper Company to make the mining operation more profitable than the railroad would ever be. It was they who first suggested that the copper ore was not as abundant or of high enough quality to bring a good return on investment. They identified a more valuable mineral present in the shafts: nickel, which was so hard that it might be of use in armament manufacture.

Perhaps their advice, which served to make Warren a very wealthy man, was the reason he had kept track of Clarence and assisted him so much. And Clarence would always be grateful for such an angel watching over him. The rich man had gotten the track welding job for him, had arranged a cabin for him and Emma, and had paid him to go to Maine to inspect business interests there. Thank God for Warren.

27

Telegraphy had been in use since the 1830s, but Clarence was unsure if there was a telegraph office in Yarmouth. And he had no idea how this modern technology worked. Writing letters he understood, but all this new electrical communication was hard to fathom. He was interested in learning how such systems worked, but it seemed to him that the technology was meant for the richest folk and large corporations, not poor people like himself. It was logical that a telegraph machine might be in the train station, so went to the station ticket window and asked for the person in charge.

"That would be me, my good man. I am the Station Manager. How can I help you?" The manager was dressed in a crisp blue uniform with red piping and wore a visored cap with *Dominion Atlantic Railway* embroidered on the front. As the man rose from behind the window and stepped out to speak with Clarence directly, he stood no more than five feet tall.

"Mr. Station Manager, I am looking for a place where I might send a telegram to a friend in the USA."

"You can do that here, but you will need a telegraph station's call letters and your friend's home address to be able to send one."

Clarence presented a slip of paper on which he had written the necessary information. "I want to have the message delivered to his business address."

The man looked at the paper, then back at Clarence with a suspicious grin. "Mr. Albert Warren, Akron, Ohio. Not a complete address, but the office in Akron may know where to send a courier. Warren will likely be very well known there in Ohio. Oh, and you must have three Canadian dollars to pay for transmission. I won't accept any American coins."

Clarence reached into his pocket and offered the man a solid gold nugget. "Will this do?" he asked.

The manager rolled the gold around in his hand for a moment and then bit down on it. "Yes, this will do. Please, what is your message? And it must be less than twenty-five words."

28

Hattie Hallett and Mary Ritchie sat across from each other at a small wicker table on the Halletts' screened porch. They were enjoying a quiet breakfast while gazing across High Street to Highland Lake, where their daughters sat on the beach. During the two days they had been visiting, not a civil word had passed between mother and daughter. Hattie finally worked up enough gumption to speak about the situation to her guest.

"Look at those two girls. They seem to get along so well, don't you think?"

"I guess so. Although it is often difficult to know what my Lottie is thinking. She might not even like your Francena. It's so hard to read her."

"Oh, I think they're very affectionate."

"I hope you're correct, Mrs. Hallett."

"Please, please, call me Hattie. No need to be so formal."

"Yes, all right, Hattie. I will try to remember to address you less formally."

"Mary, hopefully you will not find me too nosy in asking you why you and your daughter do not get along."

Mary was silent for several moments as she sought to recover her composure after such a personal question. Hattie, too, was silent. Perhaps she shouldn't have pried.

"Dear, I am surprised that you would ask such a question," replied Mary. "The relationship with my daughter is a private matter. Suffice it to say that she and I have differing views about how a young woman should conduct her life. She is unable to live according to the rules of decorum that are required if one is to be chosen as a wife by an acceptable husband."

"She is so beautiful and intelligent," said Hattie. "I would be surprised if any young man would not be attracted to her."

"Is that so, Hattie? I would think that you would have concerns like mine about your Franny. She is so rough and unrefined in many ways. Do you know what I mean?"

Now it was Hattie's turn to be shocked. She began to rise

from the chair, but then sat back down and said in a tense voice,
"No, I do not know at all what you mean. Perhaps both girls do
not fit the standards that you hold so dear because of your aris-
tocratic city airs. You want every girl to be refined and delicate,
cultured and timid. These young ladies are strong and intelligent,
ready to conquer any challenges life throws at them. Any man
who rejects them for those attributes would be a fool."

Having said her piece, Hattie stood, cleared the breakfast
dishes, and stormed from the porch leaving her guest sitting
there with a shocked expression on her face.

Such audacity, thought Mary. She had never in her life known
a woman's scorn to match what she had just seen. Strength, indeed! That was not what a man looked for in a woman. She slowly rose from her seat and headed to the guest room to pack her
bag. Tomorrow would not be soon enough for her to leave this
horrible place.

When the girls returned from the beach, shoes in hand, Hattie met them at the front door. Seeing that their pantaloons and
skirt hems were wet, she asked them to sit on the porch bench
and shake the sand off their feet. When they rose to enter the
house, Franny went straight up to her room for dry clothes. Hattie took Lottie's arm to hold her back for a moment.

"Dear, I want to warn you that your mother has gone to your
room in a snit after a heated discussion with me. She may be quite
angry when you see her."

"Whatever happened? Did she shout at you?"

"I am afraid I asked too personal a question that angered her.
It really is my fault."

"I doubt it could be your doing. What did you ask?"

"I wanted to know why you two are always disagreeing."

"Surely she told you that I am a tomboy and not a lady and
too rural in my ways. That's her opinion about everything I do. If
it weren't for my dad, I would run away from home and move to
the country."

"Lottie, I'm sure she has your best interests at heart."

"No, Mrs. Hallett, she does not. She hates me and thinks I am ruining my life and hers by being myself. I am so glad she's going home tomorrow and leaving me here with your family for two weeks. I wish it was for the rest of my life." With that, Lottie threw her arms around Hattie and began to cry. The two sat on the bench holding hands until Franny returned. Then the friends walked away hand in hand, one wearing dry shoes, the other still barefoot.

29

The following telegram was delivered to Albert Warren's office in Akron:

GREETINGS. STOP. HAVE RECEIVED YOUR RECENT LETTER. STOP. CANNOT RETURN TO TRACK WORK. STOP. CHILDREN TO SUPPORT. STOP. WILL CHECK ON MAINE MINES. STOP. NEED FUNDS FOR TRAVEL AND FAMILY. STOP. PLEASE ADVISE.

Within twenty-four hours, a telegram was sent to Clarence in response.

PLEASE RECONSIDER RETURNING TO WORK. STOP. IN-CLUDED PLEASE FIND FUNDS FOR EXPENSES. STOP. LOOK FORWARD TO HEARING YOUR MAINE APPRAISAL. STOP. IN FRIENDSHIP, A.W.

The telegram arrived while Clarence was at the mines, so he did not get it until the following weekend. When Mother Sherman informed him that a courier would not leave the message without his signature, he went once again to the station ticket window and asked an agent if he might speak to the manager, who was in his private office.

"My dear sir," the manager addressed him as he hurried from the office. "Please, come inside with me. We might be able to transact our business in private."

Quite surprised by the man's friendly manner, Clarence

slowly followed him into the office through the door that was being held open for him.

"Sir, I've come to retrieve a telegram sent to me from the US."

"Yes. I know quite well why you are here, Mr. Potter. Please use my given name, Malcolm. There are *two* telegrams for you. One is the telegram and the second is a moneygram which I have exchanged here for Canadian dollars, not American."

"Well, Mr.—uh, Malcolm, I am pleased with your service. Do you need any identification?"

"No, Mr. Potter. Not at all. I can see who you are," he said as he presented Clarence with the telegram and $1,000 in cash. "Please sign the receipt."

30

"Where in God's name did you get so much money?" asked Mother Sherman as her son-in-law handed her $500 in Canadian bills. "I've never seen that much at one time."

Matthew, who had just returned from work, sat down on his rocking chair as if he had fainted, his hand on his heart. "Damn, Clarence. Who are these folks who gave you such a fortune? How did they find you?"

"The money came from Mr. Albert Warren. He's the owner of Canadian Copper. Many years ago, my father and I did him a great favor, which he has never forgotten."

Ellie counted the money a second time before pushing the wad into her apron pocket. "This is enough money to get some new shoes for all of us before winter and get more wood for the fire. Are you giving all this to us or keeping some for your own needs?"

"You get it all. I can take care of myself from what I earn each week."

Ellie Sherman reached out and placed her left hand on his chest and her right hand on her own heart, an intimate gesture Clarence never would have expected.

Matthew said, "Emma would be proud of you for this. I'm sure she is looking down on us with a big smile." He reached into a covered bucket next to the hearth, pulled out a bottle of brandy, and filled three tumblers. "To your health, Clarence! May you keep the ball rolling!"

31

Nathan had been on the road with Nate for five days, so they missed both the arrival of the Ritchies and Mary's hostile departure. Usually when he arrived at home after time away, the family would pester him for stories about his adventures. This time was different. Hattie, Franny, and Lottie had so much to tell *him* that he couldn't get a word in edgewise. He and Nate sat in near total silence at the dinner table while the women told of both the good and bad happenings of the week just passed. Each time one of the men took a momentary break in the conversation as a chance to tell a story, a woman would interrupt. Finally, a frustrated Nathan held up his hands and made a plea.

"My God, ladies, don't you have any interest in what we gents have to tell you? We, too, have had a few full days. Nate, here, prospected for gems. He found a rare watermelon tourmaline on top of a hill near Bethel. We learned to run a planer machine in Waterford and climbed Hawk Mountain. Tell them, son, what you've accomplished this week."

Hattie held her index finger to her mouth while looking at the girls. "Franny, Lottie, let's give the men a chance." The young ladies smiled at each other, then turned their attention to the young man.

Nathan Junior was pleased to have everyone's attention, especially that of Lottie. The tall beauty was six years older, but he wanted to impress her with his accomplishments. All the time the girls had been telling their stories, he had been transfixed by her wit and melodic voice. Her laugh was boisterous and infectious; it made him chuckle. And such a fabulous face and form!

"The prospecting was the best thing. We stayed in Bethel with Dr. Abbott and his wife. You should see the huge collection of gems and minerals he has. It nearly fills an entire room on shelves that go up higher than I can reach. He drove us up to a mountain in Newry where all the trees had been cut down and a big pit dug below a rocky cliff. It's what they call a pegmatite mine, where you can easily break out big crystals with a chipping hammer."

"Show them what you found," said Nathan.

Reaching into his shirt pocket, the boy pulled out a handkerchief in which was wrapped a shiny crystal measuring two by three inches. When he held it up to the ceiling light, both lime-green and bright-orange colors radiated from it. Lottie was the first to reach out her hand for a closer inspection. Nate rubbed the gem on his table napkin before passing it over to her.

"Be careful of this, Lottie Adelaide Ritchie. It's my treasure. You can see rocks like this all over that place. Not this big, but pretty just the same."

Lottie held the crystal up to the light and peered through it, then placed it atop the ring finger of her left hand. She tried to fool Nate by putting it in her own pocket, but Franny reached for it.

"Hey, Lottie. Give that to me. I want it for my own wedding ring. I'm sure my brother would be glad to give it to his best sister."

Nate was none too happy with the girls. He demanded the gem's immediate return. "Give it here," he said. "No need to fight over this one. Dad can take us all up to the Newry mine, and we can all get our *own* treasures."

Nathan reached out to Lottie and took the stone before returning it to his son. "Hattie, you know, that might be a great outing for the family, and we could show Lottie another part of Western Maine. Dr. Abbott and the mine's owner, Mr. Dunton, would surely be happy to let us dig for a few hours. I'm sure we could get accommodations in Bethel."

Hattie was in complete agreement with the plan, so the following Friday, all five of them set off in a two-seat buggy to become prospectors. In addition to the duffels they each brought for their clothes, a wooden box in the back of the buggy contained hammers, small chisels, leather gloves, and several buckets to hold any specimens that might be found. Nathan and Nate sat on the front seat, leaving the three ladies packed tightly into the backseat. The road was smooth from Bridgton through Waterford and west to Lynchville, but when they turned north through Albany Basins on Bethel Causeway, the wheels bounced along on rough surface still ungraded from winter erosion. By the time they reached Bethel, they were all covered with dust and very irritated with the failure of local road crews.

The Alpine House where Dr. Abbott had made reservations for them was set back from the road in heavily wooded Mason Park, an isolated area just out of busy Bethel Center. In shady coolness, they disembarked and retired to a large parlor where the proprietor, Abiel Chandler, arranged for a light lunch and iced tea. Another guest, a man who sat by himself staring out to the evergreen grove, sat at a small table on the far side of the room engrossed in reading a pamphlet.

Nathan watched the man pour himself a glass of tea. "Hattie, don't we know that man? He looks very familiar."

"Yes, I believe I have seen him before. Perhaps you might go over and introduce yourself and invite him to join us."

As Nathan walked across the room, the gentleman turned to face him and said, "Hello, sir. You look familiar to me. Have we met?"

His accent made Nathan recognize him instantly.

"Yes, I believe we have, Mr. Potter. My name is Nathan Hallett. You were a guest at my house with Dr. Abbott a few months ago. Please come join my family for the remainder of your lunch."

Approaching the family, Clarence bowed deeply. Hattie reached out to shake his hand, but he gently took her hand in his and kissed it. Seeing this, the two young women stood as one with hands out to receive a kiss from the handsome man. Nate kept his seat and waved.

"Do you remember Mr. Potter?" asked Nathan. "He was in for supper with our friend Dr. Abbott."

"Oh, yes," said Franny as he kissed her hand. "I remember meeting you. Aren't you from the Provinces?"

Clarence held the young woman's hand tenderly. "So nice of you to remember me, Miss. Yes, I'm from Nova Scotia. So wonderful to see you again in such a pleasant hotel." He was unable to take his eyes off her. Either he had missed her beauty the last time they'd met or she had become more radiant since then.

"Mr. Potter, may I introduce my friend Lottie Adelaide Ritchie. She's visiting us from Massachusetts," said Franny.

Lottie extended her hand to accept his kiss. Her heart raced. She could think of nothing to say, feeling awkward and shy. Clarence, too, seemed awkward and tongue-tied. They stood hand in hand for a moment—until Franny cleared her throat loudly and pulled her friend back into a seat.

Finally, Clarence released Lottie's hand and said, "I'm here as an agent of a man from Ohio who is considering investments in Mr. Dunton's mine in Newry. He has asked me to inspect the initial pit to assay the prospect." Clarence took a place at the table across from the two young ladies. He thought about how fortunate he was to be in the company of two beautiful women of marriageable age. The younger one was beautiful in an alluring way, with silken skin and dark-blue eyes. The other was taller and had the better figure. She had held onto his hand for the longest time, as if there was a magnetism between them. He was sure that one of these two would soon be his new wife.

Nathan was the first to speak. "Mr. Potter, we are here as guests of Dr. Abbott, who is already a partner of Dunton in both his lumber and mining businesses. Abbott is to meet us here in the morning to drive us to the mine head to search for gems. Perhaps you will join us?"

32

After a splendid dinner at the Alpine House, Clarence asked Lottie to accompany him on a stroll through the plantation of pines that surrounded the immediate grounds. She willingly accepted the invitation and, as they wandered the pine needle–carpeted paths, listened intently to what he had to say.

"The Halletts are wonderful hosts. My time with them at their home was very short, but they made both Dr. Abbott and me feel very comfortable during our visit. You are so fortunate to be enjoying their hospitality for a longer time. Are you here on your own?"

"Yes; my mother accompanied me on the journey, but now I am alone for the next ten days before returning to Boston with Francena and Mr. Hallett. My time in Bridgton has been so wonderful, and I'm looking forward to visiting a real gem mine tomorrow. I do hope you can join our party."

"I look forward to it. The main reason I'm here in Maine is to visit the Dunton Mine as a representative for my employer—to inspect the pit to see if it would be a good investment for him."

"He must be very trusting of you to put such faith in your judgment. Do you have experience in mining?"

"My family owned two very small tin mines in Nova Scotia when I was a wee lad. Neither mine amounted to much, so my father became a blacksmith and trained me to do the same. When I was thirteen, Mr. Warren hired my dad to head a crew of smithies. They laid tracks for an extension of his railroad into the wilds of northern Ontario. I went along with him. When copper was discovered along the track right of way, we were given work in setting up two large mines for Warren and his partners in the Canadian Copper Company."

"Your experience sounds impressive. I can see why you're being trusted."

"More recently, following the death of my wife, Emma, I returned to Nova Scotia, where I'm currently managing a very productive gold mine."

"Clarence, I'm so sorry to hear about your wife."

"Thank you for saying that. She died less than two years ago during a wicked Ontario winter. Nothing could be done to save her."

"Do you have children?"

"Yes, there are three young ones. They live in Yarmouth with Emma's parents right now, but only temporarily. I'm thankful to Mr. Warren for providing money to help me care for them. Lottie, we don't have to talk all about my life. Tell me how yours is going."

"Yours is much more interesting than mine. I live at home with my parents in Winchester, Massachusetts. Dad is a physician and Mom takes care of our home. I'm studying at Burdett Business College and will probably get a boring office job when I graduate next year. You see how boring it all sounds."

"Not at all, my dear. It's only because you are so young that your life seems boring. How old are you, anyway?"

"Just turned twenty, but I feel like my life is still stuck at sixteen. Being on my own for two weeks with the Halletts is the most exciting thing I've ever done. I don't want it to end."

Coming to a rustic wooden bench fashioned from branches and twigs, the two sat in silence, staring back along the path they had walked. Clarence took out a cigarette, but before striking a match, he said, "I hope you don't mind if I smoke. It is a vice I have taken on recently. Helps to calm me."

"Please feel free to light it. Though I don't indulge in tobacco, the aroma is appealing."

"Perhaps you might try one of mine. I do have a holder you could use so as not to stain your hand. You don't have to inhale if the smoke bothers your throat."

At right: Specimens of tourmalines found at the Plumbago mine near the Dunton Gem mine in Newry during the 1980s by Tony and Gardner Waldeier of Waterford. Photos by author.

"Well, why not? There really aren't that many opportunities to have new experiences back in Winchester. My mom keeps an evil eye on me all the time."

After he placed the cigarette in a holder for her, she held the tip to her mouth and inhaled slightly as the match touched the tobacco. She made a little cough, then cleared her throat and inhaled more deeply. A smile came across her face as she exhaled.

"Clarence, it will surely be very difficult to raise three children by yourself and work at the same time. How do you plan to do that?"

"Well," he said, as he looked straight at her, "I don't plan on doing it alone for very long."

33

The road from Bethel to Newry had recently been graded, so the surface was wide but not particularly smooth. The Halletts rode in their chaise much more comfortably than the day before because Lottie rode with Clarence in a small wagon loaded with mining gear and a large box of lunch provisions. In the warm air, Franny and Hattie wore short-sleeved brown cotton dresses, while Lottie wore her denim jeans and jacket over a short-sleeved blouse. A wide-brimmed hat completed her outfit. Like the men, she was dressed to climb the hill and work the mine. The Hallett kids sang "Row, Row, Row Your Boat" over and over until their mother asked them to stop and watch for a road sign for the turn toward Andover, where the mine was located. Abbott rode alongside Clarence's wagon as the two shouted back and forth in conversation while Lottie listened. Her greatest attention, however, was not on their words but on the wondrous views to the rocky mountain peaks rising to their north and west.

"Excuse me, sirs. I don't wish to disturb your business, but can either of you tell me the name of that bald peak on the left? Never in my life have I seen a view like this. How wonderful!"

"I believe the one you point to is called Old Speck. It's part of the Mahoosuc range that runs from New Hampshire to north of Rangeley," said Abbott. "It's beautiful country up there, wild and undeveloped. Wasn't too many years ago that this road was just a muddy Indian path, and the country between Bethel and Newry was just as wild. This was Micmac country then, and you had to be well armed to make your way."

"Lottie, this country *is* beautiful, I'll grant you that," said Clarence, "but you would be impressed at the scenery in Ontario where the copper mines are located. I don't think a white man ever set foot there before the tracks were laid. Most of the time I was living there, snow sat on top of the hills and mountains and the wind never let up. Here you have more of a chance to appreciate nature without being blown away."

The entrance path to the mine was so rough that the chaise could go no further. Abbott loaded as much gear as he could on the back of his mount. Nathan unhitched the horse from the chaise and did the same. The others gathered together in the wagon for the slow climb to the mine. Soon they came upon two trees lying across the road as a blockade. It was there that the journey ended and the horses were tied to branches still attached to the giant logs. Standing behind the barricade was a short bearded man wearing a cowboy hat and dark sunglasses. He carried a shotgun on one arm and had a revolver in a holster strapped under the opposite arm.

"Hollis! Hollis!" yelled the good doctor. "No need to be shooting any of us. We've come for an inspection."

"Oh, 'tis you, Hiram. I've been waiting on you," said the mine owner. "Oh, and you've brought back Nathan and his boy. Please be at ease."

After the gear was unloaded, they all gathered around Hollis Dunton, who stood at the top edge of a wide, shallow pit. He made a big circular gesture with both arms. "Folks, this-here pit is the Dunton family mine. Don't look like much now, but the prospect for finding gemmy crystals in abundance is real good. Ask Mr. Hallett, here, what he found a week ago. Just ask anybody who's poked around in this pit. There are good pockets to be found.

"Yer welcome to dig for yerself. Just be careful. We blasted some dynamite two days ago, so the rock is all broke up and loose. You fall, and you'll likely cut yerself. You ladies might want to sit off to the side where there's still some grass growing. Perhaps yer men might bring a few rocks over for you to clean in one of those rain barrels.

"Before you start prospecting, I need to make one request. Since several of you are partners in this-here mine, I don't think you'll disagree with me asking you to let me inspect every stone you might want to take home. This is a profit-making business, and we partners may want to keep any gemmy crystals that could be sold for jewelry-making purposes."

As he spoke, Nathan and Nate hurried to the spot they had been working on the last visit, buckets and hammers in hand. Franny, who knew that Lottie would not be sitting ladylike in the sun, stepped behind a wagon, removed her crinolines, and tucked her skirt hem into the waist of her pantaloons. Hattie thought the idea of a safe seat was a good one, so she carried the lunch basket off to the grassy area where she might keep an eye on everyone. Clarence took a seat on a big boulder near Hattie and stared silently across the rough rubble caused by the blast, while Franny and Lottie stood behind him.

"Okay," he said after a few minutes. "Okay; I think I know where there might be a good little pocket for the opening. Why don't you two come with me and see if I'm right?"

Making their way carefully across the field of broken stone, the three went directly to an area of shattered white quartzite. These smaller rocks were crystal-like fragments that could be broken off with the tap of a hammer. Clarence knelt and began to clear debris away from a small dark hole.

"What are you doing?" asked Lottie. "These rocks that you're tossing aside are so shiny and lustrous, perhaps we might break them apart to find a crystal."

He paid no attention until he had cleared a space large enough for the three of them to sit. Reaching into the hole, he pulled out some wet white gravel. Again he reached in and pulled out the same, but when the gravel was laid out on the ground, a single green stone stood out. When it had dried, He passed it to Lottie and said, "Please wipe the film off this stone. Let's see what it looks like in the sunlight."

She spit on the stone and rubbed it on the cloth of her jeans. It was no bigger than a rock-salt crystal, but when held up to the sun between her fingers, it's lime-green color caught their attention. "Oh, Franny...Clarence...look what we've found!"

Once more, he put his hand into the hole. This time, the gravel that came out was filled with little green crystals the size and shape of pencils. Lottie was so excited she jumped to her feet and nearly fell back against a jagged boulder. Franny grabbed her leg just in time to stop the fall.

"Lottie," whispered Clarence, "why don't you reach in with your hand and see what you find. The water is cold, but you can feel around to locate the bigger pieces. There's nothing in there that will hurt you."

Now on her knees, Lottie squealed as her hand disappeared into the hole. "Oh, so cold and clammy! I don't like the feel of this stuff... Wait! Wait! I think I have a larger piece. A couple of them!"

"Well, dummy," demanded Franny, "will you just take them out so I can see what you found? Don't just sit there stammering."

Pulling her hand from the slimy hole, Lottie threw a mix of wet gravel and clay on the ground and then wiped the slime on her jacket. Clarence sorted through the mix and pulled out three green crystals, each more than two inches long and about an inch wide. There were more of the smaller pieces as well, but these larger ones were staggering in their beauty and luster. Both girls began to scream so loud with delight that the others stopped what they were doing and approached the trio.

Abbott and Dunton, who had been sitting and chatting on one of the downed hemlocks, also approached—as did Hattie, who only went as far as the edge of the rubble field. Lottie and Franny ran to her and placed all the gems in her outstretched hand. "Here, Mother, please hold these wonderful tourmalines for us while we harvest more!"

By now, Clarence had enlarged the hole with his chipping hammer until it was wide enough for him to dip his bucket into the little chamber. Out it came filled to the brim with the white solution. To the astonishment of all, as water drained off and sludge settled, dozens of green, white, black, rose, and orange crystals lay in a pile. They had found a pegmatite lode that none of them would ever forget.

Abbott and Dunton were slower to arrive on the scene, but when they stood close enough to observe the others, Hollis clapped his hands and shouted his congratulations. "Folks, what a find! Now you see why I decided to buy this rocky place. Let's wash all this gravel down and see what we have."

"Thanks be to our Canadian friend," said Nathan. "He's the one who figured where to dig."

"Yes, he has a good nose for the lode, that's for sure. But I say 'thanks be to God' who put these beautiful stones together for us to find!" Dunton exclaimed as he filled a bucket with a small shovel drawn and unfolded from a sheath on his belt.

The others placed their own pails, four in all, next to the muddy pile to be filled. Then they carried them to one of the rain barrels near where Hattie had been sitting. When each load was dumped on the ground, Hollis and Nathan took pails of water from the rain barrels and poured them over the gravel.

"Oh, my God," said Hattie as white mud was washed away revealing many shiny crystals. "There are so many different colors in the mix."

As Lottie, Franny, and Nate went down on their knees and began clawing through the piles, more stones glistened in the sunlight. There were green tourmalines, both clustered in white quartz and standing alone. There were black splinters that Dunton called schorl, which broke easily as they were uncovered. Several glittering specimens showed a layered mix of green and orange crystal that Nathan identified as watermelon tourmaline. Some pieces of white quartz contained colorful specks of rose and smoky gray. Most of the tourmalines were small, no more than a half inch long, but one was huge, more than three by four inches, and one end, or termination, came to a pyramidal point. Dunton picked up the large crystal and spit on it to make its facets cleaner.

"I'll have to take this one back to my shop. And maybe a few more of those small gemmy ones, too. As I said, we can sell these to a couple of jewelers in West Paris. These will help us cover our costs. Don't you agree, Dr. Abbott?"

"Of course, you're right. It may be disappointing to the children, but I think Nathan and Mrs. Hallett will agree. After all, we are all partners."

"And you, Clarence," asked Dunton, "do you understand what I'm doing? You were the finder here, and I don't want to offend you, but it is my claim."

The Canadian nodded in agreement. "Just as long as the kids can keep all the smaller crystals and the specimens. These will prove to be the start of a wonderful collection. I don't need anything for myself, at least at this point. If in the future you might have a job for me, I would have a great interest in working such a valuable mine."

Everyone looked at him, and the four partners nodded their heads at that prospect.

Lottie held her hand out to shake Clarence's. "Thank you so much, Clarence. You have given me an experience today that I will never forget."

As the group took seats on some nearby boulders and ate lunch, Clarence sat off on his own. In his pants pocket were the three gemmy crystals that he and the girls had first found. These had not made it into any bucket, and, in the excitement, no one had noticed their absence.

34

Hattie and Nathan sat on the front bench of his buggy as they returned from the Dunton Mine. Franny and Lottie, sitting in the rear seat, started the trip by giggling and carrying on while they sifted through a metal cookie box nearly filled with crystals. After a while, they fell asleep with their heads touching. Behind them, Nate rode in the buckboard with Clarence, pointing out roadside features to the miner as they passed through the countryside.

"Nathan, my dear, this has been one of the best family days we've enjoyed since that outing to Waterford a year ago. Everyone had such a great time. Finding all those gems is something none of us will ever forget."

"Hattie, it always makes me happy to see you enjoy yourself. Sometimes when I'm on the road, there are things that I see which I know you would love. To be able to share the discoveries with my family brings joy to me."

She hooked her arm through his. "Having Lottie with us to share the experience has been special. She's been so happy with us, not like she was when her mother was here. Those two are like black and white, complete opposites. I can't imagine how the father keeps the peace. I remember back in Waterford he was so friendly, while Mary was so difficult."

"Franny told me the girl wants to leave home," said Nathan. "Said something about wanting to stay with us in Bridgton."

"She may be twenty and old enough to leave if she desires, but I think it is only girl talk. I'd probably have felt the same way if home life was unbearable when I was her age. Remember when we met, I was only fourteen and happy about life with my grandparents. Still, I was happy to leave and get out on my own. Especially with *your* companionship, my dear." She whispered these last words in his ear.

"Well, if you ask me, she's looking at this Potter fellow as a means to the end of getting away from her mother. The two have been nearly inseparable since last night at dinner. I'm not sure that would be a good idea. I *am* sure the idea of a relationship would not be appealing to the Ritchies."

They rode along in silence for a while until Nathan freed his arm from hers and put it around her waist. "There was something that happened last week that I forgot to tell you. I was in South Waterford again at Watson's box factory, and that Stevens woman showed up. She was looking for a handyman to do some work at her place. Watson told me that he thought the job she needed doing was the same one Lizzie's old friend Bert was doing for her before he disappeared."

"I don't trust that woman at all. Lizzie might not agree, but I just don't think it wise to let someone like that into her life. You heard about the strange early-morning visit to the dress shop last month, didn't you? Very unusual. That woman is haunted by many demons, and it's good to keep her at arm's length."

"Oh, I agree. It is my fear that she may be more than just a crazy person. She may be responsible for more than driving both her husband and Bert out of town. Lizzie is right to be concerned about what happened to Henry Greene, and when she learns that Bert Learned also disappeared, I'm sure she will want to investigate further."

"That may be true, Nathan, but I don't want *you* to get mixed up in something that really has nothing to do with you. Please promise that you won't have anything else to do with Miss Greene or Stevens or whatever her name is."

He said nothing for several minutes, considering the serious tone of his wife's request. "Well, dear, I will stay as far away as possible from the demented woman and only investigate third-hand. Is that all right with you?"

Remembering the tough years of childhood when she and Lizzie had grown up without a father, she said, "I'll not try to dissuade you from helping Lizzie if you want to. Just stay clear of Stevens, and for your family's sake, never go out to that cursed farmhouse."

It was the final evening of the Bethel stay, and the Halletts,

Lottie, and Clarence sat around a sumptuous banquet table at
the Alpine House. Sitting adjacent to a large bay window facing
the west, they basked in the orange glow of a spectacular sunset. Nathan asked everyone to join hands as he said grace. "May
we praise God for the bounty which we have before us and that
which we found in nature today. Amen."

All said amen, but Hattie added her own addendum to the
blessing: "And let us all thank the Almighty for the wonderful
place in which we live."

Lottie, who was seated between Franny and Clarence, held
hands with both and added, "I don't remember ever feeling so at
peace as right now. Thank you all for having me with you."

35

Lottie was crestfallen. Her freedom was about to end. She feared
that when she got home her mother would have many leading questions for her and Franny about what they had done
during the visit, probing for things that she might have done
wrong. If only I could stay here, she said to herself over and over
again while reluctantly packing. Dad will tell me she does it for
my own good, but he doesn't understand how it makes me feel.
She's trying to control me. She was also concerned that she might
never see Clarence ever again. He was so handsome and clever
that she thought him the best man she had ever met. He seemed
to like her in return, but one could never be sure with young men,
they were so changeable. One day, a boy might be gallant and
kind, only to turn cross and cruel the next day. Perhaps this man
was different. She wanted to have the time to learn more about
him, but now she had to leave.

She asked the innkeeper if Clarence was still a guest and
found out that he was out for a stroll in the park. The innkeeper
pointed toward the *pinetum* where the couple had walked before.
There she spied Clarence sitting on their bench reading a pamphlet. Although her first thought was not to disturb his solitude,

she knew that a delay in saying a personal goodbye would mean that he might never know how she felt about him. She walked on the path toward him and called out a greeting. "Mr. Potter. Clarence, do you have a minute to chat?"

"Of course, Miss Lottie. Of course. I have as much time as you want. Please come sit by me." His eyes lit up and a smile spread across his lips as he watched her approach. She was dressed in her denim travel outfit, with her hair pulled back in a tight bun beneath a green scarf. When she stepped from bright sunlight into the shady grove, he could make out her face and figure more clearly. She was so beautiful! Franny was also quite attractive, of course, but this one was more his style. She appeared to be better suited for life in the country.

"My friend," she said, pulling up close to him on the bench, "I'm leaving today and wanted to say farewell."

"Leaving? Oh, that makes me sad," he said as his hand reached out for hers. "I have so enjoyed our time together, as short as it has been. Are you returning to Bridgton to continue your stay with your friends?"

"I have only two more days left in my visit. Day after tomorrow I must return to my home in Massachusetts. Thankfully, Franny will be my guest there for a fortnight. Her dad is chaperoning us on the journey."

"This place you live in Massachusetts, is it Boston? That's supposed to be a busy port like Yarmouth. Some men I know have sailed there many times."

"No. I live in a town near there: Winchester. It's not as large as Boston City, but it is a busy town. My father is a physician who often goes to the city."

"Does your family often travel to Maine?"

"No. We were here one time before because Dad wanted to look into investing in the Dunton lumber operation. Wait 'til he hears that I actually was in the mine on that same property!"

Her excitement was contagious, causing him to laugh and put his arm across her shoulders. "Lottie, do you think I might visit you in Winchester? Do you think your parents would allow it?"

"Dad would, but Mom would not be pleased. She and I do not get along very well."

"Well, it would be worth a try. I must speak with Nathan, see what he thinks. Seeing a new part of New England would be great fun, especially if I were with you."

They walked back toward the inn arm in arm. She felt as if they were two old friends reunited after a long separation. He thought that perhaps he was with the woman who would be his new wife.

Nathan was on the rear porch enjoying a cigarette. He was so rapt in studying a file of business papers, he didn't notice them.

"Nathan," Clarence began, "my friend here tells me that you're getting ready to leave me here all alone."

"Oh, 'your friend,' is it?" Nathan smiled. "Yes, you'll be losing your friend on the morrow. We return to Bridgton, and then we are off to Massachusetts by way of Westbrook. My sister-in-law wants to meet this young lady."

"Is that Aunt Lizzie, the dressmaker?" asked Lottie. "Franny has told me so much about her. Will we be staying overnight in Westbrook?"

"Yes, that is the plan. I am to pick up some dresses and deliver them to a shop on Boston's Beacon Hill on the way to Winchester."

"Nathan, Lottie and I have been discussing the possibility that I might be able to meet her family. Would it be possible for me to travel along with you? I won't be a burden. I'm sure there must be public lodgings available in Westbrook and Winchester."

Surprised that the couple had become so close, Nathan studied them for a moment before responding. "I'm not sure how that will go over with her parents. Surely Lizzie will have room for you to stay. I already have three tickets on the B&M Express. You'll have to check on a ticket of your own when we get to Union Station."

"If you don't mind, I will take that chance. If I can't get a ticket to Boston, there's always a train running north to Canada," he said with a smile.

"Suit yourself, Potter. You'd likely be hoping for a ride south with pleasant company and a warmer destination."

"Yes, sir. That is what I hope."

Nathan watched as they walked away, hand in hand this time. Their infatuation was obvious. He wondered how Hattie, Lizzie, and the Ritchies, especially the mother, would take to them as a couple.

36

The extremes of Maine weather are always difficult to gauge. It was August third when the party of six left Bethel. There were a few clouds beginning to build over the White Mountains to the west, but the hot sun turned a cool early morning into an uncomfortable ninety-degree afternoon. By the time they reached Waterford, the light southerly wind had backed around to a stiff northeast breeze, and the temperature had dropped like a stone. Riding horseback, Clarence had begun the day wearing jeans and a cotton short-sleeved shirt, but was soon wrapped in his vest and a leather jacket. Nathan, driving his wagon, was wrapped in a blanket with his hat pulled so far down that it protected his ears. He did not have warmer clothes with him, for it was, after all, still summer. The others wore every item of clothing they had packed for the trip. Hattie and Franny sat close together under a coarse blanket, trying to stay warm. Lottie did somewhat better with her denim riding outfit, but even she huddled next to the other two. Nate appeared to be warmer, but only because he didn't want to show any weakness in front of Clarence. At one point, he took the reins from his father, who wanted to warm his hands under his arms.

"Mr. Potter!" shouted Nate above the noise of horses' hooves and wind. "I bet you get weather like this up in Ontario all the time, don't you?"

"We surely do. It's pretty much like this all the time except for an occasional warm day." He laughed at his own joke, but no one else got the humor.

The weather had moderated by the time they got to Bridgton, though the wind was still gusty. With the exception of Nate, who'd been given the job of putting the horse in its stall, the party was quick to get inside the house. Clarence carried all the luggage into the parlor and then turned to leave.

"Hey, where are you going?" asked Nathan.

"I saw several rooms-for-rent signs in the town center. Just wanted to get a place to stay before it gets any later."

"Please don't bother," said Hattie. "There's room for you here on the cot in Nathan's office. It won't be too warm, but neither will any other room you might take at this hour. Nobody is heating guest rooms in this season."

"I'm not wanting to be a bother," said Clarence. "You've been kind enough to let me tag along, and I don't want to be presumptuous."

Nathan closed the door. "No bother, sir. We enjoy your company," he said, looking over at Lottie and winking.

Nate came in at that point and, overhearing the conversation, said to Clarence, "You can stay in my room for the night. I'll take the cot. I sleep there sometimes because it's so sunny in the morning. You'll be warmer upstairs."

"Thank you, my young friend," said Clarence. "You do me a great favor that I shall not forget."

After dinner, everyone except Clarence set off early for bed. He sat by the parlor hearth, where a crackling fire blazed, and tried to write a letter to his family in Yarmouth. Ten days had passed since he'd last sent money, and he knew that the Shermans would be thinking him a scoundrel for abandoning the kids. As he stared into the fire thinking of words to say, Lottie entered the room from the darkness of the kitchen. She had left the bed she shared with Franny and was wearing a thick green cotton bathrobe over her nightgown.

"Clarence," she whispered from behind him, "can we talk for a moment?"

He turned quickly and was shocked at seeing his new friend in her sleepwear. "Oh, please, come sit beside me. I'm penning a letter to home, but have not been able to find the right words." Moving over to make room on the small sofa, he patted on a place for her to sit. "Couldn't you sleep?"

"I didn't want to sleep. Francena and I chatted for only a moment before she fell fast asleep. I have wanted to speak with you in private since our last chat on the park bench. Hopefully you will not think me too forward, but I like you, feel very close to you. Don't you feel something between us?"

"Yes, I feel that we have much in common. We've only known each other for a few days, but we are friends already. I'm sure you would have many other admirers in your life and might not pay attention to a backwoods miner." As he spoke, his hand gently brushed hers, and when she did not pull away, he took a firmer hold of it with both hands.

"Clarence, my admirers are few, and the life that you demean as 'backwoods' is very appealing to me. I love it here in what my mother calls 'the wilds of Maine.' There is no place anywhere near Winchester where I might dig a hole and take crystals out of it. There are no mountains and forests in Massachusetts as big as these in Maine. And there is no one like you, who have the bravery and strength to make a life in the Canadian woods."

The intensity of her words made her voice become louder; so he held his fingers to her lips to quiet her. "Forgive me," he whispered, pulling his hand away abruptly. "I did not mean to touch you so personally."

She looked at him with a blank expression for an instant before pulling his hand back to her face where she placed a kiss on its palm. "You have done nothing for which you need to ask my pardon. Tenderness becomes you."

"Lottie, so much time has passed since I've had a tender moment with a beautiful young woman like yourself. Perhaps I have forgotten how to respond to affection. It is not my intention to push myself on you."

When she placed her head on his chest, he kissed the top of her head. "Please, Lottie, go back to bed. I wish nothing to happen which might push us apart. Tomorrow we will be traveling together and may have more private moments along the way."

Lottie tiptoed back into the bedroom and slid between the sheets with Francena, who was aware of her friend's absence and sat up straight. "Dearie, where have you been? Were you sitting with Clarence?"

"Yes, he and I had a friendly chat near the fire."

"Did you kiss him?"

"No, silly. Nothing of the kind! Just simple conversation about our travels in the morning."

37

The day dawned warm and sunny with perfect road conditions for the trip to Westbrook. They arrived at Lizzie's just before noon, surprising the seamstress, who had not yet prepared lunch. Moses met the group at the front door and ushered them into the showroom. Liz entered from her office carrying an outfit to use in dressing a mannequin. When Franny saw her aunt, she rushed forward, grabbed her arm, and nearly stepped on the hem of the dress.

"Francena Hallett," Hattie chastised, "act like a lady. Don't knock your aunt over and ruin the dress."

"Oh, I'm sorry, Auntie. It's been so long since I saw you that I got excited."

Liz laid the outfit on a table and, turning to Franny, gave her niece such a hug that the young woman's feet came off the floor. "Young lady, I have missed you terribly." Before she could embrace Hattie and the others, Franny pulled her by the arm toward Lottie, who stood next to Clarence.

"Auntie Lizzie, please meet my friend Lottie Adelaide Ritchie.

She has been staying with us for a fortnight. She's from Massachusetts. This man is her friend, Mr. Clarence Potter, who lives in Canada."

"Ma'am," said Lottie as Lizzie took her hand. "Franny has told me so much about you. It's a pleasure to finally meet the woman who makes all the lovely clothes my friend always wears."

Clarence bowed and said, "It is indeed a pleasure to meet you."

Nathan came in carrying two overstuffed duffels, accompanied by Moses, who toted a smaller one. Dropping the heavy bags, Nathan gave his sister-in-law a hug, and Hattie gave her a warm kiss.

After lunch, Moses, Lizzie, and Nathan sat together on the front porch watching traffic on Forest Avenue. They talked about changes happening in the local economy.

"Moses, I don't wholly agree with your assessment of our Maine economy. There is much to be excited about. I see lots of investment opportunities in many new businesses—sardine canneries and pulp mills, for example. And even the mining of feldspar holds promise of a great future. Granted, the older industries might fade, but isn't that always the way with progress?"

"Perhaps that is the way, but unless these new enterprises are able to create permanent jobs and healthy profits, like our mills, the future will likely turn out to be bleak."

Lizzie was bored with her husband's continual complaining about the future of manufacturing. She interrupted in order to change the subject. "Nathan, Moses and I have been discussing that investment we made in the Newry sawmill. How has that operation fared?"

"Very well. Very well, indeed. Have you not received payments from the Duntons? If not, I'll have to check on that for you. They have nearly cleared both of the Newry lots, and the Rumford mill has been recently expanded to keep up with local demand. For several months, this spring they were operating nearly twenty-four hours a day."

A guilty smile came across Moses's lips as he listened. "Liz, my dear. I am so sorry to have misled you. We've gotten three drafts from Mr. Dunton's bank over the last few months. I must have forgotten to tell you about them. Please forgive me for being so distracted by my health worries."

"Wait, didn't we have a conversation just last week about the mill's failure to pay us? How could you have forgotten to tell me? Why were you complaining if the drafts had already been deposited in our bank?"

Realizing that the couple might need to discuss this matter in private, Nathan switched topics. "Lizzie, you and Hattie both have a fascination with the potential for gem mining from Dunton's new quarry. You may be pleased to know that young Potter has been sent here to inspect the mine and assay its value for a very wealthy investor from Ohio."

"Does Potter have the experience to be able to judge the value of a prospect?" asked Moses. "What's his background? I know that Lizzie is interested in the mine, but I am skeptical. After all, so many of these mineral excavations have proven to be worthless. I heard that gold had been discovered in Franklin County, but that turned out to be a total hoax."

"Moses, your skepticism is warranted, but I understand from Dr. Abbott that Clarence was instrumental in establishing several copper mines in Ontario and an iron mine in Nova Scotia. And after witnessing the young man's ability this weekend to identify where a pocket of gemstones was located, I must say he has an impressive skill at sniffing out minerals under the ground."

Moses rose from his seat and headed toward the door. "Nathan, I may have to agree with my wife now about investing further in Dunton's endeavors. Please get us the details of how we might best be involved. Now I'm going out to the garden to have a smoke."

38

The two sisters had an opportunity to separate from the others and go for a stroll along the cart path that ran between the rear of the house and Pride's Quarry. Tall pines and ancient maple trees still lined the way, providing shade and screening noise from the nearby highway. The women had not been together in private for months, but as they walked arm in arm, their lifelong intimacy was quickly renewed.

"Hattie, I'm afraid that my husband is failing. He's fallen a few times recently and broke his leg the most recent time. His mind wanders and he forgets so much now. His faculties are regularly sound, but there are moments when I think he may not be aware of his surroundings. The fact that he forgot to tell me about those recent bank drafts gives me pause and makes me worry that there may be other things he has done but cannot remember. It scares me."

"Lovey, I'm so sorry to hear this. What a good man and a good helpmate he has been."

"You know the problems I had with men better than anyone else. When Henry Greene dropped me, it was like a bolt out of the blue—a real shock. All those years at home and then at the Pepperell, I couldn't bring myself to trust any man who approached me."

She hesitated for a moment before continuing. "Hattie, I knew there might be some problems marrying a man twice my age. Now, with his increasing health issues, I'm concerned that he will leave me alone with many more years to live. Not having children is all right with me, but losing my love would make me miserable."

"Liz, just enjoy the time you have together with him. We both have been fortunate to find good men. Hopefully, young Francena and her friend Lottie will be as fortunate. There are so many dead-end paths in relationships."

"Do you think that the Massachusetts girl has perhaps found a good man in the Canadian? They seem to be hitting it off quite well."

"That situation is very troublesome. My concern is that when Clarence meets the parents, especially Mrs. Ritchie, there will be a row. Lottie is mature for her age, but he has a separate life up there in the Provinces. He may want her to join him there. You don't know about his wife dying and leaving him with three young children. It would be burdensome for a twenty-year-old to have to adjust to being a mother of three at the same time she would be growing into a relationship with a new husband."

"Three little ones? Very troubling, indeed. However, it really is not our concern, is it, my dear? We can only hope for the best."

39

Franny was angry with Lottie. Their trip to Massachusetts was supposed to be a time when they might enjoy each other's company. With Clarence along, she would likely be spending more time with her dad than with her friend. At the start of the trip, it had been her understanding that "the miner," as she now referred to Clarence, would be leaving them either at Portland or Boston. Now he planned to travel all the way to Winchester in order to meet Mr. and Mrs. Ritchie. As the party prepared to leave Westbrook, Franny pulled her friend aside.

"Come, sit next to me in the wagon. It's a short ride to Union Station, but we can chat. I haven't had a chance to enjoy your company since we left Bridgton."

Lottie smiled at her younger friend, but explained that she was going to ride behind Clarence on his horse. "It will be exciting to ride up higher and get a broader view of the countryside. You and I will have a long train ride ahead when we can sit together."

Knowing that Lottie would find another excuse for sitting with Clarence on the train, Franny said, "Do you not like me anymore? I thought we were going to be very good friends, but all you want to do is be with that miner. Do you love him or something?"

"You and I *are* good friends and will be spending a lot of time together when we get to my home. Right now, I want to enjoy his company. He may not be with me for long. After all, my parents may not like him, so I need to be with him while he's around. Don't you understand how I feel?"

"No. Not really. It seems to me that you're in love and want to be with him all the time. Why don't you just get married!" Her words were said with a sharp staccato as she turned and mounted the carriage.

Both her mother and her aunt observed what had just happened. Hattie mounted the rear seat and patted her daughter's shoulder. Lizzie stepped up close to the side of the carriage and whispered to her niece, "I know that you are offended by your friend, but please try to forgive her. Her affection for the man may not last for long. Young love can be like that. On the other hand, perhaps the relationship will last. Remember that your friendship with Lottie will have its ups and downs, but may turn into a bond that will last a lifetime. Don't lose that possibility by being too quick to judge."

Franny leaned over and gave her aunt a kiss, but said nothing. Hattie whispered in the girl's ear, "Take you aunt's advice to heart. Through all of my life, my sister and I have seen each other through trials and triumphs. This girl could be the sister that you don't have. Please be patient. Things may change."

"Thank you," Franny said with a grim smile. "I'll try to be patient with her as you say."

40

Aphia stood at her front door watching the young man spread topsoil on the Hill of Death. The lad Mr. Watson had sent to work for her was a newcomer to Waterford, exactly as she had requested. When he arrived, she had asked a few questions. He lived in Lynchville, just outside of North Waterford, in a rent with a farmer who had himself recently moved to the area. The boy's family was back in Connecticut. He had run away and hoped his parents would never find out where he was. When she asked him why he ran away, he laughed at the question and wouldn't answer.

The hill was in need of a deep coating of soil because of the swarming flies. Every year, Aphia purchased a wagon full of topsoil from a local farmer and hired someone to spread it in order to increase the soil depth until it was thick enough to stop the annual infestation. Bert Learned had been the last one to do this same job, but he had done such a poor job she'd taken away the shovel and finished it herself.

She watched the young man very closely as he began to poke at the pile of soil. "Miss Stevens," he shouted, "what's all this stuff sticking up from the ground? Someone left a hat here and a boot."

"There's a bunch of old stuff buried in there," she called back. "I'm not paying you to dig things up. I'm paying you to bury things. If you don't want to finish the job, just go away."

"No, ma'am, I'm fine with doing your work. No more questions."

Aphia began to worry that the same thing that had occurred before was about to happen again. Why don't these people just do what they are paid to do? Hell, everyone has to ask so many questions, and they're sure to spread rumors. She watched the helper continue to do as told until his shovel caught on something that caused him to fall.

"Hell, lady, what the heck is buried under here? I just stepped into a hole full of maggots!"

Running to the hill, she took the shovel away. "Oh, son, your boots are quite a mess. Why don't you come inside and let me clean them for you. This is such hard work that you might want to take a break and have a bite to eat for lunch."

At first he was reluctant to go inside with her, but since he had not eaten anything that day, he followed her to the house. At the door, he stopped, staring at bunches of dried herbs hanging from the kitchen rafters.

"Ma'am, why do you have all that grass hanging from the ceiling? Don't it make a mess of your place?"

"I use them to make dried flower bouquets and herbal remedies. That is a way I make a living."

She led him to a wide table in her kitchen that was covered with piles of green flowers and leaves. Brushing some cuttings aside to make room for him to eat, Aphia served an earthenware bowl of steaming broth and a piece of brown bread spread with butter. He sniffed the bowl and studied the bread.

"Go ahead. I made this vegetable soup myself. It's delicious and very good for you. The bread was baked only yesterday." Seeing that he was still reluctant to eat, she poured herself a bowl and stood at the stove with a spoon. He thought she was eating, so he tried some of the food himself. The bread and butter were very tasty, so he held the bowl up to his mouth and nearly drained it in one gulp. His face suddenly flushed bright red and sweat began to run down his brow.

"What is in this soup? Are you trying to poison me? I feel like I'm going to puke!" He jumped from the chair and ran toward the open door, but halfway there he lost balance and fell to the floor. As he lay there, he vomited what he had just eaten all over the floor. He grabbed his stomach and rolled onto his side. He tried to get up but fell again and lay still.

She knew that he was dead.

"Why does this keep happening to me?" she asked herself out loud. "People just don't know how to pay attention to the work. They ask too many questions. Now I'll have to dispose of another body and still spread the damn soil by myself. What a life!"

Having been in this predicament several times before, Aphia wrapped the dead boy in a hooked rug and rolled the bundle across to the threshold. Then she secured the end of the rug with a long rope, tossing the end out the door. The efficiency with which she worked impressed her.

"I don't make any wasted motions. So smooth."

She went into the barn and returned with one of the Morgans all saddled up. Tying the rope to the saddle horn, she led the horse across the front yard to the pile of soil. After digging a two-foot-deep hole, she undid the rope, pulled up the edge of the rug, and rolled the body into the shallow grave. A few shovelfuls of dirt completed the job, and once the horse was back in its stall, she returned to compact the soil by jumping up and down on it.

With her work done for now, Aphia returned to her kitchen, thoroughly washed the bowl and plate used by her victim, and sat down to rest. That will do for the time being, she thought. It will soon be winter and the ground will freeze. Once I spread the remaining soil and plant some grass seed, nothing will seem amiss. In the summer, I may still have the same problem with flies, but I'll figure out a new solution before then.

41

Will Cain offered to drive the party to Union Station, twelve miles away, and then bring the wagon and horses back to Westbrook for safekeeping until Nathan and Francena would return in two weeks. As he shook the reins and the horses began to move forward, Clarence reached his strong arm down to Lottie and pulled her up behind him in the saddle. Franny sat next to her father in the rear and, slipping her hand behind his elbow, smiled at him and then at the couple as they followed behind. Following her aunt's advice, she would remain patient and give the relationship with her friend a chance to grow despite "the miner's" presence.

At the station, Clarence was able to purchase a ticket on the Boston Express so that he might travel with the Halletts to Massachusetts. Once again, a bit of jealousy sprang up in Francena's heart when she realized that deepening her bond with Lottie would have to be further delayed. There was still the possibility that he would not be with them by the time they reached Winchester, but she was beginning to think that once Nathan left for his appointments further south, she would become a lonely third wheel. Her hope was that Mrs. Ritchie would be so set against her daughter having a relationship with a foreigner that he would be driven away.

Francena had never been on such a fast train before, and during most of the four-hour trip, her attention was drawn to the towns, fields, forests, and seashore through which they sped. Nathan was so busy explaining to his daughter the landmarks they passed that neither of them was aware that the other two had left the compartment soon after departure.

The couple had hidden away in an empty compartment at the other end of the car.

"Lottie, please come and sit beside me and watch the countryside pass by. If you recognize places along the route, please tell me about them," said Clarence as they entered the cabin. She moved quickly to his side, pressing as close as possible on the seat cushion. He put his arm around her shoulders and pulled her even more tightly against himself. She removed her hat, allowing her hair to fall free. "Such a beautiful woman you are," he whispered in her ear and placed a kiss upon her cheek.

In the hours since they had been alone at the fireside, she had wondered how it would be to kiss him on the lips. When he gently pulled her face up to his, she closed her eyes and breathed deeply before tasting his mouth. Boys at home had stolen kisses from her, but they were not like this. Her heart raced, and when she opened her eyes, she noticed that his were closed, too.

"Clarence, please kiss me again. I love how it makes me feel."

This time, their mouths met passionately and his tongue entered between her lips. She gasped and pulled back, but he held on to her so tightly that she had to either push him away or surrender to his strength. Sensing that she might be reluctant to go any further, he loosened his grip and turned his face away.

"No, Clarence. Do not stop. I want to kiss you and hold you against me."

They both removed their coats and wrapped their arms around each other so forcefully that they fell across the length of the seat. He reached out to touch her breasts through her blouse, but she drew back again and moved away from him, straightening her camisole.

"Oh, Lottie. I don't want to offend you, but I think I'm falling in love with you. Please forgive me for saying that, but it's true. I love you."

"I've never been in love before, so I'm not sure love is what I feel. I know I want to be with you, close to you, as much as is possible. Lest we go any further in our passion, let's find our way back to the others. They must miss us by now."

When they returned to the shared cabin, both Nathan and Franny were napping, so the couple entered as quietly as they could. He pulled his watch from a vest pocket and judged that the train would be arriving in North Station within minutes. Small houses set on treeless spans of sand dunes stood along the western side of the tracks. Open water of the Atlantic came nearly up to the tracks on the east. The conductor tapped on the door and stuck his head in to announce that Boston was just ahead. As the Halletts awoke, a whistle squealed and the train began to slow.

Nathan pulled two bags down from the shelf overhead and looked over at Lottie. "Glad you came back to join us. I was thinking I might have to tell your father you had left us somewhere along the way."

"Mr. Hallett, please don't joke about that. I would not want Dad to hear such a thing. He and my mom might get some wrong ideas about my friendship with Clarence. We were only next door in a vacant cabin enjoying the scenery run by, like yourselves."

"Young lady, I will leave it to you to explain why we have a fourth party member," he said, nodding to Clarence, who returned the nod in silence.

As he grabbed his and Lottie's bags and went to the door, Clarence said, "Mr. Hallett, I will handle any explanation to Mr. Ritchie about my presence. After all, it was my idea to come along and it is now my idea to tell him how his daughter and I feel about each other."

Franny nearly fell back into her seat. What did he mean about himself and Lottie? Such arrogance, to assume that he could change everyone else's plans! She knew it had been a bad idea to let him come along in the first place.

Lottie took her bag from Clarence and turned back to her friends. "Your family has been so kind to me. This vacation will be something I will always remember. Though I don't want to offend you or lose Franny's affection, please allow Clarence and me to explain our relationship to my parents." She had taken his hand as she spoke.

Once again, Franny was shocked. What was going on? These two had only known each other for a few days. How impulsive!

Nathan, too, was taken aback by the young woman's statement. He had believed that Clarence was pushing himself on Lottie. Now it was becoming clear that the two of them were hatching some sort of plan to be a couple and to break her away from the family. There would be hell to pay if this happened on his watch. Surely the Ritchies would blame him and Hattie.

42

John Ritchie waited for them at the platform, just as planned. He shook Nathan's hand and then turned toward Clarence to do the same. Instead, the Canadian bowed deeply so that John was left standing with his hand extended. Lottie greeted him with a hug and a quick kiss. She then reached for Clarence's hand.

"Daddy, this is Clarence Leslie Potter, a good friend of

mine who has been traveling with us from Bridgton. He comes from Canada, a place called Nova Scotia. He is a miner and a blacksmith. Clarence, this is my dad, John. He's a surgeon here in Boston."

"A pleasure to meet you, sir, I'm sure," said Clarence as he shook Ritchie's hand. "Lottie has told me much about you and your wife. It has been a pleasure to get to know your daughter."

John peered at the man over his rimless spectacles. He was trying to figure out how this stranger had become such a good friend to his daughter in only two weeks. Surely the Halletts would have made sure that their "friendship" had gone according to accepted customs.

Ritchie reached for Lottie's bags, but Clarence refused to let go of them. "Sir, it is the least I can do after she and the Halletts have been so kind as to let me travel with them."

The older man looked the younger man straight in the eyes and said, "Sir, I'm sure that you have other places to be, now that you are in Boston. I can handle the luggage."

Lottie stepped between them, turned to her dad, and said, "Father, Clarence will be coming with us to Winchester. I want him to meet Mother and see our home."

John glared at Nathan for a second and then said to his daughter, "Lottie, dear, there is only room for four and their luggage in my barouche. I'm afraid your friend will have to make other arrangements. I know he understands."

"Father, I want him to come with us. If necessary, I can sit on his lap to make room."

Clarence, realizing that his presence was making everyone uncomfortable, dropped her bag and asked Nathan, "Could you direct me to a stable where I might rent a horse for several days? And Mr. Ritchie, could you please provide directions to your home? I will travel on my own." To Lottie he said, "My dear friend, don't worry about me. It may take some time to work out the details, but I will not be more than a day away from meeting you in Winchester."

Relieved by the Canadian's offer, Nathan took out a pen and on a scrap of note paper wrote the address of a man in Charlestown, across the Charles River Bridge, who might have a horse he could hire. As the party of four began to walk through North Station to board the carriage, John reluctantly provided the requested directions, which Clarence scribbled on the back of the same scrap of paper.

Then, as Clarence walked away, an angry father threw his daughter's luggage into the rear compartment and said, "Lottie, you have a lot of explaining to do to me and your mother about this man and why you think he is such a friend."

The two-hour ride to Winchester was tense and nearly silent except for an occasional comment from Franny on the beauties of scenery and Mr. Ritchie's explanations of what she was seeing. The journey took them over the Charlestown Bridge, where a panorama of Boston Harbor filled with hundreds of barges and sailing ships opened to the east. Then they followed Main Street in Charlestown to a bridge over the Mystic River, which offered a clear view of the Bunker Hill Monument across pastures and rows of brick town houses along Bunker Hill Street. The route then ran along the remains of the former Middlesex Canal through Somerville and Medford, until the party approached the Wildwood section of Winchester where the Ritchies lived. The house was a handsome shingle-style cottage located on Woodside Street, a few blocks from Wildwood Cemetery. A small pond sat opposite the house, across the heavily wooded street.

Distracted by so many wonderful views in so short a time, Franny had nearly forgotten about the trouble her friend might be in until they pulled in behind the house. As John stepped down from the high driver's perch, he opened the carriage door and offered his hand to assist his young visitor to the ground. Lottie rose from her seat expecting the same courtesy, but he ignored her completely and walked to the luggage secured to the rear. Nathan gave the young woman a hand down before he himself disembarked.

Mrs. Ritchie stepped onto a brightly painted porch and waved at the group. "John, you have made such good time. I hope you drove slowly enough for our visitors to take in our lovely scenery. Welcome, Halletts. You've chosen a beautiful day for your arrival."

She then stepped to the pavement and tried to pull her daughter into a gentle hug, which the girl resisted. "Lottie Adelaide, can't you give your mother an affectionate greeting? You may not believe it, but I missed you."

"Mother, my time away flew by so quickly! Maine is such a wonderful world. I have been lucky to be there."

Carrying the luggage toward the stairs, John turned to give his wife a peck on the cheek. "Dear, our daughter has made several new friends this fortnight, more than just Francena and Nathan, here."

"Whatever do you mean, John? Lottie, what is he talking about?"

Nathan and Franny, who had reached the top of the porch steps, quickly moved through the open door to avoid witnessing what they knew was going to be a family argument.

"Mary, she has met a man up in Maine whom she now refers to as a 'good friend.' He accompanied them from Bridgton on the train. He's not here now, but will likely show up soon. I thought you should be prepared."

"Lottie Adelaide Ritchie, for what is your father preparing me? Who is this friend? Why did he travel with you all the way from Maine?"

"Mother, his name is Clarence Potter. I met him on an outing we had to a gem mine. He is such a lovely young man, quite different from the boys here in town. He has worked hard all his life in Canada, where he comes from, and is really a nice man. I like him."

"Like him? What do you mean? What is going on in that complicated little mind of yours? Tell me the truth."

The rising volume of their voices made John step between them before they might come to blows. He dropped both bags.

"Mary, I met this man at the station. He seems to be quite intelligent and courteous, but he is much older than Lottie, and he lives in Nova Scotia, of all places."

Lottie interrupted her father and started again with her mother. "Mother, the boys I meet around here are all children. Clarence is a man. He has lived through some hard times in some very rough places. He is stronger than anyone I've ever met."

"So, you have met a real man, you say, and you like him. But you have only known this *man* for two weeks. That is just not long enough to get to know what type of man he is. Now, you bring him home to meet your parents. What? Are you going to be courted by a man who lives two thousand miles away? It makes no sense."

"You haven't even met him. You can judge him for yourself when he arrives. Right now, I do not want to speak another word to either of you. My friends are inside waiting for a warm welcome. If you will not give it to them, I will. Don't embarrass me any further with your haranguing." With that, she walked into the house and slammed the door.

Her parents stood in shocked silence for a moment. Then John grabbed Mary's shoulders and spoke softly and directly into her face. "We have often wondered if our girl would ever find the right man. Now, she shows up with one who is all wrong for her and for us. What can we do?"

43

Clarence didn't show up until the following afternoon, and by that time, a semblance of peace had settled on the Woodside home. Not that the underlying tension had disappeared: Lottie and her parents had hardly spoken at all, and when they did, the conversations were short. Nathan and Francena had been provided with a guest suite just off the porch where they might be able to relax from the road. There they were also able to keep to themselves when they wanted to.

Franny and Lottie did find time to explore the historic neighborhood. They had not been able to bring themselves to speak of the row caused by Lottie's new boyfriend, but they were able to enjoy each other's company as they strolled the shady lanes of the nearby park-like cemetery.

The Ritchies and their guests were gathered for a light lunch on the porch when the sound of an approaching horse drew Lottie from the table and down the steps. Clarence rode up on a small quarter horse, and as he dismounted, she ran to his side for an affectionate greeting. Instead, he bowed to her and swept his hat almost to the ground. She grabbed the hat from his hand, threw it across the drive, and jumped up to wrap her arms around his neck in full view of the others, who had also left their seats.

"Young lady!" shouted Mary. "Behave yourself. Stop throwing yourself at this young man. Act like a lady!" Glaring back at Nathan she continued, "We didn't raise you to act like a rural cowgirl. You must have learned this behavior recently."

Ignoring Mary's words, Lottie said, "Mother, this is Clarence Leslie Potter. He is my dear new friend. Clarence, this is my mother, Mary. I have been waiting to introduce you to her."

John stepped forward and offered his hand in welcome. He knew that the argument between his daughter and his wife was about to ignite again, and he wanted to maintain some common decency in front of the others. "I wasn't sure if you would be able to follow my directions."

Clarence looked him up and down and said, "Mr. Ritchie. I am able to understand English, you know. It is my native tongue." To Mary he bowed and placed a gallant kiss on the back of her hand. She drew back in shock and wiped the hand on her apron before speaking.

"Mr. Potter. Is that your name? Mr. Potter, I am afraid your presence is not to my liking. You and my daughter may have become friends; however, my husband and I do not appreciate her being swept off her feet by a man who lives so far away. She has only just met you."

Clarence acknowledged Nathan and Francena, but knew that he had walked into a hornet's nest. "Mrs. Ritchie, I can understand your concern. She and I have both come to feel very close over the past few days. It is a surprise to me, as well. I wish to get to know her and her family more, if you will allow me. I have taken a room at an inn I passed near the center of your village so that we can have more time."

Lottie stepped to his side again and placed her arm around his waist. She was smiling directly at him, avoiding the shocked looks from everyone else. "You are such a dear, Clarence. You really do like me. How thoughtful to have such a plan."

John clenched his teeth in rage. "Young man, you are wrong to think that my wife and I are pleased to have you in our town. Neither of us welcomes your advances toward our daughter. She may be taken in, but we are not so naïve. You may stay as long as you want in Winchester. Spend the rest of your life here, as far as I am concerned. You will not be welcome in our house."

Mary could not control herself. She walked in a wide circle around the couple, waving her fist in the air and stamping her feet. "Get out of here, you scoundrel, you devil! You'll not see my daughter again, if she obeys me. Lottie, let go of this man and go to your room immediately. You both should be ashamed of yourselves."

The couple stood their ground against such anger for several minutes before Lottie burst into tears and ran up the porch stairs. Clarence, who now faced her parents' rage alone, stepped back to the horse and led the animal toward the street. Not knowing what else to do, he mounted and rode off toward town.

The Halletts didn't know how to react to the situation. They had come to pay a friendly visit, yet now it was clear their presence had become a mere distraction in a Ritchie family tragedy. Nathan took Franny into the parlor and said in a low voice, "I don't think it's good for either of us to be here any longer. John and Mary already blame me for what has happened, and you are not clear of suspicion. You can't stay here alone for a fortnight; it might be dangerous. Let's return to the suite and pack up to leave in the morning. I'm sure I can make an acceptable excuse for leaving. They don't want us here, either."

"Dad, if we could leave *now* it would make me happiest, but tomorrow will have to do. Lottie may be my friend, but she is on the verge of destroying her own life. I don't want to get caught in the explosion."

John agreed to drive Nathan and Franny to the Boston and Lowell railroad stop in Medford Square the next morning, where they would board a train to Boston. Before leaving, Franny accompanied Lottie on a short walk around the block.

"Lottie, I hate to leave now, but you have to understand how hard it would be for us to get any closer during this fight. Our time together in Maine made me realize how much I love you. I can only hope we can get back together when things are settled."

"Settled, you say?" She laughed. "My parents are not likely to allow any settlement on terms other than theirs. I need them to accept Clarence as possibly my future husband, yet they won't even allow him to pay court to me. This has nothing to do with our friendship, and hopefully, you will not be turned away."

"Lottie, I love you dearly. How could I not see you again? Please, please, please do not make any decisions that might ruin your life. Canada is so far away. You may not know this man enough to leave your family and friends behind for him. Please be careful."

The two hugged and cried on each other's shoulders before walking hand in hand back to Wildwood Street.

Climbing into the carriage, Franny dried her eyes on a sleeve and waved to her friend as they drove away. At the station platform she waited with John as Nathan bought two tickets and checked the schedule.

"Mr. Ritchie," she began. "Your daughter is very dear to me. We've grown very close in a short time. I can't bear to see her so sad. Clarence may not be to your liking, but perhaps they should be given a chance to get to know each other. I don't think fathers like all their daughters' friends, do they?"

"My child, you speak very wisely for a young person, but you must believe that Mary and I have only Lottie's best interests at heart. He is a man of the world. She is quite innocent. He comes from a place far away. How would you feel if she moved so far away that you would never see her again? That is my greatest fear about her being with this Clarence fellow."

"Sir, I understand you completely. It is just that she wants to be happy. Isn't *that* in her best interest?"

"Happiness is not all that it's cracked up to be," he said.

44

John had much time to consider his conversation with Franny as he drove back to Winchester. By the time he arrived home, he had begun to think that perhaps, just perhaps, there might be a way to let Lottie learn enough about the Canadian to realize that it would be wiser to meet and wed a local man. He and Mary might not have been fair in making their happiness more important than their daughter's. As he drove the carriage into the garage, Mary came running with a piece of notepaper in her hand.

"John, John!" she cried hysterically. "She has left us—run away with that man! She left this note. I can't believe it. I can't believe it! She left us." She fell against the front wheel before he had a chance to dismount and thrust the paper in his face. He read it aloud.

Dearest Parents,

I have decided to go and live with Clarence. Do not think that you can catch us and bring me back. He is the man to make me happy, happier than I have ever been. We may live in Canada or in Maine. I know not where, but it will not matter. We are meant to be together. We are soul mates. I will let you know where I land.

Lottie Adelaide Potter

45

*A*ugust 1896

The Portland Express sped northward as Lottie watched the shoreline fly past. Wheels on the tracks clicked in a constant rhythm, and telegraph poles in sharp repetition nearly hypnotized her into a trance of reflection on how fast her own life was moving. It had not been her intention to fall in love so quickly. Clarence had entered her life only a month ago, yet now she had given up everything to be with him. The business degree, which she had just one term to complete, was thrown away, as were her plans to grow her friendship with Francena Hallett. Suddenly, without forethought, twenty years of safe, ordered living were behind her.

Clarence saw things in a very different light as he stood on the exposed platform between two cars and enjoyed a cigar. Each beach house and stunted pine that zipped past brought him closer to his goal of having a new mother for his children and a beautiful young woman for himself. In just a few days, he would be returning to Yarmouth Town, packing up his repaired family, and returning to his work in Ontario. Life would be back to normal in his world. As he stepped back into the train and returned to his seat beside Lottie, she turned to him and smiled.

"I was just thinking of how quickly we have come to know each other. Almost as if it was destiny. Perhaps we are soul mates."

"Lottie, I'm not sure what that means. I can only say that I love you and want to make your life happy."

"Surely you will do that. I trust you with my heart and soul. You will bring true happiness to my life, something that was unknown back in Winchester. Mom and Dad were so cruel to you and unreasonable to me. I had become accustomed to their efforts at control, but you've helped me strike out on my own adventure."

His optimism was buoyed by the roll of cash he had received in exchange for the three gemmy crystals he had pocketed at the Dunton Mine. In a conversation at the inn in Bethel, Nathan had mentioned a lapidary on Tremont Street in Boston who might be a contact for future business. Clarence had called on the man immediately upon arriving in the city. Mining was becoming his easy path to money, whether it was gold nuggets, sparkling tourmalines, or payments from Mr. Warren.

46

Upon arrival in Boston, Nathan decided to postpone business travel further south in lieu of a return to Bridgton, where he could return his daughter and explain to Hattie what had happened in Winchester. Franny had been looking forward to a fortnight of adventure away from home, so he reserved a suite at the Parker House for two nights. He was sure a short stay in downtown Boston would fulfill her expectations.

From the large window of their suite, they looked down on the front of the French Second Empire Boston City Hall with its three stories of double columns and deep-set arched windows. "Dad!" exclaimed Francena. "Look at that statue in front. Is that Benjamin Franklin?"

"Yes, the great American was born very close to this spot. There are many historic places within walking distance of the hotel, locations which I'm sure you have read about in school. You know, your mother and I spent our honeymoon in this hotel seventeen years ago. It was one of the best times of my life."

"Mom has told me about that time. She was so excited to be in the city where our country was born. I told her I would go to see the place where the Boston Tea Party happened and where Paul Revere used to live. But what I really want to do most of all is visit Faneuil Hall. You know, it's called the Cradle of Liberty."

"We'll stop at Faneuil Hall on our walk around town tomorrow. For now, I want to buy you an excellent meal in the fine restaurant downstairs. It has been a rough few days for us, and we deserve to be gaily treated."

Franny woke before dawn so that she could make the most of her time in the great city. She woke her dad from a sound sleep, and while he dressed, she sat at an open window looking down on the corner of Tremont and School Streets as pedestrians made their way to work. She had never seen such a diversity of people. Well-dressed men on their way to law or government offices rubbed elbows with men and women in less formal attire who were likely craftspeople or merchants. She watched one boy for the longest time. He stood directly on the corner holding a tin cup of what appeared to be pencils. Every so often, a man or woman would take a pencil and deposit a coin in the cup. She could hear the coin clank on the metal cup bottom. He was dressed much like her brother would be, with brown short pants, a tunic that appeared to be a faded yellow, and a baseball cap. As Nate liked to do, too, he wore no shoes.

"Come on, my sweet," said her father, emerging from his toilet. "I assume you've gotten me up at this dark hour to be able to visit as many sites as possible in one day. Let's not loiter at the window when we can submerge ourselves completely in the urban beast."

Grabbing a bonnet from the settee where she sat, Franny flew from the room before her father could put on his canvas jacket. "Wait, dear. Wait! You'll need to wear your ankle boots; the streets are often dirty." She returned long enough to change her shoes and grab Nathan's hand. "We're off," he said. "I want to show you a shop run by an acquaintance of mine, just around the corner on Boston Common."

Walking Tremont Street to West Street where the jeweler's shop was located was a history lesson for Francena. At the top of School Street lay the King's Chapel and its ancient burial ground, where many of the greatest early citizens were interred. Then they passed the Granary and the majestic Park Street Church steeple. Nathan pointed across the spacious green Boston Common where the golden dome of the State House shone in the bright sun. Franny had never seen buildings so large or streets so wide and full of hustling citizens. By the time they reached their destination, she was in awe of the urban world.

An elegant six-story brick building anchored the corner of Water and Tremont Streets. On the second floor façade was displayed a huge golden eagle, symbol of the Shreve, Crump and Low jewelry company, founded in 1796. Nathan explained that this new building had been built to replace the original one on Washington Street, which had burned in the disastrous Great Fire of 1872.

A man in uniform swung the large door open for them as they entered a huge sales floor with twenty-foot ceilings decorated with gold leaf. Walls were covered with marble and gold, and there were rows of gold display cases holding trays of diamonds and rubies, bracelets of shiny gold, and cloisonné in French and Italian motifs. Mounted high on one wall was a large clock adorned with another gold American eagle, its wings spread wide. Such grandeur was unlike anything Franny had ever seen. Nathan led her down a wide marble stairway to a workshop where craftsmen and women seated at big wooden tables carved and engraved custom designs on silver bowls, clock crystals, and gemstones. A man in the front row of tables raised his hand to Nathan and called his name.

"Mr. Nathan, you bring such a beautiful diamond with you this time. So pretty." He gestured to make clear that he spoke of Francena. Not only did his accent show he was a foreigner, the thick black hair and bushy eyebrows gave him an exotic look.

"Simon. Simon Levitz," returned Nathan. "This is my daughter, Francena. I've brought her here to see a world quite different from what she sees in Maine."

"Oh, yes," the artisan said, giving himself a second to understand the English words of his friend. "I have not the English tongue very well, but I understand beauty. She must be a blessing to you and your wife." He was faceting a large green crystal on a disk that spun rapidly in front of him. Removing the stone from its holder, he passed it to Franny, who grabbed it with both hands.

"Oh, Dad, look at this gem! It is so green and translucent. You can almost see through it. What a ring this could be!"

Nathan took the stone from her, held it up to a lamp, and looked at its purity. "So marvelous. Si, this looks like an exquisite tourmaline of many carats. What is its source?"

"Mr. Nathan, you do not recognize an elbaite from your own home state? A friend of yours came here two days ago. Said you sent him to ask for me." He slid open a small drawer and pulled out a cloth bag containing two more stones identical to the one he was cutting. "He say these three are from Maine. Are they not? So much more clear than ones I found in Russia."

Nathan and Franny stared at the stones, then looked at each other. These were the stones Clarence had found at the Dunton Mine several weeks before. "Yes, Si, these *are* from Maine. I was with the man who sold them to you when he found them, but I didn't know he still had them."

Franny said, "Dad, weren't these supposed to be given to Mr. Dunton?" He held his finger to his lips to keep her from going any further. There was no need to worry the Russian with suspicions that the stones might have been stolen.

Once they left the man and returned to Tremont Street, he turned to her. "I didn't want you to make the man nervous. He likely spent a good deal of money on the rough crystals. As cut stones, they will be worth much more. He's not a rich man and needs his profit to feed and clothe his family."

"Father, Clarence stole those stones from Mr. Dunton, didn't he. He failed to follow the terms of their agreement. I fear now more than ever that Lottie does not know the character of the man she loves."

47

Will Cain met Nathan and Franny at the Riverton trolley platform. Hattie, who had been spending a couple of days with Lizzie, was with him. Franny spied her mother before the trolley came to a full stop, jumped from the car, and ran to her before Nathan had even left his seat.

"Mother, you should have seen all the places we visited in Boston! It was such a treat. We stayed at your hotel and ate in that restaurant that has all the oysters. Dad took me to Faneuil Hall and the marketplace. And we saw so many ships in the harbor!"

Hattie hugged her and kissed her on the cheek. "Hold on there, sweetheart. You have plenty of time to tell me about everything. No need to cover all your stories at once."

Nathan approached with their luggage and, passing the bags to Will, kissed his wife. "Yes, dear, we have had quite a time. She wants to relate all the good things we did; but there were also several bad days. We don't need to speak of those, either, until we get to Aunt Lizzie's."

Franny was so excited about all of their adventures that she continued in a frenzy, as if she would explode unless she got everything out. "Oh, yes, we lost Lottie on the train. Not lost her, really, but lost track of her. She and Clarence sneaked off and sat alone in an empty compartment. She said they only talked and watched the scenery, but I think otherwise. Especially after the shouting and arguing that went on at the Ritchies' place. You should have seen how they went at each other! Not Clarence and Lottie, but her parents."

Franny was babbling; her words would not be stemmed. Nathan took her hand and led her several yards away from the carriage.

"My dear girl, please calm yourself for a while. We both have much to tell your mother, but there is no reason to burden Mr. Cain with all that happened. Heaven knows we don't want to start rumors about things which really are none of our business. Let's wait until we're alone with her."

Franny agreed to get herself under control and jumped up on the rear seat next to her mother for the short trip to Lizzie's. Mother and daughter conversed about the sights along Forest Avenue and the upcoming school year. Franny had almost forgotten that it was nearly September—the exciting summer had flown by. Nathan sat up in the driver's bench seat with Will.

"My friend," said Nathan, "I've had a wonderful time these last few days getting to know my daughter in a different way. I guess I've been so tied up with my business interests that I did not realize how she has grown into a wonderful young woman. She is not a little girl anymore."

Will was silent for a moment as he considered his response. "Nathan, they grow up so fast, it's hard to keep track. My young Faith is so smart that she can stump me at that game Twenty Questions. Not that I'm a genius or anything, but—" He hesitated for a minute. "You know, your daughter is a lot like her aunt."

"Yes, and a lot like her mother, too," said Nathan. "Hattie and Lizzie both have made the most of life after a rough start."

"You're right on that. The sisters struggled after their father abandoned them. I met them at the very end of that period, when they moved in with their grandparents. You met them right after that, when they were only beginning to blossom into the strong women they both are today."

"Will, Hattie and I hope that we have given our two children a much better start." He reflected for a moment on what he had witnessed in Winchester. "You know, we may not have the wealth that others have, but, in God's name, we have the best interests of our children at heart. I have seen families torn apart because the parents do not pay attention to the feelings and yearnings of their children. Especially the daughters. They are often trained to blindly follow the elders' wishes."

After a few moments, Will said, "I must consider your words very carefully. It is so easy for a parent to believe that their way is the only way, but I'm not sure how one can allow a child to set its own way. Could be dangerous."

The two men watched the passing scenery for a while, commenting on how many new houses had been built recently. Then, as they passed Brook Street, Nathan informed Will of what he had witnessed on his last visit to Waterford.

"I know you have family in Waterford and are there occasionally, so you are likely aware of the turmoil created by the woman

Aphia Stevens. Do yourself a favor and do not get anywhere near that woman. She is trouble in the making for anyone who gets involved with her. William Watson tells me that your old friend Bert Learned was falling for her…until he disappeared off the face of the earth."

"Bert Learned? I was wondering what happened to him. I asked after him last time I was there, and none had seen him in a while. He's had an occasional drinking problem, though I heard he had been sober for quite some time. Lizzie has already asked me not to waste any more time investigating the witch because she worries that something bad might happen to me, as well. Fine by me, I told her, but between you and me, if that woman creates any problems for Miss Lizzie Millett, I might *have* to get involved."

"Exactly what I said to Hattie, but be cautious, my friend. Neither of us would want to see Liz or anyone else be hurt by her, so you must keep your own interests at heart."

Soon they passed Mr. Pride's quarry, where granite blocks and slabs were stacked on pallets on both sides of the road ready for shipment to Portland builders. One mile on, they came to the small driveway and sign directing them to Millett's American Designs. Liz sat on the porch, and when she saw the wagon approach, she rose to greet the Hallets. Hattie and Franny stepped down from the carriage and went to her, but the men stayed in their seats talking quietly.

"Nathan, you know of the visit Aphia made to Lizzie here at home, don't you?" asked Will. "I caught sight of her racing away on one of her prize horses. She was slapping the animal's flanks with the end of the reins and laughing like a mad person. I wanted to stop her and give her a piece of my mind, but she was away too fast."

"I heard about that visit. Hopefully she will not come this way again."

"I will take your warning to heart, Nathan, and not poke my nose into her shenanigans. But if she dares to come back when I'm working here, there will be hell to pay."

"Lizzie. Why so quiet?" Hattie asked her sister as Nathan, Franny, and Will headed into the house. The two women remained standing on the front porch as the summer sun began to fade. Lizzie had been sitting there for two hours waiting for her guests to arrive. She had a book with her in hopes that reading might calm her mind, but it was impossible to drive out her worries.

"I can't keep a thing from you, can I? Sometimes I think you can read my mind."

"We may not be together as much as we were growing up, but the life we've lived together often makes us think alike. What is bothering you?"

Liz sat back down on the settee and motioned Hattie to sit next to her. "It's Moses. He has just returned from an appointment with Dr. Weymouth in Casco. The diabetes has gotten bad enough to seriously weaken his legs. That's why he's been falling so often. When we were in Saco last month, he tripped over his own feet and fell on the sidewalk. Now the good doctor says that his heart is being affected, making him feel tired all the time and out of breath."

"Oh, my dear. So sad to hear that. Is there anything that he can do for himself? You know, to help him get better."

"Weymouth suggested that it would help for him to lose thirty pounds, but even that cannot cure the diabetes. I'm not sure what can be done."

Liz placed her head on her younger sister's shoulder and let out a great sigh. "Little Sis," she said, using a term of affection from their childhoods, "you have been so fortunate to share your life with a wonderful husband and to watch your children grow into fine young people. I remember how our grandparents worried when you and Nathan wanted to marry so young."

"I am so grateful," said Hattie, "that I found a man who is kind and generous, not like our father. When he abandoned us after Marm's passing, I was only three, but I can still recall how cruel he was to you."

"My years with Moses have helped to heal the wounds and fears built up in those early years. He has been so kind and supportive of what I wanted to do with my own life."

"Hey, Big Sis, let's not let our imaginations run wild here. Moses is still with us and will be for a long time, if God is willing. You and he have made an exciting life for yourselves, a life that should make it possible for you to be happy, even if alone."

Liz lifted her head and looked straight at Hattie. "Girl, give me a big kiss and hug me hard enough to shake me out of this misery state. You have always known what to say to me at times like this."

48

During the final hours before the Express pulled into Portland's Union Station, Clarence's mood turned sullen. He sat apart from Lottie, staring out the window and drumming his fingers on the seat arm. He had been so friendly and amorous up to that point, holding her close to him and speaking about how wonderful life would be now that she would be sharing it with him.

"Clarence, what is distracting you? You seem to be so far away."

"I'm considering what we might do next, where we might be headed. There's a train from Portland to Montreal, which would put us close to my home in Ontario. We could also wait for a few days to board a clipper ship that carries goods and passengers from Portsmouth to Yarmouth. I'm not sure what I want to do."

"Don't you want to gather your family in Nova Scotia and take them with us? I thought that was your plan. I've been thinking how wonderful it would be to meet your children."

"I suppose you're right. Although I might just send more money up to the grandparents and tell them it will take a little more time to return. They don't know where I am, after all."

"No!" she said with tension in her voice and a sharp frown on her face. "It would be wrong to let the children linger on in near poverty with two elderly ones, when you have already found a new mother for them. I am ready for the task, make no mistake about that. To turn your back on them now would be immoral."

Immoral? he thought to himself. It is not up to her to judge my actions immoral or otherwise. It is my family, not hers. He turned to her with glaring eyes. "Woman, it is not up to you to tell me what I should or should not do. You may be ready for the task, as you say. I may not be ready to gather all those hungry mouths back into my life."

"My dear," she responded, "you may do what you want, but I am heading up to Yarmouth with or without you. I have a conscience, you know."

He stared hard at her for several minutes. She imagined the thoughts spinning in the brain behind his glowing eyes. A tight little smile finally came to his lips. He reached for her hand.

"Forgive me, dear. Life often offers me so many options that choosing the right one is difficult. Perhaps you are correct. We should continue by water to Yarmouth. But I warn you, this decision may make our life much harder than if we struck out on our own."

49

Clarence was entering Yarmouth Harbor for the second time in a year. His situation was much improved from the first visit. This time, he was accompanied by a lovely young woman who would soon be his wife and a mother to his children, and there was a good deal of money in his pocket. There were sure to be bumps in the road ahead, but he felt prepared to take them in stride. In darkness, the clipper on which they sailed carefully approached Cape Forchu at the mouth of the harbor in a blanket of thick fog. The revolving lamp of an old lighthouse barely made it possible for the ship's pilot to avoid the forked sandbars for which the Cape had been named by Samuel de Champlain. A piercing fog whistle shrieked out its warning.

When he and Lottie disembarked from the schooner, it was

break of day. They quickly made their way up the wharf onto the main street and then down the muddy alley where his in-laws lived. Stopping in the middle of the street before the little cottage, he asked her if she would care to rest before meeting the family.

"No. We've come all this way," she answered, "let's charge right ahead with our purpose. No time for second thoughts."

They crossed to the door and he knocked lightly. There was the sound of people speaking loudly on the other side. Then the door opened up to a narrow slit. Clarence could make out Ellie Sherman squinting out at them, unable to make out who was there until her old eyes adjusted.

"As God is my witness," she said, "I never believed the man would return. Matthew, it is Clarence, risen from the dead."

The old man joined her at the slit, then drew her aside and opened it wide to see the prodigal himself. "Come in, son. You are welcome to our house. Who is this with you?"

Matthew had aged a great deal in the short time Clarence had been gone. His gray hair, usually shaggy, was now down to his shoulders in dirty snarls. His forearms, the only part of his body not covered by several layers of worn clothes, were as thin as shovel handles. When he stretched his hand out, Clarence was afraid to shake it lest the bones be crushed. Ellie, standing with the children gathered about her, frowned at the couple. She was dressed in a well-worn shift that reached to the floor. She also appeared to be much thinner than before.

"*Welcome*, you say, husband? What is *welcome* is the money he has been sending off and on, us not knowing when to expect it."

Turning to the couple, she gestured toward two empty chairs at the fireside. As they passed near her, she reached out to feel the material of Lottie's denim jacket. "You've found a well-dressed one, Clarence."

Lottie felt like a horse up for sale at an auction. She sat in her assigned seat and waited for Clarence to formally introduce her before opening her mouth. Hazel and Bessie left their grandmother's protection, trudged to their father for a kiss and then drew near the stranger. Hazel, now five years old, held out her hand to feel the cotton of Lottie's long skirt.

"Here, little girl" said Lottie. "I've a pretty lace handkerchief you might like. It comes all the way from China."

Hazel eyed the offered cloth suspiciously, but Bessie jumped in front, grabbed it, rubbed it on her face, and began to giggle. Then both girls grabbed onto the handkerchief and started to pull. Lottie reached into her jacket pocket and displayed a small silk purse containing a sachet of pine needles. She handed it to the girls. Hazel let go of the cloth and pulled the purse to her nose.

"Dearie," said Ellie, "you have a way with the wee ones, don'cha now. They're not used to such fancy baubles, these girls. You're not from a poor family, are you?"

Clarence, who had not taken a seat, stepped to his fiancée's side. "Mother Sherman, Matthew, this is Miss Lottie Ritchie of Boston."

Matthew, still standing at the open door, smiled at Lottie and made a timid wave. "A blessing on you, young lady, and welcome to our humble home. From Boston, you are. Such a grand place it must be."

"Boston, you say?" said Ellie. "That's a far way for you to come. Are you visiting, or do you plan to stay with us in Yarmouth Town? You'll not be liking the life here, I'm sure."

"Mother Sherman, Miss Ritchie and I are engaged to be wed. We have been traveling for many days since leaving her home and have not had the time to make proper arrangements. We plan to live in Ontario, near the town of Cobalt, where I hope to have work in the copper mines. I will be able now to take back the children and make your lives easier. Just as I said I would."

Matthew went to the fire and placed a branch on the hearth. Ellie, however, exploded in anger. "Plans? Plans? You are always making big plans, aren't you? I told our girl before she married you that you were big on plans and dreams, but short on reality. She wouldn't listen to me. Too dreamy-eyed in love with you, the big dreamer."

Shocked at the woman's outburst, Clarence took a step backwards. Lottie, who had never considered that his in-laws would be so hostile, jumped from the chair and stood behind her fiancé as the woman continued.

"Now you *say* you will marry, but have not. *Plan* to live in Ontario? *Plan* to work in another mine? The only real things I know about you are that you let my Emma die and that you send a few dollars to us when you feel like it."

Afraid that the woman might attack them, Clarence spread his arms to protect Lottie and began to back toward the door. "Ellie, Matthew, I don't know what I've done to deserve such treatment. I asked you to help me with the children while I made arrangements to set up a new family home. You were gracious to help. I've been sending dollars to you regularly to support both you and the babies, as I said I would. Now I am here to deliver on my promise. Isn't that enough for you?"

Now it was Matthew who spoke. "Son, it has been a struggle to take care of Emma's three, but Ellie and I have grown to love them as our own. You may have brought this lovely girl back to Canada to be their new mother. Yes, you may. But these are not hers. They have our blood, are Shermans, not Potters. We do not want you to take them back. You must continue to send money for their support, but they will be staying with us. We will raise them right."

"You will do nothing of the kind!" shouted Clarence. "These are my children. I've not traveled halfway 'round the world to find a wife who might help me raise them, only to have you two crazy old people claim them as your own. Lottie and I will leave now, but we will return with whatever help we need to get them back. If I need to, I will have you arrested for kidnapping."

"Do what you want, Clarence," said Ellie. "We have our rights. Now, get out of our house and do not come back."

50

"Lottie, I am sorry. This is not the way I wished to introduce you to my life." Clarence sat across from his fiancée at a small wooden table. In the sparsely furnished room were an unmade double bed, a small chest of drawers propped up on one side by bricks, the table, two chairs, and a stand on top of which stood a small white china ewer. A chamber pot sat beneath the stand. Next to the table was one window with no shades, its cracked panes taped together. The dark view was of a muddy alley terminating at a tall stockade fence.

"I'm sorry, too," Lottie said. Her hands were shoved deep into the pockets of her jacket to keep them warm. "Who would have thought that the Shermans would be so unreasonable? How long do they expect to be around to raise those young ones?"

Three weeks before, the couple had rented a room in a sailors' boardinghouse near the wharves when it became clear that they might have to stay in Yarmouth for a time in order to secure release of the children. Originally, their expectation was that they would not have to stay very long to accomplish this goal, but now winter was nearly upon them and they had made no progress.

They had hired a solicitor, a Mr. Ripley, who was very pessimistic about the possibility of taking back the children. The first problem was that they were not legally wed, so they went to a local Presbyterian Church and asked the pastor to marry them.

"My children," said the reverend after listening to their story, "I am afraid that it would not be legal for you to get married. When you apply for a license, the magistrate will ask why you did not marry back in the United States at her family's home. That is the custom, after all. There is sure to be a suspicion that either you, son, have forced this girl to marry you, or that you, my daughter, may be marrying only to escape to Canada for some reason. Both of those acts are illegal."

"But sir," said Lottie, "we both are of age and choosing freely to spend our lives together. How can that be illegal?"

"I am sure you mean well, my dear. But it might be easier to return to your family and marry there before returning here as husband and wife."

"Reverend, I apologize for being so blunt," said Clarence, "but we are getting married here one way or another. Either you will help us or we'll find another way." He was so angry that he turned to leave before Lottie grabbed his arm and pulled him back.

"Sir, we will find a way to get the license and come back to you," she said. " Thank you for your advice."

The solicitor threw another obstacle in their path. "The Shermans' representative is an arrogant young barrister who takes work from that type of people. He takes the position that if you return to the wilds of Ontario, where their daughter died without medical treatment, the lives of your children will be in danger. He says that if they are raised here in Yarmouth, they will be happier and safer."

"Even though they live with elderly folk who have very limited income?" asked Lottie.

"Well, that lawyer has already asked the court to leave them with the grandparents and to require Clarence to provide money for their support each month, as he has already been doing. I hate to say it, but it is going to be very difficult for you to get custody of your children. You may find that many months of investigations and hearings in front of a court justice will come to naught. I encourage you to reach agreement with the Shermans and continue on with your lives together. You are young. There will be more children to come."

Now the two found themselves in a cold room, wearing sweaters and outdoor jackets to protect themselves from the damp sea breezes. It was time to make a decision about their life together. If they stayed and fought the legal battle, their lives would be miserable during the coming cold and snowy months. Neither of them wanted to set up house in Yarmouth and live from hand to mouth as Clarence had done previously. Yet, sacrificing the children to what was at best a meager life of poverty might be long regretted.

"My love, I have chosen to spend the rest of my life with you," Lottie said. "And I will be with you whether in Ontario or here in Nova Scotia. It is your decision to make—after all, they are your children. You must be happy with the choice you make or the rest of your life, as well as mine, may be miserable. Choose carefully."

Clarence had never faced such a moral dilemma. Both of his options had the potential for great sorrow. As he looked at his beloved and thought about their future, he knew right away that she would help him start a new family.

"Lottie, I am ready to strike out on our adventure together in Ontario. Life will surely hold more joy for us there than if we stay in this damnable place. Yet, we cannot strike out for the wilds now. Winter must have already devoured Cobalt. My cabin will be invisible beneath the drifts."

"Is there not a civilized town near your settlement where we might stay until spring arrives?"

"You are very brave, my dear. No matter where we go, the journey will be difficult and tiring. The town of Sudbury is near-by. We will find a decent room there for the winter months. If we stay here, we will freeze to death."

"Clarence, you are strong and I trust you to lead me safely. Let's away."

51

Winter was Aphia's favorite season. In early December, when the icy north winds blew down from Mount Washington and across Albany Mountain carrying that first blanket of snow, she found relief in isolation. In January, white drifts built up around her simple home so that the heat did not escape so quickly. She liked to view the mosaic of rime ice that grew like primitive plants on windowpanes during the coldest days. The sun low to the horizon would illuminate the icy crystals, casting a magical glow about the interior of the house. Between the rear door of the house and the horse barn, she kept a path open all winter. After each storm, she would shovel the way clear, throwing snow up along both sides of the path into piles that reached above her head. Her six horses were wrapped in rough woolen blankets, their breath steaming from both nostrils and forming small specks of ice on their hairy noses. Being with them each morning was all she needed to feel that she was not alone. Firewood cut and stacked for her two years ago by Bert Learned still stood high to the ceiling of a shed just off the kitchen. He had been the only person in town who had been good to her, and now that he was gone, she was completely on her own. In her kitchen, the range continuously burned. It provided a comforting heat for the living space. It also enabled her to process many baskets of herbs collected during the summer and fall. Winter was her time to cook and mix and distill the herbal elixirs and remedies that provided her income. The aromas of steam rising from pots on the stove and from tinctures dripping from a copper still filled the house. Most of the smells were sweet and calming to her, except for those emanating from an occasional batch of bitter herbs like wormwood and monkshood.

This morning, the wind was calm for a change. Light from the sun rising through her pine grove at the top of the pasture had begun to melt powder from yesterday's light snowfall. For the first time in nearly a month, Aphia was able to open the front door. After shoveling snow that had drifted above the windows, she stood at the gate and stared up at Beech Hill's rocky face. On the hilltop, she noticed a patch of pale blue sky showing through a gap in the grove where giant pines had been felled and were lying atop the snowpack. Sounds of men shouting to each other, clangs of axes on wedges, and thunderous tree falls broke the silence. At first, she cursed those who might be taking her trees. Then she realized that the work was taking place on the lot just above hers owned by farmer John Kimball. She recalled that her late grandfather had sold him the woodlot and that Kimball had some interest in opening a mica mine after the lot was cleared. Since nothing had ever happened up there, she assumed the farmer's plans had been forgotten. There was nothing to be done about it right now, so she returned to her own work.

At dusk, as she prepared to bottle a cooled distillation of rose flowers, there came a knock at her door. It was a sound to which she was unaccustomed in the dead of winter. At first, her attention was so focused on not spilling the rose water that the rapping went unnoticed. As it continued, she cursed about the interruption on the way to the door. She turned the knob, opened it a slit, and peered out. On the landing stood a man wearing a heavy woolen coat, a flat leather hat with ear flaps tied beneath his chin, and a pair of snow-covered leather boots that reached up to his knees. He was fully bearded, making it hard for her to recognize him. By his short height and gray hair, she assumed it was neighbor Kimball, whom she had met several times in North Waterford village.

"Who is it that calls?" she nearly shouted out to him. It had been so long since she had spoken to another human, she was not sure how loud to speak.

"Ma'am, it's John Kimball. You remember your neighbor, don't you? My son and I are lumbering up on the ridge. I saw you standing outside for a moment and wanted to speak with you."

She opened the door wide enough so she could step onto the threshold. "Yes, Mr. Kimball, I do remember you. How have you been doing with this cold weather?"

"Oh, it ain't that cold, really. Not much colder than other years. The wind's been quite bitter, but not as bitter as other winds."

She considered inviting him inside, but decided against it. "What can I do for you, John Kimball? I'm sure you haven't just stopped by for a friendly visit. Not in this cold."

"Well, ma'am, I only wanted to come by and inform you about the work we're doing up in that stand of ancient pines." He hesitated for a moment as he began to pick up the aroma of her herbs and sniffed several times. "That lot I bought from old Abe, rest his soul. It seems never to have been cut. Some of those pines stand well over a hundred feet and are, some of them, twenty feet

around at the shoulder. I'm not set on clearing the lot, just thin-
ning enough to pay the taxes. Oh, and to make room to excavate
for mica we know is up there."

Although she was not dressed for it, she stepped forward and
drew the door almost closed behind herself. It was clear he was
curious about her cooking, but he said nothing. "John, I appreciate the courtesy of your advising me on your plans. I remember
my grandfather telling me about your buying the lot a few years
back. As long as you're not taking any of my trees and staying off
my pasture, I don't mind a bit."

"Appreciate it, Miss Stevens. We'll not set foot on your land
except to remove a fallen trunk if it falls across the line. In the
summer, however, I might ask your permission to run a wagon
across the corner of your land up near where we dig. I will pay
you fairly for the right-of-way."

"Isn't there any other way to get in and out of there?"

"Yes, ma'am. But we don't want to use it. Hard to drive a
wagon off the edge of that cliff and have it survive the trip." He
laughed at his own joke.

She stared at him with a straight face.

"I suppose if you pay me for the use, it will be permissible.
But please make me an offer in the spring, when we can walk the
area. Now I have to get back to my chores."

"Fine. I'll see you after mud season, then."

As he turned to leave, she opened the door to go back inside. He hollered back to her, "Miss, what is that you're cookin' in
there? Smells mighty sweet. My wife tells me you're an herbalist.
What is that you are makin'? Smells like perfume."

"Rose water, John. Rose water. I use it to make soap. Your
wife bought some from me last year."

"Such a sweet smell. I'll tell her to get more this year."

Once he left and she returned to her bottling, the idea that
he wanted to use her land for part of a messy mining operation
began to gnaw at her. Miners were notorious for the lack of consideration they had for the property of others. It's all about their

getting rich quick, she thought. She would have to set a very high price for cooperating.

52

"Daddy! Daddy!" Francena shouted out to Nathan as he walked into the house. She had been waiting for him to return from his long-delayed business trip. "Look what I have! Lottie has sent me a letter after all this time. She and Clarence must have eloped while we were in Boston."

Giving his daughter a big hug and draping his raincoat across the back of a wooden kitchen chair, he took the letter and read it aloud.

March 15, 1897

Dear Franny,

So many times I have sat down to pen an apology to you and your father about how horrible I was to you in August. Please forgive me. I did not mean to put you both in such an uncomfortable position. Please understand that, once I realized how much I love Clarence, my emotions got the best of me. I know my actions were headstrong and that perhaps I should have waited for my parents to accept him, but it seemed at the time that they hated him and would never give us their blessings. Unfortunately, you and your dad were innocent bystanders whose friendship I threw aside. Again, I ask your forgiveness and hope that we can continue to be dearest girlfriends.

We are moving to a small mining camp in Ontario called Cobalt. It is not on any map. It is hardly a town at all, only a few seasonal cabins, a blacksmith shop, and two copper mines. Our temporary home during the long hard winter months has been a room in a boardinghouse in nearby Sudbury, a bigger town which is year-round. Clarence will be managing a crew of smithies who are to lay tracks from here to mines further north. He makes a good wage, enough to cover our expenses and to put aside a monthly payment to his former in-laws, who are now raising his children from the first marriage. When I see you next, I will fill in the details.

There is not much work in the woods for a woman, so I am a stay-at-home for the time being. I am learning to cook and sew and to be a good wife. Please write to me. I don't know how long your letter will take to get here, but know that I will await your news and relish every word.

> With love and sincerest apologies,
> Your best friend Lottie

By the time Nathan had finished reading, Hattie had come into the room. "Nathan. So wonderful that you are home. We all missed you terribly."

He looked at her with a smile and a quick wink. He removed his dripping boots and placed them next to his briefcase before standing and giving her a hug. "Hattie, my love, I assume you have been privy to the contents of this letter. I fear that Lottie and Clarence may soon be needing a change of life."

"Father," asked Franny, "whatever do you mean?"

"Young lady, you have seen where your friend grew up and met her parents. How long do you think she will be satisfied to live in a muddy wilderness?"

53

Lizzie had asked her two partners to meet in her kitchen. Maeve, who was seven months pregnant, sat on one side of the big table with arms folded across the top of her very large stomach. Mary sat next to her clutching a white handkerchief with which she rubbed her eyes to dry her tears.

"Liz, we don't want to give you bad news," began Maeve, "but our Ma has died and Da' is left on his own."

"Oh, I am so sorry to hear that. When did it happen?"

Mary stopped weeping for a moment and blew her nose before speaking. "'Tis sad. The post is so slow. I received the letter yesterday, but it is dated nearly a month back. He has had to bury her himself and now has lived alone in that drafty cottage for weeks. For all we know, he may be dead himself by this time." She began to weep again.

"Did they remain in the same house you grew up in?" said Liz.

"Yes," said Maeve. "That drafty old place! They never wanted to live in a more modern house. Her mother was born there, for God's sake."

Mary dried her eyes once more. "Liz, I must go back to Clare to see what can be done for the old guy. It is a busy time for you, I know, but there really is nothing else to do. Perhaps I can convince him to move to a home with others his age."

"There isn't other family? Can't someone else over there take care of that for you?"

"Both of my brothers are in Australia. They're married and have families and jobs. Maeve can't go. It is up to me to see to it. I may be gone for a short time...or it could be that I might have to stay indefinitely. I'm so sorry to leave you shorthanded."

"Mary, taking care of you father is much more important than making a dress or two. We will handle the work, won't we, Maeve? Love of one's family is the most important thing in life. I respect you for what you are choosing to do."

54

Lizzie was beside herself. With Moses ill again, they were not spending as much time in Saco, so orders were down from the past years. However, there was work that had to be done, a schedule to be met, but there was not enough work to keep herself and two seamstresses busy full-time. Maeve Cain was unlikely to be working much. She was having some difficulties with her fourth pregnancy. And now that Mary had left for Clare, Liz had to figure out some other way to get the work done.

Wait, she thought, perhaps Hattie might be able to help me. She knows how to sew. The children are old enough to be left alone at times. Nathan would have to agree, but I'm sure we can work something out. As she thought about the plan, the entire Hallett clan arrived outside. Wonderful, she thought. This is a propitious sign. God is at work here.

She rushed to the door and threw it open, waiting for the family to enter. Hattie came in first and grabbed her sister in a big hug. "My dearest Lizzie," she said, "we are just returning from a weekend on Cape Elizabeth. Nathan has an associate who loaned us his family cottage. It was such fun. We just dropped in for an instant to say hello and use the toilet."

Nathan stayed in the driver's seat of the carriage, but the children ran to their aunt and told stories about how much fun they'd had at the seashore. When Hattie came back to the showroom, Liz offered her a job.

"Sis, I've just received a number of orders from old customers for my new designs—"

"And Mary's away and Maeve's pregnant. Leaves you all alone to handle the work."

"Yes, it does. But I've been thinking you might be able to help me. Just a few hours each week. And I would pay you at a seamstress's rate."

"It would be lovely to spend time with you, but I'm not sure how it would work. The children are still at home and Nathan is away so much, who would take care of the family? No, I don't think it would work, but I will think about it." After a few seconds, she said, "Franny would be a great helper for you. She knows how to hand stitch, and after she graduates from Bridgton Academy in May, she will be looking for work. She might stay with you during the week and come home on weekends or whenever Nathan came through Westbrook. Isn't that a good plan?"

Liz turned to her niece, who stood listening to the conversation. "Dear, what do you think of this idea? You would learn how to sew on one of my big Singer machines and make a bit of money each week. What do you think?"

"Auntie, I am not very good at stitchery right now, but I believe I could learn pretty fast. Especially with a teacher like you. Wouldn't it be something to have you teach me the skills that your mother taught you so many years ago? When do I start?"

Hattie and Lizzie smiled at each other then each took one of Franny's hands in theirs.

"Francena taught me, and now I will teach Francena," sighed Lizzie.

55

Flies buzzed around Lottie's head. She sat on the timber slab step at the front door of a log cabin she shared with Clarence. Their "house" was one of five clustered along the edges of what was called a road. In truth the street was little more than a flattened ribbon of clay wide enough for a horse and wagon to pass. Between her place and the next, tree trunks ready to be turned into railroad ties were loosely stacked. Behind each cabin sat an outhouse that drew flies. Five months had passed since they'd left Sudbury, and she was getting worried about the winter already. Where would they live during January and February? Certainly not here where the cold north wind already whistled through chinks between logs and shook the oilcloth windows. Maybe they could find a warm room again in Sudbury or in the new town of Haileybury. Clarence said the Matabanick Hotel there would likely be vacant during the cold months, and a room there would be available at a reasonable rate.

In March, when they had arrived, her excitement about the adventure knew no bounds. They were in love, and love would conquer all inconveniences, even the lack of running water. She knew Clarence would be working full-time and making enough money to keep them happy. She threw herself into making a home for them by learning to cook on a campfire, lug water from nearby Long Lake, and keep the indoors as clean as possible. She had time to read, write letters to her dear friend Francena, and go swimming. And there was always the lovemaking, which filled her heart and body with joy. He was away much of the time during the week, but on weekends they spent most of their time in bed.

She was one of only three, or occasionally four, women in camp and the only one who was married. The others were quite wild and seemed to live with more than one man at a time. One woman—a girl, really—not more than fourteen or fifteen, had shot one man dead and been hanged. The women considered Lottie strange because she was loyal to Clarence. When she started to show her pregnancy, they avoided her entirely. An old lady who passed through one day advised her to go over to Sudbury or Haileybury, where she was sure there was a doctor or a midwife, but there had not been time to make the trip. She was only a couple of months along, as best she could tell, not having been pregnant before. There would be time when the weather began to turn and Clarence was around more.

As the setting sun began to burn clouds into red and orange flares, she grew fidgety. It was Friday, payday, and anytime now the horse and wagon would arrive carrying the men back from laying track all the way to Liskeard. Clarence would return with supplies for their weekend together.

When it grew dark, she went inside to rest until the noise of squeaking wheels and singing men brought her to the door to welcome her dear husband home. He rode barefoot with muddy boots tied together and draped over one shoulder. His jeans were streaked with dark creosote used to cure heavy pine ties. As he crossed the threshold, she threw her arms around his sweaty neck.

"My love, your ride home at the end of each week is getting longer and longer. A month ago you returned before sunset. Now it's dark before you are home. I've missed you."

"And I you," he replied. "Yes, we are nearing the end of the line. I'd be surprised if it takes more than a month to complete this phase." He reached down to pat her stomach. "Have you been resting yourself this week? There's two of you in that body now."

"Clary, I'm as fit as a fiddle. You're the one who needs to rest up—you look exhausted. Please sit down. I have water heating for your bath."

He took a seat at their dining table and placed a leather duffel on top. From it he pulled a corked bottle, pulled the stopper, and took a swig. He then offered it to her with a grin.

"Do you think it's all right for you to drink a bit of whiskey? Not a lot, mind you, but enough to make you feel as good as I do?"

"Have you been drinking this all the way home? No wonder you're tired. I will have a nip, but no more. I don't know much about being pregnant, but I'm sure a doctor would tell me to be careful with that stuff. Where'd you get it?"

"There's a French moonshiner, a *trafiquant*, as they call him, who sells the stuff every Friday as we leave the track site. It's good, clean stuff."

"Hell, aren't we getting fancy. How do you say it? A *trafiquant* is it now? Soon you'll be wearing a wig and tight breeches like the rich French do in Montreal."

"My dear, we may not be dressing like the rich, but we will be spending like them as soon as Warren and his partners hear how quickly the new line has been completed—a full year ahead of schedule."

She thought for a moment before commenting. "Clary, when the line is finished, will we have enough money and time to relocate to a better place to live in the winter? Perhaps that hotel in Haileybury or back to Sudbury? Don't think I want to live here during the winter. It is already getting cold when the sun goes down."

"I don't see why we would have to leave, but if you want to move for a time, we will certainly be able to afford it."

Lottie smiled and kissed his cheek. She reflected on how rough it must have been for his first wife to give birth without a midwife in attendance and how much stress must have been involved in raising those three babies. It was not the life for *this* wife.

56

Francena had all she could do to concentrate on her studies during the last month at Bridgton Academy. She kept getting distracted by the thought that she would be embarking on a new adventure living with Auntie Lizzie and learning how to make dresses. Yet, despite her daydreaming, when time came for graduation, she was ranked the highest of any female in her class. In July, when the day came to move her belongings to Westbrook, her mom had accompanied her for the first few days, helping to unpack and get her acclimated. Her new home was so large that she was able to have her own apartment on the third floor with luxuries of a private bath and small kitchen. The furnishings left behind by sisters Mary and Maeve were alien to her: overstuffed chairs and settee, mahogany dresser, hooked rugs, and lace doilies everywhere she looked.

The morning after her mother left, she was feeling lonely when Lizzie knocked at her door. "Auntie, please come in. It's so strange to have all this space and privacy. At home, I had my own room, but there was always someone else walking around, making noise, hogging the bathroom."

"Don't worry. You'll become accustomed to it soon. If you need to have company, Moses and I are right downstairs. As a matter of fact, I think you'll be able to hear us making noise if you only open the door and stick your head into the hallway. You'll especially hear Moses."

"I don't mind the noise at all. You never lived with Nate. He is so loud!" she said with a laugh.

"This letter came for you," said Lizzie. "The post office is mighty fast transferring your mail to the new address." She handed the envelope to her niece as she left the room. "Oh, by the way, why don't you join us for dinner tonight?"

Francena eyed the writing on the envelope and realized that it was from Lottie even before she noticed the return address of "Cobalt, Ontario, Canada." She sat on the velvet settee and began to read:

20 August, 1897

Dearest Franny,

Time has flown since last I wrote to you, and I am sure you have forgotten me entirely. Thoughts of you fill my mind so often that I sometimes sit on my front step without recognizing the wild world around me. Say that you remember me also.

Write and tell me of your life, please! I need to know what is going on in a more civilized world than the one in which I live. What is it like to have the comfort of running water? Here our water comes in buckets from a common spring. Not that the place is without charm. The evergreen forest is so magical, full of deer and many kinds of birds. Spring and summer have been very comfortable. On the hot days, I am able to enjoy the cold water of our lake, like those waters we shared in Maine.

Clarence is the sweetest of men. He works so hard to make our life as comfortable as he possibly can. Not like the other men who are always drunk and fighting. The women here are not to my liking, so wild and wanton. There's no one here like you.

I have some exciting news! I am pregnant and looking forward to being a mother. My stomach has just begun to show the baby, so I'm sure there is a way to go. We will be leaving Cobalt before winter, so the birth will happen in the nearby town of Haileybury. We will be living there for a few months in the Matabanick Hotel.

It takes so long for the mail to travel up here, I suggest that you write to me in care of that hotel. Please write to let me know what you are doing. Didn't you finish school this year? I am so far behind in knowing how your life is going.

Yours in love,
Lottie

Franny rose from her seat and went to a floor-to-ceiling window that looked out on Forest Avenue far in the distance. How fortunate she was to have her family and to be able to begin the next stage of her life in safety and comfort. Her friend was also embarked on a new life of adventure, but, as Nathan had said, it seemed that both Lottie and Clarence would soon be in need of a "change in life."

57

Months had passed since Nathan was last in Bethel. Business at the Rumford sawmill had slowed to a single shift, and land had been cleared for construction of a new village center. His services were no longer needed to arrange for shipments outside the area. He received a letter from Dr. Abbott requesting that he join Hollis Dunton and him in Newry at the site of the new gem quarry. The operation was entering a new stage with the purchase of hydraulic drills and hammers, which would make it possible to dig deep below the surface. A crew of experienced miners from Oxford, Waterford, and Norway had been assembled. When he arrived on site, dust raised by blasting filled the air. As Nathan climbed down from his carriage, Dunton shouted out to him. Amidst the din, he could not hear what the man was saying until he was nearly next to him. The mine owner stood on a ledge high above a rock-filled pit thirty feet deep. Below, he watched six men, bandanas tied across noses and mouths, moving wheelbarrows of broken stone into a pile against the opposite side of the pit. Finally, he was able to make out the mine owner's words.

"Hallett, glad to see you could join us. This is the day we've all been waiting for. The ledge was blasted away on Monday. We've found a pocket of Cleavelandite and quartz crystal which runs the length of this ledge. As soon as the boys have moved debris out of the way, we can really see what we have." The noise of two jackhammers attacking the quartz was so loud that the men had to continue shouting.

"Hollis," hollered Nathan, "I didn't realize how far along you were. The good doctor led me to believe that work was only about to begin."

"Sir, when I make a decision to move, I move quickly. Who

knows what we will find? What obstacles? What rewards? 'Tis best to move quickly, especially at the start. I need to figure out how much work needs to be done before winter sets in. It is already October."

Dunton gestured that Nathan should follow him to a shed set back twenty yards from the work site. As the miner stepped down and maneuvered around the many rocks, he limped and had to steady himself on the jagged boulders. Nathan reached out to assist, but was met with anger.

"Hold off, young man. I can get around on my own. No reason to be helping me. I'm not a cripple."

"I'm sorry, Hollis. Just wanted to help."

"Don't bother. It's my arthritis bothering again. It comes and goes," he said with a grin, pointing to his knees. "Sorry to have shouted at you like that. After being on a site like this for a few days, I forget how to speak in a regular voice."

Already in the shed, Abbott opened the door and heartily shook Nathan's hand as he and Dunton entered. There were three chairs around a single table made of a rough plank spread across two apple barrels. On the wall next to the room's one small window was tacked a map of the site showing elevations and places of interest. The doctor reached under the table for a large cloth bag which he emptied, spilling gemstones of green and red, white and rose colors.

"Nathan, we have asked you to join us today because we've discovered one of the greatest deposits of gems ever found in the pegmatite mines of Oxford County—perhaps one of the greatest ever in the world. This sack contains but a small percentage of gemmy stones dug out of one pocket. Hollis believes we can look forward to many more such pockets along the length of a vein which runs for at least a thousand feet. We believe it's time to put together that team of investors and miners we've been discussing these last two years."

"You know that my wife and I are on board as investors, and possibly her sister and brother-in-law," said Nathan.

"Yes, that is what we expected. There was that other man from Massachusetts, that doctor. What was his name?"

"Oh, you mean John Ritchie. Yes, I believe he was interested, though I haven't kept in touch with him on that subject. I know how to contact him and will check with him and his wife."

Hollis drummed his fingers on the table as he studied the gemstones lying there. "What of that Canadian? Do you know how to get in touch with him?"

Yes, sir," said Nathan. "My daughter is a pen pal with his wife up in Ontario. I can contact him as quickly as the mail can be delivered. You probably do not know, but Clarence Potter, the man you want, is now married to the Ritchies' daughter."

"Strange how the world works," mused Hollis. "Fate weaves so many strands together into a strong rope."

"Not sure how strong this rope might be," warned Nathan, "but I am certainly the one to braid the strands."

58

April 1898

Standing in her doorway, Aphia stared out across the still-drifted pasture. All morning, the door and two sunny windows had been open to allow fresh warm air to enter her stuffy house. Snow that had been rolled hard on the road past her gate was turning brown as it melted. Spring was on its way and with it the return of her perennial problem, flies. Both outside and inside the house, flies tormented her during the damp warm weather of May and early June. Perhaps this year will be better, she thought. That extra layer of topsoil spread on the pasture might have been enough. It was the third layer in as many years. At some point, the flies will have to go away. She was convinced it was decomposing horse flesh that attracted the swarms, not the other bodies she had added. Her grandfather was the one at fault for creating this problem and leaving it for her to solve.

As she peered around her lot, she noticed with surprise that the pine grove beyond her pasture was completely cleared. It appeared that neighbor Kimball had gone beyond the selective clearing he'd mentioned to her. And, to her further amazement, a path had been cleared across the corner of her lot where his oxen had dragged the tree trunks. So much snow still lay upon the land that she was unable to judge the extent of his trespass. It would be weeks before she would be able to inspect for herself.

"If he has trampled across my land beyond what was to be allowed, there will be hell to pay," she said out loud. "These men think they can step all over a single woman, not pay attention to my rights. They are all the same."

59

Thank goodness this winter had passed more easily than the last. In her pregnant condition, Lottie had enjoyed the relative warmth and comfort of Haileybury's Matabanick Hotel in a large suite complete with a full bath and a small kitchen. Unlike the drafty boardinghouse room she and Clarence had rented in Sudbury the year before, the windows were tight against unchecked north winds blowing down from Hudson's Bay. Although the town, like Sudbury, was nearly deserted when miners departed for their homes in October, the year-round population was large enough to support the Sisters of Providence Hospital. The medical staff there, including a midwife, were available to help her come to term. Thankfully, there were no unusual complications. She was young and strong. When baby Clarence Conrad Potter was born on April 17, the hotel room was a warm landing place. While his wife lay in bed with the infant son nestled in her arms, Clarence opened both windows to let some fresh warm air enter. The day was sunny, and a breeze wafted in from the south as if spring had arrived.

"Clary, the air is fresh and warm, but we need to think of what a chill might do to this little one. Please close one of the windows."

He closed both sashes down halfway. "It is good for all of us to feel the freshness and warmth of this day. Pressed in the comfort of your breasts, he will not feel any chill. Such a healthy baby! You must be so proud to have brought him into the world. I am proud myself."

"We must tell everyone about this," she said. "My parents, Francena and her father. We must tell them how happy we are."

"I've already wired Mr. Warren with the news. He wired back with congratulations and a moneygram for five hundred dollars. There is also a new job for me when we're ready and able to travel. Do you want me to wire your father?"

"Yes, please let them know how happy we are and how beautiful our son is. Perhaps Mother will be glad to have a grandson. What is the new job?"

"It's the gem mine down in Maine, the one we both visited in Newry last year. Along with Hollis Dunton and Dr. Abbott, Warren has invested in what they believe will be a very profitable operation. They want me to manage the mine. We will have to move there, but I doubt that would bother you."

"Bother? Are you serious? To live where winter doesn't last so long and where spring and summer are a joy to behold? That would be an answer to my prayers."

That afternoon, Clarence went to the Western Union office in the hotel lobby and sent a telegram to the Ritchies in Massachusetts. It was the first time he had reached out to them since their unfortunate confrontation. He was sure they would be pleased with the news, but just in case, he had the telegraph operator sign it with Lottie's name. A wire was also sent to Albert Warren thanking him for his gift and assuring him that he would report to Bethel when the family was ready. Another went to Dr. Francis Abbott, telling him that he was both aware of the job offer and ready to take it by the summer, but no earlier. He left the communication with the Halletts up to his wife, when she felt up to it.

60

Sometimes the things you want, but don't think can come about, actually happen because you decide to try a different approach. That is exactly what happened when Lizzie hired Francena to work instead of sister Hattie. Her niece quickly learned basic skills with the big Singer Professional machine and had even taken on some of her aunt's design work. She also turned out to be a very good housemate, able to help with cooking, cleaning, and other chores, as well as being a companion for Moses as his aging process quickened. Another surprise was that Hattie became a regular visitor, spending weekends at first and then, as time went on, several days each week. During the fall, she would show up unannounced at the office to check in on her daughter's progress. When spring arrived, she began to plan her visits to last for three or four days. It wasn't that she only came to visit, she began to pitch in and help with the workload. Lizzie finally had to sit her down at the kitchen table for a chat.

"Sister, I don't want you to think that I'm ungrateful for your volunteer work. It makes my own life much easier. I'm wondering how much time you plan on being here so that I can get you on the schedule and begin to pay you."

"No, no. You don't have to pay me. I'm here to visit Franny and you, not to work. In order to share your time, I have to do what you are doing. I don't want to interrupt you or pull her off the job."

"But dear, have you kept track of how many times you've been here recently? I have. Since March first, you have been with us two full weekends, including either Friday or Monday. Both, in one instance. Last week, you worked with us nearly three full days and then cooked suppers all three nights. What about your family? What does Nathan think about this?"

"He is away so much now, working up in Newry on the new Dunton mine. Nate is with him on weekends. They love working together."

"I was wondering why he hadn't been around to visit. The

prospects for that gem mine must be good if Nathan is spending so much time there. Moses and I are interested in being investors."

"The two of them talk about nothing else at home. When school ends, I doubt that Nate will be home at all. Dunton has offered him a full-time job over the summer."

"Are you saying that you'll be here even more come May and June? If so, I won't let you talk me out of making you a paid seamstress like your daughter. The three of us will run right through the new orders."

As the sisters chatted, Franny came down the stairs from her apartment. "Hey, you're both here. I received a letter from Lottie today. What excitement she is having. They have a new son, and guess what—they are moving to Maine to live! Clarence has been offered a job managing that gem mine in Newry. They'll probably be here by July at the earliest. How wonderful!"

"My God," said Hattie. "This is going to be one big happy family!"

61

When spring arrived on Beech Hill, Aphia began her gardening season. She cleared dead foliage from her perennial herb beds as soon as insects began to emerge from the mud and slime of rotted vegetation. She could not wait for the soil to dry because the growing season was so short. On days when the sun was bright, she would rise very early, have a simple breakfast, and work with rake and hoe until her back gave out. Snow still remained on the upper pasture, so she still awaited a visit from John Kimball to view the damaged corner of her lot. Thus far, there had been very few flies arising from the front hillock. It was early to be making any judgments as to the success of last autumn's regrading, but so far, very few flies had emerged. Perhaps, she thought, this might be the year to plant grass and ground cover on top of the new soil.

One warm morning, a stranger approached her house riding

a handsome quarter horse. She thought he might ride past, but when he stopped and dismounted, she rose from her knees. She tried her best to wipe dirt and stains from her work dress, and went to meet the man who first went to knock on her front door. He was quite tall and had a full beard that was neatly trimmed. He wore a three-piece riding outfit made of brown and tan tweed and tall riding boots of polished leather.

"Miss Stevens?" the man called out. "Are you she?"

Surprised that the stranger knew her name, she waved and bobbed her head. "Yes, I am. Who is it that asks for me?"

He came close enough for her to see a pair of pince nez glasses affixed to the bridge of his nose. "Lady, I am Dr. Francis Abbott. I'm glad to have found you on such a fine day. Just rode down from Bethel to meet you."

"Sir, I'm pleased to make your acquaintance. Please pardon my appearance. Gardening is not work which allows one to be tidy and ladylike."

"Indeed," he said looking her up and down with a smile. "From the description given me by Mr. Kimball, I thought you would be an older woman, but you are a beautiful young woman. You have no husband, dear?"

"Doctor, whether I am married or not is really none of your business, is it? As I see this is not a congenial social call, please tell me why I have the dubious pleasure of your company this morning. I do have chores to do while the sun is shining."

"Good lord, Miss Stevens, I assure you I have not meant to offend you. It is just curious that you live all alone out here in the woods and manage your own farm, as small as it might be."

"Sir, what you meant is of little matter to me. What is it that you want?" Her hostility toward the doctor had nearly come to the point of asking him to leave, when he drew a neatly folded piece of paper from his waistcoat pocket and handed it to her.

"Madam, I have recently purchased Kimball's small lot at the top of your pasture, the one which he has been clearing during the winter. It is my plan to mine that land for the mica and to make arrangements with you to have a right of way across your land. Kimball tells me that you have already given approval to my plan and that you only await a fair payment in exchange. I offer you a generous ten percent of the value of material which my miners find."

As she looked at the legal document, she grew angry. How dare he present her with such a demand and expect approval on the spot? What of the damage already done to her property? Who would pay her for that? She passed the paper back to Abbott and began to stamp her foot. "Sir, you have surely misunderstood John Kimball. I made no such agreement and will make none under duress. Yes, Kimball and I had a quick discussion of his mining plans, but nothing was decided. To tell the truth, the only decision I am making today is to ask you to take your offer and your attitude and your snotty glasses and get off my land immediately."

"Miss Stevens, I've come all this way today to make a very generous offer to you only to be attacked as a piker or scoundrel. You may drive me away and refuse to consider this proposal, but I will return with the sheriff and my attorney to convince you of the fairness that is being offered. Take the offer now or take a more difficult one later."

Aphia said nothing, only glared at the man and pointed at the road for him to leave. She was sure that John Kimball had not lied to this man. Rather, he himself had arrogantly assumed a single woman would quickly accept his plan.

62

Nathan Hallett sat at the wooden card table in Dunton Mine's head house, a leather-bound ledger and two piles of paper slips stacked in front of him. He had been asked to determine how successful the first half year's production had been. One stack was expense records: time sheets for each laborer, invoices for materials and subcontract services. The second contained slips on which were recorded the amount of production in weight and an estimated market value. Hollis Dunton usually did the accounting, but with the warm dry summer weather upon them, the owner wanted to supervise his crew directly. Work went on from dawn to dusk. Not an hour was to be lost between now and November. Once information on each slip was recorded in the ledger, that slip was folded in half and dropped in a file in case further inquiry was needed. Nathan was a good bookkeeper and always knew the status of each client's account on a transaction-by-transaction basis. The fact that no accounting for mine business had been kept for six full months made him suspicious that the partners were not good businessmen.

Dr. Abbott came into the office, sat in a chair opposite Nathan, and lit his pipe. "Hallett, how have we done so far? Should I have a shot of bourbon to celebrate or to drown my sorrows?"

"Can't answer that as yet, Francis. It takes forever to decipher the little scratch marks on most of these slips. I have to wipe dried mud off some in order to read the figures. Who makes out these records each day?"

"Likely the only man nearby who has a pencil. These are miners, Nathan, not notaries. They can blast and drill and pick out crystals without breaking then to bits, but they don't really give a damn about keeping records."

"Look at this one, Doctor," said Nathan. "Can you make out whether this says one-half ton or one-eighth?"

After staring and squinting at the paper for a second, Abbott answered, "Can't tell for sure, but I would record it as one-half. Give it the best guess, so to speak."

Nathan was thinking that even the good doctor didn't care about accuracy. "Why am I bothering to do this work?" he asked. "We could just as well write down any old figure in each column."

"No, son, someone has to do this recordkeeping. We can't make these things up for the bankers. You can understand that."

"Yes, but don't you yourself want to see how we did with some accuracy?"

"Well, I am of course interested, but I am not going to worry about my investment in this particular mine. If it goes bust, I won't be ruined. There are plenty more prospects in the Oxford Hills that will pay off a large enough stake to cover my losses. Some are worth a million, some nothing."

Nathan kept working away, wanting to complete the calculations before the end of the day. As the receipts and expenses began to balance out, he felt better. It looked as if they might have broken even or come close to it. He reached the bottom of the final columns and turned to Abbott, who had not left the table. "Mr. Abbott, I think we have nearly turned a profit. The only reason we did not break even is that our labor costs are too high. Too many wasted hours."

The doctor clapped his hands and slapped Nathan on the shoulder. "If that is our only problem, the future will indeed be bright. I have sent for a Mr. Clarence Potter to manage this operation. He accepted my invitation in a wire this morning. He will be sure to whip this place into shape and make some money for us all."

As Abbott prepared to leave, he knocked his pipe on the table edge, spilling ashes on the floor. "I had a friend in Waterford who was a naturalist, or a scientist, who made the collection of crystals, rocks, and minerals part of his life's work. James Shaw began collecting when he was a boy running through his father's fields on the slopes of Beech Hill. When I was but a sprout, he would take me to the deep holes he had dug where all types of specimens had been found. Not just pretty crystals, but pieces of granite, shale, sandstone—things he could put in his display case as examples of natural elements.

"Why would he collect so many common rocks?"

"He wanted to have a piece of every stone in the world and even sent away to have exotic pieces shipped in by mail order. When he died earlier this year, the family offered to sell me his enormous collection, but I have no place to put it. I did take the best pieces: green and orange tourmalines, purple amethysts, lovely blue and green beryls. Gave them a good price for those pieces. They put the rest in a couple of boxes for storage in the attic."

"Did he ever sell the best of the pieces he found?"

"Not that I know of. It was the collecting that he wanted, not the selling. He was very comfortable financially. And it wasn't only minerals. He collected leaves and branches from trees, every sort of plant. He had a conservatory for his palms and tropicals."

"So, as you said, he was a scientist."

"Very much so. I'm not that way. Collecting is a hobby I enjoy, but the selling is a way to make my fortune swell. James was a man of an earlier generation who had a great desire to learn about the natural world. He taught me enough to know how to use nature to my advantage. I don't know if any venture will be boom or bust, but each one shows me more of the world. If this gem mine fails, there is always another."

Nathan was anxious to leave before dark. Abbott wanted to continue their discussion. "I currently have another prospect in mind, a mica mine in Waterford that was one of the holes James Shaw showed me so many years ago. You might have some interest in becoming a partner. Early excavations by the farmer who sold the lot have yielded books of mica large enough to justify further digging. Some are a foot square or slightly larger. I've already offered this new man, Potter, a chance to manage that prospect as well as this one. Combining the two salaries might give him a better income than just the one."

"Won't that take him away from our operation?"

"Perhaps, but if he's learned how risky it can be to put all of one's eggs in one basket, he will welcome the opportunity." He hesitated for a moment. "You know, perhaps you would do me the favor of assisting in Waterford. I know you are there quite often and have many contacts. Do you, perchance, know a woman by the name of Aphia Stevens?"

"I do. She's quite a local character. Has raised quite a few eyebrows in town with her outlandish ways. My sister-in-law has adopted her as a personal enemy."

"Outlandish? Yes, a good description. She has blocked my access to the mica prospect, denying to sell me a temporary right-of-way across the corner of her pasture, an area for which she has no use. I've threatened her with legal actions, but you might be able to grease the wheels and buy her off."

63

Hearing a loud knock at the door, Mary Ritchie walked to a front window and saw a bicycle leaning against their mailbox. When she opened the door, a Western Union courier handed her a tan envelope and asked her to sign a receipt. When she opened the envelope and saw that it was from Lottie, she nearly fell to the floor in shock before staggering to the long velvet sofa. Over a year had passed since that Canadian scoundrel had stolen—no, *kidnapped*—her daughter. This was the first message of any sort from her.

The message was short and to the point. After reading it, she threw the paper on the cushion beside her and reached into her housedress for a handkerchief to wipe away tears. After all the months of worry, anger, and feelings of abandonment, at last she knew that the girl was still alive. After a moment, she picked up the telegram and read it again, this time much more slowly.

DEAREST PARENTS. STOP. CLARENCE AND I HAVE JOY-OUS NEWS. STOP. WE NOW HAVE A SON. STOP. A GRANDSON FOR YOU. STOP. HIS NAME IS CLARENCE CONRAD. STOP. STILL LIVING IN CANADA. STOP. WILL BE MOVING SOON TO MAINE. STOP. ALL THE BEST.

This is it? Mary thought. After all this time, a four-line telegram to announce her baby? Of all the nerve! No return address.
No other information about what she has been doing with her life,
how she is, how he treats her. Again she threw the paper down on
the cushion, but this time, she stood and swiftly went to a Chip-
pendale tallboy and drew a decanter from behind a glass door.
Pouring herself a tall glass of vodka, she went out to the porch
and sat on a wicker chair while sipping the liquor until it was
gone. She had another, then another until she was unable to walk
and fell asleep in her seat. When John returned from the hospital
that evening, he found her slumped over and snoring loudly.

Unable to raise her, he draped his long overcoat across her
like a blanket. He saw the open cabinet and the half-empty decanter, which made it clear that his wife had been drinking to
excess for some reason. It had become a habit for her to imbibe in
the evening after dinner, but such an early spree was unusual. He
spied the telegram on the settee, picked it up, and, as he read it,
he realized what had driven Mary to drink. So many months had
passed that it seemed to him a blessing to get even a short message from Lottie. She was alive and healthy enough to give birth
to what he hoped was a healthy baby. This was good news, but
he knew that to Mary such a curt announcement might stir her to
anger. He decided that since the evening was warm, he would let
her stay on the sofa until he had prepared a small meal. It was not
likely she would be able to cook tonight.

As he fussed over scrambled eggs, bacon, and toast for supper, Mary entered the kitchen and supported herself on a pressed-
back chair. "Oh, John," she mumbled, "you're home. Didn't hear
you come in."

"Not surprising, dear. I see you've been drowning your sorrows tonight."

"Don't be funny." Her voice grew louder and she stood up
straight. "So what if I am? There's good reason to be sorrowful.
Did you see that telegram? She's married. And she has a baby!
Just drops me a short line about two of the most important things

that could happen to her. After all this time. How dare she?"

"Would you like me to prepare a plate for you while I'm at the stove? Something in your stomach might help you accept the fact that our daughter is living her own life now. She is happy and healthy and looks to be planning to live closer to us."

"Don't bother," she snapped back. "I couldn't sit at the same table with you tonight. How can you accept the news that Lottie has turned her back on us and done as she pleases? I'm going to bed."

He watched her stumble out of the room and said as she left, "My dear, your heart is much harder than mine. She is safe and happy. Given the manner of her departure, isn't that a blessing?"

64

Moses fell again—tumbled off the porch steps onto the gravel driveway. Doctor James came to the house, but other than a few bruises on his head and left hip, there was no evidence of serious damage, no broken bones or sprains, just a headache. Still, he was to keep to his bed for a few days. Lizzie, who was planning a trip for them both to Saco to deliver several custom-order dresses, was left to travel alone. She nearly canceled the delivery until young Francena volunteered to keep an eye on Moses and prepare meals. After all, her absence would be only for a day or two. Will would take her the two miles to Riverton to get the trolley. Before leaving, she went upstairs to check on Moses, to make sure he was still in bed and that he was not smoking. She went to the room and saw that he was asleep with a book under his chin. He looked peaceful enough and she didn't want to disturb him, so she tucked in the comforter around his legs without waking him.

He is such a sweet man. It's sad to see him slow down, she thought. He has been so good to me, brought me happiness I thought I would never know.

Franny met her at the bottom of the stairs with the boxes

which held the dresses. "Auntie, please don't worry about Uncle Moses. I will check on him every hour or so to make sure he is following doctor's orders. I've packed the dresses as carefully as I know how. Don't you think the ladies will love their new outfits?" She was very excited.

"I'm sure they will. Especially the blue one. The bows you attached at the waist are stunning. The customer will be so happy. Franny, the talents you have with stitchery must have come down in your blood from my own mother. If you stay at it, you will be the best seamstress in the family."

The girl blushed and curtsied before taking the boxes out to the waiting carriage. When Liz and Will drove off, she sat on the porch bench to contemplate what had just been said to her. No one, other than her parents, had ever paid her such a compliment, and she beamed with gratitude. What little sewing she had learned in school had been boring and led her to believe that she was not cut out for such creative work. Now, here was her very talented aunt saying that she only had to apply herself in order for a new door to open on her future.

Returning to the workshop to complete cleaning up from yesterday's projects, she had just begun to sweep when there was a loud noise. She ran to the stairs and saw Moses lying on his stomach with his face resting on the bottom step. His left foot was caught in the railings and blood was spattered on the carpet runner where his head had apparently hit the bannister. She let out a scream, then calmed herself enough to make her way carefully to her uncle and put her hand beneath his face. He was breathing, but with much labor, and making a loud wheezing sound. She was able to move his foot from between the two railings and then slowly move his heavy body down to the floor. He remained unconscious and continued to bleed profusely from the side of his head. She ran to the bedroom, grabbed a blanket off the bed, and returned to cover him. At least he might stay warm while she figured out what to do next. The Cain place was close, just a hundred yards down a well-worn path behind the house. Perhaps

Maeve might be there and know what else should be done.

Maeve was working in her vegetable garden when she saw the panicked girl run past her toward the house. "Wait, Franny!" she cried out. "I'm over here. What the devil is wrong with you? You look like you've seen a ghost."

"Come quick! Please come quick! Moses has fallen down the stairs. I don't know what to do. Please help me."

The two women ran together back to the big house. Maeve noticed that his neck was bent to the side in an odd fashion. "My God, Franny," she said, her voice cracking with emotion. "My God, he has broken his neck." She felt his forehead. "And he is cold to the touch." After reaching for his wrist and squeezing it for a moment she turned to Franny and whispered, "I think he is dead."

65

The morning had turned cold, and a brisk breeze kicked up from the northwest as the wagon made its way along Portland Road. Suddenly, Liz closed her eyes and began to sigh deeply over and over again. Her eyes were shut so tightly that small wrinkles formed at the corners. She began to moan loudly. It was as if she was seeing something that wasn't there, a vision.

"Stop, Will. Stop! We must go back!" shouted Lizzie. "Something is terribly wrong! Something has happened to Moses!" Lizzie grabbed Will's arm so hard that he nearly fell from the seat. He firmly but gently pulled on the reins until the wagon came to a full stop. They had come almost two miles, and he could see the station on the Presumpscot River just ahead.

"What's wrong, Liz? You're so pale, as if you've seen a ghost."

"I have. I have seen Moses dying. Almost as if I am still back at home. We must turn around and return immediately. I must be with him."

Will hesitated at first, but seeing how distressed Liz was, he turned the wagon around as soon as there was no other traffic on the road. She looked to be in a trance: eyes closed, hands clasped across her chest, her head and torso moving from side to side. He spoke to her, but she paid no attention. As they approached the house, she began to moan and keen, making Will think that she had gone mad. It frightened him to see his friend so transfixed.

The carriage pulled up at the porch. Maeve came to the door, surprised at their quick return. Tears were already running down her face, but upon seeing Will, she too began to cry like a banshee. He didn't know which woman required consoling, but since Liz wouldn't budge from her seat, he climbed down and went to his wife's side. He threw his arms around her and placed her head on his chest. Francena exited the house and, seeing Lizzie, threw herself onto the porch sofa and began to cry out like the others.

"What has happened? Why is everyone in such a state?" asked Will.

"Oh, Will, Moses is dead! He fell down the stairs and broke his neck. Franny and I could not revive him. There was nothing we could do."

Overhearing Maeve's words, Liz quieted and began to simply cry. Her frightening vision had come true. What had been a momentary nightmare was now a stark reality. Her husband was dead. He must be mourned and then buried. With no help, she stepped down from the wagon and mounted the stairs. Her left hand reached out to Maeve, her right hand to young Francena. "I'm sure you both have done all you could do. I must see him now."

She went silently into the house while the others stood outside, allowing her time to be alone with her husband's body.

66

Moses was buried in Biddeford's Laurel Hill Cemetery in the Webber family plot next to his parents and first wife. That had been his wish, and Lizzie wanted to abide by all the terms of his last will and testament. She had known in advance that he would return to his blood relatives in death, just as she knew that the town house would be left to his cousin, who had cared for the place since the wife died. Turnout at the burial service was impressive. Of course, the Cains and Halletts were there and members of his own family, but what surprised Liz was the number of mourners who knew him from his work at the Pepperell. She had expected managers and his partners, but the number of workers, both men and women, made her realize how much love there was for Moses Webber. After the service, an elderly woman wearing a long brown dress, a black bonnet, and a frayed shawl came up to Liz.

"Please, Mrs. Webber, please accept my condolences. Your man was so dear to us who worked for him. Not a mean bully as some managers were to me. He will be remembered gratefully."

Then the woman took a photograph from her pocket and handed it to Liz. It was of a group of factory girls dressed in the factory outfit of brown skirts and white blouses made from the mill's cotton. In the rear of the group stood Moses looking just as he had the day he'd hired Liz back in 1877, twenty years before.

"Please, ma'am, take this with you as a reminder of the years you shared your life with a good Christian man."

Liz said nothing, but took the photo and held it to her heart. She squeezed the old woman's hand for several minutes until the woman withdrew with a curtsey.

67

Abbott and Dunton met in the Newry head house early one humid August morning to discuss the long delay in getting Clarence to take over the operation. Their offer had been made during the spring, and it had been expected he would run the crew during peak summer conditions when work might go on twelve or more hours each day. Several wires had been sent to him in Ontario, but his only response was to say that he was reluctant to relocate until his son, born in April, was strong enough to withstand the trip. He said that he was excited about the opportunity, but his wife wanted to wait until later in the year.

"Do you think he's being honest with us?" asked Hollis, as he drummed his fingers on the cluttered tabletop. "After all, the railroad or Canadian Copper may not want to give him up, might be offering him more money to stay."

Abbott tapped his pipe on the table corner to empty its ashes on the floor. He refilled the meerschaum before answering. "Hollis, there's no amount of money that will keep him in Ontario for another winter. His wife wouldn't allow it. She is used to a lot more comforts than what he's able to offer her up there in the wild."

"Well, perhaps he's being coy with us, wants to play us for more money or better terms. If I were in his shoes, I'd've been down here in a jiff no matter what the wife said. We're offering him a good position and a good wage."

"I agree," said the doctor striking a Diamond match and drawing its flame into the bowl. "It is a damn good deal, but it's a risk on his part, just as it is on ours. We've plowed good money into this pit, believing that its lode will turn a profit, but it might fail. You and I both know from experience that a few good buckets of minerals are nothing but a good beginning. Here's a boy just married and a new father who is thinking to leave a proven source of income and jump into what is little more than a big hole in the ground."

"Francis, we have a good prospect here. We both know it, as do the other investors. Figures show that we nearly broke even in the first season. You have to admit that, don't you?"

"Oh, yes. And I'm looking forward to a great run here, but you and I are a lot older and more settled than is this boy. Both he and his wife must be looking for a bit more security from us. I have a suggestion on how to sweeten the pot. Last month, I purchased a mica prospect from a farmer in Waterford. It sits just below the rocky summit of Beech Hill with easy access through a right-of-way across a neighbor's unused pasture. Farmer Kimball has cleared the lot and showed me books of the crystal larger than twelve inches square. If we were to offer Clarence the management of that future mine, perhaps that might lessen the risk for him."

Dunton smiled at his friend, but did not move his head in agreement or disagreement. He sat stone-still for a moment as he considered the proposal. "Dr. Abbott, your idea has promise for several reasons. First, of course, is the possibility that it will bring our lad down here faster. The second, and more important reason, is that the prospect may prove a good investment for myself as well as you. Why haven't you told me about this?" he grinned. "Holding out to enjoy the wealth yourself, were you?"

"Friend, let's walk that prospect before the snow comes. Will you reach out to Potter with this new proposal or shall I?"

"Leave it to me. He seems to agree with much that I say," said the doctor.

68

It was the final weekend of October and the mine pit where Nathan and Nate worked was no longer warmed by the summer sun. The field of broken stone was cold enough to suck heat from their bodies as they dug at the remnants of a tourmaline pocket from which most of the showy crystals had already been removed. Nate was back at school, but the two had so enjoyed working together during the past few months, they'd decided to get in one more day before snow might close the mine until spring.

Nathan rested for a moment, watching his son work the wall of the pocket with his chipping hammer. Muscles built up through hours of hard work during the summer brought his hammer down hard, sending shards of cracked stone flying in all directions. The boy had grown into a man before his father's eyes.

"Dad, look here. There's a good-size crystal with what looks to be a sharply pointed termination. If I can carefully chisel away the surrounding quartz a little at a time, we may have a fine specimen." He splashed a cup of water on the spot to wash off loose chips and dust. "It looks real gemmy to me!"

Nathan peered over the boy's shoulder at the cleaned green crystal. "You might have a valuable gemstone there if you're careful. Take your time. We still have a couple of hours before dusk. Even if we were to come away with only that one specimen, the day will have been well worth it."

The two were so wrapped up in their work that neither of them noticed a single figure standing on the top edge of the big pit with a duffel bag on his arm. It was Clarence, who had arrived in Bethel two days before and had come to make an inspection of his new workplace. His plan to inspect the mine when no one else would be there was not working out. Already he had run into a mechanic who worked overtime repairing one of Hollis's hydraulic jackhammers. Now he watched the Halletts from afar. When Nate shouted out a loud "Huzzah!" he slowly made his way down the precipitous path to see what had been found in his mine. Father and son were both kneeling in the pocket, which was about five feet wide and four feet tall. Neither of them was able to stand. Clarence made his way up behind them until he was able to see that the boy had a green crystal in his hand.

"We have it!" Nate shouted. "What a beauty this one is!"

"Hand it to me. Let me wash it off," said an equally excited Nathan. "Then we can see what it really looks like." When he turned around to dip the stone in a bucket of chalky water, he was shocked to see a stranger standing tall above him. "Sir, can I do anything for you?" he asked.

"Mr. Hallett, if I am not mistaken, you may be doing something for me already. That looks to be a perfect elbaite specimen that would add to the total yield for the year."

Nathan stared up from the hole, studying the man's face. "My god, is that you, Clarence Potter?" He couldn't be sure because the man was backlit by the lowering sun.

"Nathan, yes it is I. Let me see what your boy has found." He took the crystal in his hand and held it to the sun. "This is about as perfect a piece of tourmaline as I have ever seen." It was a six-inch-long, four-inch-wide hexagonal crystal with a perfectly pointed termination. "If this is an example of what can be found here, it will be easy to make a profit. This rock should draw a good price." From his jacket pocket he pulled a cloth bag into which he placed the stone. As he returned it to his pocket he turned back to Nathan and said, "How is it that you two are the only ones working on such a warm autumn day? If it were up to me, I would have a full crew out here."

Both Nathan and Nate crawled backwards on hands and knees from the tiny pocket, stood up, and slowly straightened their backs. They stared at the Canadian, whom they had not seen for over a year, as they stretched. Nathan thought he looked much older. His hair had not been cut for some time, and his beard was streaked with gray.

Nate walked up to Clarence and put out his hand. "Can I please see my crystal for a closer inspection?"

"It isn't yours, son," said Potter. "It's the property of the mine. The rule is that any crystal of significant value found here becomes the property of the mine."

"Sheez, Mr. Potter, I just want to take a look at it, see how pretty it is." The boy extended both hands and stood face to face with the man.

Nathan pulled his son's shoulder gently and said, "Nate, you know the rules. Clarence is right. As the new manager, it is his job to take and protect all valuable specimens. Perhaps he'll show it to you if you are not so demanding."

"I said please, didn't I?" Nate said. "I'm not asking to keep it or anything. Not going to take it to some jeweler to sell."

Nathan was shocked that Nate would make reference to what Potter had done with the three gemmy tourmalines Lottie and the family had found. Clarence also was taken aback by the boy's comments, though he said nothing, only frowned as he turned away.

Later that day, as Nathan locked the gate and returned to the mine office, he sat at the table and wrote a note to Dunton that would be read on Monday morning. "Successfully harvested a complete terminated tourmaline crystal. Gemmy quality. Sixty or more carats. Given to Clarence Potter this day for safekeeping." No valuable gemstones would be misplaced *this* time around if he had anything to do with it.

69

It was nearly Christmas. Moses had been dead for more than four months, and although black crepe was still wrapped around her green drapes, Lizzie's wardrobe was no longer a widow's black dress. Her personal grieving continued at night, when tears sometimes overcame her as she read, or when she was alone in the house. There were reminders of him wherever she looked, his favorite chair near the hearth, his worn-out slippers under his side of the bed. She was unable to sleep in the middle of the mattress because, even after all this time, the indentation left by his large body still remained. Lizzie sat in her kitchen looking down at the traffic on Forest Avenue and at the wreaths Will had hung in her windows. Unlike most winters, there had been so little snow that the green grass was still visible. Franny had hung an advent calendar in the office, but Lizzie didn't feel motivated to do any decorating of her own. She just couldn't find the Christmas spirit. Perhaps, when she was with her family for the holiday, the spirit might find her.

Precisely at noon, Nathan's chaise pulled up to the front porch. He bounded up the stairs to knock on the door. As Lizzie opened it, he threw his arms around her. "Merry Christmas!" he shouted. "The day is so bright and warm. What a day for a ride in the country!" He was so excited about the holiday that he seemed ten years younger. When Franny heard his happy voice, she ran down the stairs wearing a holiday outfit she had made for herself. He stared at her for a moment with a huge smile on his face.

"You will be the best dressed at the party," he said. Then,

turning to Lizzie, he said, "Thank you so much for making her such a wonderful outfit."

"Daddy, I made this completely by myself. Even designed it. Auntie says I will be the best seamstress in the family."

She spun around on her toes to show the white bows attached at the waist of her party dress, as her father exclaimed, "She's right, daughter of mine, you've learned very quickly from your aunt. Thank you so much, Lizzie."

He carried both ladies' suitcases and helped them to mount the wide seat, then secured their bags to the rear of the carriage. Jumping up to the front bench, he shook the reins and shouted, "Over the river and through the woods to the Halletts' house we go!"

As they left the driveway, both women chimed in. It would be a jolly ride the Bridgton.

70

The low winter sun shone brightly as Nathan, Francena, and Lizzie rode west on Forest Avenue. Many carriages and wagons rolled by in both directions, some decorated with red ribbons and wreaths. People shouted out holiday greetings as they passed.

"We have a surprise guest for the holiday party," said Nathan as they approached Bridgton. "Clarence Potter will be joining us for Christmas Day. I hope you will be cordial, Franny. It would not do to mention what happened when we were last with him."

Franny, who had been telling stories and singing carols for the entire ride, suddenly became very quiet. "Daddy, what is he doing here? Is Lottie also coming with her new son? How long will they be staying?"

"Whoa with all the questions. Slow down. Let me explain. The man has taken a job as manager of the new Dunton mine. He's alone while he searches for a suitable winter home for his wife and baby. When he finds one, Lottie will be joining him. There, I think that answers all your questions, if I am not mistaken."

Lizzie, who had met Clarence only once before, was surprised to hear that he had been invited to what she assumed would be a family party. Wasn't his presence likely to dampen some of the enjoyment she expected? Like her niece, she had many questions, but hers concerned the stories she had heard about the Canadian's questionable behavior toward Lottie and her parents. These she decided to keep to herself.

As they pulled up to the barn door, Hattie and Nate greeted them. "Merry Christmas!" shouted Hattie to her daughter. "Welcome back home, stranger! We've missed you."

Franny stepped down from the carriage, grabbed her bag, and handed it to Nate. Hattie threw her arms around the girl and swung her around as she had so often done. Fanny screamed with delight before pushing herself free.

"Mother, be careful! You'll hurt yourself. I am not your little girl anymore."

Hattie took her sister's hand, then kissed her cheek. "Lizzie, so wonderful to have you join us. So many times during the last few months, when the family came together, your absence made my heart ache. I've been worried about you."

"Little Sis," said Liz, "I've missed you all, but you must believe you were always with me."

When Francena saw Clarence step onto the porch, she smoothed her overcoat and fussed with her bonnet to make sure it was on straight. "Mr. Potter," she demurred, holding her hand out to him. He took the hand and made a slight bow in her direction.

Seeing all this, Nate began to snicker and bowed deeply, nearly touching the ground with his hand. "My dear sister, I humbly greet you, Your Highness."

"So happy to meet you once again under what are better circumstances," said Clarence, "as I hope you will agree. Lottie sends her best wishes to you for a joyous holiday. She wired me yesterday that she is preparing to join me here in Maine and will travel no matter what the weather."

"What wonderful news. Father tells me that you work up in

Newry at that mine where we all prospected together that day. I remember those three remarkable crystals we found."

Nathan stepped forward between Potter and Franny, shaking Clarence's hand. He felt that the topic of the three missing gems would be best forgotten for the moment. "Come with me, Franny," he said, taking her by the hand. "We don't want to be keeping Mr. Potter. He has a long ride to his rooming house in North Waterford before the sun sets. He'll be back on Christmas Day, and we can chat more with him then."

71

Franny and Lizzie stood in the second-floor sunroom and gazed at Highland Lake across the roofs along Main Street. Christmas Dinner was over. The men had gone for a walk along High Street, and a few flakes of snow had begun to float down from very dark clouds building to the south and west.

"Perhaps we'll get our first snowstorm tonight," said Franny. "It's not like Christmas to have no snow on the ground."

"Oh, it will come, you can be sure of that. I remember winters where snow didn't come until much later than this, but then before spring the banks climbed higher than your head."

"I'm sure winter will soon raise its harsh head, but it's been nice to be able to get around so easily. I wonder what conditions are like where Lottie is in Ontario."

"In that remote area of Canada, I've been told they always have a lot of snow and brutal cold. I've not been there myself and am not likely to visit. I'm sure your friend will be glad to come down to a more comfortable clime."

"Auntie, there's so much room in your house now with Mary away and Uncle gone. Perhaps we might be able to make room for the Potters, at least for the winter. I know that Clarence will want to live closer to Bethel, but he hasn't been able to find a good warm place where he and Lottie could settle this winter. Could they live in his small room?"

Liz turned from the window and stared into the dancing flames of the fireplace. "I'm not so sure that he would want to take up a temporary residence. There are some times during the winter when there might be meetings he must attend for work."

"Yes, but it would be so much fun to have Lottie and her baby with us. It would help to make the winter go by more quickly."

Liz was silent for a moment as she stared into the fire. "Well, perhaps we could make the *offer* to Clarence, see if the arrangement would be of interest. We certainly have the room, and there is always so much to do at this time of year to keep the place up and running: fires to build, snow to shovel, water to carry in from the well. It might be good to have a man around."

"Will you ask him, Auntie? Will you?" Francena's eyes flashed with excitement, but she tried to keep her emotions in check.

"Yes, dear, I'll ask Clarence before the day is done. Now, please calm yourself. You look like you're about to explode!"

The party was gathered around the sparkling Christmas tree when the two came downstairs. Hattie and Clarence sat at a small table playing at cards. When Hattie saw them coming, she patted a third chair at the table. "Come here, sister. Why don't you join us? Clarence is teaching me how to play a game called forty-twos. And you, too, Francena."

"It's a game for four people," said Clarence. "I used to play it as a kid in Yarmouth, but nobody down here has ever heard of it."

Although neither woman really wanted to play cards, they took seats at the table. Clarence shuffled the deck and began to deal, but Liz interrupted him. "Clarence, Franny and I were just discussing the possibility that your family might want to live with us here in Westbrook for the next few months, until winter breaks." He stopped dealing and turned abruptly toward Liz with a frown on his face. Was he angry, or was he just confused? She couldn't tell. "If you were to have a temporary place to live that is warm and safe, would you be interested in joining the two of us in my big house?"

"Miss Liz," he said, "you are so kind to make this offer. My preference would be to find a permanent home in Oxford County close to one or the other of the mines, but your kindness is of great interest. I will take it up with Lottie. She wants to join me here, but she, too, seeks a house we could live in as the family grows. Can I speak with you in a few days, after she and I have a chance to discuss your offer?"

"Of course, please talk it over with her."

Franny couldn't hold her tongue any longer. "Tell Lottie that I am living in Auntie's house and would love to help take care of your son. She and I will make the house comfortable for us all!"

72

The first storm of the season came three days after Christmas, bringing six inches of slushy snow to Westbrook. For the next three weeks, a storm blew into the area every third day until, by January 20th, drifts had piled up against Lizzie's parlor windows. She and Francena, unable to venture out for days at a time, had plenty of time to prepare the third-floor apartment for new residents. As expected, the invitation to the Potters had been accepted. Clarence had gone to Ontario to help pack up the household and bring his family to their new temporary home. Their arrival had been expected for nearly a week, but delays at this time of year were not unusual. Franny was sweeping the floors one more time when her aunt arrived back from market with a bag of groceries which the young woman jammed into the icebox and the pantry.

"Auntie, there's no more room in the icebox for anything. Why have you bought more milk? There's still a gallon in there from this week's delivery. We haven't eaten the carrots you got last week. and here you've bought more."

"Don't worry. When the Potters get here, most of that perishable food will be moved to their own icebox. You forget that there are three of them. A man eats much more than we two girls. I didn't know what to get for the baby, but we'll figure it out when they're here."

"Whenever *that* might be. Dad said they might be here once the last storm blew by yesterday, but it's taking them so long. I wonder how Lottie and her son are coping with having to travel in fits and starts."

When a large sleigh pulled into their driveway a short while later, the two women rushed to the showroom window and saw their visitors stepping down from the enclosed passenger compartment. Franny rushed to the door, throwing it wide open to the cold wind. She was wearing no coat and had slippers on her feet, but the sight of her dear friend kept her from feeling the cold.

Lottie, dressed in a roughly made coat of some sort of animal pelts, with a hood drawn tight around her head, shouted a greeting. "Franny! My dear, dear friend, seeing you is such a blessing after this ordeal of a journey!"

They clutched at each other and the taller Lottie lifted Francena off her feet. After putting her back down, she leaned back into the compartment and picked up what appeared to be a parcel wrapped in leather and tied with heavy cord. Through an opening at the end of this bundle the small head of a young child appeared. The boy's hair was long enough to cover his eyes. A big smile lit up his face.

"Oh. Look at this beautiful boy," said Franny, reaching to touch his rosy red cheeks. "He is so wrapped up. He must be very uncomfortable. Can I carry him for you?"

"Yes, please do, but be careful to keep his head uncovered so that he's able to breathe. We've wrapped him in a blanket of beaver pelts each morning of the journey as the native tribes do in Ontario. I'm sure he can hardly wait to be freed."

Clarence, who had been riding up front with the sleigh driver, had stepped down, unloaded their bags, and entered the house before the two friends had stopped embracing. He went up to Lizzie and said with sincerity, "Mrs. Webber, many thanks for your gracious offer. After the arduous journey we have just completed, your lovely home is the most welcome haven I've ever seen."

73

It must be the steam from my kettles that brings on the dreams, Aphia thought as she stirred a pot of lavender. The steam rising from the bubbling broth surrounded her head like a foamy wreath, leaving droplets on the hairs poking out from a linen kerchief. As spring approached, there remained dozens of herb bundles hanging from strings run between the rafters of her kitchen. The dreams were becoming more and more common as the winter wore on. There was so much time between sunset and sunrise that three or four visions would disturb her sleep some nights. Not all her dreams were nightmares. In some, she traveled to distant places where the sun was always shining, the sands were bleached white, and her every need was satisfied. Other times, she flew above the house where she had grown up and watched her parents caring for each other in their old age.

Last night's visions had been a frightening series of scenes in which her husband, Henry Greene, returned from the dead to relive sad events of their relationship. Once again, he touched her for the first time that night her grandfather's seven horses were killed by a lightning strike. The feel of his hand on hers brought back the acrid aroma of burning flesh and drove her from the bed. Then came the horror of a passionless kiss at their Waterford wedding. She remembered how it felt to wipe the filth of his kiss from her lips. One pitiful scene after another ran across the screen of her mind until a vision of his death caused her to jump back under the covers screaming.

"Leave me! Leave me, Henry, you devil! As God is my witness, I did not kill you on purpose! It was your own fault, you bastard!" Why did he come to torment her? If he hadn't tried to rape her in the herb beds, he would still be alive. Though who would want that? He was cruel to her. He deserved what happened. Yes, she had poisoned him, but not on purpose. He had brought it on himself. "Yet, you curse me. Blame me for killing you. Won't you please leave me alone now?" she moaned.

Once in the past, she had seen him rise as a ghost from the

shallow grave on the Hill of Death where she'd buried him among the rotting horses. He had come to her side in the herb garden, picked up toxic leaves of *aconitum*, the same leaves that had killed him, and waved them in her face. She knew with certainty that he was still waiting beneath the layers of soil, waiting amongst the fly pupae to rise up in summer heat and drive her mad.

74

During the winter, Lottie and Francena decided to try their hand at raising vegetables when spring came. They would use the same area where Franny's great-grandmother Beattie had had her garden. Neither of them had ever grown vegetables before, and although it would be a lot of work, they looked forward to working closely together. Clarence, however, took a different view of their plans. One afternoon in late February, the friends sat at one of the dress shop worktables laying out a plan for garden beds on a large piece of sketch paper. He came into the sunny room and stood over them.

"Girls, I still don't know why you're planning to do this. Lottie, you and I will be gone soon to live closer to the mines. Franny has a lot of work to do for Lizzie. Who will take care of all these plants?"

"Clary, we have been through this all before," said Lottie. "Franny thinks she can handle the gardens with a little help from Maeve and her kids. Auntie says she will lend a hand now and then, and we will be visiting once in a while. It will all work out."

"I don't know how often you'll be able to help. We're going to be hours away from here. You'll have to take care of your own place, and I will be working most of the time."

"I know we do not agree, but please give me the opportunity to learn how to garden. I've never done this before, and the experience may come in handy when we have our own house."

Throwing his hands up in frustration, Clarence walked away. She was being unreasonable again, but he had learned that if he tried to stop his wife from doing what she wanted, it would back-fire on him. She would continue following her desires, sometimes in secret, and would gloat on successful completion of each project. Besides, the things she wanted to do usually came out to be good for him as well. It was so different from his first marriage, when Emma would be a pessimist about things that *he* wanted to do. Lottie was so much more optimistic than he was. The years of seeking financial success had dampened his enthusiasm a bit, made him more realistic about his goals.

Once Clarence left, Franny put her hand on Lottie's shoulder and said in a hushed voice, "What is his problem with our garden? He has criticized the plan from the very beginning."

"He's just anxious about getting to work. Sometimes he paces from room to room, stopping occasionally to peer out the window at the drifts. I know he's wishing for the arrival of spring, when he can reopen the Newry mine and break ground at the Beech Hill prospect. It's hard on him to be shut in like this."

"There are other things he might do to be busy during the winter, you know. Will Cain is always looking for someone to help him finish the interiors of his projects. Clarence could be painting woodwork for him right now."

"I've suggested that to him, but he wants nothing to keep him from running off to Bethel at the first hint of warmer weather. He believes that mining is a good way to get easy money and wants to do nothing else. His friend Dr. Abbott has already found us a house in Bethel to rent at a good rate, and it's ready for us to move in. Clary would be there today if I would agree to move with young Con, but I won't do it until the snow is gone."

At mention of "easy money," Franny thought of the three crystal gemstones stolen from the Duntons and sold in Boston. The subject had never come up with Lottie, and she wondered whether it might prove argumentative. She wanted to find out if Lottie knew of her husband's dishonesty.

"I hope you don't mind me bringing up something about Clarence, but it has been bothering me for a while. When you and he rushed off from Winchester, Dad and I must have been right behind you. We stopped in Boston for several days so that I might visit places in the city. He took me to see an old friend of his, a lapidary who makes gems from crystals. The man showed us three crystals of tourmaline he was working at the time. He told us the stones were from Maine and that he had purchased them from a friend of Dad's. I knew right away that those were the ones we found that day at Dunton's mine. Clarence had stolen them from the mine and sold them to cover the expenses of your elopement."

"Oh, Clary told me all about that. At first I was angry, but then I realized that he was not trying to make himself rich or anything, but was concerned that our life together not start out in poverty. He also needed to come up with money to send to the parents of his first wife, who are raising his three children in Yarmouth. I couldn't stay angry at him after he explained his motives."

"Dad is concerned with his honesty, but I don't think the other partners in the mines know anything about it. Didn't want to give him a bad reputation."

"Oh, he's honest to a fault. He told me that he took a few gold nuggets from the Nova Scotia gold mine where he worked after his wife died. He didn't have to tell me, but he wanted me to know. That time, too, he had to find some money for his kids. He sends a sum to them every month. How can I be angry or not trust him? He has a heart of gold."

Lottie looked into Franny's eyes with an expression that revealed her complete devotion to her husband and acceptance of his flaws. "He is so kind and generous to his children up in Yarmouth, children who have been taken from him by Canadian law and whom he may never see again, I can have no doubts about being able to raise a family with him. He is the love of my life. I hope that you will find a man as good as this one for your own someday."

Franny had nothing further to say in light of Lottie's complete devotion to Clarence. It was possible she herself was wrong about the man and that, as Lottie said, his stealing arose from the desire to be a good father and husband. Still, in her heart she felt that the man needed to be watched.

75

Nathan sat in his carriage at the foot of Beech Hill on Greene Road waiting for Clarence. The momentum of spring was building, and the day's warmth melted snowdrifts along the road so quickly that gurgling runlets splashed down the gullies on either side. At last he spied the miner riding in the distance. Sprays of water were being thrown up by the horse's hooves each time they hit the ground. When Clarence arrived, his boots and pants were soaked and pocked with mud.

"No need to ride so hard," said Nathan. "I would have waited for you as long as it took. Sitting here has given me a chance to observe how the world is changing with the seasons."

"No time like the present to get this mining season under way, my friend. Winter has been so damn long. Before I came down here from Ontario, I was told to expect an easier winter, but now it's clear that the Old Man will have his way even in Maine. Wasn't it you who sold me on the idea of a mild winter?"

"No. Not me. It must have been your wife. She comes from Massachusetts, where it hardly ever snows."

The men chuckled and chatted as they rode uphill toward the rocky summit. When Aphia's small farmhouse came into view, neither looked forward to what they knew was going to be an uncomfortable meeting with its owner. If they were going to make a go of the mica mine above her pasture, a legal agreement was needed to allow their wagons to run across the corner of her lot. Abbott had given them the freedom of offering $500 for her to grant a temporary right-of-way to them, a large sum for such a small privilege. Clarence had a written agreement with him. As manager of the prospect, he was to be the one to ask permission. Nathan, who was known to the woman, was there as a witness.

Pulling up to the front door, the men dismounted and inspected the place, looking for evidence that Aphia was at home. Clarence stepped to the granite landing and knocked. There was no answer, so he knocked again. As they looked at each other, shrugged their shoulders and turned to leave, Aphia jumped from the door of her woodshed with a small pistol aimed at them. Instinctively, they held their arms straight up in the air.

"Miss Stevens, you've no need of that gun," said Nathan. "We're here to discuss some business with you, not to harm you."

"Business is it? What business?" She lowered the pistol to her side. When Clarence moved closer to her, the pistol came up again.

He stepped back and spoke loudly. "Miss, my name is Clarence Potter. I am new to this area. I believe you know this man, Nathan Hallett." As she squinted at Nathan, he continued. "Miss, we have come to speak with you about the mica prospect we own above your field. Our partner, Dr. Abbott, spoke with you of our plans this past summer. Do you recall him?"

Putting her pistol into her apron pocket, Aphia stepped closer to the men and said, "Yes, I remember a man who came here and so arrogantly spoke about wanting to cross my land. I drove him away. The nerve of him." She still studied Nathan's features as if trying to remember where they might have met. "Your friend does look familiar. How do I know you, mister?"

"We met at Bill Watson's box factory in the city some time ago. I was with my wife and children. Bill is a good friend."

"Oh, yes. Now I remember. Isn't your wife a Millett born here in Waterford? Isn't she a sister to that fancy seamstress Lizzie Millett from Westbrook?"

Nathan did not like the way this introduction was going, but he had to make the best of it in order to get her agreement. "Yes, Miss Stevens. My wife and her sister were both born in Waterford." He kept his answer simple, hoping to end her questioning. Apparently, it worked.

"Mr. Potter, I do not have all day to entertain you. What is it that you are offering for use of my land?"

"Miss, we are only in need of crossing a small corner of your unused pasture. Most of our access will be on Greene Road, which is a public way."

"Am I supposed to accept the racket of wagons back and forth past my house at all hours and horses dirtying the road for me to clean up?"

"Miss, we will clean anything that lands on the road surface and repair all marks on the right-of-way. We want to be a good neighbor to you and everyone else along the route."

"What use is it for me to argue? You will get your way. Everyone knows the town will go along with you—they always do. What are you offering me for the pleasure of allowing a crew of ill-mannered miners to make a mess of my land?"

"I am authorized to make a one-time cash payment of three hundred dollars to you, if you will approve the paperwork." He pulled the contract from his jacket pocket and passed it toward her with a pen. Nathan was pleased that the additional $200 was being held back for negotiation.

"Whoever authorized that amount must think me a fool. I may be a woman, but I am not going to be inconvenienced for a mere pittance. Go back and tell that doctor that he can go to hell."

Clarence continued to hold the paper in front of her. "Miss Stevens, I am to be the manager of this mine. My livelihood and that of my wife and children will rely on my being able to work our claim. If you are willing to let me do my job, I promise to do it in a way that is the least offensive and respects your property. Please accept my final offer of *five* hundred dollars and approve this document."

She stared at him for a moment and then at Nathan, who said nothing. "Mr. Potter, though it grieves me to agree, I will approve your contract, not so much for you or your doctor friend, but as a way of doing something in return for an affront I made long ago to Mr. Hallett's family. Please let seamstress Millett know that I do this for her."

That said, Aphia led them into her house, where she sat at her kitchen table to sign. Clarence gave her the cash and reached out to shake her hand, but she refused. Instead, she leaned in close to Nathan and whispered, "No need to let anyone else know about my reasoning. Let it just be between me, you, and the seamstress."

76

In the months after Moses's death, business at Millett's American Designs dropped off precipitously. With the transfer of the house and shop in Saco to new owners, orders came mainly from Lizzie's local customers and word of mouth. There was enough work to keep her and Francena busy most days, but she had more free time than at any other time in her life. When spring arrived, she was able to enjoy sightseeing trips to nearby Portland, peaceful walks on the shore of Highland Lake, and an excursion to Riverton Trolley Park with the Cain family. She spent hours sitting on the front porch watching the world go by and reading, something that she had enjoyed all her life.

For the first time since Hattie's children were young, she spent hours enjoying the company of a young toddler. She often babysat little Clarence Conrad. He was quite big for his age and full of so much energy that she was often very tired at the end of the day. On one warm early evening, she rested on the porch swing after putting the boy to bed. Will and Maeve emerged from the well-worn path between their house and hers.

"Lizzie, how are you this nice spring day? We've been out for a walk to clear our heads—mine in particular," said Will.

"What seems to be the matter, Will?"

"I received a letter today from Bert Learned's sister in Epping, New Hampshire. She tells me that she, too, has heard nothing from our old friend for over a year. He has just dropped off the face of the earth."

"Last summer, Nathan told me Bert had been sweet on Aphia Stevens, if you can believe that," said Liz.

Maeve came up to the porch and sat next to her friend. "We

heard that story, also. Now, I never met the man, but from what Will says about him, he wouldn't be the type to fall head over heels for a loony like that one."

Will walked up and perched on the railing. "She *is* quite pretty, and he has always had an eye for a pretty woman. The man who told that tale to Nathan, Mr. Watson, is supposedly a good, honest Christian. I've known him since I was in long pants, and I trust his word. But, gosh, even if Bert fell in love with her, once he learned enough about her mad ways, he would have dropped her. He wouldn't run away."

"Remember," said Liz, "he did run off and turn to drink after the tragic death of his wife and son in the house fire. How long was he gone? Must have been a couple of years. Yet, he was done with his demons, from what Nathan said."

"Yes, he was living a good, righteous life, as far as I know." Will rubbed his hands together. "We got together once in a while. He was doing well. That's why I wrote to the sister. If she hasn't seen hide nor hair of him for a year or more, I have to believe something bad has happened to him."

Liz rose from her seat and brushed the folds in her dress. "I'm not sure what we can do to find out more. Nathan said no one has suspicions of foul play. If there were, the sheriff would have looked into it. And Miss Stevens is certainly not going to provide any information."

Will descended the steps as he spoke. "I know both you and Maeve do not want me to get involved with the woman. You've told me several times. Please forgive me, but I will be going over to Waterford sometime soon to do some digging of my own into what happened to Bert."

"I can't stop you," said Liz. "You must be careful not to let your investigation get you into trouble. Perhaps you might contact the sheriff and get his advice."

Maeve followed after her husband. "Will, don't you dig so deep a hole that you can't get out of it. We need you around here."

77

Francena hurried into the kitchen, where Liz was preparing dinner. She was in such a rush that she caught her foot on a table leg and almost fell. "Auntie, you must come with me! There's someone at the door to see you, a wild-looking woman who has tied her horse to our railing out front." Her words came so rapidly and at such a high pitch, Liz could not understand her.

"Slow down, girl. You'll hurt yourself. Now, take a deep breath and start over."

"I'm sorry, but you really need to come with me right now. I answered a loud knock on the front door and saw this woman standing there. She is *wild*-looking. She shouted at me that she wants to see you immediately. Said you know what it's about."

As Liz walked into the shop with her niece close behind, she was shocked to see Aphia Stevens, who had entered the room and now stood next to one of the design tables. She was dressed all in black from her knee-high leather boots to the sweaty kerchief that held back her hair. Her black dress was dirty with mud spatters along the hemline, and large sweat marks had formed under her arms. Jammed behind a sash at her waist, the handle of a pistol was clearly visible. At Liz's entry, she laughed maniacally and drew her arm across the table, scattering papers and pencils about the room.

"I warned you, Miss! I warned you the last time I was here. You were not to delve into my private life anymore. You paid no attention to my warning. Now I am back."

Liz stood stock-still, then pushed Francena back into the kitchen. "Miss Stevens. Aphia Stevens, get out of my house." She pointed to the open front door, but remained standing near the kitchen entry ready to jump out of the way if her visitor became violent. "You are not welcome here," she said firmly.

"Miss Lizzie," Aphia sneered, "I'm likely as welcome here as you and your friends are at *my* house." Her voice grew louder. "Why do you continue to torment me? Send your friends to investigate me? I'm the one who should be angry, not you."

186

"I don't know what you're talking about, Aphia. There has been no effort on my part to bother you. Now, please leave my house—right now!"

The wild woman turned, screamed, and rushed toward Liz with both arms in the air, but Liz held her ground and put up her own hands to fight off the attack. Aphia suddenly came to a dead halt within a foot of her target and put her right hand on the gun handle. "My dear," she said quite calmly, "I have brought my Colt pistol with me. I am skilled at its use. Do not put me in a position to draw it."

Liz said nothing and lowered her hands to her sides. Franny, who had exited the kitchen and entered the office from the rear, poked her head out from behind one of the sewing machines.

"Miss Millett, I understand that your husband has died. I would not want you to join him so early in your life. Now listen to me very, very carefully. You are not to send your man Nathan Hallett, his friend Potter, or any other of your people to bother me anymore. This is the second time I have warned you, and I want it to be the last. They came to my place on the pretense of getting permission to cross my land. They even gave me money to be cooperative. But I am not easily fooled, miss. I know what you're doing. You are trying to get even with me for stealing your fiancé. Now that you are alone again, you want to ruin my life so that it is as miserable as your own."

Liz stared at her assailant in disbelief. Yet, she said nothing, realizing the potential danger that threatened Franny and herself. What could she say to reason with a person who was insane? She went along with Aphia's demands. "Miss, I apologize for the intrusion in your life made by my friends. It was not at my request, I assure you. I will warn them against bothering you anymore."

"I'm glad you see my situation, Miss Millett. You must realize that I do not need any help in making myself miserable." With that said, she turned abruptly, dashed through the open door, and jumped back up on her horse. Before riding off, she smiled at Liz and shouted, "Please forgive the mess I made of your shop!"

Franny came out of hiding and grabbed her aunt's hand. "What is wrong with that woman?"

78

Clarence and Lottie's rental was a little raised cape located on the noisy corner of Railroad and Bridge Streets. Even though it was a temporary home, Lottie did everything she could to put her stamp of ownership on it. She hung heavy curtains on the front windows to cut down on the sound of trains and wagons traveling past at all hours. Mismatched pieces of old furniture that came with the place were not completely to her liking, but they could not afford many new pieces. She was able to make the place more comfortable by moving some pieces to the garage, painting others, and covering the sofa and stuffed chairs with colorful throws. Clarence was pleased with the place because it was close to Newry and within a day's journey of Beech Hill. He didn't plan on spending very much time there.

One morning, as Lottie returned from shopping with her son, she was surprised to see a young man standing at her door with his bicycle leaning against the house. He was knocking on the door as she approached.

"Good day, sir," she said. "What can I do for you?"

"Ma'am, I have a telegram for Miss Lottie Ritchie. Be that you?"

"Yes, though my married name is Potter, not Ritchie."

He handed her an envelope. "Please sign for it with your maiden name. I am only supposed to give a telegram to the addressee. Could be trouble for me if I don't follow the rules."

She put the message in her shopping basket and went into the kitchen, first setting the basket down on the table and then placing Con in his high chair. She opened the envelope and began to read.

DEAREST DAUGHTER. STOP. I HOPE THE ADDRESS IS CORRECT. STOP. I GOT IT FROM NATHAN HALLETT.

STOP. IT PAINS ME TO TELL YOU YOUR MOTHER HAS
DIED SUDDENLY FROM A FALL AND CEREBRAL HEMOR-
RHAGING. STOP. IF IT IS AT ALL POSSIBLE PLEASE
COME HOME TO HELP ME. STOP. YOUR FATHER.

"Oh, my God!" she said aloud, falling into a chair. Her mind was racing. She had never gotten along with Mary, but she did love her. Her father would be devastated and would need help getting his life back together. Tears flooded her eyes as she knelt beside the chair and prayed for the soul of her mother and for her grieving father. What could she do? There was her own family to consider now, and she was sure that Clarence would not be able to travel during his busy season. She would have to carry her son on the journey unless other arrangements could be made. Perhaps Liz and Franny would be willing to take him for a few days…

When Clarence learned of the predicament, he at first wanted to accompany her and the boy back to Winchester. He thought it would be a good opportunity to mend bridges with John, especially now that the mother who hated him was gone.

"Clary, you are kind to offer, but how can you do that at this time? You just opened the pit again and have already taken on a crew. Wouldn't Dunton and the other partners have your head if you left for a week or so?"

"It would create many problems for the mine and for myself," he acknowledged. "No question about that. Yet, we have always talked about healing the wounds caused by our elopement. This would be the time to do that."

"Dad would appreciate your effort at reconciliation, but he would think less of you once he realized you were walking away from your responsibilities. He has always demanded I follow through on commitments even if it was difficult. No, you must stay and make a living."

Clarence sighed. "You are right, my dear. I'm sure there will be other chances to make my amends. I can go with you to Westbrook to ask Miss Liz to help by caring for Con while you're away.

I can also make all of the travel arrangements for you. At least I can assist in some way."

"Tomorrow you will send two telegrams, one to Lizzie and one to Dad. Tell him I will let him know when I might arrive in Boston. Tell her that we would like to visit her and Francena this weekend, and ask if they will take Con for a few days."

Though the thought of traveling all that way alone was daunting, there wasn't anything else to do. She did love her father, and both she and Clarence wanted to make up for the pain they had caused him. By the time the family left for Westbrook two weeks later, she was confident that she would enjoy a few days on her own despite the tiring journey. If she had been able to make it all the way down from Cobalt during the worst of winter, a springtime trip to Massachusetts should prove to be a lark.

79

By the time the Potters arrived in Westbrook, it was late afternoon. Both Lottie and her son were asleep in the rear of the chaise Clarence had borrowed from Dr. Abbott. Clarence reined in the horse at Lizzie's front door and stepped down from the driver's seat. He stood for a moment watching his sleeping family, as Franny came out to the porch to greet them.

"Clarence, you must wake them and come inside before it gets dark and chilly," said Franny. "You certainly have made a full day of it, haven't you?"

"I'll let Lottie tell you all about what a wonderful day we had," he said as he woke his family.

When Lottie saw her dear friend, she handed her son to Clarence, climbed down from the carriage, and mounted the steps to wrap her arms around Franny. The boy was so tired that he continued to sleep in his father's arms.

"Dearie," said Franny, "you took forever to get here. Were there any problems along the way?"

Smiling from ear to ear, Lottie replied, "Not at all. The weather was perfect. We saw such beautiful spring displays along the way, and we just had to stop and enjoy the scenery. Come, let's go inside where I can fill you in on the marvelous Maine sights we visited."

They strolled into the house arm in arm, leaving Clarence to take care of the boy, unload the bags, and put the horse in the barn. Liz came to his rescue by taking the sleeping child in her arms and carrying him inside. When Clarence returned to the house, a full dinner was set out on the kitchen table, and the two young women had begun to eat while still talking. They would not stop even when Liz sat down with the infant in her lap and spoke to them.

"Girls, please stop your chattering for a moment so that Lottie can tell me what she wants to do with this little darling. Since you two don't seem up to serving Mr. Potter a plate of dinner, I would also like to take care of that."

"Oh, Aunt Liz," said Franny, "give that little fellow to me. After all, I will have to entertain him for the next few days. Might as well get started." She rose and took the boy in her arms just as he awoke and started to squirm and cry. Lottie reached out for him, but Franny shook her head. "No, I can handle him. You just relax and enjoy the meal we've prepared for you. I have a cookie to please this little one."

The next day, Clarence drove Lottie to Riverton Park, where she would board a trolley to Union Station for the train to Boston. On the way, she gave him a list of things to be done in her absence. At the platform, they stood holding hands while they waited for the trolley to arrive.

"Do you have enough money? I have more cash. Just in case, please take this hundred."

"No, Clary, I don't need any more money. You have already given me much more than it will take. I'm only going to Boston, and we already have the round-trip ticket. I'll be fine. It is you I worry about. Make sure you get enough to eat. And don't work all the time just because you are alone for a few days."

"I'll be fine, but I will miss you. The worst part will be sleeping alone. Hope I'm able to get enough sound sleep, and not lie awake all night thinking of you."

"Silly boy. You're so sweet to say that. You will be fine. All three of us will be fine. I will send you a telegram when I know the date of my return."

80

When Lottie's train pulled into Boston's North Station, all four platforms bustled with activity. There were people running and hollering, whistles and bells sounding, so much commotion that she became confused. In the two years she had been living in Canada and Maine, she had become accustomed to a rural way of life. The rush of an urban scene was no longer to her liking. After stepping from the coach and claiming her duffel, she proceeded to the front of the station on Causeway Street, expecting to quickly find her father and get out of the pandemonium. The furious hubbub continued unabated as passengers carried luggage to and from waiting wagons. There were several buggies, with no horses in front of them, moving quickly, making loud noises and puffing smoke from their back ends. She had heard of motorcars, but seeing them was a shock.

The crowd finally thinned enough for her to identify her father standing directly across the street in front of a theater. She waved to him, but he didn't see her until she walked almost up to his carriage. He looked as if he had aged a decade in the two years since she'd left.

"Daddy, what a ruckus there is here in the city! How things have changed." He stepped down from the carriage, nearly losing his balance. She reached for his hand. "Are you okay, Father?"

"I guess I am just so excited to see you that I wasn't concentrating on where I put my feet." He reached for her bag, but she put it on the buggy herself. "You've grown much taller than I remember, Lottie. And you look so healthy. The northern climate must be good for you." When he put his arm around her shoulders and leaned in to kiss her cheek, she felt his tears on her face. She could not remember that he'd ever cried before. "Your mother never thought she would see you again. I tried to tell her that you would come back to see us when you were ready, but she went to her grave thinking you were lost to us."

"Daddy," she said as her own tears welled up, "I didn't want to hurt you, either of you, but you both refused to believe I had found my love in Clarence. Would she even accept it to this day?" She hugged his chest, her tears wetting his shirt. When the show let out at the theater behind them, people stopped to stare. Finally she pulled away. "Let's go home. We've made spectacle enough of ourselves."

As they mounted the carriage, John turned to her and said, "Whether or not she would accept the truth today is unimportant. We are here together because I *do* accept it. Now, tell me about my grandson."

81

By early June, the summer sun had melted any remaining snow in the shady patches of underbrush on the muddy pathway to the pit. Runoff and groundwater springs filled the gaping hole, requiring two gas-powered motors to constantly pump water into rivulets across the mine's refuse piles. Early-season work was tedious, and Clarence had difficulty finding local men and boys who were willing to work knee-deep in mud and cold water. When crew members failed to show for the day, he was forced to do much of the work himself. He would take his place at one of the pumps, directing the flow into a dump. Occasionally, a small crystal that had been overlooked in the excavations would be exposed in the debris. Whenever he saw one, he would turn off the pump and slog through the sludge to retrieve the valuable speck. Once the water was drained, the crew began the strenuous work of clearing an overburden of muddy soil and gravel, stumps and roots in an area that would then be dynamited. This was work the men could handle on their own. They were farmers and used to clearing land for pasture and planting. Clarence felt comfortable leaving at this point and returning to the opening of the Beech Hill mine in Waterford 25 miles to the south.

During the previous visit to North Waterford, he had rented a small room at Mr. Lewis's boardinghouse in the village center. It would save him the long ride home on summer days when he might work from dawn to dark. With both Lottie and his son away, he decided to spend several days in town, where he could recruit local men to work for him.

On the first day, he rode to the site on his own, and as he passed the Stevens place, he saw Aphia rise from her garden work to stare. He waved to her, but got no response. Just as well, he thought. The less contact I have with her, the better. When he reached the muddy right-of-way across the woman's lot, he turned back and saw that she was standing on a small hill at the low end of the pasture with hands on hips, continuing to stare. He thought it might be best to let her know who he was and why he was there before going any further, so he turned the horse and rode back toward her. As he approached, he noticed that she held her pistol in one hand.

"Miss Stevens," he hollered, and raised his hand in greeting. She pointed her pistol in his direction. "Miss, I am Clarence Potter, the miner with whom you met several months ago. Remember? I was with your neighbor, Nathan Hallett."

"My neighbor, you say? I know no neighbor of that name." She continued to stare and squint into the sun as her visitor came closer. "Come no nearer, sir. I warn you."

"Ma'am, you and I have an agreement that I and my crew may cross the corner of your pasture to gain access to our mica prospect on top of the hill beyond. I paid you five hundred dollars, and you signed the agreement. You do remember, don't you?"

"Oh, yes. An agreement. I do remember, and I will live by my bargain with you, Mr. Potter. But before you begin to mess up my land, I want *you* to agree to do one more thing. You must place a fence or a row of stones on either side of your access. You must promise to stay within those curbs or else I will void our agreement. Is that clear, sir?"

He stayed mounted and gazed down on her. He was angry at her demands, but wanted to keep the peace. Annoying this mad woman would cost the mine partners valuable time—and increase the risk of getting shot, as well. "Yes, ma'am. I will do as you say. Those markers will be set up as soon as we start working. Right now, I'm here to inspect the site and will carefully cross your land on foot, leaving my horse tied to a tree on the edge of this public road."

Aphia dropped the Colt to her side and waved him off. "Begone with you. Cross on foot if you must. I will inspect after you have gone to make sure you've stayed within the path and not done any damage. I've too much to do in my gardens to waste any more time with you today." She turned her back and walked away.

Clarence said nothing, but rode back up the hill to a large oak at the road verge, where he tied the horse. The shady ground was still somewhat slushy. Perhaps tomorrow would be the final day before the ground would be firm enough to support the equipment wagons. Small pines and hemlocks were starting to take over once again. It would not be easy work to open the ground because of all the stumps left by farmer Kimball two years before. Kicking at several muddy branches and looking at the ground beneath them, he was able to see small crystals of mica reflecting the high sun. To find such small amounts of the flaky mineral was not proof of the quantity and quality of what lay beneath the forest duff, but when he picked one up that was two inches by four inches and peeled back one of its pages, he believed there was a good prospect for success.

82

In the nearly two weeks that Lottie had been away, Clarence
had heard nothing from her about returning. He was beginning to worry that something had gone wrong. Franny was also
concerned because she had expected that the responsibility of
caring for little Con would last only a few days. Both received a
letter from Massachusetts on the same day. Clarence's read:

Dearest Clarence,

So much has happened here in Winchester that I do not
know where to begin. Father has been so kind in welcom-
ing me back to my old home. I thought he might have held
a grudge, but he only wishes us well. Can you believe that?
While I have been here, he has put the house on the market at
a price which should make it sell quickly. We have been packing up all his belongings, including furniture, in preparation
for his move to an apartment in Boston. I haven't seen it yet,
but he says it is quite the high-brow place near the Statehouse
on Beacon Hill. I told him he would become a grand mucky-
muck.

My apologies to you and of course to Franny and her
aunt for my staying so long. I will return to Portland on June
1. Hopefully you won't mind that I have invited Dad to join
us for a short vacation. He is in need of some time away, so he
will be returning with me.

I have sent a letter to Westbrook with all of this information. They will expect us to stay over on the night of my return.

I hope you haven't been working from dawn to dark
every day.

In love,
Your Lottie

I know I should be grateful John has forgiven us, Clarence
thought as he fried an egg for supper, but having him as our
house guest is unwise. What if he has only forgiven *her*, but not
me? Where will he sleep? There is only the one bedroom. What is
she thinking?

When Lottie's letter arrived in Westbrook, Franny and Lizzie both had a similar reaction. "My God," said Franny. "She is so headstrong and independent. What can Clarence be thinking right now?"

"I'm sure he's a bit nervous about having his father-in-law in their tiny house for very long," said her aunt. "I think there will be some reckoning when she gets home."

83

"Lottie! Over here!" Clarence shouted as Lottie and John stepped off the Boston and Maine platform at Union Station. After waiting for two hours among other carriages and wagons in the heat of St. John Street, he was relieved to see them and anxious to get away from the stench of horse manure.

She saw him and rushed to his side with her father following at a slower pace.

"Clary, my darling. I missed you so," she said as he grabbed her in his arms and gave her a long kiss—which she returned with equal passion until John reached them.

"Mr. Ritchie, I'm happy to see you looking so well," greeted Clarence, reaching out to shake hands. "It has been a long time."

John looked the miner up and down as if he was having trouble recognizing him. "Yes, Mr. Potter. It has been a long time. My daughter and I were just speaking about the circumstances of our last encounter. Perhaps that is best forgotten."

"Please call me by my given name. We're family, after all."

"Yes, family. Hmm. I guess you are correct, Clarence. And please call me John."

A porter brought over two large steamer trunks. "What's this?" asked Clarence. "Have you been shopping down there in Boston?"

"No. I really didn't have need of anything. These are Dad's trunks. He's brought some items he wants to leave with us, as well as his clothes and a few other things. I want him to be comfortable, you know."

As he loaded the trunks one on top of the other into the rear compartment of his borrowed brougham, Clarence couldn't help but wonder how much of the contents were actually John's clothes and "a few other things" and how long the visit would last. Lottie had yet to mention whose idea it had been for him to come. When he had successfully secured the trunks and her two bags with a length of rope purchased from a nearby teamster, he gestured for her to come with him and speak in private on the opposite side of the carriage.

"You know I have missed you deeply and that I am very relieved to have you home once again." She nodded her head in agreement. "But I have to ask how this visit came about. Did you invite him, or did he ask to come?"

"It was my idea. He has gone through a very rough time since Mother passed. He is so lonely and has been unable to go to work. I would call it melancholy, but he says it is just a stage in his grieving. I know I should have spoken with you, but how would I have done that?"

"Do you want him to stay until his grief passes? How long might that take?"

"Clarence, I have no idea. Perhaps when he has a chance to meet little Con and sees how cramped our house will be, he will leave. I must do something to help him. He is my father." She began to sob on his chest as he embraced her.

"Please don't cry. We shouldn't make a public scene. We can discuss it more when we're alone. Now, let's all get going to Westbrook while the sun is still out."

On the ride west, the couple sat together on the high bench, while John lay across the seat of the enclosed passenger compartment and napped. Lottie was so happy to be back in Maine that her mood improved the instant they passed Woodford Street and left the city behind. She related to Clarence all the things that had happened in Massachusetts, where the pace of life was now too fast for her. He had little to say about what had been going on in the two mines, and she didn't ask any questions until they neared Lizzie's.

"Clary, I think it's time we had another baby, don't you?" she asked.

He smiled and took hold of her knee. "Oh, yes. I think it is. I wonder if we will be able to work on that while your dad is in our house."

Franny and little Clarence Conrad, who had been waiting on the porch all day, finally saw the carriage approach. The boy at first began to laugh. When Lottie climbed from the seat, he cried and held his arms out toward her. "Conny, look how you have grown!" She held him up to the window for John to see before passing him to Clarence. "Dad, look how healthy this boy is."

John, who had slept through most of the ride, jumped from the passenger compartment, cut in front of Clarence, and enveloped his grandson in his arms. Clarence stood back, arms to his side, and watched. He knew that he should not be jealous, yet such an aggressive move by his father-in-law brought back the same worry as at the train station: How long will this man be with us?

84

Oxford County Sheriff Moffett stood nose to nose with Dr. Abbott in front of Nason's Store in North Waterford. The good doctor had come to town in response to a request for help made by Clarence following the miner's latest run-in with Aphia Stevens. By chance, Moffett had just tied his horse at the store's hitching post and was walking across the street. Abbott and the sheriff had met many times in Bethel, where they both lived, and since they were both Democrats, had gotten along well. This time, it was a different story.

"Sheriff, what brings you to this little village? I was planning to call on you at your office, but you have saved me the ride."

"Doctor, what a pleasure to see you this fine summer day. I see you've survived the winter once more."

"And you are looking well. And the wife?"

Before the sheriff had time to respond, Abbott launched into a complaint. "I want your help to protect my employees from threats by a crazy woman up on Beech Hill. She has drawn a gun twice on two of my men who were going about their business in a mining prospect just past her place on Greene Road. Twice this has happened! The woman is a menace, I tell you." By this time the doctor stood directly in front of Moffett, blocking his path.

"Hold on here, Abbott. Calm down and help me understand what has happened. Where is the mine? Do you own the property? Does the woman have a right to complain about something your partners may have done? Is this woman that same Aphia Stevens who Bill Watson has told me about? The one who seems a bit loony?"

The doctor, taken aback by the interrogation, backed away. "Why are you asking me all these questions? If you've heard about her from Selectman Watson, then you know she is completely *mad*, not just loony. My mine manager paid the woman good money to allow us to access the mine site across one corner of her property. We have a signed agreement with her."

"Okay, I've heard that she is unbalanced. Threats made toward other people with a gun is much more serious than previous complaints. I may ride up to her place and get her side of the story."

Satisfied that some action would be taken to control Aphia, Abbott shook hands with the sheriff and returned to his horse as Moffett continued into the store.

Later that day, Moffett rode out to Aphia's house, stopping a few hundred yards from her gate. Nothing was going on outside the place, but smoke rising from the chimney led him to believe that someone was at home. He approached the gate, dismounted, and tied his horse to the gate post.

Aphia, watching the rider from her front window, came to the door but didn't open it. When the man knocked, she opened the door a crack, just enough to see a badge on the visitor's coat.

"Miss Stevens, I am Oxford County Sheriff Amos Moffett. I'm

here because of a complaint made about you by one of the owners of a mine up that hill."

"Sheriff, I wondered when those trespassers would stir up trouble. They've been bothering me for a year or more."

He could hardly make out her words through the small opening. "Ma'am, please open the door and speak to me directly."

Before complying, she pulled the pistol from her apron pocket and hid it in the pocket of her storm coat, which hung on a rack beside the door. The sheriff stepped up onto the threshold and began to inspect the interior of the house. There was very little furniture in the place, but he could see a number of large, bubbling kettles on the cookstove and a good-sized still on top of a wide plank table. The fumes of whatever was in those kettles made him cough and then sneeze.

"Miss Stevens, Dr. Hiram Abbott of Bethel assures me that his partners have an affidavit signed by you allowing his crew to use a right-of-way across your land. Is that correct?" He sneezed once again, drawing a handkerchief from his pants pocket and blowing his nose.

Noticing his discomfort, Aphia said, "I'm sorry if my herbs are irritating your nasal passages. Perhaps we should step back outside to have our discussion."

"No. No, I'm okay. I only need to sit down for a moment to catch my breath." He was feeling a little dizzy, but wanted to stay inside long enough to get a better inspection of what she was doing in the kitchen.

"I must insist that we step outside," said Aphia. "If you have no warrant to inspect my home, I insist."

"Ma'am, I have not come here to pry into your affairs other than to clarify the legal arrangements you have or don't have with Abbott and his miners. Do you have an agreement? Did they pay you a fair sum for access?"

"Yes, the miners and I have an agreement of sorts. I erroneously signed the paperwork before getting assurance that only a well-marked path will be used. These miners usually leave an awful mess wherever they work. One of them, a Mr. Potter, was here the other day and said he would carefully mark their wagon path and make sure no other areas were used, but I don't trust him."

"Miss, I will see to it that the crew clearly designates the right-of-way and that the path be fully repaired when they finish. If other areas of your land are entered and damaged, it would be customary to have them pay you more than the original amount. I will see to that, if it happens. However, I want you to agree not to threaten these men with a gun as they go to and from their site. Will you agree to that?"

She walked past him, leading him out the door as she responded. "If the miners go about their work without pestering me, and they stay within the right-of-way, they will get no threats from me. I don't want to use my pistol, but I do have to protect myself. I will do what is needed. Now, would you please leave so that I may return to my work? I have broken no law that I know of unless you people have come up with some new ones recently."

As the sheriff walked away, his head was spinning, and by the time he reached the gate, he had to lean against the fence to regain his balance. He had no idea what the woman was cooking in there, but it had to be something quite powerful. After a moment, he mounted and rode away, making a mental note to return to inspect the right-of-way and to keep an eye on this odd woman.

85

Lottie sat on the square stone terrace her father had laid between the rear of her house and the lawn, where Conny played on a worn woolen blanket. John had gone for a walk into Bethel Center, leaving her alone for the first time in three days. Clarence was in Waterford once again, where he had been most of the time since her return from Massachusetts. She wondered if she really had to work that much on the Beech Hill mine, or whether he was trying to keep away from the crowded house. Their tiny cape had a kitchen to the right of the entry, and on the left a parlor that had been temporarily converted to a guest bedroom. Behind the central brick beehive oven was the couple's bedroom, shared with the boy for the time being. When four people were under the roof at the same time, the only way of keeping out of everyone else's way was to stay outdoors. Thank goodness it was summer.

Conny was his grandfather's pride and joy. In Clarence's prolonged absences, the boy became strongly attached to his granddad.

John came around the side of the house with a small apple in his hand. "Conny, look what I have for you." He walked past his daughter as if she was invisible. "You'll like the flavor of this Baldwin," he said. "I got it from the fruit man just for you."

"Dad, you know he can't very well chew on that. Let me slice off a few pieces for him to nibble on."

"Oh, Lottie. I didn't see you there. I can do that for him with my pocket knife."

As John began to slice into the apple, Clarence appeared inside the back door. He watched the three others in silence for several minutes before making his presence known.

"My dear," he addressed Lottie and went to her side. "So grateful to be home again." He held out both hands to her.

"Clary, you're back! What a surprise!" She stood and took his hands before throwing herself into his arms. For a moment, they were oblivious to everything around them, until John approached with the child in his arms.

"Here, Clarence, take your son from me. He's getting so heavy."

Passing Con to his dad, John stood back and peered at the three. "You certainly make a wonderful family. Such a blessing to an old man."

Surprised at how Con had grown in the short time he had been away, Clarence put his hands under the boy's arms and held him up for inspection. "What a handsome lad you are," he said with a big grin. "You'll be joining your dad in the mines before we know it."

"I know you're joking" said Lottie, "but just in case, I certainly am against child labor." At that, they all laughed, even the child.

Later that night, after Con was in bed, the three adults sat in lawn chairs next to the garden while the men enjoyed their pipes. Lottie sat off a bit from them to avoid the tobacco smoke as much as possible.

"I think it's time for me to return to work," announced John. "The time here in the country has brought peace unto my soul. Given me a chance to recover from my grief."

"Dad, are you sure? You know we welcome your company, and Con loves you so," said Lottie. "I think I speak for both of us when I say you might stay as long as you wish."

Clarence said nothing at first, considering his response very carefully before speaking. "John, you are certainly welcome here, but I can appreciate a man's need to get back to his work. I'm sure your patients have missed you nearly as much as we have enjoyed your being with us."

"Yes, the time has come to return to my practice and get back to a regular life, such as it will be without Mary. Besides, it's time that the three of you had your own life back. You have been lovingly putting up with my presence long enough."

Over the next two days, arrangements were made for John to return to Portland and then to Boston. On the night before he was to leave, he and Clarence smoked together, sitting on the front step. They watched wagons and carts run back and forth to the train station and waved to neighbors who walked by on the hot late-July evening.

"John, please feel free to come back for a visit whenever the spirit moves you. I know we had a rough start to our relationship, but now I feel that you are part of my American family."

"Yes, both Mary and I resented the manner in which you entered our lives. She was especially outraged. Likely, she never forgave you. But I have now had the chance to know you as a good husband and a caring father. You are a hard worker and will make your family secure. This has been a good visit, but there is only room for one man of the house. That is, until the little one grows up. Then you will be in trouble."

"Don't worry," said Clarence. "We will have a bigger house by that time."

86

In the days following her father's departure, Lottie enjoyed her family life more than ever before. She watched as Clarence and Con played together in the evenings after supper, pleased that her husband seemed to dote on his son. The couple had never been closer, their lovemaking never so passionate and tender, and their chats about the future never so hopeful. Clarence was off to the gem mine each morning at dawn, but unlike the days earlier in the year, he returned each night eager for supper and a chance to be with his family. One afternoon, however, he arrived home at two p.m. in a sullen mood.

"Is there something wrong?" Lottie asked him.

"No, I'm just tired. Not feeling well today."

"Did something bad happen at the mine today? You look so down and sad. And you're home very early."

"Well, Hallett was in the office today to start the tally of production for the season. We separated all the expense sheets, time cards, and production reports. He hasn't added everything up, but it looks to me like we may not have made a profit this year. Big disappointment."

"Oh, I'm sure you're worrying for no reason. When will the accounting be finished? Don't be in such a rush to be dispirited."

"Maybe you're right. Nathan will be there again tomorrow to finish the books. I'll wait to see his results. The thing that bothers me is not so much the expenses or labor costs. Those were expected to go up. It's the production that bothers me. We didn't find as many marketable crystals as Dunton expected. There were lots of tourmalines dug, but the quality was not there—not enough gemmy ones."

Lottie walked to his side and put her arms around his waist. "Clary, I'm sure the accounting will prove better than you fear. Please take Con outside and play with him for a while. That will take your mind off the mine. It always does."

"Yes. He is such a blessing to us. Maybe we can go for a walk down to the station. He loves to watch the trains and all the busy people there. You know, I'm very glad I have the two jobs. Prospects on Beech Hill look good, even though excavation has only begun. If Dunton's fails, we can always move to Waterford and live off the mica."

He took his son's hand and together they walked out the front door into the fading light of a sunny September afternoon. Lottie knew winter would soon arrive and the three of them would be together most of every day. She prayed that the news from the gem mine would be better than expected so Clarence would rest easier. If not, a move to Waterford would bring her closer to the Halletts, Francena and Lizzie.

87

Clarence and Dr. Abbott met at the Beech Hill site to close it for the season. A local farmer was hired to help, and as he used his brace of oxen to block the entrance with two giant hemlock logs, the two partners chatted. After the worrisome conversation with Nathan about the future of the Newry site, Clarence wanted to get Abbott's evaluation.

"Dr. Abbott, Hallett has told me that the Dunton may not be the prospect you originally expected. He said it might be closed down."

"I wouldn't be as worried as Nathan about the future. Yes, the first year has not been as profitable as expected, but that is often the case with a new mine. Once the overburden is removed, you'll usually see the best prospect is in a different location than was planned. It takes a while to find the true deposits."

"So it does, sir, so it does. I worked on one mine in Ontario where the owners thought they had a good copper vein, but it turned out to be nickel instead. Took nearly two full years to figure out the nickel was worth more than the copper."

"Don't be worrying about the first year. Your job is safe."

Once the heavy work was done, Abbott bid farewell to his manager and headed back to Bethel while the sun was still bright. Clarence and the farmer were left to tidy up the area in order to keep nosy Miss Stevens from finding cause to void their right-of-way agreement. With that done, Clarence had one last errand to complete before leaving. He wanted to rent his room in North Waterford for another season. He would then have a place to rest his weary body and not have to go home each day when spring work began. As he drove his wagon back to town, he passed Aphia's place and noticed a small one-horse shay tied to a hitching post just off the road. Wanting nothing to do with her, he pushed his steed to a fast trot.

There were several boardinghouses in the village center, but the best, in his estimation, was Forest House run by John Rice. It was the only one with an attached stable. He was surprised that, even this late in the season, the hotel was so busy. Mr. Rice explained that with so many new buildings being constructed in town, the Knight sawmill on Crooked River was working six days a week, and several new men working there had taken rooms. Clarence renewed the same room at the end of the building. Its window faced the crossroads of Valley Road and 5 Kezars Road and offered a clear view of the Congregational Church. Beyond the four corners, he saw splashes of reds and yellows, flaming oaks and maples scattered among towering hemlocks. Majestic elm trees planted along both sides of Valley Road were draped in autumn dress of pale yellow. Daylight was already fading, but men were still working on frames for three new houses. In the distance, a white picket fence, the only fence in the village, nicely fronted the one-room schoolhouse and a smaller building next door to it. His plan was to stay the night and return to Bethel in the morning at sunrise, so he would have his supper at Rand's Store on the other side of the intersection.

As he walked downstairs to the street, he heard a commotion and caught site of Aphia Stevens whipping her horse with a crop, driving her buggy too fast. A man who was crossing the road leapt aside to keep from getting pummeled and landed face first in the gutter. The victim jumped up and chased after Stevens yelling, "You witch! You witch! Stop beating that animal!" When the wagon slowed, he jumped in front of the Morgan, grabbing its halter and bringing the animal and wagon to a sharp stop. When he attempted to pull the reins from the driver's hands, she began to strike *him* with the crop.

"Back off, you brute! You have no right to stop me! Back off or I'll make you pay for your insolence." She swung the crop at him again, but he grabbed it and pulled her off the wagon. She fell to her knees in the dust.

"You could've killed me, you witch! What gives you the almighty right to ride through the village like it was a racetrack? There are children playing in the street. Look there." He pointed to a mother pushing a carriage and two small children walking behind her.

As Clarence watched, a crowd gathered around the scene and began to egg the victim on to punish the woman. One young man in short pants threw a stone at Stevens. Another kicked dust in her direction. When a woman stepped forward and grabbed her by the hair, Clarence thought the crowd would kill her if no one stopped them. "Hold on!" he shouted, stepping into the street. "Don't hurt the poor woman."

"Poor woman, you say?" said an old woman who sat on the Rand's Store porch. "She really is a witch. Sits up there in her cabin on the mountain making God knows what. *Remedies*, she calls them, but they're poisons. You're from away. You don't know how evil this one is."

Voices were raised at the mention of Aphia's concoctions,

and people stepped back in fear. The victim took his hands off her and broke the crop in two, throwing it back in her face.

She took advantage of being free for the moment to reach into a canvas bag that had fallen on the road beside her. She threw some white powder into his face, then a second handful into the crowd. The man grabbed his face and fell to the ground. He began to thrash about in a fit and cried out for water. "Please! Someone please splash water on my face before I burn up! I can't see anything. She has blinded me!"

Several others in the crowd also held hands to their faces and began to rub their eyes.

Clarence spotted a rain barrel at the corner of the store, filled a bucket that lay beside it, and emptied water on the man, who had begun to retch and cough. He called others to reach into the barrel and splash themselves.

Aphia saw that she might now be able to get out of town, so she jumped back on the wagon seat and jerked hard on the reins until her horse turned away from the scene. As she headed away, she spoke directly to Clarence. "You, miner, I thank you, but you see what I can do. Do not cross me in the future."

88

Following the end-of-season closings at the Dunton and Beech Hill mines, Clarence spent the winter considering the fact that the gem mine might be closed permanently. Neither Mr. Dunton nor Dr. Abbott had mentioned that possibility to him. However, Nathan again hinted as much during a visit to Bethel just before Christmas, when the Potters had invited their friend for dinner. Nathan had brought them holiday gifts from his own family. As the three sat by the Christmas tree in the parlor, he brought up the subject

"Have you two considered what you would do if Dunton decided to close the pit come spring? Mind you, I'm not saying it's going to happen. He may have a plan to expand the excavation, but if so, he hasn't shared it with me. I'm only going by the numbers I put together last month."

Clarence, who had known such a development was possible, said nothing in response. He stared straight ahead at the colorful tree as if he hadn't heard Nathan's words, puffing on his pipe before answering. "In the mining business, closure is always a possibility, especially at the beginning of the operation when costs of excavation are so high. We're still seeking the best pockets. So much of the work involves speculation based on knowledge of the site's geology. You can be lucky and hit that lode right off, or it may take a few misses before you strike it rich. Sort of like the doctor finding a vein in your arm to get a blood sample."

"But everyone has been so confident that we would make a lot of money. Now you say that might not happen," said Lottie.

"Like all prospecting," said Clarence, "there is always as much a possibility of failure as there is of success. I, for one, will wait to see what happens in the spring. Our worry may be nothing more than idle winter chatter."

"I didn't mean to worry you, Lottie," said Nathan. "My comment was only based on speculation arising from my bookkeeping. Only that. As Clarence says, let's wait and see what happens in a month or two. Besides, there is always the Beech Hill operation to keep you busy. The prospects there are quite good, according to the Bureau of Mines inspector. He says it shows the greatest potential for mica production in all of Oxford County."

Lottie sat with her sleeping son's head propped on her chest and thought for a moment before turning back to Clarence. "If what you both say is true, then mining is like a roll of the dice or luck of the draw. Might we never be sure that our future is secure?"

"My dear," began Clarence, "I've been in this business since I was a lad not much older than our Conny. My dad taught me how to be both a miner and a blacksmith, so that I would always have a job. As a miner, I've been able to make a lot of money in very short times. As a smith, I've made much less and had to work much harder. Don't worry now about what might happen in Newry. If the worst happens, we can relocate to prosperous North Waterford. We might find a better home than this place. One that we could purchase."

Nathan had been silent for a few minutes as he listened to the couple's conversation. He felt guilty of throwing a shade over what should have been a happy holiday season. "I'm so sorry for bringing up all this worry. Please be assured, Lottie, I work with many blacksmith shops. A skilled smithy is always in high demand, and if all else fails, a job would come easily."

Clarence reached over to gently straighten a curl on his son's blond head and to touch Lottie's cheek in order to calm her anxiety. She smiled, but a fear for the future now lurked in her mind.

89

January 6–8, 1900: The Storm

Thirty-nine-year-old Lizzie Millett sat at a large dining room table sorting through her mail. On this January day, heavy snow, pushed by steady eastern gales, was rapidly piling deep drifts against the windows. Business mail was set aside in one pile. Personal mail, making up a much smaller stack, contained a legal-size envelope with brother-in-law Nathan Hallet's Bridgton return address. Breaking the seal, she was surprised to find a worn and weathered pamphlet. Clipped to the cover was a note from Nathan.

Liz,

This pamphlet was given to me by Hollis Dunton, owner of the gem mine where Clarence Potter works. Although it is a bit tattered, it contains some news about doings in Oxford County some time back.

We all look forward to your upcoming visit.

Nathan

Lizzie was barely able to read the print on the cover. She reached for the magnifying glass, which was becoming more and more useful as her eyes began to weaken from years of close work on dress designs. The pamphlet was titled:

The
History of Mount Mica
of
Maine, U.S.A.
And
Its Wonderful Deposits of Matchless
Tourmalines

The book, published by Augustus Choate Hamlin in 1895 was in terrible shape, as if it had been rained upon and crushed underfoot in the dirt. When she turned to the first page, dirt dropped onto the table in front of her. This will have to wait for a later time, when I have better light, Lizzie thought as she looked at the title page. The large type on the second page caught her interest, so she began to read the booklet rather than insert it back into the envelope.

Author of A Treatise on the Tourmaline, Leisure Hours Among the Gems, Fellow of The American Association for the Advancement of Science. Member of The Royal Society of Antiquaries of Northern Europe, Chevalier of St. Anne of Russia, etc.

I have no idea what this has to do with Oxford County, she thought. But if Nathan and Hattie found it interesting, I will have to give it a read.

As she read, Francena entered the room and took a seat across from her. Not wanting to disturb her aunt's reading, she stared out at the howling blizzard. She was wearing a heavy wool cable-knit sweater and a blue shawl draped across her shoulders, but even with a fire burning in the kitchen range, she was cold. Both windows rattled in the gale.

"Franny, you must be wearing every piece of winter clothing you own. You look like an eskimo," said Lizzie. "It's not that cold."

"Perhaps it's looking out at the storm that makes me so cold. I can't keep from shivering. I even have my boots on."

She peered across the table at the pamphlet her aunt was reading. "Oh, I've seen that book before. Clarence Potter was reading it up in Bethel that time when Lottie and I worked with him to find the tourmalines."

"Did you read it? The print is so small and the pages so worn that it's a bother for me to make out the words."

"No, I haven't read it, but Lottie says the writer's descriptions gave Clarence an idea of how to find gems. You know—what to look for. Do you want me to read it to you?"

They moved their chairs next to the range and sat for the rest of the morning while Franny read Hamlin's entire story of the accidental discovery of tourmalines on Oxford's Mount Mica in 1820 by two college boys out for a hike in the woods at the end of summer. Both women were fascinated by how easy it had been for them to find the initial green crystals caught in the roots of a fallen tree. How frustrating it must have been for the boys when an early snow made it impossible to return to the site the following day.

"I bet those kids dreamed and talked about returning to their discovery all the time during the school year," said Lizzie at one point. "You know how young boys are once they get a thing planted in their brains. It must have been difficult for them to wait for spring to come."

"That's how I would have been," said Franny, "and I'm not a boy! It would have driven me to distraction all winter long."

At the part of the tale where the young men returned to their prospect and carried buckets full of crystals back to their homes, Liz interrupted. "Oh, how I wish Moses was still with us. He would have loved this story."

At the end of the reading, Franny excused herself for a minute, leaving her aunt musing by the stove. When the girl returned she carried a small cloth sack which she handed to Liz. "Here, open this and see what I've been treasuring since my one day as a miner."

Liz pulled a small tissue wad from the sack and opened it to reveal two stunning green tourmalines no bigger than the nail on her pinkie finger. One was broken on both ends, but the other had one pointed end with five facets. When she held it up to the filtered light coming through the snow-encrusted window, she exclaimed, "Oh, my! This is truly a gemstone. Why haven't you had this one fit into a ring or a pendant? It takes my breath away, it's so beautiful."

"When I look at these stones, it reminds me of the way I felt when I first found them. A magic moment when such a wonder of nature caused me to bow my head in prayer. They are God's creations. I could never have them fabricated into showy baubles."

90

"Clary, the snow is blowing under the back door again! Isn't there something we can do to stop it?" shouted Lottie as she swept white powder away from the threshold. Wind, sounding like a locomotive, shook every window in the house. A drift had already covered the front windows and another was rapidly spreading up against the windows on the east side. If the blizzard were to continue much longer, their little house might be buried like the sheds next to the railroad station already were.

Clarence was in the bedroom driving wooden shims between window sashes and frames to keep them from vibrating open. He rushed into the front room at the sound of Lottie's voice.

"Christ!" he hollered above the roaring din. "I've never seen a storm like this one, even in Ontario. The wind will just not shut up!" He raced from the room and returned with nails, hammer, and a pine board, which he proceeded to attach to the door frame, closing the gap between door and threshold. As he finished, a puff of smoke came from the Franklin woodstove in the parlor. As he moved toward the smoky room, he shouted, "Lottie, where is the boy? Don't let him near that fire! With his fever, the smoke will drive him to a shivering fit of coughing. Are you in the kitchen? Is the range smoking like this?"

In that very instant, the wind abated and a glint of refracted sunlight entered the parlor windows. Was the storm ended, or was this only a momentary respite in the ordeal? As the sunlight became brighter, Clarence threw himself on the sofa and took a deep breath. Lottie entered with Con in hand and sat down next to him. They gazed at each other with relief. Perhaps they had just weathered the worst conditions winter had to offer, even though it was only the seventh day of January.

Clarence left his seat and went to the front entry. He opened the door to find that the snowdrift had taken on the impression of the door itself. No light filtered through the dense drift. He knew that if they wanted to get out of the house, he would have to remove the board to open the back door. Yet, he didn't trust that the storm was completely over, and until such time as the wind died down completely, he was content to stay inside. Tomorrow was soon enough to start digging out.

"You know, Clary, I'm so glad to have you at home at times like this," said Lottie. "It was all I could do to keep Con calm these past couple of days. He usually likes to play in the snow, but with the wind howling, he was frightened. I was frightened myself."

"We are a good team, my dear. No question about that. However, this house is not built well enough to withstand such an onslaught. When spring comes, we will find a better place to live, no matter where it might be."

91

The blizzard that had blown in from the coast on Friday evening blanketed the area with nearly thirty inches of snow. Gales piled drifts as high as eight feet on the sides of houses, barns, and stores. Then two nights of bitter northwest winds under starry skies blew the snow onto Valley Road, where it lay in sculpted swirls. Monday, the eighth of January, finally brought people into the village from the homes where they had been hunkered down for two days. Just as had been the case each day of the previous week, temperatures did not budge from below-zero levels.

By the time the first grammar school students arrived, teacher Burton Sanderson had lit a wood fire in the potbelly stove. The room temperature began to rise, but no one wanted to remove their heavy coats, hats, boots, and chopper mittens. Those who had gotten wet stood close to the stove to dry their clothes.

Florence Brown and Fonti Manning, two of the older students, went outside to get more fuel for the fire. They ran back with empty arms shouting at the top of their voices, "FIRE! FIRE! FIRE!"

William Nichols, thirteen, who lived in the rental above Nason's Store, across the road from the schoolhouse, arrived just at that moment. Shouting and waving his arms, he pointed back toward the store at thick black smoke rising from a front window of the top floor.

"Mr. Sanderson," shouted the boy, "my house is on fire! I saw the stovepipe upstairs shaking and smoking. I could have stopped it with a bucket of water, but Mom told me to run and warn everyone."

Sanderson hollered to Bertha Hamlin, who was teaching in the next room, "Miss Hamlin, we must get these children out of here in case that fire spreads in this direction." He quickly had his students lined up and marched them toward the parsonage, out of harm's way. Hamlin led the elementary students to her own house near the church on 5 Kezars Road. As the children walked to safety, they all screamed "Fire! Fire! Fire!" to alert the neighbors.

216

Church Sexton Bisbee rushed to the Congregational Church and rang the steeple bell. Pulling on the bell rope over and over, he tolled the alarm to residents who lived in the outskirts of the village or those who might not have seen the smoke and flames that had already enveloped Nason's Store.

Bucket brigades were set up at the two wells in the village that were not frozen. As more and more people gathered, progress was being made—especially when intense heat melted snow-packed roads and driveways. Resulting rivulets ran down the street, making it easier to get buckets of water onto threatened structures without running back to the wells.

Postmaster Saunders arrived just in time to snatch bags of mail from the Post Office, which was in the store. Fonti Manning and Florence Brown, once again working together, saved two baskets of books from the Rebekah Library located in a shed next to the burning store. True Brown went into the nearby Oddfellows Hall and carried the lodge's portable organ down an old ladder just before the building ignited.

Sparks and cinders were blown high into the air before falling like hail on the nearby James Brown house. Dressmaker Edith Knight was barely able to escape from her shop on that house's first floor. Effie Matheson, who lived with her two preschool children on the second floor, barely had time to dress her son and daughter and flee into the cold. Ellis Rand, whose store was next door to Brown's, dynamited an attached shed—which was already afire—in order to save his business.

John Lewis's rooming house was separated from the Nason store by a narrow alley. His roof began to smoke and then burst into flames. The large dance hall on the second floor was quickly engulfed. Risking his own life, Lewis threw chairs, furniture, and other valuables through the windows into the street.

Wind blew flaming shingles from Nason's onto the front of the now empty schoolhouse, which burned to the ground. Will Fiske's freshly painted white stable next door to the school also burned to ashes in a matter of minutes. In the rush to try and save these buildings, people trampled the lovely white picket fence that stood along the road in front of both buildings. At this point, citizens realized they were fighting a losing battle. The wind switched direction and drove flames back into the village, igniting buildings on both sides of Valley Road. Mosher's Store burned next, along with all grains stored in the rear. Gene Andrews's blacksmith shop exploded in flames. The last place to go was the Mosher House next to the store.

In all, eight families were left homeless. Two stores and all the goods within were lost, as was the school and six other local businesses, including Lewis's boardinghouse, which had no fire insurance. The stately elm trees that grew along Valley Road were gone, never to be replaced. However, the citizens were not defeated. They had bravely risen to the occasion. The Rand House and Dr. Coolidge's place were saved by courageous men who stood on the roofs taking buckets from those below to pour on the shingles. Several brave men and women fought to resist destruction by soaking quilts and blankets in meltwater and draping them over roofs.

"Look on the bright side," said Tim Nason. "No one was killed. And it was a day fire, so it was easier to fight. The snow from yesterday's storm melted to make our job easier. And thus far, there has been no looting."

92

Aphia Stevens worked in the stable clearing away horse droppings and trampled hay frozen into the dirt floor. As she emptied the last spade of debris into a metal barrel, the sound of a church bell caught her attention. It was strange, she thought, that the North Waterford Congregational bell would be pealing on a weekday. She left the stable to bring her horses back from the snowy paddock. The bell kept ringing over and over. The sound continued while she gathered her horses back into their stalls and closed the barn door.

By the time she walked back to the house, it had dawned on her that there must be an emergency in the village, likely a fire. She peered to the west but saw no smoke. It was too cold, she thought, to harness one of the horses to the cutter and drive off to investigate. After all, she had her own fire to tend in order to keep the house warm. Inside the house, she kept her coat on as she built the fire back up in the Franklin stove. With January temperatures hardly getting above zero for more than a week, it was only at night when she crawled beneath her bedding that she shed the outerwear. Even then, it was often necessary to wear long underwear and a sweater, especially since she had to get up several times each night to feed the fire.

"That damn bell keeps ringing and ringing." She spoke out loud as if someone else was present. "This must be a serious fire to have the call for help go on for such a long time. I'll have to ride out there tomorrow to see what's happened."

She prepared herself a simple lunch of coleslaw and a cake of hardtack. There was no butter left to put on the bread, so she dipped it into the slaw juice. "I must remember to get a firkin of butter at Nason's Store tomorrow when I'm down to North Waterford. And there are a few other provisions I need to get, too."

93

Spring arrived late in Oxford County, as it is wont to do. Snow drifts against the north side of the house in Bethel stayed until mid-May, but Clarence and Lottie did not wait around to see it fully melted. With the Dunton Mine now temporarily closed, there was no good reason to stay. Clarence had spent several days in late February visiting the Halletts in Bridgton to search for a reasonably priced house in Waterford near the Beech Hill mica mine, but he found nothing to his liking. Nathan had learned of a seasonal apartment available in Waterford City on the third floor of a carriage shop. Clarence inspected the apartment and was willing to live there while the search for a permanent home continued. He knew that Lottie would be disappointed to live over a manufactory with its noise, smells, and smoke, but when he reported his misgivings to her, he was surprised at her willingness to at least visit the place.

She held tightly to a flimsy handrail attached to the wall of a narrow stairwell with one hand, while clutching Con in the other arm. Clarence walked closely behind her in case she slipped back. Raising her voice above the noise from the factory, she asked two questions. "Are the machines so loud all the time or only once in a while? Would we be staying here for only a couple of months?"

"Dear, we do not have to stay here at all, if you don't like it. We would likely have more options if we keep looking. Bethel is not all that bad in the spring and summer, you know."

As they stepped into the apartment's kitchen and closed the door, noise from below was muffled. She stood the boy on his feet and began to inspect the space with him in tow. Clarence followed after her, opening closets and cabinets to see how dirty they might be. All the small windows were open, admitting the pleasant sounds of City Brook. Out of the west-facing kitchen windows, they saw cows and sheep in small enclosures attached to several dilapidated sheds.

"It is certainly very different from Bethel," she said as she watched chickens running free on the dirt road below, pecking at what little grass sprouted in the spring sun. "It leaves much to be desired. The rooms are small. The summer kitchen is large, but it needs a good painting."

"As I said before, Lottie, we do not have to live here. We can find other options. Nathan has a lot of contacts in the area."

"Yes, I know, but I am done with living in Bethel, especially if you'll be working down here all the time. We need to be together as a family. This is so close to Beech Hill, you could nearly walk to work. And I could bring lunch to you. When we find a better place, we can easily leave. There is plenty of room here for the little bits of furnishings we've collected."

"No doubt it is close to work. No more traveling back and

forth from town to town. That part appeals to me. I could spend more time with the boy. So, is it here you wish to stay?"

She said nothing for a while, staring out at the bubbling brook flowing down to a mill pond where ducks paddled. "Yes, I think so. It is not completely to my liking, but we'll enjoy the summer here. Our vacation place." He placed his hand against her cheek, then leaned over to kiss her there.

"We'll be happy here, even though it is but a stop on the way," he said.

94

Lizzie hated to close the shop on such a warm spring day. God knows, there is scarcely enough business these days to make ends meet, she thought, and a "closed" sign on the door might turn away a potential customer. However, she and Francena— who was now as good a seamstress as could be found—had completed all the bespoke orders that had come from the shops that still used her for quality custom work. There really wasn't any reason why she and her niece couldn't take a few days off to visit the Halletts in Bridgton. Neither had been there since Christmas.

Nathan had agreed to pick them up on his way back from an appointment at the S.D. Warren paper mill in Portland. His new one-horse runabout wagon was such a light vehicle that there was no roof to protect from the weather, so the women were glad the day was warm and calm for a change. While they waited, the postman arrived with the mail, including a letter from Lottie Potter. Since there had been no word from her friend for several weeks, Francena tore open the envelope and sat down on the top step to read it.

Dearest Franny,

So much time has gone since I last wrote. Please forgive your loving friend—she has not forgotten you. There has been little time to let you know how busy life has been here in

Bethel, but I will leave most of the news until we are together once again. Hopefully, in a short while.

I write to tell you that Clarence, Con, and I are leaving this busy town and moving to Waterford. Perhaps by the time you get my news, we will be living in an apartment in "The City," as they call South Waterford village. Our wish is that we stay in the place only for a short time while we search for a permanent home.

You must come visit us at your first opportunity. We are so close to Bridgton. I so much look forward to your cheery smile and loving embrace. Thoughts of you are always with me.

> Looking forward to being with you,
> I am,
> your Lottie

"Auntie Liz!" she cried out, jumping up so fast that she nearly lost her balance. "You'll never guess what has happened!"

When Lizzie came to the front door, Franny ran head first into her. "Slow down, girl! Watch where you're going. Tell me your news."

"Lottie is moving to Waterford! Isn't that wonderful? We must go visit her. I've missed her so much, and I want to see her little boy again. She's so lucky to have a family."

As she spoke, her dad's carriage turned into the driveway. Not waiting for him to reach the house, she ran to the side of the vehicle and walked along speaking loudly to him through a front wheel.

"Look out, there, missy! Don't come too close to that wheel! What is all the hubbub about? Can't it wait till I get down?"

"Daddy, did you know the Potters are moving to Waterford? Lottie wrote me that they are probably there already. We must visit this weekend!"

"That's news to me. I knew that Clarence was looking for a new place to live because the gem mine closed down, but I didn't think it would happen so fast."

"Can we go over to South Waterford tomorrow? I miss Lottie so much."

"Of course, Franny, if the weather allows. I'm curious if they took the apartment in Frisbie's carriage mill."

After throwing their duffels in the rear compartment, Liz and Franny climbed up to the padded bench seat, and Nathan squeezed himself in between. "I apologize for the lack of room. These little runabouts are really made for one or two. Thankfully, the road from here to Bridgton is smoother than most. I will go slow on any rough places so as not to ruffle your feathers, ladies."

"Feathers? We aren't chickens, you know," joked Francena.

And she did not stop talking about her girlfriend for the entire four-hour ride to Bridgton. Neither of the others was able to get a word in. As they crossed the bridge over Stevens Brook, Nathan drew the wagon to a halt. "Daughter of mine, I beg you kindly to gather your wits about you before we get home. You wouldn't want your mother or Nate to think you've become a silly ninny. Your aunt and I will never tell a soul how you have gone on and on during this trip."

Franny sheepishly stared at them both and then at the river below. "Oh, please forgive me. It's just that I'm so excited about being reunited with darling Lottie."

When they arrived at the Hallett house, Hattie greeted them with news that Lottie, Clarence, and Con had visited. "They were here just yesterday on their way to South Waterford. She wants to see you as soon as possible. I invited them back to dine with us tonight, but their furniture will be delivered tomorrow, and she wanted to clean the apartment beforehand. Perhaps we might go over for a visit tomorrow."

95

"Oh, my," said Hattie to her sister as Nathan pulled the wagon onto the dirt road off Cross Street. "I know this place. It's where you and that Aphia woman had your standoff so long ago. Hard to believe that a city girl like Lottie would come to live in an apartment over a carriage factory in such a dirty neighborhood."

Franny whispered, "Look at all the rusty barrels and rotting wood all over the place. And the street smells of chicken manure. This can't be the right building."

"Franny! Franny!" came a shout from the second floor of a three-story factory. Lottie leaned out an open window and wildly waved a small broom. She wore a gray kerchief and had a handkerchief tied across her mouth and nose. "You're here at last! I'll be right down to get you."

The two friends raced to each other in the middle of the dusty road as frightened chickens scattered and curious cows came up to watch, their heads leaning on the metal fence of their enclosure. A bearded man wearing a brown leather welder's apron came to the door of the first-floor shop to see about the commotion.

"Mr. Frisbie," called Nathan. "Didn't mean to disturb you. We've come to visit your new tenants."

"You're certainly welcome to visit. I thought some of the neighbor's sheep had got out again, with all the noise." He quickly returned to work, adding the hissing burr of a grinder to the din.

Lottie led the company up the precarious stairs to the empty apartment. As they entered, Franny whispered to her mother, "How can she live here? It's so shabby. Not her style at all."

96

When Clarence had last visited the village of North Waterford in late March, debris from the January fire remained scattered about. The charred and collapsed remains of eight houses, six businesses, and the school were leaking dark water into the streets as snowdrifts melted. Depending on the wind direction each day, the smell of burned wood reached as far as Albany to the north or to East Waterford and Waterford Flat, both five miles away. Mr. Lewis's hotel, where he'd rented a room, was a pile of rubble and blackened foundation stones. Now, nearly three months later, as he entered the village in his buckboard, he saw how much of the rubble had been removed. Determined residents were beginning to rebuild atop foundations that had survived. A man with a white bandana across his nose and mouth was throwing half-burned boards from a huge rubble pile into his farm wagon.

"Hello there, mister. Can you tell me if Ray Lord still lives around here?" asked Clarence.

The man removed his bandana, cleared his throat, and spat on the ground.

"Why, Tim Nason," said Clarence. "How have you been doing? I was told you lost your house and store and all your worldly goods."

Nason peered at his questioner for a moment before recognizing him. "Oh, Mr. Potter. Haven't seen you since last summer. I wish I could say the news you heard was wrong, but I lost pretty much everything. Found a few cast pots and pans in the store basement, and my foundations are still good. The missus, Timmy, and me are still alive. That's a blessing. And my neighbors have been another blessing. They made it possible for us to make it through the winter."

"You people are doing a great job cleaning up the place and rebuilding," Clarence remarked.

"I'd say you won't find Ray here in town today. Down by the Chalk Pond or at his mica mine, I'd say. He'll be home in the evening. Lives behind the Church on 5 Kezars Road, in the big white house with red shutters."

"I know about Ray's mine, but what is Chalk Pond? Strange name for a pond. Is it one of these muddy farm ponds?"

"Oh, no," said Nason. "Chalk Pond is up near the Albany town line at the foot of two hills where people have been prospecting for feldspar. The water drains down from those pits into the pond. Turns the water chalky. For as long as I've lived here, farmers been taking buckets of mud from the bottom of the pond and using it to clean their plows and harrows. One man I know uses the muck as fertilizer. Been going on for generations, I'd say."

"Mr. Nason, when I have the time I'll inspect that pond." He knew of a household cleanser or polish that was made of feldspar powder. That chalk in the pond might be the same material, but he would keep that to himself. "I'll be going home myself in the evening. My family is living in a rent over Frisbie's carriage shop in The City. Would you tell Ray that I'm starting to excavate at Dr. Abbott's mine up on Beech Hill? You know the prospect. Used to belong to John Kimball. I'd appreciate it if he would help me find two or three men to work the site."

"Will do that next I see him. When you go up Beech Hill way, you be careful of that mad Stevens woman. She lives right next to your prospect. You know of her, I'm sure. I heard she nearly caused the sheriff to die from whatever concoctions she's cooking in her kitchen. Threatening folks with a pistol, too, I hear."

"I know very well about her. She has pointed that Colt at me once or twice, but we seem to have reached some sort of peace agreement. We've agreed to leave a big distance between her pistol and my body."

97

Franny and her aunt sat on the front porch on a warm and sunny afternoon. "This is the kind of day that helps make winter enjoyable," said Lizzie. "Gives you something to look forward to when the snow is flying."

Franny paid no attention to the small talk. Ever since returning from the visit to South Waterford, she had been preoccupied with one thing. "I can't believe that Lottie would put up with living in such a dirty place." She stood and paced back and forth with hands behind her back. "Clarence must have some sort of control over her, making her do what *he* wants. She deserves better."

"She is deeply in love with him and will try her best to satisfy his wishes. He wants to be close to his work site and she does, too, so that he can be home every day. Must have been difficult to have him away so much of the time when they were in Bethel."

"Yes, I guess so, but she has always stood on her own two feet. I liked that about her from the very first day we met, when she stood her ground against her mother."

"She's still strong. You will see. You told me about how she ran away with Clarence to Ontario to live in the wilderness. Moving into that mill apartment can't be as hard as being in that rough wilderness, now can it? Then she got him to leave Canada for Bethel, then Bethel for Waterford. Seems like she's getting her own way, doesn't it?"

"Maybe you're right. I don't know, but there's very little I can do to change things. It's her life, after all. Perhaps I should be grateful for having her so close by."

"Franny, if the time comes when Lottie needs your help, you can count on me to be there for both of you. We have a good home here, and I am willing to share. There's so much space that we might accommodate a growing family with little difficulty."

98

Clarence climbed to the top of the narrow stairs, careful not to bump his head on the third-floor stringers above him. Even in the long days of summer, the windowless stairwell was dark. He tried to make it up to the apartment door before the first-floor door closed behind him. This time, he almost made it, reaching the tiny landing just as all went dark.

"Lottie," he called out, "I left early today to be here for Con's birthday. What a wonderful sunny day!"

There was no answer, so he walked from room to room looking for his wife before realizing she was not at home. Walking back down the dark stairs and out the heavy wooden door, he strode directly to the spot where she liked to sit and play with Conny atop an earthen dam where Mill Brook spilled over a wooden coffer. He was right: The two of them sat watching sheep grazing among tall reeds on the stream's opposite bank. Noise from the falls muffled his steps as he sneaked up behind them across the grassy berm. Just as he was about to jump out at them, his son turned and pointed.

"Daddy! Daddy!" he cried out with glee, standing and jumping up and down.

Lottie, too, then turned and clapped her hands. "You've come home early on such a day! Come join us in our party."

He laughed with delight and sat down on the damp grass. Their party fare consisted of nothing more than an apple sliced in quarters and a pitcher of water set on a sheet of canvas where the boy was sitting. Lottie poured her husband a cup of water, and Con handed him a piece of apple. Together, the family celebrated in the shadow of a giant pine growing on the mill pond's embankment. Soon Con grew tired and lay on the canvas with his head on Lottie's knee. While he slept, she and Clarence sat in silent meditation on the sound of the water. She reached for his hand and drew it to her cheek.

"I think I am pregnant again."

"My God, are you sure?"

"Not sure, but I have missed my time for the second month. We can make an appointment with Mrs. Bishop and see what she has to say. However, I think we should be prepared."

Clarence moved closer and placed his hand on her stomach. "What wonderful news. We have wanted another. Perhaps a daughter this time. Ever since we had to leave my children in Yarmouth, I have wanted more than one. And you have wanted more children."

"Yes, there will be room in our lives for a large family. Not here in this space, but in a new house. We will find a new place to live with room enough for more."

He lay back on the grass and stared up at a white cumulus cloud so large that the bottom had turned a shade of gray. "Looks like a storm may be coming from the looks of that cloud. Let's take this party inside where the boy can sleep, and we can talk about the future."

99

"Have you told Franny the news about her friend's pregnancy?" said Hattie as she and Nathan walked out toward the garden. He had just returned from Waterford after a visit to the Beech Hill mica mine with a Bureau of Mines inspector.

"No, but I'm sure Lottie has sent word to her about it. Clarence was so pleased about the prospect of a new child that it was like pulling teeth to get him to concentrate on the inspector's questions. He kept bragging to the man about his family, so much so that he likely will be surprised by the BOM report when it arrives."

"Is there a problem with the mine? Last year's assay was so positive. Any changes this time around?"

"Maybe. The quality of the books remains good. A little smaller than last year—right around a square foot—but still big enough to get a good grade. But there's some concern about the production rate. The pit may have to be expanded higher on the hill. That means a lot more work and possibly a need to expand the Stevens right-of-way."

"That'll be a new kettle of fish. Getting another agreement with that woman will be no easy task. Perhaps we were wise not to get too deeply involved in this mine. Hopefully, things will work out for the Potters, especially with a new baby coming."

"I don't think it would be a good idea to share these concerns with Franny. She is so in love with Lottie that her emotions might well get the better of her."

"I agree. Let's just let them handle their own communications about this. Our worries may come to nothing, after all."

100

Franny walked the gravel path that ran from the rear of her aunt's house along the edge of Pride's granite quarry, the one her great-grandfather had operated so many years ago. As usual on a Saturday, the men were not working. No singing saws or hard hammering disturbed the way along the pit edge. She loved to wander here, sit on moss-covered boulders, and peer down at the blue sky reflected in the deep puddles at the pit bottom. This was a place of weekend solitude where she might walk and think about her life and the people in it. Today, her thoughts were of Lottie and why her friend had accepted a life so much different from the dreams they had discussed as girls.

Was Auntie right? she thought. Was Lottie patiently guiding Clarence toward a stable family life that would have them eventually living close to Westbrook? It was clear that he had matured and was no longer the rake who'd stolen his wife away from her family. Still, he jumped from job to job looking for his quick fortune. Maybe I'm overreacting to what I see her doing with her life. I can only pray that their future brings Lottie great happiness.

Up ahead she saw Maeve Cain and her brood, now numbering four, coming toward her on the path. The youngest, a boy born eight months ago, was in a stroller being pushed along by the eldest girl, who was now ten. Such a happy family, Franny thought. She and Will enjoy having so many young ones around them, almost like the farm families of old. Or more like the Irish way. They always have large families.

"Franny, girl," hailed Maeve. "How you been keepin'? It's been some time since I've seen you. How is that auntie of yours?" In all the years she had lived in Maine, she had not yet lost the lilt of her native accent. Many immigrants wanted to lose any characteristic which marked then as foreigners, but not Maeve. She was proud of her heritage.

"Oh, we are both doing well. What a marvelous summer day."

"Couldn't be better."

"Aunt Liz is off to Portland today on the trolley. She has an appointment with a good customer who has a dress shop on Congress Square." As she spoke, five-year-old Willy Cain grabbed her hand, beginning to swing her arm back and forth.

"Willy. Stop that bother. You'll make the lady angry."

"No, no. He's only being friendly. You're so fortunate to have such healthy children. I hope when my day comes, I will be as fortunate as you."

"Don't you be in any great rush to be a mother. You'll have to find the right man first. One true to you and your family."

Franny thought to herself how fortunate Maeve had been to find Will. Aunt Liz might have married him, if her life had been different. He was a man that both Maeve and Liz had relied on to help them through life. She herself had not yet met anyone who was mature enough to be so reliable. But she was only nineteen. Maeve was right, still plenty of time. As she walked along beside the Cain family, she again thought of Lottie and wondered if her friend had found such a trustworthy man in Clarence. She wondered if Lottie had even taken the time to consider such thoughts when she rushed into marriage to escape her own mother.

"I suppose you're happy about your friend Lottie being pregnant again," said Maeve.

"What? How did you know? I was with her last month and she said nothing at all to me. Are you sure?"

"That's what Will told me. He's been working two days a week with Mr. Potter at a mica mine in Waterford. Says the man is overjoyed. Wants to have a daughter, he does. And he wants a big family like ours. I'm surprised you didn't know. Your dad must have been told by the man."

Thoughts about Lottie having another child in that ramshackle apartment brought back the worries. Franny said nothing for a while as she tried to figure out why her parents had not told her about this. When she saw them again would be time to ask. Now, she wanted to put her best face on the news. "Oh, that is wonderful! I know that they both want more children. They'll be likely to look for a new home now, a big house they can fill with a big family."

"If Clarence is as happy as Will says he is, that is a good sign. Buying a big house might be the next step. Perhaps they can get my man to build them a big new modern house, like he did for me."

101

Dr. Abbott continued to believe that the Beech Hill mine was a good investment. He decided to increase his investment enough to make it possible to clear the overburden and expand the pit nearer the Stevens boundary. A test hole had unearthed several dozen books more than twelve inches square at a depth of four feet. Will Cain and two North Waterford men were hired temporarily to excavate, and a farmer agreed to transport the gravel and topsoil to his own fields. It was so near the end of the season, success of the expansion might not be judged until spring, unless the clearing could be completed for blasting to begin before November.

Working closely together, Will and Clarence shared stories of their pasts and their families. The other men stayed much more to themselves. One afternoon after the others had left, the two men rested on a granite boulder protruding from a ridge of glacial till that marked the boundary with Aphia's lot.

"This is about as close to that witch as I ever want to get," Clarence said. "I don't trust her one bit not to shoot me the next time she sees me."

"Shoot you? Christ, I thought her potions were what makes her dangerous. I had a good friend who once fell for her. Seems he was thinking of marrying her. She must have put a hex on him with those concoctions and lured him into her web, like a spider does to a fly."

"So, what happened to him? If he's still around, I'd like to hear his stories."

"Not sure where Bert is now. One story is that she turned him down and he left in shame to marry another woman. I think she might have done something to him. My wife thinks so, too, but made me promise not to pry into the matter."

"Maeve is a wise woman not to trust Stevens one bit. I ride as fast as I can by her place coming and going."

"Don't you think she'll bother us when she realizes how close we've come to her lot line?"

"Will, let's close up shop for the day and get out of here. Just speaking about the woman bothers me. If she puts up a stink about the expansion, you can discuss it with her. Abbott is sure to pay you extra for it."

"Maybe I could find out more about what happened to my friend. Pleased to do it, if it comes about."

102

When the weather changed abruptly from late October's calm coolness to early November's hints of winter, the men completed their pit expansion. A brisk wind from the north-west swept down Albany Mountain, and snow flurries left white traces atop the carpet of fallen leaves. With great disappointment, Clarence and Will, realizing that they would be unable to blast until the new year, had a farmer pull trunks of fallen hemlocks from the woods and lay them across the access. As they worked, a shot rang out from the Stevens pasture. Aphia was approaching them at a run with her pistol pointed at the sky. Will and Clarence quickly hid behind the trunks of two sturdy oaks, and the farmer ducked for cover between his oxen.

"Hold on there, you damn miners! What do you think you're doing, crossing over more of my land?" She shot again and came to a halt at her boundary line, where a berm of boulders and gravel blocked the way.

"Miss Stevens," shouted Clarence from behind his tree, "we've done nothing wrong here."

"Nothing wrong, you say?" The woman was furious. Tossing the Colt back and forth from hand to hand, she tried to scale the rough berm. "You have broken the terms of our agreement. You call that 'nothing wrong'?"

The farmer wanted nothing to do with the woman. He addressed her directly without revealing himself. "Miss Stevens, please don' harm me or my animals. I've done nothing to you, jus' doin' some work to make a bit of extra before winter comes. You know me, Ezra Ward. My wife, Molly, is a good customer of yours. Buys salves and liniments from you."

"Mr. Ward, of course I won't hurt you. My argument is only with the miners. If you wish to leave, do so quickly, before I run these two off my land with their tails between their legs."

Ward emerged from between the oxen, grabbed the long reins, and strapped the team to move down the road and out of harm's way. The other two men, seeing that Stevens was distracted for a moment, rushed to where their horses were hitched to a roadside fence post. Seeing them run, the mad woman took a shot in Clarence's direction, stirring the dust just to his left.

"Run, you bastards! Run for your lives! And don't come back!" She had reached the top of the berm and could now clearly see where the horses were tied.

Clarence had already mounted and was turning to leave. Will lay flat on the ground under his steed, unwilling to move a muscle. She pointed the gun in his direction and fired a shot at his cap, which lay two feet away from his head. "You, too, mister. Get on that horse and ride away from here as fast as you can." When he didn't move, she pointed the pistol and shot at the hat once more. At this shot, Will turned over onto his back and stared at her. Blood was running down his face and flowing from his mouth.

"Get up, stranger! Don't lie there and play dead," she said, but he didn't move. Coming closer, she could see that one of her shots had apparently ricocheted off a stone and struck the man. She leaned over him and shook his shoulder. Clarence, who had stopped several hundred yards down the road waiting for his friend to escape, watched as the woman knelt beside his friend and began to rock back and forth. He heard her cry out, "Why have you died? I meant to scare you, not kill you! Why has this happened to me again? I meant you no harm."

Clarence turned to ride away as she rose from her knees and ran in his direction waving the gun in the air.

Suddenly, Aphia halted, stared at the pistol for a moment, and then heaved it into the tall grass. She turned in the direction of her house and didn't stop running until she reached the barn, where the door was wide open. She chased three horses out of their stalls. "Run from me!" she yelled and picked up stones from the barnyard, throwing them at the Morgans until they ran down the road.

Clarence rode slowly up to the woman's front gate so he could observe her behavior more closely.

One of the horses returned to the yard, but was frightened away when Aphia threw more stones and started yelling again. "Begone, you fool animal! Where I am going, I have no further need of you. Get out of my sight! Find a home where you are needed. There will be no more care for you in this place."

She's gone mad, Clarence said to himself as she ran from the barn carrying a long-handled shovel and began to dig in the mound at the edge of the pasture. Dust rose as clods of earth flew in all directions, some flying back onto her, dirtying her hair and clothes. He couldn't make out what she was looking for and dismounted to come nearer. She was standing in a shallow pit about six feet long and three feet wide. When the depth of the hole reached three feet, she turned and looked directly at him, offering the shovel handle.

"Here, miner, do me a great favor." She tossed the shovel at his feet and lay down on her back in what he now saw was to be a shallow grave. "Do *everyone* a favor, miner. Bury me with the other bodies that lie here in this hill of death."

Taking a coil of rope from his saddle pack, Clarence approached the prostrate woman and bound her arms and legs. She offered no resistance. "Miss Stevens, I fear you will kill yourself if I leave you on your own. Come with me." He lifted her up and carried her to the barn. Securing her to a post, he mounted his horse and headed toward the village to get the sheriff or some other local official who might hold her overnight until the sheriff could take her into custody.

"Don't bother to get help, miner," she hollered after him. "I don't deserve to live any longer. Take me to my kitchen, where I can poison myself."

103

Maeve Cain was stoic in her grief. For the children's sake, she didn't cry, but after they were all asleep each night she would rush to her double bed and weep into the pillow until fitful sleep would come. At first, she refused to tell the kids, even Faith, the ten-year-old, that Will would never be home again. Lizzie suggested that Hattie might take all four to Bridgton to avoid the funeral services, but when five-year-old Willy began to wait in a porch chair from morning to night for his father to return, Maeve realized she needed to tell her children the truth. It might help her to have them all know; then the dreadful secret would be shared, a weight lifted from her heart.

On the day Will's body was laid to rest in the Cain family site at Pulpit Rock Cemetery in North Waterford, the entire family was present along with the Halletts, the Potters, Lizzie, and five of the dead man's cousins who still lived nearby. As everyone gathered around the grave on a cold autumn day, Pastor Brown led them in saying the Lord's Prayer while Will's casket was lowered. One after another, Maeve and three of the older children each tossed a handful of soil on top of the casket.

Liz approached the widow. "Maeve, may I please join you in tossing soil onto his casket? He was always such a dear person to me from the very first time I met him at my grandparents' boardinghouse. He was always helping me get on in my life's journey."

Maeve nodded, and Liz grabbed up a bit of soil and tossed it into the grave as the gathering began to move away. Bursting into tears, she reached for Maeve's arm so as not to fall into the hole. Arm in arm the two stood for a moment, then turned to weep on each others' shoulders. Hattie and Francena, seeing that the other two women were lost in shared grief, stepped in to take the hands of the smaller Cain children and guide them out of the cemetery.

Dr. Abbott, who had been invited to the service, sent his regards to the widow and apologized for not being able to attend. He had pressing business matters concerning the Beech Hill mine following the shooting. With Aphia Stevens out of the way and

winter fast approaching, there was a short window of opportunity to expand the mine entrance across the Stevens lot in order to
make access much easier in the spring. Although there was some
question about the legality of such a plan, Abbott felt that no one
in Waterford would notice. So, while the funeral service was taking place, Abbott and three men from Bethel removed a section
of temporary wire fencing that marked the boundary and reset
it twenty feet further onto the Stevens lot. By spring, the witch
would be in an asylum in Portland, and the property would sit
idle for quite some time after that.

104

"Where are we going to live during the winter?" asked Lottie.
She was careful not to speak loud enough to wake their
young son, who slept in his crib close to their potbelly stove. She
and Clarence sat across from each other at the small dining room
table in the mill apartment. They both wore heavy sweaters, and
she had a shawl wrapped around her head and shoulders.

"It is mid-November," she continued. "We must get a warm
place or all three of us will catch the flu. The boy already has a
cough that won't go away. If I get sick, will it affect my pregnancy? Something must be done quickly," she said, her voice rising
with urgency.

"Lottie, please. You'll wake Con."

"You're not listening to me. I'm frightened by the prospect
that we might be stuck here for the winter. Already the cold winds
off Bear Mountain are beginning to rattle these flimsy barn windows. I've put newspapers between the sashes, but it does no
good."

Clarence left the table to take a stick from the wood box and
shove it into the stove. "What do you suggest?" he asked, returning to the table. "You know we don't have enough money to buy
a house, even if one that you liked was up for sale."

"Are you saying it's my fault for being careful about a place to live? All the places you have shown to me are little more than hovels. Places for animals to live, not humans. If there really aren't any worthwhile houses for sale, we must at least find a better rent before we all freeze."

Clarence was shocked at his wife's anger. She was hardly ever like this with him. Perhaps it was caused by her condition. When he reached for her hand, she snapped it away, tucking it under the sweater.

"I'm sorry to be so cross with you, but you don't seem to share the same fear I have about the future. Perhaps it's because of the way you lived in Ontario. You may be used to a miner's wilderness life, but I will not put up with such discomfort and danger. Franny told me that she and her aunt Liz have plenty of room in that big boardinghouse, and they've invited us to stay with them again for a time. It might not be our own place, but if it means we can survive the winter—"

"If we move to Westbrook, it will be too far from the mine. I must be nearby when the thaw comes. And how do we pay for rent? I have some carpentry and painting jobs all set in North Waterford for the winter, but I can't travel back and forth from Westbrook all the time. Maybe we could accept their invitation and also keep this place. Then I might have a place to stay during the days I work."

"You might do as you wish. I'll not have my son or myself struggling in this frigid place for the whole winter. I'm sure that rent would be affordable, but if you want to keep this apartment as a retreat from a women's world in Westbrook, by all means, suit yourself. Keep in mind that in the spring there will be another little member of our family. A safe and comfortable home of our own will be required before then."

Clarence could see that her mind was set firmly on moving to be with her best friend, and it was clear that nothing would change such resolution. He agreed that the summer apartment was not suited to year-round family life, but it would fit his needs as temporary quarters even in the worst weather. As for not being able to return to the mill in spring, there would be plenty of time to discuss that over the next five months.

105

North Waterford had quickly completed its cleanup from the disastrous fire and was nearly rebuilt by early summer. People from away, drawn to the village for jobs at prosperous Crooked River mills, were building new homes. A new school was rapidly built and ready for the new term. A new hotel, the Forest House, and several new stores were under construction at the intersection of Valley and 5 Kezars Roads. During the summer and fall, Clarence observed so much progress in the village that he began to consider building a home for his family on Greene Road, halfway between the mine and Waterford Church. By the end of September, he had yet to find time or funds to purchase land, so he put it off until spring. As winter approached, it became clear to him that he might find off-season work finishing the structures that were being built. A local farmer, Pliny Henley, and his young son Elmer started up a winter painting crew, and soon they had so much work they took on helpers, including Clarence. He could work as many hours each week as he wanted.

After moving the family to Westbrook, he returned to the mill apartment in order to be close to work. Travel to North Waterford and back was easy, and he would easily be able to earn enough money to pay the small amount of rent Liz was charging for the third-floor apartment. Each day, he left at the crack of dawn, rode through the woods along Mutiny Brook Road, and spent eight to ten hours painting interiors of the newly constructed buildings. Returning after dusk each evening, he quickly lit a roaring fire and ate a simple dinner before heading off to bed. Twice during the night he would be awakened by the cold and have to feed the fire. He worked seven days a week. There was no time to do anything else. He even worked on Thanksgiving. Soon he had a coffee can full of cash and was ready to take a couple of days off to be with his family.

He also had interesting news to share with Lottie about the prospect of a new mining venture he had learned about while painting at Forest House. Young Elmer Henley had arrived at work one morning wearing boots caked with a tan-colored mud. When he removed the boots, a fine whitish powder marked the outline of each boot on the floor. As Clarence attempted to clean up the dust with a dirty paintbrush, he noticed that so fine was the powder, it filled pores in the floorboards.

"You'll be hard pressed to clean that powder off the planks," said the boy. "That's mud from Chalk Pond. It's as fine as the dust from a blackboard eraser."

"What were you doing down in that pond so early in the day?" asked Clarence.

"Had to get a couple of buckets of the muck for cleaning rust off the plow and harrow. The stuff is a fine abrasive that don't scratch the metal. Farmers around here been usin' it for years. Once the water freezes over, won't be able to get any till spring, and then the metal will be really corroded."

"This is the same stuff I saw a farmer dump into a barrel at the old Rand store before the fire. Is it of any other use?"

"Gosh yes. My uncle dumps the mud on his pastures. Says it's a good soil conditioner. He uses it every summer. Says the hay grows better with it."

"You'll have to take me to this Chalk Pond sometime. Sounds like interesting stuff." He had heard about a new polish made by a Connecticut outfit called J.T. Robinson Soap Company. They were using dried mud containing the mineral feldspar to make Bon Ami, a household product that could be used to polish silverware without scratching. He had heard from Abbott and Dunton that people were prospecting for feldspar in Waterford. He wondered if this pond might be cloudy with powder running down from hills where the digging was taking place. If so, this might be a good prospect to add to his Beech Hill income in the year ahead. Such news might make Lottie feel better about their future.

106

That night, the weather changed. Threatening winds howled across the small mill pond and rattled all the windows. It was early for a blizzard, but when the snow began to fall it quickly drifted against the front door and then across the dirt road to stack up against Hamlin's chicken shed. *Looks like my plans to beat this storm are for naught,* Clarence thought as he huddled near the stove. *I can always venture out tomorrow.* Although he wore his warmest storm coat, boots, and woolen sweater, the wind made him shiver. Mittens, wet from lugging wood in from the downstairs pile, hung on a hand-forged hook nailed to the wall behind the black stovepipe that spit smoke from its seams every time a wailing gust blew. His face and hands were red and chapped.

This was not the way things were supposed to have worked out when he'd convinced Lottie to move to Maine. *We're supposed to be living in a fine house with all the comforts money can buy. Now we live apart, she's pregnant and I'm facing winter in the same condition I was in back in Ontario.* What had he been thinking? Perhaps he should have stayed in Yarmouth, where there was always a steady job as a blacksmith. The pay would have been much less than a mine manager might make, but at least there might have been steady employment. The weather in the Provinces was horrible more than half the year, but it was the same in southwestern Maine. If only he had taken the time to do more research and ask more questions about these Yankee mine operators. He might have seen how weak was their financing and how unskilled they were at judging the quantity and quality of the minerals they dug. Then he might not have budged from a life that at least offered some stability.

He stared around the room trying to bring his attention back to the realities of survival in such cold and harsh conditions. The stove was fed once again. A kettle set on top provided hot water for a cup of bitter herbal tea in which he dipped a chunk of stale bread. Then, fully clothed, he lay on his straw tick and fell asleep under two coarse horse blankets.

Hours later, a sound from the carriage shop woke Clarence up, and he rose to feed the fire once again before going downstairs. The owner of the shop, Timothy Frisbie, had slid the barn door aside and was removing snow that had blown in under the door. Like Clarence, the man was wrapped in so many layers of clothing that his thin frame looked to be that of a much heavier man.

"Mr. Frisbie, why are you out on such a frigid day?"

Frisbie turned abruptly and held his shovel out like a weapon to protect himself. "Hell, man!" he shouted. "Don't sneak up on me like that. I could have hit you with this."

"Please forgive me. My thought was that an animal had stolen into the building. I came down to see."

"You almost gave me a heart attack with your creeping around. I thought the place was empty. Thought you and your family had vacated. The smoke from the chimney made me think the place was on fire."

107

The blizzard raged for two days, making it clear that plans would have to be changed once again. Clarence no longer wished to brave the winter in a frigid little apartment when the comforts of life in the Westbrook rooming house were available. As soon as Waterford Road to Bridgton was rolled, Clarence packed his essential belongings, including the little nest egg, saddled his horse, and headed east. Roads within the immediate villages of Bridgton, Naples, Casco, and Raymond were passable, but in many places, he had to dismount and lead the animal on foot. It took all day to reach Westbrook, and by the time he arrived at Lizzie's house, it was completely dark. Light from recent-ly installed electric fixtures shined through the windows.

Lizzie and Francena, sitting together on the sofa facing the hearth, each had their heads deep in a book. Lottie was upstairs with Con, sitting on the edge of his little bed, reading him a bed-time story. All three women were startled by sudden noise in the front yard and rushed to the nearest windows.

"Auntie, I think there's someone out in the stable," said Fran-ny. "Should I carry out a lantern to see who it is?"

"Who would be out so soon after the storm on such a cold and windy night?" answered Lizzie. "Don't go outside, dear. I'll turn on the front porch light."

When they looked out through the icy window, they were barely able to make out the figure of the man who opened the barn door and led his horse inside. A gust of wind blew the hinged door wide open, crashing it into the barn wall. The horse spooked and tried to run away, and the man, holding tight to the reins, was dragged back into the driveway, where the animal stepped on him before freeing itself and galloping into the darkness.

Lottie rushed—almost flew—down the stairs. "Oh, my God, it's my Clarence!" She ran past her friends, threw open the door, and hurled herself into the gale and snowdrifts wearing only a shift with a cotton shawl thrown over her head. Her feet were bare.

Clarence lay on the ground, face down in the snow. "Clary! Clary! Are you hurt?" she yelled as she fell on her knees next to him. When he did not answer, she lowered her face to his and saw a bruise and some blood on the side of his head. "Clary, can you hear me? Please get up from the ground and come inside." She heard a murmur from him, but he didn't move.

"Franny! Aunt Liz! Please help me. He's badly hurt. Come, please help me get him inside before he freezes!"

"Francena, we must help her," said Liz. "She's so far along, we don't want her to do anything to hurt the baby!"

After donning storm coats, they dashed outside, and together the three women were able to lift Clarence up the steps and lay him on the floor just inside the door. Lottie undid his coat and removed his hat while Liz wiped his hair dry enough to be able to inspect a gash just in front of his left temple. He was not bleeding badly, but a bad bruise was beginning to spread from his forehead down past the ear where a hoof had struck.

In the warmth of the room, Clarence finally regained consciousness. Looking around at the three women, he propped himself up on one elbow and said, "Is that you, Lottie? And Francena? And Lizzie? Thank God! I thought I would never make it." Then he sat up, felt the lump on the side of his head and looked at the blood on his hand. "What have I done to myself?"

108

"I think I've learned my lesson, sweetheart. What was I thinking when I decided to stay in that apartment? And I was trying to get you and the boy to stay with me." Clarence shook his head. "Could have been the death of all of us."

"You wanted to provide for us, that's all. But you hadn't thought it through to the end. You'll make me so proud when spring comes and you're managing the Beech Hill prospect. And we will have a new child. We'll have so much money we'll be able to get a house of our own. There was no need to risk it all for a few dollars."

Two months had passed since Clarence's dramatic arrival in Westbrook. It was true that he had arrived with a roll of cash sufficient to pay rent and get through the worst of winter. Yet, he had put himself in great danger. The horse's hooves had concussed his head so soundly that he suffered dizzy spells and headaches so severe that he was unable to walk without a cane for three weeks. Thankfully, he enjoyed the care of three good home nurses and the attention of an adoring young son to boost his spirits.

"You're such a good woman, Lottie Adelaide. I pray to God I am able to get you the home you want back in Waterford where our family will thrive. It's almost time to get ready to reopen that mine, and I'll make it work this time. There's also another side prospect that you don't know about: a muddy pond in North Waterford that may bring us extra cash."

"Hold on, Clarence. Don't get your head into too many prospects. That is so like you, running from one thing to the next. Just get that mica mine going, and we will be in fine shape."

"Please don't worry. Mining Chalk Pond is such a small thing that it doesn't really need a manager. I met a couple of farmers who would do all the work. We would get only a small percentage, but it would help get the house."

She looked at him for a moment with a blank expression. "Okay, my miner. Let's just make sure that Beech Hill pays off."

109

Lottie's second pregnancy was much easier than the first. She knew that the care given by her friends in Lizzie's house had a lot to do with it, and when she gave birth to a second son, she wanted to name him William after Maeve's late husband. Clarence had another idea. He wanted to honor his mentor and boss, Dr. Hiram Francis Abbott of Rumford. He reasoned that it was the good doctor who had chosen him to manage the now dormant Newry mine and entrusted him with running the Beech Hill works. The man had put great faith in the Canadian and deserved the honor more than a man who had only entered the Potters' lives a short time before he was murdered.

"Clary, please consider my wishes. Along with Liz and Franny, Maeve has given so much support to me in the last few months."

"Oh, I know, but Abbott has made it possible for us to live here in Maine, where you have wanted to be. Will was a fine man, no question on it, but he really did very little for either of us."

Lottie thought for a moment before responding. She didn't wish to get into an argument with him about the naming of a child.

"So, would Hiram be the boy's name?"

"No, he would be christened Francis Abbott Potter. Hiram is such an antiquated name."

"All right, it will be Francis Abbott as you wish, but when we have another child, whether boy or girl, I want to give the honor to one of my friends here in Westbrook."

"I can agree to that, but you must realize that we are only living here temporarily. Our home will be in Waterford by the next time you are pregnant."

"Clarence Leslie Potter, you are wrong to think our friends here will forget us, or we them, when we move to our own place. They are *now* my friends, if not yours, for as long as I live."

110

Longer hours of sun in late April brought warmer southwesterly breezes that began to melt patches through drifts so deep that it was feared they might last into summer. Now strong enough to travel, Clarence borrowed Will's farm wagon from Maeve and drove back to Waterford. He would be gone for several days, and knowing that the mill apartment would still not be habitable, he planned to go straightaway to North Waterford. There he would be able to take a room in the new Forest House, which he had helped to finish. At Bridgton's Pondicherry Square, he decided to make a quick stop at the Hallett house on nearby South High Street. He had not heard from Nathan recently about the Beech Hill mine and wondered how the family had weathered the winter. Nathan and Hattie were not at home, but Nate, just back from school for the day, greeted him at the door.

"Mr. Potter, nice to see you," said the boy, who was now a senior at Bridgton Academy and had grown to over six feet tall. "Dad's not here right now, but you're welcome to wait. I'll hitch your horse for you."

"No need, Nate. I'm trying to get to North Waterford before it gets dark. Just wanted to say hello."

"I'll tell Dad and Mom you dropped by. Sir, can you tell me if you might be looking for help on Beech Hill this summer? I'll be done with school in early May. You know I have some experience at mining."

"Son, there might be a job for a strong lad like yourself, but you'll have to clear it with your father. I don't know when we'll be opening. I'll know more when I see what the place is like after such a rough winter."

"Dad says the place is still under deep drifts. I don't think he expected to see you back at work so early."

"Let him know I'll be staying at the Forest House for three nights. I sure would appreciate being able to speak with him. Oh, by the way, I might have another job open for you at a pond in North Waterford. Not really mining, but still a chance to make some quick money. Your Dad knows nothing about it, but he still would have to give you permission."

"Who would be my boss on that job?"

"Me, son. Just me."

111

Maeve knocked at Lizzie's office door one sunny May morning. Seven months had passed since her man's casket had been lowered into the ground. During that time, she had worn the black widow's dress every day. When Liz opened the door, she was surprised to see her friend dressed in a yellow cotton dress with a gold sash and wearing a pale-blue bonnet. She beamed with a glorious smile.

"My dear, you look radiant today! It is a blessing," said Liz.

"Yes, I have done my time of grief. It is over. I've been working on this outfit for days. The first one I've made for myself in years."

"Indeed, you have made so many clothes for your children. Time to treat yourself for a change. Did you have a pattern to follow?"

"Lottie loaned me a copy of your *Delineator* fashion magazine. This was one of the designs to catch my eye. Didn't need a pattern."

"You certainly haven't lost your skill, Mrs. Cain. You always were quick at picking up the details. I guess it's like riding a bicycle."

"Of course! Or like making love." She stuck out her tongue and hid her face with one hand, faking embarrassment.

Very surprised that her friend was so impudent, Liz placed both hands on her hips, then shook a finger at her. "You haven't lost that dirty mouth, either, have you? You rogue!"

"Lizzie, it was that side of me that first drew Will's attention. Now that he's gone, the love we had together continues to bring me joy."

The two stood staring at each other for a moment until Liz grabbed both of Maeve's hands. Neither cried, but the great love they felt for Will was in their eyes. Then they linked arms and walked out to the warm porch to sit in the sun.

"It's a joy to see you so bright after all these months of sadness," said Liz. "I have grieved along with you for so long. He was my helper and defender at a very bad time in my life. His death at the hands of Aphia Stevens brought back horrid memories of those old times."

"She took from you both a curse of a man and one who was a blessing to you."

"The first murder doomed that sad woman to a life of torture from which I was freed. The second act of cruelty struck me to the quick with loss and grief. She and I are tied together by fate. Sometime I might visit her in jail to see if she is worth forgiving."

"At home in Clare there is a saying that forgiveness frees both the giver and the receiver. Perhaps we might visit her together at some point. But it will take a bit more time."

112

Clarence was surprised to run into Elmer Henley at the front door of the hotel. The boy was dressed in overalls spattered with paint, and he carried a wooden stepladder.

"Elmer, I thought you would have been done here a long time ago."

"Me too, but the owner ran out of money during the winter and cut us off. Only started up a couple weeks ago. Dad gave up. Said he had enough work to do on the farm. I been working alone and am almost done. How've you been doing, Mr. Potter?"

"Please use my Christian name—call me Clarence. We've worked together enough to do away with formality. Doing okay, but for a while there, I was laid up."

"Yeah, you up and disappeared just before we got laid off. I think Dad has an envelope with some money for you. Where you been, Clarence?"

"Been in Westbrook most of the winter living with my wife and son. We have friends who put us up. They have a fancy big house almost in Portland."

Elmer excused himself, and as he was about to leave, Clarence remembered the discussion the two had had about Chalk Pond last fall. "Elmer, I'm in town for a few days to inspect the mine up on Beech Hill. I would be much obliged if you would take me to Chalk Pond during my stay. The way farmers around here use that mud is very interesting. I'd like to learn more about it."

"Sure, Mr. P—Mr. Clarence, I'd be happy to do that. You know it's a bit muddy down there in the valley below Sawin Hill. I believe most of the snow has melted, but the way down is messy. You might want to wait until May."

"No, I want to see the place while I'm here. There might be some business to be done there."

"Business? What do you mean? It's just a muddy little pond. I cut ice off it and sell blocks to neighbors. They use the muddy stuff to keep milk cold."

"Let's go day after tomorrow. I'll tell you my plan after I inspect it."

When they met on Sawin Hill Road to follow the wooded path down a steep slope to the pond, ankle-deep mud made walking very difficult. A few days of warm sun followed by showers had created rills of runoff they had to avoid. Maples lining both sides of the path were pastel green with new foliage. Robins sang and pecked for emerging worms among the leaf debris. It had been warm on the road, but the temperature dropped quickly as they descended. By the time they neared Chalk Pond, both men had donned jackets. Looking to the east, Clarence could make out two shallow streams splashing down across exposed boulders from low hills. Wherever sun struck the water turned it white.

"Elmer, do you know where that water comes from?"

"Yes, sir. Comes from up where Roy Lord has a small prospect. Up behind that stand of cedars, close to Hunt's Corner. He's looking for feldspar and mica at a place he calls the Ledge. It's the highest point between the pond and Crooked River. The water has always been cloudy like that, according to my dad, even before they started excavating."

Clarence pulled a small notebook from his jacket pocket and jotted down everything Elmer had said.

"Can we get any closer to the pond where the streams enter?"

"Not this time of year. The water's too high. The only access right now is from the south, where we saw blocks of ice."

Their path turned to the right, up a small rise to a spot high enough on the banking that mud had already dried in the sun. A flat landing of sorts marked the path where ice must have been carried in ox carts along a low trail toward Bisbeetown Road to the east. Clarence noticed a pile of buckets on the shore. He grabbed one with a rope attached to its handle and threw it into the water. Dragging it hand over hand up to the ox path, he dumped it on the ground at his feet.

"Elmer, is the water light gray like this all year or only in the spring?"

"All year long, though in August, when the water level is low, a green scum often sits on the top. That's when I stay away from the pond. There are so many snakes here at that time. I don't like snakes."

Clarence pulled out another bucket. This time, he took a jar from his pocket and filled it with mud from the bucket bottom.

"What you going to do with that mud, Mr. Clarence?"

"I'll set it in the sun for a while to dry. See what the particles of earth look like. If this is what I think it is, we may have a valuable material here. They call it infusorial earth, something that might be harvested and sold."

Elmer stared at the man for a moment and then laughed. "Clarence, this is *mud*. Who would buy mud? All anybody has to do is come down here and get some of their own!"

"You never can tell the value of what comes out of nature. There are riches in the damnedest places."

"If there's money to be made off this-here pond, I'm the man to work on it for you. I catch trout out of it every year. And I cut ice from it each year for all the people around here. And I take out a lot of buckets of mud—have my own system. I'd say I know Chalk Pond better than anyone around here."

"When I get back to town in a couple of weeks, you might be able to introduce me to a couple of your friends who'd be interested in working this claim with me. We can all meet at the Town Office in Waterford Flat village. We need to get permission from the town to mine. We can discuss all the details there. It'll be easy."

Elmer grinned. "I'm your man, Mr. Clarence. I've always wanted to get rich quick."

113

For nearly two months, Clarence rode by the Stevens place on his way to the mine each morning and on his way back to his room at Forest House just before dark. The house and barn reminded him of all the troubles caused by its owner, so he never appreciated how well-maintained it was. When Lottie and Con came to visit him with their new son, Francis, for a weekend in August, he took them to the top of Beech Hill for a picnic. As they passed the house, Lottie asked him to bring the buckboard to a halt at the gate.

"What a cute little house," she said. "Is that the place where that Stevens woman lived?"

"Indeed it is. That witch used to sit on the porch with her gun in her lap. Even with the woman in prison, I can almost see her there."

Lottie climbed down from the seat, passed the baby to him, and leaned against the fence. "How much land goes with this house? Do you know? Seems like a nice big pasture running up toward the mine. Maybe five acres or so?"

"Abbott tells me she owns about twenty acres including the stand of hardwood past the right-of-way. Come on, let's get going. This place spooks me."

"I like the place. Do you know if it's for sale? Maybe we could buy it. I want a closer look. I'll be right back."

Before he could stop her, she opened the creaky gate and walked slowly toward the front door. Stepping onto the little porch, she noticed a six-pointed star had been etched into the wood of the door. She touched the carving and the door opened. Looking back at Clarence, she shrugged her shoulders then went inside. Although the place had been uninhabited for almost a year, it was spotlessly clean. With the exception of some spider webs in the sunny windows, it seemed to Lottie that someone had been living there. In the kitchen, big metal vats still sat on the stove top, and empty jars were lined up on shelves above a stone sink.

"Lottie, come away from there!" shouted Clarence from the

wagon. "I'm sure we're not supposed to be trespassing."

His words made her realize that she had been standing there almost in a trance. Perhaps aromas from Aphia's herbal tinctures and potions still permeated the air enough to affect her.

As she stepped back out onto the porch, she was shocked when the door shut so quickly behind her that it bumped her rear. "Clary, let's find out if this little farm is for sale. It does have a weird feeling about it, but it's the type of place we've been discussing. We could make a good home here, and being so close to the mine would make it possible for you to be home with your family every night."

114

A summer heat wave was upon the entire southern part of Maine. Temperatures had been ninety or higher for four days and the humidity stifling. With Lottie and Con leaving for another weekend in Waterford, Lizzie and Francena volunteered to keep four-month-old Francis Abbott. They could find no place where the boy wouldn't sweat and squirm in the heat except down in the cool basement. The floor was cleaned two times and the spider webs removed. An extension cord had been run down the stairs from the kitchen, and an electric fan was aimed directly at his crib. He still complained bitterly. Liz walked around the cool, dark room with the baby in her arms, his head laid across her shoulder. She found that rubbing his back and soft sweet humming would make him fall asleep for a few minutes at a time.

Franny opened the door at the top of the steps and whispered so as not to disturb the child. "Auntie, there's a man here to see you. He says he's an old friend from both Westbrook and Waterford."

Liz approached the steps. "How's that? I can't hear a word you're saying."

Franny came partway down the steps and spoke a little louder. Standing on the landing behind her was a tall man whose white beard reached down to his chest. "I said, there's an old friend here to see you."

Liz passed the child to Franny and peered up the steps at the visitor, who was so thin that his worn blue coveralls hung loosely on him. She couldn't make him out until he removed a wide-brimmed hat and brushed back long hair with his hand.

"Bert? Bert Learned, is it you?"

"Yup, Miss Lizzie. It's me. Just stopped by to say hello."

Liz started up the steps. "My God, Bert, where have you been? We all thought you had died on us, you've been gone for so long."

Reaching out his hand, Bert helped her up the last step. At first she shook his hand, but then she put her arms around his back for a hug. "Miss Lizzie, I asked the young lady here about Will. She said he has died. What happened to our dear friend? Does his widow still live around here? I would like to give her my condolences."

"Come with me out to the porch where there may be a bit of a breeze. I'll tell you the whole sad, complicated story. Can I get you a cold drink? You might want a beer for this."

"No, ma'am. I am sworn off all alcohol. It has almost killed me twice, and I want to live a few more years. How 'bout a cold glass of soda water?"

She brought the water to him, and they sat for a moment while Liz found the right words to tell Bert about his friend's death. As she spoke, Bert dropped his head to his chest and cupped the ear closest to her so as not to miss a word. When she finished, he took a white handkerchief from his back pocket and blew his nose several times, not saying a word.

"You know," he began, "I thought I loved that woman. She fascinated me with her beauty, intelligence, and talent. When I moved into her house during the autumn, I was the happiest man alive. I'd never met a woman like her."

"No question she was a fascinating woman. Didn't you notice her strangeness?"

"Well, in the spring she began to change. There were swarms of flies in the house, the barn, the pasture, everywhere. When I figured out that the insects were breeding on top of a mound at the pasture edge, she swore at me. 'Go get some dirt to cover up that damn hill of death,' she yelled. When I asked her what she meant, she told me her grandfather had buried six horses there years ago, and the soil he used to cover 'em was too thin."

"Her torment has been going on for such a long time," said Lizzie.

"While I was spreading the soil, my spade hit upon a man's boot partially buried in the mound. I asked her about it, and she went screaming and pulling on her long hair. She ran around barefoot in the pasture like something was chasing her. I tried to calm her, but she pushed me away and fell on the ground, beating it with her fists. 'Damn you, Henry Greene!' she screamed. 'Damn you to hell.' And then she confessed she had accidentally killed her husband, poisoning him with a powerful herb. I was scared then."

Lizzie sat in shocked silence, her hand over her mouth.

"That night I packed up as much of my belongings as could fit in a duffel and left town. I was ashamed that I'd so easily succumbed to her guiles and beauty. I was afraid she would kill me because I knew her darkest secret. I went out to western New York where my cousin told me a friend was looking for a hand. I worked there for a couple years, but got fired when I started drinking real heavy. Since then, I've been a traveler."

Liz didn't know what to say. Bert's story was just as Will Cain had imagined. Perhaps if he had returned much earlier, Aphia might have been convicted of her first murder and Will might still be alive.

"Bert, old friend, your story is a sad one. You faced great loss when your wife and son were burned to death many years ago. And you've also suffered at the hands of this evil woman. Yet, you are still here with us. I wish Will was here to see you again."

He wiped tears from his eyes and rose from the seat. "Where

does his wife live? I want to meet her and give her my regards."

"She and the four kids live just down the path behind my garden. I'm sure she will appreciate your caring words."

"My God, she is left with four children?"

115

The newly expanded Beech Hill Mine ran full-time all summer. Clarence and his four-man crew would arrive just after dawn in order to get in part of the day before the sun might turn the pits into ovens. In early afternoon, the local hired men would go home for a few hours, then return to work until it was nearly dark. Early in the season, Clarence rode to his room in Forest House for the break, but after a few days, he took to resting on the porch of the Stevens house, where he was able to do his recordkeeping in the shade of a tall maple. He was still unwilling to go inside the place and actually placed a padlock on the door, keeping the key in his pocket.

One afternoon as Hiram Abbott rode toward the mine, he saw his manager sitting on the porch, reined in his horse, and called out, "Mr. Potter, you've arranged a comfortable outdoor office for yourself, I see." The good doctor dismounted, tethered his mount to a fence post, and walked to the porch.

"Dr. Abbott, what brings you out here on this stifling day? Not much goes on in the pit when it's this hot."

"I was privy to a bit of news today which might be of interest to you. It's about that Stevens woman and this house. Didn't you tell me your wife was interested in living here?"

"Yes, she wants me to buy it. I told her it might be four years before the town could take it in foreclosure because of back taxes. Until then, the property would continue to be owned by the murderer."

"I guess you haven't heard of Maine's 'slayer rule.' The law says a person who kills their spouse cannot inherit the property of the victim. Some lawyers call it 'no profit theory' because it does not allow a murderer to profit from the act of murder."

Clarence closed his accounts book and paid close attention.

"I was discussing with a lawyer friend the recent revelation that Stevens murdered her husband. He claimed that she must surrender the house and lot to Oxford County, which would then sell it. Granted, she has not yet been tried for that earlier crime, but it is only a matter of time, now that there is a witness to her confession."

"If what you say is true, Mrs. Potter will be a very happy woman. We might finally have a house fit to raise our family, and her husband would be home every night after work. Even so, it may well take months for this to come about."

"Clarence, if you agree this property would fit your needs, I believe I can wheedle a way for you to live here immediately."

"I don't want to do anything illegal. I'm sure Stevens would be able to make my family's life miserable if we acted too soon."

"Son, leave it all to me. I will handle the details quickly and you will have a happy home in no time."

They shook hands on the deal before Abbott rode back toward town. Clarence reached a key out of his pocket and removed the padlock. Maybe I might start to do my paperwork inside where it is a bit cooler," he thought.

116

Elmer Henley, Roy Lord, and Role Littlefield arrived at the Waterford Town House in Lord's buckboard so early in the day that the office was not yet open. Late summer haze hung over the tops of hills across Tom Pond, and wood ducks swam just a foot off Town House Beach. A boy in his rowboat near Kokosing camp cast his line into the mirror-still water. Clarence had taken a room at the Lake House in Waterford village for several nights, and he'd asked the others to meet him at the Town House when the Town Clerk arrived in order to complete the application to mine Chalk Pond, devise their plans, and be back at work before conclusion of the long lunch break. He had filled out most of the required papers during the evening before and showed up at the exact moment as the clerk.

"Boys, this is Town Clerk Mr. Clyde Bennington. He told me yesterday that all we need to do is sign the applications and pay a ten-dollar processing fee. Because Roy is the pond's owner, and you other two are town residents, we may proceed with my plan."

The plan had taken several months to come together after his visit to Chalk Pond with Elmer. First, he had written to the J.T. Robertson Soap Company in Manchester, Connecticut, to ask if they might be interested in purchasing dried feldspar mud from the pond to be used as raw material for Bon Ami household polish. They were interested, but only if a small sample was sent to them for testing. Roy Lord had pulled up a few buckets of mud, placed it on a drying rack for a week, and then sent it in a large can to Robertson. That first sample had passed the test. Now the local team prepared to fill an order for fifty wooden barrels.

Lord, who already owned two small mines in North Waterford, sat directly across the table from Clarence. He said very little until it was his turn to sign the document. "Mr. Potter, I know that you have great experience in mining, both in the Provinces and now in Oxford County, but this here is not really mining, is it? How do you plan to get hundreds of buckets of mud out of the water? Enough stuff to dry and fill fifty barrels? We can't take a year to do this. The soap company wants a quick delivery. We know what they will pay, but what will it cost? Will we make a profit?"

The three men all stared at Potter, waiting for answers. They all had other work to do, work that might not pay as much as selling the chalk, but no one wanted to waste time on a failed experiment.

"Boys, I have this all planned out. I've even projected costs and receipts. We may not break even on this first run. And much of the work will be done by hand until the first order is filled. After that, there will be a healthy profit for all of us." He pulled a small notebook out of his pocket. It contained sketches and notations explaining the mechanics of how the extraction and drying could be done efficiently. A steam-driven motor would be anchored on a base of granite blocks. It would turn a large wooden gear wheel that would carry a continuous loop of wooden buckets attached to thick rope. Each bucket would drag across the bottom of the pond, filling with mud, and then be emptied onto drying racks by hand. The dripping racks would then be stacked on timber frames along the sunny shore and dried until the material could be shoveled into barrels. The men passed his notebook around, turning pages slowly and reading every word.

"What do you say, partners? Are we ready to make this project a success? We may not become millionaires, but our lives will be made easier."

Littlefield passed the book back to Potter. "Clarence, I'm still unclear as to what this soap company does with the mud. I mean, we have been using it for years to clean farm machinery and to condition soils. I wouldn't call this lumpy mud a household product."

From his coat pocket Clarence pulled a metal can of Bon Ami and poured some of the butter-colored powder on the table. He drew a hunting knife from the same pocket and spit on its tarnished blade before placing a pinch of powder on it. As he rubbed on the blade with his sleeve, the damp product removed discoloration from the metal.

"That is how it works, Role. They grind our mud into this fine powder, package it in small jars, and sell it throughout the country."

"Ain't nature wonderful," said Lord. "Maybe we can change the name of the pond to Crystal Polish Pond."

117

Hiram Abbott was a man of his word. Within a week of his discussion with Clarence about Aphia losing ownership of her farm, he met with a Bethel lawyer to plot a way to get the place for his mine manager's family. It would take a few months before the witch would be tried for her husband's murder, but there was no doubt the property would be up for sale. The doctor then met with the Oxford County Sheriff, who said that he would not stop the Potters from occupying the house on a temporary basis. His next stop was with the chairman of the Waterford Board of Selectmen, who pointed out that if the new residents stayed in the house for a year, they might have first claim under rules of adverse possession. He then asked Clarence to meet him in the lobby of the Forest House at his earliest convenience to discuss this information. Clarence convinced him to wait until Lottie and Con would be visiting the following weekend.

When they met, the three adults sat at a round card table adjacent to a large picture window while the boy played with his toy soldiers.

"My boy," said Abbott to Clarence, "there is no question in my mind that you can begin living in the Stevens place immediately. You have a few good weeks to set yourself up for winter before the weather turns."

Clarence looked askance at the doctor. "How can you be sure our moving in would not be ruled illegal and we would have to move again?"

Lottie, who had not been addressed directly, chimed in. "Listen to the man, Clary. He has spoken to a lawyer, the sheriff, and the Board of Selectmen. If there was going to be a problem, it would have come up already."

Abbott looked blankly at the woman, noticing how attractive she was, but barely listening to what she said. "Dr. Abbott," she asked, "am I right about this? Haven't you looked into every angle?"

"How's that? What did you say, Mrs. Potter?" After a second, he realized that she agreed with him and her husband didn't.

"Yes, yes, you are so right, Mrs. Potter. I can't see any possible complication that might keep the house in that woman's hands. And if you are living there, you would have the first claim."

Clarence was still not convinced. "Dear, perhaps you are not aware of Aphia's devious ways. I know she will stop at nothing to get back at someone she thinks has wronged her. If there is a loophole in the property law, she will find it. Then we could be facing winter once again without proper housing. You don't want that, do you?"

"Look," said Lottie, "you placed enough trust and faith in Dr. Abbott that we named our new son after him. Please allow me to put enough trust in the man to have researched all the possibilities. We need a home. No one lives in this lovely house. I say we jump at the chance to make it our own."

He saw that he had little chance to oppose the team of his boss and his wife. "Doctor, how do we proceed? Since Lottie is convinced we will be okay, I will go along."

Instead of reaching his hand out toward Clarence to shake on their agreement, Abbott first moved toward Lottie and touched her elbow. Surprised at the attention, she reached her hand for his and shook it firmly. It was the first time she could remember a man thanking her that way rather than with a kiss on the cheek.

118

"Bert Learned, my, aren't you a sight! How'd you get so old?" Aphia laughed at him through the wire grid separating them. He wore the same outfit he had worn to visit Lizzie: baggy overalls worn in places, a stained long-sleeved shirt, and a wide-brimmed straw hat. Her drab prison housedress and uneven haircut gave her an impoverished look, but her spirit had not been broken. He spoke so softly, she laughed in his face once again.

"What's that you say? Speak up! What has happened to you to make you so weak? You don't look at all like the man who used to make love to me in the garden."

He sat on a chair, watching and listening as she insulted him until, as last, he placed his face right up to the wire and winked at her. "Still such a fiery woman? I thought prison might have taken some of that wildness from you. That was what I liked about you. Also, what scared me enough to make me run away."

"Yes, you coward. You ran away! I suppose you've come back to make fun of me now that you think I can't hurt you. You'll probably be trying to get my farm, won't you?"

"No, Aphia, I'm only here to visit. Then I'm off again to New Hampshire where I s'pose I will die after a time. Besides, there is already a family living in that house of yours. The Beech Hill mine manager has moved in with his wife and two kids. They will be able to buy the place once it's taken from you by the government."

"That will never happen. The place is lawfully mine and will stay that way until I get out of jail. That bastard miner can't take it away from me. I own it outright. No mortgage or liens."

Bert shook his head. "Not so. Once the state convicts you for the murder of your husband, you lose all rights to the place."

She stared at him in shock, her mouth wide open, eyes so big they looked ready to pop out. "What? You bastard! You told them about Henry, didn't you? I should have killed you when you dug up his boot. Bastard! *Bastard!* You came back to ruin me, didn't you? Bastard!"

As she forced her fingers through the wire and began to shake it, a matron stepped forward and grabbed her by the collar. "Prisoner Stevens, stop the racket or I will return you to your cell."

Aphia spit through the wire at Bert, who by this time had moved from the chair and stood back from the insane woman. He removed his hat and bowed deeply. "Woman, you have ruined my life and ended three others. When the sheriff found Henry Greene's remains, they also found the body of an unidentified man buried close by. If justice is served, you will be here for the remainder of your miserable time on earth."

"Go! Return to your pathetic life. I'm glad I played a small part in the process of ruination. Tell that Lizzie and the miner who is in my house that I am not done with them. Not while I am still alive!"

Bert watched her being handcuffed and led away by the matron. Then he noticed that his hands were shaking while his pulse raced. He hoped that he would not die on the road back to New Hampshire.

119

Clarence refused to have his family move into the lovely little cape until Lottie and Francena worked for a week to clean away every trace of Aphia Stevens. Although the place was fully furnished and the Potters had little furniture of their own, Lottie was dead set against using the woman's belongings.

"It isn't so much that her furnishings are not acceptable. Indeed, many of the pieces are of high quality. I just don't like sitting in my own kitchen on a set which has been tainted by that witch. We must start over as much as possible," she said to Franny as they swept the floors once more. "I wish I knew how to get rid of the smells."

"Yes, I know. Who is to say which aroma is that of a medicinal herb or of a toxic, poisonous one? I say it's a damn good thing you have your own clean beds to sleep in."

Clarence's main concern was the herb garden. He did not want his children to be exposed to any plants that might be harmful. With Nate's help, he dug out all the plants and disposed of them in the mound where the two bodies had been found. He wanted to burn the plants, but realized smoke from some of the herbs might make everyone ill.

"Bury each plant as deep as you can, Nate. We don't want my boys digging them up. I'll get a load or two of mine tailings on top to make it hard for them to dig."

"Mr. Potter, I wouldn't dig too deep, if I were you. Don't want to unearth all those horse bones."

"Good point. I can always bring down more tailings from the

mine. God knows, we have enough to spare. We could build a mountain of refuse and debris down here and not miss a speck."

While the two men worked behind the house, Hattie, Liz, and Nathan unloaded chairs, a kitchen table, and two beds from a farm wagon. The beds had come from the rented Bethel house. The kitchen set was a gift from Maeve Cain.

"Not enough to fill this fine house," said Nathan.

"No, but they have the essentials," said Hattie. "We were fortunate enough to start out with all the pieces your mother didn't need when she moved out of the farmhouse. But Lizzie, you remember how little we had when we were living on Temple Hill."

Her sister laughed. "Little, you say? I don't think Marm had a piece of furniture that wasn't borrowed or hadn't been repaired a few times. Think of how many times our bed broke, throwing us off. Didn't we end up sleeping on a tick on the cold floor?"

The bits of furniture were set up in the clean house by late afternoon. Lottie opened a picnic basket containing enough chicken, potato salad, and porter to feed them all and toast to their new home. All was ready for the arrival of the two boys, who had been left with Maeve.

After the others departed, Lottie and Clarence were left alone to watch the hazy autumn sun backlight crimson oaks as dusk spread across the flank of Beech Hill.

"Do you think you can be satisfied living here?" he asked.

"It is not a grand house by any means, but when we own it outright, we can add on. Make it a home for a large family. Just the kind of home where children may live healthy lives."

As they retired to the kitchen, he lit a fire in the range. They sat across from each other at the table holding hands. "There is a chill in the air tonight—might be a frost. We'll have a chance to see how the place holds heat."

She rose from her chair, crossed to his side and took a seat on his lap. After kissing his cheek, she bent her head down and whispered in his ear. "If we are going to fill this place with a big family, I say we had better get working on it."

120

December arrived with a startling cold air mass. Snow squalls covered the pasture in a white sheet. A warm, late-autumn sun melted the cover by early afternoon, but winter had begun. The mine entrance had already been barricaded with hemlock trunks, so Clarence now had time to address preparations of their new home for the new season. Recently delivered cordwood needed to be stacked in the barn. Bales of hay had yet to be laid against the house's foundation to combat the bite of winter gales. As he loaded a wheelbarrow with firewood, a tall, thin man approached the gate leading a sagging horse.

"Sir," shouted the stranger. "Is this the Stevens house?"

Clarence set down the barrow and addressed the man. "'Twas the Stevens place, but not anymore. Are you looking for the former owner?"

"Not at all, sir. You must be Mr. Potter. I am Bert Learned. You may not know of me, but I lived here for a while some years back, when Aphia Stevens lived here."

"Oh, Mr. Learned. You're the man who told the sheriff about how she killed her husband. Thank you for that. Without your witness, my family might not be living here today."

"I've only done my civic duty. Not a favor to you. No need of thanks. I'm stopping by to deliver a message from Aphia. I just visited her in prison. The message is for you, your family, and any friends who might be helping you set up your home—especially Lizzie Millett and Nathan Hallett."

"Surely the message is an angry one. I can't imagine she is too pleased with loss of the place."

"Yes, and when that one is angry, it scares me. She has some powers that I can't begin to understand. Her message is that she will do everything within her power to make life miserable for you and anyone else who might have done her wrong by taking her property. Now, I don't know you from Adam, but I wanted to tell you that your family needs to be careful. Be wary of strangers. Don't be surprised if any of you have weird dreams or

266

visions. And for God's sake, don't let your children touch any of the plants in her gardens."

"Mr. Learned, thank you kindly for your concern. I don't know how she would be able to affect our dreams and such. It's doubtful she would be able to put a hex on us from behind a prison wall. Now, I must return to my work. Winter will not wait for me to worry about black magic and incantations."

Bert climbed onto his swayback nag and moved slowly down the hill. Watching him leave, Clarence said a silent prayer he hadn't used for years: May all in this house be blessed.

That evening after both boys had been put to bed, he sat with Lottie in front of the Franklin stove set into the fireplace. He told her of the strange visit and the warning brought to them by Learned. She sat with her face to the fire for a few moments as if she had not heard his words. When she turned to him, tears were running down her face. "Clary, we must pay careful attention to that man's message. I've been having disheartening dreams these last few nights. Dreams that I don't understand."

"I'm sure it has nothing to do with that woman. Haven't you had many odd dreams in the past?"

"Not like these," she sniffled. "In them, I am all alone. My babies are gone. You are gone. I am left here without you all. And the old herbs have returned and grown so tall that the house is covered. I am a prisoner behind doors and windows that cannot be opened." Her hands began to shake and she coughed uncontrollably.

When he put his arm around her, he could feel how she shivered. Her skin was cold and clammy to his touch. "Lottie, please, we must not let such dreams frighten us into believing that we are not welcome here. You and Abbott have convinced me that we *are* welcome here, that we're *meant* to be here. Nothing will keep us from making this a happy home. You do still believe that, don't you?"

Her crying stopped. She looked directly into his eyes and said, "Yes, there is no legal way this property will not be ours. It is not the ways of man's laws that I doubt, but the dark influence of evil powers we cannot control."

121

The winter of 1902–03 was the easiest people in Oxford County could remember in a long time. There were only two cold spells severe enough to freeze wells and keep everyone inside for days on end. There were fewer blizzards than in the two previous years. Smaller storms came so often that, once the ground became covered, the thinner blanket stayed as long as usual. Most storms would start with lovely white powder, then turn to sleet and end with a layer of freezing rain, making it almost impossible for folks to get around. By late March, rural roads like the one that ran past the Potter home were seldom traveled and never rolled. Their icy cover made even walking difficult. Clarence spent the winter feeling confined, often sitting at the kitchen table for hours at a time staring out at the blank white pasture. Sometimes, he was oblivious to Lottie and the boys. In late February, as daylight hours lengthened, he itched to get the mine open again.

"Clary, why don't you take Con with you up to the mine today?" asked Lottie one sunny morning. "It bothers me to see you sitting here silently for hours at a time. You could pull him along in his sled. It would do you both some good to enjoy the sunshine and get some exercise. I can take care of the fire for a while."

"I'm afraid to go up there. Fear that it will make me more melancholy because I will not be able to start working."

"You might be able to get into the head house now that ice has started to melt. Shovel out the door. Then you could at least set up your office and get ready for spring."

Following her advice, he bundled the four-year-old into his warmest clothes and donned his own woolen overcoat and miner's boots. He pulled the sled down from the barn loft. Strapping on snowshoes, he pulled Con out to the road, only to find the ground surface very slushy. Melting snow built up under the shoes' leather net. It was easier to walk in his boots. Con was so excited to be outdoors with his daddy that he talked a blue streak, giggling each time his sled hit a bump.

When they reached the head house, there was no snow drifted at the door. Clarence was able to open it easily and lead his son into the small shed adjacent to the mine pit. Tools of all descriptions hung on the walls, blocking light from entering through the two small windows. A rolltop desk stood to the left of the door. A small stand-up desk consisting of a box with a slanted top was attached to the rear wall. Except for a potbelly stove set on a stone pad, the room was filled with stacks of empty buckets. Once inside, Con made up a game of turning buckets upside down. He would sit on one as he turned another until he had created a circle of buckets. He then sat in the middle of the circle playing with rocks and pebbles that had fallen from the pails.

This is a peaceful place at this time of year, thought Clarence. Perhaps Lottie is right. Maybe I can open the desk and begin to plan for the season. To take the dampness out of the room, he filled the stove with scraps of board and lit it with a match. As the fire grew, the place quickly warmed. He removed his coat, hung it on a hook, and sat at the desk reviewing past records and setting up report pages for the future.

A loud rattling came from behind him, and when he turned, he saw the metal stovepipe shaking. Smoke began to fill the place. Knowing at once that it was a chimney fire, he jumped from the chair, grabbed Con by the arm, and dashed through the door. The shack quickly ignited, making it impossible for him to go back to get his coat and the sled. Standing safely away from the conflagration, they watched as the structure tumbled into a pile of burning lumber. Con was in awe at first, but as the flames began to slow, he threw his arms above his head and began to laugh. Unable to find any humor in the situation, Clarence took him by the shoulders and gently shook him.

"Stop that laughing, Con. Stop it right now. This is not funny. We could have died in there."

Con pushed him away and broke into loud crying until Clarence picked him up and started to walk back toward home.

When they returned, Lottie stood at the gate with infant Francis in her arms. "What happened? Are you both okay? I saw the fire and immediately thought the worst."

"We are okay, Lottie, but the head house will now have to be rebuilt. And I'm afraid all my records have been lost."

"Clarence, dear, I don't want to be an alarmist, but this is just the type of calamity that man warned us about. Let's pray it is the last. Loss of a building is a small setback, but loss of you or Con would be a tragedy."

He looked at her and then up at the gray smoke still rising from the mine site. "Please do not draw any conclusions about the cause of this. I started the fire without checking to clean the chimney. Simple as that. Don't give in to the fear that Aphia has any responsibility for it. If you do, you will allow her the power to create more havoc."

122

One month later, Clarence had built a new and larger head house with the help of Nate Hallett and Elmer Henley. They performed so well that he hired them to work for him during the upcoming season. Spring arrived early, but it rained nearly every day the first week in April. Still, both hemlock logs were moved away from the access road, and the pit was opened two days before May first. Dr. Abbott, Nathan, and Clarence were excited at having such an early start, and all forecast a banner year. Orders had already been placed by an electrical component manufacturer in Concord, New Hampshire, and a Waterford foundry.

Early digging produced mica books as large as twelve by eighteen inches, which could be used as windows for stove doors. Quality of the smaller books was high enough to meet requirements for manufacturers of electrical components. On June first, the partners were to meet at the Potter home and assess where they stood and how to become more profitable. Nathan arrived on time for the ten a.m. meeting, but at noon the two men sat on Clarence's porch still waiting for Abbott.

"It's not like the doctor to be late. He's always so punctual," said Nathan. "I can't remember him ever being late to a meeting."

"Whatever is keeping him must be pretty important. He was here last Thursday with the Bureau of Mining Inspector. They took a few samples from the new pit. I didn't meet the BOM man himself, but the good doctor said he was very impressed with our operation. Based on last spring's sample, he said the potential was better here than at any other mine in Maine."

As they spoke, a chaise could be seen bouncing along the road at a high rate of speed from North Waterford. Clouds of dust rose above the vehicle. When the buggy stopped at the gate, Abbott jumped down from the seat, tethered the horse, and walked quickly to the porch.

"Doctor, why are you in such a lather?" hailed Nathan.

"I've been talking with inspector Warren all morning in Bethel. You will not be pleased with the news I bring." He pulled an envelope from his valise and shook it in the air.

"Please, sir. Please sit yourself down and rest until you are able to catch your breath," advised Clarence. "Can I get a glass of cold water for you? You must be thirsty."

The man sat and accepted the water gratefully. His tweed jacket was coated with dust, and when he removed his derby, a shower of dust fell on the envelope in his lap.

"Here, Hallett, you read this report and see what I mean. Warren says his samples in the new area show that our production is not holding its level of quality. Two new mines in Rumford Falls, the Elliott and Black Mountain, have opened in the past two years and are now producing more and better books. Using the power of the Androscoggin River to operate a plant, they can process their material so quickly that our customers are sure to go to them."

While Nathan read the report, Clarence paced back and forth

on the porch. If what Abbott said was true, two and a half years of effort would have been wasted. "Doctor, we've all heard about how ground mica will become more useful in manufacturing electrical insulators. Surely we can compete in that market."

"We have the material to do that. Yes. But we are not able to process it here. How would we grind it? The Rumford men have water power to do the work. It looks to me like the end of Beech Hill mine. What do you say, Hallett?"

When Nathan had finished reading, he dropped the report on the porch at Clarence's feet. "You can read it if you want to, but I suggest you just kick it out of your way and start making other plans."

Clarence was already thinking of the next plan—the mining of Chalk Pond—which he had kept secret from his partners. He said nothing for a moment, then picked up the envelope and gave it back to Abbott. "Boys, if the best thing to come into my life from this failed mine is this-here house, I will be forever grateful. This is, of course, a great disappointment, but as you both have taught me several times, mining is a great risk. You are more likely to lose your investment than to strike it rich."

Both men looked at him with shocked expressions. Then Nathan spoke. "At least you have made a gain. We have only big losses."

"No. No, Nathan. We will find a buyer for this site," said Abbott, "one who has the yearning for adventure and risk. Mark my words, we will break even once again, as we did in Newry."

123

After his partners left, Clarence went around to the rear of the house, where Lottie sat next to a play area where the old herb garden had been. Both boys were playing in a sandbox.

"I have both good and bad news, Lottie Adelaide. Which do you want first?"

She was silent for several seconds, staring across the freshly mowed pasture at a stand of ancient hundred-foot pines.

"Clary, you might as well start with the bad news. I bet I already know what it is, but go ahead."

"Beech Hill Mine will be closing soon. There is no way we can make it a profitable operation, according to the Mining Bureau man. Both Abbott and Hallett agree. They will be selling the property as soon as they can find someone rich and foolish enough to buy it."

"I knew that would be the bad news. Must a miner's wife be ready for failure and always be ready to make new plans? What will we do this time? Will we be unable to buy this place? Is it to be sold with the mine lot? How will you earn a living now? Don't tell me. I already know. You have another scheme in mind to get rich quick."

"Yes, of course. Last fall, I signed on with three other local men to process and sell mud from Chalk Pond in North Waterford. We discussed that. Don't you remember?"

"I do recall that conversation, but I didn't pay much attention at the time. Thought it was just another of your schemes."

"I also said there was good news. Let's focus on that. We will not lose the house, because it is not part of the mine lot. As soon as Aphia is tried for her husband's murder, we'll be able to purchase it outright. That must be comforting to you."

"My dear, of course that part is comforting. It's just that I see the failure of another mine as one more misfortune brought on us by that woman. If so, who can tell what else is in store."

"Lottie. Lottie, my love, you mustn't assign this problem to Aphia. Like every mine, digging in the ground for wealth is exceedingly risky. That is all it is."

"I pray that you are correct," she said. She had planned on telling him that she was pregnant once again. He would be so excited. But faced with his news, she decided to wait until a better moment.

124

During the summer, Clarence split his time between closing down the Beech Hill operation and implementing his plan for Chalk Pond. At the former site, he and Nate filled in most of the pit and emptied the head house of all its tools and furniture. A new one-room shed was constructed on the pond shore, and the furnishings of the old office were placed inside. They built four-foot-square drying frames and portable racks to hold the frames. On a heavy granite slab, Roy Lord and Elmer Henley raised a six-foot-high A-frame holding a hand-operated winch used to pull a line of buckets across the bottom of the pond to collect mud for drying.

"Mr. Clarence," said Elmer, "seems to me we are about ready to start this machine. What do you think?"

"I wouldn't call it a machine," said Lord. "More like a contraption. You'll be wishin' for a real machine after a couple days of turnin' this crank. See for yourself. You'll be puttin' your shoulder to the test."

"Roy, if you can come up with a better way to do this, be my guest," said Clarence. "No doubt it will be tiring to extract the mud this first time. We'll all have to take a turn. Once we make a profit, there will be improvements to be made. Perhaps we could use an ox or mule to do the hard work. For now, it's just the four of us. I say the young ones give it a go first. They have stronger backs."

Nate and Elmer worked together to attach a long thick rope to the winch. Tied to the rope at regular intervals were metal buckets that dragged across the bottom of the pond filling with mud. As each bucket neared the winch, one of the other men would unhook it and empty the contents onto a drying frame. Once all the buckets had been emptied, they were reattached and the rope carried out into the pond by one of the partners.

"Christ almighty," Elmer griped to Clarence, "how many times do we have to drag this line until the racks are filled? I'm ready to fall into the water and drown myself."

"Just two more times should do it for today. We won't have to come back until the muck is dried. Likely at the end of the week."

"Okay, boss, but when we return, I want you to take a turn. After all, this scheme is all your idea."

During the next four days, Clarence returned every afternoon to throw off a black tarpaulin that had been spread across the racks and turn the drying mud with a garden hoe. On the fifth day, he and Elmer shoveled the cakey material into ten wooden barrels. These were then carted to Lord's barn where they might dry a bit more. In one week's time, they had completed only twenty percent of the order. In four weeks' time, the order was completed.

Role Littlefield stood at the barn door watching the others unload the fiftieth barrel. "Damn, but I hope we can figure out a way to do this faster. I just can't believe that the soap company will be able to wait a month for each order. What if we get more than one customer? Then we won't be able to do anything but dig, dry, and barrel this crap while everything else goes neglected."

"Role, don't fret about success," said Clarence. "Once we get paid for this load, there will be money to follow through on improvements according to my plan. When we can afford the motor, the process will be easier."

"I hope so, Potter. I have a farm to run. I can't be mucking about in this goddamn pond all the livelong day."

Lord, who was weighing each barrel, stopped for a moment and peered at the two. "Role, if you can make as much money with mud as you do with your farm, why would you want to continue the chores from morning to night, seven days a week? Hell, you might even be able to take a few days off once in a while and show the wife a vacation trip. Something I presume you have never done."

"Listen, Roy, we farmers may work hard and make modest money in return, but at least the work is regular and makes us a reliable living. You miners might get rich on one scheme, poor on another. When it comes down to steady, honorable labor, you can't beat farming."

125

Lottie sat across the kitchen table from her husband. What was once a nearly empty house was now full of furniture collected from friends and neighbors. Both bedrooms were now comfortably furnished, as was a small sitting room, where she was proud to have a plush lavender camelback sofa and easy chair that Lizzie had given them. Yet, whenever there was family business to discuss, they still chose to sit at the comfortable old table brought from Bethel.

Clarence held a letter from which he read aloud as she stared out at snow swirling past the window behind him.

Dear Mr. Potter,

I regret to inform you and your partners that the infusorial earth received from you several months ago cannot be used to make our product. Unlike the samples sent earlier, this batch contained a very high percentage of quartz particulates which can be highly abrasive. If you wish to have the barrels returned, I can make arrangements to have them shipped to you C.O.D. If not, we will dispose of the material and reuse the barrels.

Richardson Soap Company will not pay you for the material, but will reimburse you for the barrels. Kindly send us an invoice for those at your convenience.

With sincere regrets,
Samuel Richardson

"Damn it," she whispered through tightly pursed lips. "How many times does this have to happen to us? What are you going to do now?"

He saw tears in her eyes, and when he reached out to touch her hand, she pulled her arm away and walked to the window. "This is the third time our plans have been dashed by failure of your schemes. This is not the life I thought I would get when we married. There has to be something else you can do besides mining. Your father taught you how to blacksmith, didn't he?"

"Yes, I can work with metal better than most, but I won't be able to make very much money being a smithy. Dad was never able to support the family doing it. That's why he went to work for the railroad laying track in Ontario when I was a boy. And that is why he went to work at the mines in Cobalt. Mining pays the best money for the least amount of work."

Lottie walked back to the table and took her seat across from him again. This time, her quiet whispers were replaced by stern words. "My dear Clarence, I love you dearly. Of that you can have no doubt. However, you must believe that I have run out of patience. Three times, we have followed your dream of wealth beyond measure, of streets paved with gold, only to bring your family down into a muddy reality. Wouldn't it be better to have the steady income of a craftsman or farmer than to chase one failure after another?"

"Let me think on it, Lottie. Perhaps there is a way to improve our techniques at Chalk Pond. If nothing can be done, I will consider what you've said. I do apologize for causing you so many disappointments. Please forgive me."

"Clary, you are a good man, and I don't fault you for your intentions, but you have been foolish to believe that there is success to be found in mining here in Maine. We have a home here now, one which I do not want to leave. We also have found good friends. They will surely be able to help you find regular work that pays well enough to support a growing family. Please speak to Nathan about some other kind of work before spring comes."

126

In early March, Clarence received a letter from his cousin Jack in Nova Scotia. Mail from relatives at home had been so scarce over the years that he didn't recognize the return address at first. He was surprised anyone from home would know where he was living after a decade of being away. Opening the envelope, he saw that the scrawling message filled only a small section of the page. He could barely make out the writing.

Dear Cousin,

Maybe you will get this letter. Maybe you won't. Who can say? I don't trust the post very much, do you? I am well. Are you? If you ever come home, please visit me and my new wife, Evelyn. I am still in the old house in Yarmouth. This story was in the journal yesterday. Thought you might have an interest.

All the best,
Your Jack

Enclosed was a clipping from the *Halifax Journal* about a recent discovery of gold and silver in northern Ontario near the town of Cobalt. GOLD RUSH IN NORTHERN WILDERNESS read the headline, and there was a location map included. "Men from the Provinces are rushing to the outback to strike it rich," read the story. "One man described the ore he found as 'a wonder of Nature. So easy to dig enough gold to make me a happy man until I die.'"

Maybe I should give it a good look at that, Clarence said to himself. This might be the lode that rewards Lottie for all the aggravation I have caused her.

Next morning, he interrupted her from reading to the boys on the big sofa. When he showed the clipping and letter to her, he was surprised at her calm reaction. Rising slowly from her seat, she smiled and without a single word led the children to the kitchen near the stove, where toys were spread across the floor. It was upon her return that her response was as he expected.

"Why are you showing me this? You aren't thinking of leaving me, are you? You know how I feel about this get-rich-quick dream you keep having."

"It will only be for a short visit. I can judge the value of the lode with a quick inspection. If there is nothing of great value, I will be back before spring. If it's worthwhile to work the mine for a while, I can send good money back to you until the site is played out."

"No, Clarence! I forbid it. If you go, I will never forgive you."

"Make this my last opportunity to make up for all the disappointments I have caused you. If I fail again, I will follow your plan to find another line of work."

She began to cry, wrapping her arms around herself, rocking back and forth. Through her tears she said, "You will never return. I know it in my heart of hearts. When you say goodbye, it will be forever."

"You are doing it again, Lottie. You are giving into the curse that Aphia Stevens put on us from behind bars. Do not worry; I will return. I will be either richer or poorer, but I will return."

Mine Tram. *Tram used on a mining train in the early twentieth century. As seen in Jerome, Arizona. 2019. Photo by author.*

127

For the next few days, the Potters did not speak to each other. At first, he puttered around the barn splitting and carrying firewood into the woodshed. She kept to herself in the kitchen and slept with the boys in their room. Tension between them was so heavy, both boys reacted by being cranky and crying at the least little thing. One day, Clarence rode to Bridgton and arranged with Nathan to drive him to Portland's Grand Trunk train station. He would ride to Bridgton and leave his horse for Francena to ride back to visit with Lottie. Nate would then pick her up in his dad's chaise once it returned from Portland. When he returned home, Lottie would not even listen to his plans. He left the next morning without a fond farewell.

At dawn the next morning, Lottie went to answer a knock at the door and saw her dear friend on the porch. She rushed to Franny and threw her arms around her, and after sharing the sad story of Clarence's departure, they both began to weep.

"I know how you must feel," said Franny. "Your man has left you against your wishes; but he will return."

"How can you be so sure of that? The man is only able to find value in his life by digging for it in the earth. It is an obsession, a fantasy. His love of discovering gold—or jewels or silver—is far greater than his love for his family. He may find gold in Ontario far beyond his wildest dreams and send money home to me, but he will not return. I should have listened to you years ago, when you warned me about Clarence's weaknesses."

"He is a man of conflicting ideals, I agree, but he has done his best to give you a good life. Look, you have this house and two wonderful sons."

"Yes, dear friend, you may be right. He may return a rich man and reward me with his loyalty. I will pray for that outcome, not the one I fear may befall him in that cold wilderness."

She looked at Franny for a moment, as if trying to put something important into words. "Dear friend, I am pregnant again.

Clarence doesn't know. I want you to keep it a secret. He must return, or, like Maeve, I will have to raise my children without a father."

128

Clarence boarded a train in Montreal in preparation to ride it to the end of the line at Temiskaming Lake. There he found that a smaller line, the Temiskaming and Northern Ontario, had been added in the years he had been away. He rode on a flatcar all the way to mile marker 103, where a mining camp of shacks and lean-tos had been established. It reminded him of the neighborhood in Cobalt where he and Emma had first settled. All the simple structures were empty and drifted with snow except for a cabin next to the tracks that served as a station and mine office. Ducking into the cabin, he found a man sitting behind a big rolltop desk and smoking a cigar.

"Sir, can you tell me where I might find Henry Timmons? I was told that he lived here and that he owned a silver mine hereabouts."

"That would be me, son. Me and my brother opened this mine a year ago. What can I do for you?"

"My name is Potter. Clarence Potter. I used to work the copper mine in Cobalt years ago. I live in Maine now. Been trying my hand at mining down there in Oxford County."

"Guess that hasn't worked out too well or you warn't be back here in this hellish place."

Clarence didn't know what to make of the man's rudeness. He tried to ignore it in order to get the information he desired. "Tell me, Mr. Timmons, are you looking to hire a man with a good nose for finding the best deposits?"

"Not open for business right now. Come back in a month or so and we'll see."

"I can't be going home and coming back again in a month. I'll need a place to stay. If you could use a man who could give you a jump on the season by cleaning up the mine head from winter damage, I will do that in exchange for a bed and board. No need to pay me anything else."

Timmons looked Clarence up and down, thinking that perhaps he might be helpful. "Look, mister, you can take a mining tub on the tracks that lead to the head house, inspect it, and give me an idea how long it would take to get the place ready. There's a potbelly stove there and some old junk wood you can burn. Stay there if you want. Food is real scarce, but you can always take the train back to Haileybury. There's a store there."

I'm in, thought Clarence. Now I'll be able to assess how much value is in this mine. He made his way to the rear of the cabin where there was a set of narrow-gauge tracks. A train of mine trams was lined up. After unhitching the first cart from the others, he threw his duffel into the tub and hopped aboard its rear hitch. He pushed off with one foot and rode along the track toward the mine head. As he approached the shoddy head house, which appeared about to collapse, he dug in both feet on the tracks to bring it to a halt. His boots slipped along the icy track, unable to get a hold. The steel tram smashed into the structure and rolled over on him.

"Help!" he shouted. "Help!" But there was no one around to hear his cries. He struggled to wriggle out from beneath the heavy vehicle, but his legs were pinned tight. Suddenly, the damaged head house wall let go and the entire structure collapsed, burying him in rubble.

"The cosmos is filled with precious gems.

I want to offer a handful of them

to you this morning.

Each moment you are alive is a gem,

Shining through and containing earth and sky,

water and clouds."

—Thich Nhat Hanh

List of Primary Sources

Maine Treasure Chest by Jane Perham; Quicksilver Publications; Second Edition, 1987

We Walk on Jewels by Jean Blakemore; Downeast Mineral and Gem Shop; Third Edition, 1990

Maine Feldspar, Families and Feuds by Vandall King; Multicultural Book World, 2010

Mineralogy of Maine, Volume Two: Mining History, Gems & Geology by Vandall King; Maine Geological Survey, 2000

History of Mount Mica of Maine, U.S.A. and Its Wonderful Deposits of Matchless Tourmalines; written and published by A.C. Hamlin, 1895

History of Mt. Mica; Department of Earth and Environmental Sciences; University of New Orleans

Online sources such as e-mails from Vandall King and various genealogical sites

Life on Sawin Hill Road as reflected in the diaries of Elmer C. Henley (1876–1953); summarized by Edwin A. Holt, Harpswell, Maine, 2007, from the archives of the Waterford Historical Society in Waterford, Maine

Disaster Hits North Waterford by Dorothy Erickson; Waterford, Maine, 1875–1976, Pages 135–138; published by Waterford Historical Society, 1977